Graham Edwards [illegible] Somerset, in 1965, and brought up in Bournemouth. He attended art school in London and now works in a special effects design studio. He lives in Nottingham with his wife Helen and their two children. *Stone & Sky* is his fourth novel.

BY THE SAME AUTHOR

Dragoncharm
Dragonstorm
Dragonflame

Voyager

GRAHAM EDWARDS

Stone & Sky

HarperCollins*Publishers*

Voyager
An Imprint of HarperCollins*Publishers*
77–85 Fulham Palace Road,
Hammersmith, London W6 8JB

A Paperback Original 1999
1 3 5 7 9 8 6 4 2

A catalogue record for this book
is available from the British Library

ISBN 0 00 651070 1

Typeset in Meridien by Palimpsest Book Production Limited,
Polmont, Stirlingshire

Printed and bound in Great Britain by
Caledonian International Book Manufacturing Ltd, Glasgow

for dad

'Nature, like a careful gardener, thus takes her seeds from a bed of a particular nature, and drops them in another equally well fitted for them.'

CHARLES DARWIN

PROLOGUE

May 12th 1883

Ship's Log

1.00 a.m.

Wind moderate from south-west; sky clear and quite free of cloud. The coast of Java is clearly visible to the east as we enter the Straits of Sunda. It is a welcome relief to see the promise of landfall after 184 days at sea.

1.30 a.m.

Responded to a call from Jenkins the mate, on watch. He drew my attention to a discoloration in the water some two miles to the north; he was agitated, leaping from one foot to the other in a manner most uncharacteristic. I suggested that the phenomenon was most likely to be a floating raft of pumice (I understand the formation of such rafts to be a common occurrence in this region, due to the many active volcanoes which sprout from the forests of both Java and Sumatra).

However, Jenkins protested that, before he had looked away to call for my attention, he had been faced with the sight of a towering edifice rising from the waves. He described it as resembling 'an island made of glass' (these are his precise words). I looked again, and for a moment it seemed that there was something there after all, hovering above the sea like a phantom; it seemed to me like a huge, transparent mass, a ghost-island, as it were. Then the mass of pumice near it shifted and the air cleared. We agreed that what we had seen had been a trick of the light; perhaps a strange electrical discharge, again associated with the region's volcanoes. Jenkins continued his watch until 4.30 and reported no further disturbances.

5.45 a.m.

The lead brought up from thirty-two fathoms deep was unusually warm.

5.48 a.m.

When I looked north I was presented with a most curious sight. At first, what I saw seemed to promise to make sense of what both I and Jenkins had seen earlier, yet ultimately it served only to deepen the mystery. Just like the earlier vision, this latest phenomenon had an air of unreality about it, a spectral quality one might say. It was sheer, in the sense that it was partly transparent. I could clearly see the outline of the island of Krakatau or Krakatoa through it. It was indeed very much like a ghost. I am now assured that, though we are less than eight degrees from the equator, what I saw was nothing less than an iceberg. Though I anticipate ridicule at entering such a patent absurdity in this log, I feel obliged to set down all that I believe I saw.

The object – it has already become known among my crew as the ghostberg – appeared to reach to approximately one quarter of the height of the highest peak of Krakatau, that is to say, to between six and seven hundred feet above sea level. Its shape was that of a rough pyramid, with a distinct tendency to lean towards the west.

I followed its progress – it was moving to the west at a rate of approximately one knot – for some fifteen minutes, during which time I was joined by several of my crew, all of whom confirmed the sighting. It should be noted that this progress was made against the prevailing wind. Shortly before six o'clock the object had become so sheer as to be practically invisible.

6.32 a.m.

Some members of my crew have expressed fear following our encounter with this strange apparition, however I am informed that ours is not the first vessel to see such a thing. Jenkins has confided to me that some years ago the second mate of the Brilliantine *told him a story about a similar sighting, this one in the Indian Ocean. Though I am as susceptible as most to the legends of the sea, I am however inclined to believe that what we saw was indeed some peculiar manifestation of the vulcanism that is known to infiltrate the region. I have in the past encountered St Elmo's Fire, and though this phenomenon was very different, it had something of the former's electrical quality. I am confident that a rational, scientific explanation will come to light sooner or later.*

7.55 a.m.

Lead brought up from thirty fathoms deep; this time it was not warm but hot. There are volcanoes here indeed.

Captain George Tremaine

Chastity *(Liverpool), out of Newport, South Wales*

1

Krakatoa

The night was warmer than any he had known. The black sand crowding his toes felt as though it were baking his flesh; even the light of the stars seemed to bring with it something of their old, remote heat. All was dark, and green, and splendid.

He lay back in the sand. Behind him climbed the steep mountain slope of Rakata, a sheer wall of tropical vegetation that sang in the wind. The drone of the breeze through the thick leaves was counterpointed by the intermittent cries of parrots, lost deep within the foliage; nearby he could hear the soft scuffle of crabs on the shore. A tropical symphony, the song of Paradise. To the north-east rose the lesser peaks of Danan and Perboewatan, humble in the shadow of their greater sibling. Between them, the three little mountains made the idyll which was the island of Krakatoa.

Across the straits to the east sprawled the coast of Java, from which wafted the scents of a thousand spices; to the north loomed Sumatra. Krakatoa lay between in all its unremarked glory, a tiny island known to sailors the world over for its value as a marker, an exotic buoy denoting the final approach to the fabled Spice Islands, an overlooked haven that offered to weary travellers not rest but one final spur – *almost there,* it whispered. *Just a little further* . . .

'No further for me,' whispered Jonah Lightfoot into the warm, spicy breeze. 'This will suffice, thank you very much.'

He wriggled his shoulders, settling himself more comfortably into the canvas bag that had accompanied him halfway round the world. He knew its contents intimately – half a year on a barque had acquainted him more than sufficiently with the rigours of a travelling life. This bag and its contents had been his only real friend among a crew whose members had regarded him as a curiosity rather than a companion. Only his late father's long friendship with the short-tempered captain had secured him a berth on the ship in the first place; Jonah had sailed, for the most part, alone.

Still, he had preferred this to the idea of taking a passenger vessel. The money he might have scraped together, but as for the sociability . . . well, this was not some whimsical grand tour to be shared at the captain's table – this was a *mission*. After a week or two of suspicion both captain and crew accepted him as a loner who was at least willing to swab the decks once in a while. He received his share of guarded looks for most of the six months they were at sea, but that was only to be expected.

They will not like my name, he had mused when first he had set foot on board the *Caroline*. Nor had they.

Jonah did not embark on his voyage to Java because he considered himself a traveller. Quite the opposite, in fact. He was happier sitting in his small parlour, surrounded by maps and globes and imagining his way to the many exotic places that were so vivid in his mind. What need was there actually to visit these lands when he could see so much of them from the reading room of the British Library, or view their relics in London's countless museums and galleries? How much faster he could travel, how much further he could roam by staying well and truly at home! Not for Jonah was the discomfort of the adventure, the dreadful boredom of the voyage.

'Why, if one could take a flying machine to these places,' he would remark to his sister during her increasingly infrequent visits, 'avoiding the tedium of the sea crossing, perhaps it might be considered worthwhile.'

And Mary would nod and smile and look anxiously at the clock, picking at the hem of her skirt in the manner that instructed her dutiful husband that the sun was low and it would soon be impossible to find a hansom to take them back to Waterloo. And they would rise and apologies would be made, and Mary and her husband would leave, forgoing tea and leaving Jonah on his own again.

All things considered, he found he preferred it that way.

There was an annoying bulge pressing into his shoulder; he delved into the bag and pulled out the offending piece of luggage.

It was a book, worn now, its corners scuffed, its pages foxed. He traced his fingers over the title on its spine:

On The Origin of Species

and its author:

Darwin.

It was a first edition, and Jonah's father, Henry Lightfoot, had bought it for him on the day of publication – 24 November 1859. He had been eight years old. He fancied that in years to come, it might become a very valuable item indeed.

This book was where it really began. This was where Jonah's inquisitive, eight-year-old mind had been opened fully to Charles Darwin's outrageous theory of evolution, and the search for man's place in the great, unstoppable flow of time. Just now it amused Jonah to consider his life as a mirror of Darwin's: whereas Darwin's voyage on the *Beagle* had inspired a book, so in turn that same book had inspired Jonah's voyage on the *Caroline*.

Why Java? The reason was simple: against all popular belief, Jonah believed Java to be the cradle of mankind. Here, he believed, in the Spice Islands of the East, the mysterious process of Natural Selection had first elevated some ancient ape to the level of primitive man. If anywhere in the world could claim to be the Garden of Eden, this was it.

Now, surrounded by tropical forest and the hot, soothing sounds of the jungle, Jonah did not doubt it in the slightest.

He slept lightly, the rich, nocturnal symphony filling his dreams with light and colour. He woke late and remembered little of the night, except a vague recollection of a song, the words to which he could not recall.

Habit drew his father's pocket watch from the canvas bag. The sun was high and the Hunter confirmed that it was already half past ten. It was 20 May, in the year 1883. Today, Jonah Lightfoot was thirty-two years old.

He usually celebrated his birthday alone, and so the trip across the straits to Krakatoa had seemed a perfect way to remove himself of the bustle of Anjer, the Javanese port in which the *Caroline* had deposited him. Enchanted though he was by Anjer's palm-fringed bay, and grateful for the hospitality shown him by the van Dekkers – also friends of his father's and owners of a luxurious villa overlooking the southern corner of the harbour – Jonah felt hemmed in there. The beauty he had anticipated; the throng he had not.

Covered wagons hauled by steaming buffalo; the shore market smelling of spice and tobacco; the kampongs with their bamboo huts built on stilts, from which arose the squall of babies and the incomprehensible song of their mothers; the pristine white houses of the Europeans. Everyone smiling, from Dutch master to native slave; everyone secure in Paradise. Everyone so *busy*.

Java was the right place, Jonah knew it as soon as he smelt its richly-perfumed air; but he had been here a week now and today, just today, he wanted to get away from the hubbub.

Across the bay the answer loomed. A few brief enquiries confirmed that a group of native fishermen regularly made the crossing to Krakatoa to cut hardwood. It proved easy enough to secure a place in their *proa* and now here he was on his own desert island, a full year further from his birth. His watch told him the fishermen would be back in three or four hours; the sun just laughed and told him not to worry – *soon*, it said. *Forget the hours, just enjoy the time*.

Jonah laughed too, snapped the watch shut and dropped it back into the bag before strolling down to the shore to wash in the warm, eastern sea.

I would look like a cork to anyone watching, he thought as he bobbed amid the waves. *One soaked in Claret, of course*. His thick red hair was testament to his mother's Scottish ancestry; his pale skin was already glowing pink beneath the late morning sun. The rest of his slowly plumping body was hidden underwater – he had already begun to reacquire the weight he had shed on the voyage. Not that anyone would be watching, of course. Like Defoe's Crusoe he was a castaway, though by choice, and for a short time only.

The current carried him swiftly away from the pile of clothes he had left on the beach, but Jonah was not concerned. He had already decided that he would swim as far as the nearby headland, regain the shore at its tip, where a cluster of palm trees were bowed low over the water, and stroll back along the sand. There were any amount of exotic fruits which might sustain him until the fishermen returned; perhaps he would seek out some shade and doze for a while, read a little Darwin . . .

The sea was warm and buoyant; never had Jonah felt so alone. And never so content.

He rounded a fallen tree. Its brilliant green fronds were awry, some of them sticking up towards the sky in a startled fashion. Cocoa nuts ascended the shore, pushed by the waves, only to roll back into the water once more. A single parrot was perched on its trunk, watching Jonah's progress with silent amazement. It blinked, then swivelled its head towards the beach. Jonah followed its gaze – he could not help himself – and stopped dead in the water. No sooner had he stopped than he sank. He blew out a spray of water and kicked out, sculling with his arms in an effort to regain his composure.

Leaning against the fallen palm was a woman. Until now she had been shielded from view by the tree and its considerable foliage, but now Jonah could see her quite clearly. The sun beat down on him, penetrating the thick hatch of his hair; its rays turned the glossy leaves of the forest wall to emeralds. For the briefest moment, in this Paradise, he believed he had found Eve.

She was turned a little away from him, bent over as though regarding something on the sand. Her hair was long and dark – black perhaps, or very nearly so – and her skin was heavily tanned. A small collection of objects lay in the sand beside her: several small bags, a wooden box, some clothing. She, like him, was naked.

Jonah felt himself turn even pinker. He backtracked against the current, hoping to retreat behind the tree, but his splashing and spluttering had already attracted the woman's attention. She turned round quickly, evidently startled but not, Jonah thought, scared. He found himself looking straight into her eyes, found himself held by them, and although they were separated by the best part of fifty yards, he felt close enough to reach out and touch her. The woman smiled, unashamed by her nudity, and crouched down to rummage among her things.

An air of unreality had descended upon Jonah. He looked up, half-expecting to see some shimmering veil thrown across the heavens; he saw only the pure cobalt of the sky, the wide eye of the sun. He glanced to his left. His own belongings were a dark speck on the distant sand, at least half a mile away. Reason urged him to go back for them, to clothe himself at least, reminding him that no English gentleman could possibly enter the company of a lady in such a state of undress.

The woman reached up with her right hand and brushed the hair back from her face, an unconscious, childish gesture. Her body was smooth and brown, a lean shape cut from the wall of greenery ascending behind her. The scene was somehow primeval.

Paradise, marvelled Jonah. A wave splashed against his chin and before he knew what he was doing he found himself swimming towards the shore. Horror mingled with excitement, but something drove him on until his feet scraped against a coarse shelf of sand. He waded through the surf, stopping at a point where the water was just deep enough for him to be able to retain his dignity.

I hope the tide is not going out, he thought wryly.

The woman had not looked up at all during his approach, nor did she look up now. She was still searching in the box, her face creased by a frown of concentration. Jonah tried to place her country of origin and found he could not. The dark colour of her skin seemed likely to be a product of direct sun rather than original race, yet he fancied there was something exotic in her features. South America, perhaps? He could not be sure.

Then she lifted her eyes and spoke. *America, without a doubt,* he thought, *but from the north. The United States.*

'You going to stand there all day?' Her accent was light. Jonah found himself entranced by the shine of her white teeth in the sunlight. He spread his arms and shrugged.

'I'm afraid you may consider me indecent – you see, I'm not wearing any clothes,' he answered. She smiled and copied his gesture, affording him a generous view of her breasts. Jonah looked down sharply, suddenly fascinated by the sea bed, clearly visible through the water that splashed around his waist.

'Nor me,' she laughed. 'Come on, Englishman. I won't bite!'

Jonah loitered amid the waves while the strange woman sat on the sand and laughed at him. The sun was beginning to burn his shoulders – now he had two reasons to retrieve his clothes. Yet he could not tear himself away. He looked around, locating the horizon and scanning it. Sails pierced the sky many miles distant. The woman's laughter was as raw as her presence here, a rich, primitive sound. A *good* sound.

Finding her eyes again, he was surprised to see sympathy there. She beckoned him as a mother might beckon a bashful child.

'Join me, please,' she called. 'I'll look the other way if you like. Got a wrap you could use.'

There came a squawk from the fallen tree. The parrot that had been preening itself there suddenly exploded into a whirring, feathered firework, swooping low over Jonah's head, so close that he felt the draught from its wings. It wheeled in the air, heading out into the blue distance. With its departure Jonah felt the last of his reticence ebb away and, gritting his teeth, he stepped forward out of the waves.

She watched him approach, keeping her eyes fixed upon his. As he gained the sand, feeling it cling to his wet feet and ankles, he grew more confident and even managed to adopt a kind of swagger. Even when her gaze wandered – briefly – down his body he found that he was not ashamed. Everything about this encounter felt right – the utter loneliness of the location, the wall of trees that was its backdrop, the enclosing heat of the sun and, yes, even their nudity.

Later on during that extraordinary day Jonah found time to reflect that *this* was the moment when he started to cross over into a world that was wholly new. Baptised by the waters of the Sunda Straits, he emerged reborn into what at first seemed Paradise, but which he would later come to regard as the very gate of Hell. Over black sand he walked with water dripping from his body, towards the American woman who regarded him with innocent fascination. When he reached her he stopped, hesitated, then bowed extravagantly.

'Jonah Lightfoot,' he announced. 'At your service, madam.'

Still smiling, the woman nodded her head. 'Pleased to meet you, Jonah. My name's Anne West, but everybody calls me Annie.'

'Might that category include me?'

She looked around. 'Looks like you and me is everybody,

Jonah. Guess you might as well. Want this?' She held up a long strip of dark red towelling. 'I know how you English types get shy.'

Again Jonah consulted his internal workings and found that he was not feeling shy at all. Quite the opposite, in fact – he had the urge to throw himself down on to the sand and spread his arms and legs out wide, exposing himself to the full glare of the sun. This urge he resisted, just. 'No, thank you,' he stammered, shocked by his unprecedented boldness. 'I think I'll just sit here and steam, if that's acceptable to you.'

Annie nodded graciously and Jonah sat down beside her.

There was a pause, after which they both started speaking at once. A shared laugh rounded out the moment, after which they both relaxed. Jonah plucked a flake of bark from the sand and tossed it into the foam, then lay back to gaze up into the sky.

'May I inquire what brings you so far East, Annie?'

'Indeed you may inquire, Jonah, my man,' laughed Annie, mimicking his accent faultlessly. 'Though by my reckoning I've been headed west.'

Jonah frowned. She settled back, propping her head on one elbow. From Jonah's viewpoint her mane of dark hair was surrounded by a halo of sunlight. Again he was struck by the primitive nature of their situation: they might have been brought together from anywhere, from any time. *Paradise*. The thought was like a sigh.

'I joined ship in San Francisco, you see. A ship of naturalists, or so they reckoned themselves. Following some route or other. They were good enough company for a year but I persuaded them to change course as far as Java and took my leave at Anjer.' Her eyes grew distant. 'A couple of them wanted more than just my company towards the end.'

'I . . . see,' said Jonah carefully.

'Anyway, there's a lot here for a girl to see, so I said to myself, "Annie, if you don't set your feet down sooner or later there'll be nothing to take home again at the end of it all." So here I am.'

'May I ask what it is that you do plan to take home?'

Another smile, a different one this time. A little girl smile, shy and secret, full of pride. 'You really want to see?' She was excited now, and Jonah could not help but smile back. He sat up again as she turned to the wooden box he had seen from the sea, then he peered over her bare shoulder as she lifted its lid. The sun bounced off its contents with sudden ferocity and for an instant he was blinded. *Is it gold?* he thought stupidly. Then his vision cleared, and he saw.

Inside the box were what looked like hundreds of small, oblong tiles. Each one measured perhaps one inch by three-fifths of an inch; they were made from what Jonah guessed to be ivory. The box itself was dark hardwood, probably mahogany, lined with silk, and it opened on smooth, brass hinges. On one side, occupying one-third of the width of the interior, was an elaborate set of trays and drawers. A porcelain cup was resting in a recess in the uppermost tray, and from it came the pungent aroma of turpentine. A small palette lay beside the cup, on which were spread a range of pigments, mostly blues and greens and translucent, cerulean mixtures of the two. A pile of paint-soaked rags completed the ensemble.

Jonah drank in the incredible richness of the box's interior – it seemed to him like a temple whose exterior was plain, unadorned stucco yet within which lay the most astonishing array of mosaics and jewelled tiles. The smell of the turpentine mingled with the constant drift of spice from Java, causing a moment of light-headedness; it was not without reluctance that he allowed this feeling to pass.

'You're a painter!' he exclaimed. Annie nodded, still wearing her child's smile.

'Damn good, too,' she replied, almost breaking the spell.

Jonah scanned the inside of the box for evidence of a canvas, or a small board perhaps on which Annie was working. 'What . . . ?' he began, but before he could complete the question she was pointing to one of the tiles, separated from the others on a tiny, wooden plinth. Brass clasps held it in place. On its upper surface, painted with the most extraordinary delicacy, was a duplicate of the view across the straits.

He stared at the miniature painting, enthralled. The Javanese coast floated in the distance, a mass of faded green that protruded from the ocean like the haunch of some subterranean god. The sky flowed above it like liquid; the sun admitted white fire from a distant realm. Exquisite, fragile, a small and perfect splinter cut from the reality that surrounded them, the painting shone as if with its own, internal light. Jonah knew that this was an illusion, just the kick of the sun off the oil she had spread so artfully across the smooth ivory of the tile, but as illusions went it was flawless.

'It's beautiful,' he marvelled.

'Thank you. It's nearly finished.'

Jonah looked again at the tiles that filled two-thirds of the box and saw that they were divided into two groups by a removable wooden slat. Those in the larger group were plain; those below – these numbered about thirty, he guessed – each bore a miniature painting. Most of them were seascapes, a few of which featured black masts and ropes in the foreground; three showed a high mountain range peaked with snow; two more were of a busy sea port. They were all beautiful.

'The Rockies were from memory,' she explained, indicating the mountain views, 'and the port scenes I did just before we left San Francisco. I didn't do much painting until we were well on the way – I was trying to get away from the United States, not remember it.' She sighed. 'But those views seemed so lovely at the time. I just couldn't ignore them.'

'And these?' Jonah asked, indicating a pair of tiles half in shadow at the bottom of the group. Both showed the same location, but at different times of day. The first was of a sunset or sunrise, he could not tell which, over a primitive, rocky terrain. The second showed the same landscape at midday, shadowless and bald. A lizard scurried across the foreground, its scales glistening in the sun, its motion trapped by the brilliant green pigment she had chosen for it. The place looked old, and it looked familiar.

'Galapagos,' answered Annie with a shudder. 'It put me off painting for a while. I'm only just starting up again now.'

She carried on talking but Jonah was not listening. Galapagos! Of course! He had not really registered her earlier comment about travelling with a group of naturalists, or rather the relevance of her words had not sunk in. What had she said: that they were 'following some route or other'?

'Darwin!' he exploded, rocking forward on to his knees and showering sand across her clothes, which were piled neatly beside the box. 'You were following Darwin!' Annie nodded, her amusement at his outburst apparent.

'*They* were following him,' she corrected him. 'I was just going along for the ride. They picked up his trail in the Panama Bay. Tahiti was so beautiful.'

Jonah let out a long, whistling breath. It was all too much. The sensuous aroma of the spices wafting across the straits, the heat of the sun, the extraordinary circumstances of this encounter . . . and now this.

'Charles Darwin is . . .' he started to say.

A sound erupted behind them like shutters banging against a hundred windows, a clattering that filled the air suddenly and completely. Annie dropped the box; the tiles rattled, their own, small sound quite lost in the cacophony. They whirled round together, Annie's long hair sliding over Jonah's bare shoulder.

It was as if the forest had come alive. A cloud of green expanded out of the foliage as though each individual leaf had taken on a life of its own and hurled itself into flight. Then the reality broke through: it was a cloud not of leaves but of parrots, thousands of parrots bursting from the jungle in a single flock. They watched in astonishment as the sky turned green, as the slapping of wings was joined by the parrots' cackling voices: 'Kara-kat! Kara-kat!' Jonah did not believe the local tales that the island on which they had landed was named after these characteristic cries – there were any amount of these birds spread across both Java and Sumatra; they did not belong to Krakatoa alone. However, indigenous or not, something had clearly unsettled them and now they were leaving their home in their thousands, if not tens of thousands. The cloud trailed upwards and outwards, crossing in front of the sun and dipping towards the mainland, a wide thread of green in the clear blue sky.

Slowly the sound of their calls faded, leaving only the rhythm of the ocean on the hot, black sand. Jonah and Annie shared a frown, neither of them entirely happy with this strangely ominous event. There was an awkward silence.

'I should get my clothes,' Jonah suggested.

'No,' said Annie at once. 'We should stay together.'

'Is something wrong?'

'I don't know. Yes, I think so.' Jonah found himself growing uneasy. The air felt damp and cloying, as if a thunderstorm were about to break, though the sky was still breathtakingly clear. He saw his sudden fear reflected in her face.

She tossed her head then leaned forward and closed the box, lifting her eyes as she did so to the distant horizon. Jonah stared at her naked back. He was suddenly appalled by his own nudity and tilted his body forward as well, crossing his arms in his lap in an effort to regain some kind of modesty. He shivered.

'Did you come on a *proa*?' Annie asked, her frown deepening. She was paying him no attention whatsoever.

'The men who brought me are coming back this afternoon. And you . . . ?'

'A lot of fishermen come to Krakatoa.' She did not appear to have heard his reply. Her eyes were everywhere, now on the jungle, now raised to the sky. 'There's always boats between here and Anjer.'

'The *Zeeland* leaves today,' Jonah babbled. 'It's a mail packet, Dutch, if I remember rightly. It will sail quite close to us, I think.' Annie shook her head, her gaze keen. Jonah could see her nostrils quivering, the dryness of her lips. 'Can you see any boats coming near?' he ventured.

'I can see . . . I don't know. I don't think so.' She glanced at him, clearly afraid. 'I thought I saw something in the bay, close by. It was –' she gestured vaguely with her left hand, '– big, towering, like an island.' She shuddered and started to gather her clothes together. 'Come on, let's go and get your things. I don't think we should stay on the beach.'

As they stood she held the strip of towelling out to him again. This time he took it gratefully, wrapping around his waist like a kilt. It amazed him how this simple act restored his sense of propriety; it did not still his fear however.

The day seemed to *freeze*. In that long, held second, Jonah knew something was dreadfully wrong.

He looked back up the beach and his eyes widened with horror. He backed away, stumbling over the wooden box and sprawling in the sand beneath Annie's shadow. He stared up at her, eyes bulging, and pointed stupidly.

A red, flickering tongue launched itself out from the jungle and across the sand, splitting open the beach; as they watched the crack grew wider and deeper, spraying steam and gobbets of fire from its glowing depths. A line of trees erupted into flame like gigantic sulphur matches. The ground rattled; Jonah's ears felt heavy and his eyes seemed to be loosening in their sockets. Annie was raising her hands to her ears.

An invisible battering ram hurled her backwards like a doll.

Across the entire expanse of the beach the sand *levitated*. Jonah heard a brief, dull *thump*, and then he was struck deaf.

He fought against the black sand scouring his face, the idea that Annie had been injured galvanising him into action. To be here at all was awful enough, but to be here alone was too dreadful a prospect. His fingers touched flesh and he grabbed what turned out to be Annie's wrist. Terrified, he pulled her close, seeking out her face in the sudden, painful fog. She seemed unhurt, though she was gasping for breath; she was mouthing silent words, her face contorted, and only when she was close enough for him to feel the wind of her breath on his cheek did he realise that she was screaming at him. Still he heard nothing, nothing at all.

'I can't hear you!' he bellowed, feeling his cry as a rich, inaudible vibration inside his head. She pounded at her own ears, shaking her head violently.

They were grappling with each other in a blinding whirlwind of black sand, yelling hopelessly at each other as the shore collapsed beneath them. Fresh red flames exploded close by and they were thrown towards the sea. Hot water splashed across their searching feet. The whole world seemed to be shaking.

Paradise Lost, thought Jonah in panic, then he looked up, and understood.

Above the broken shore, above the vast swathe of forest, above even the green peak of Rakata, there rose a great, black column of smoke and ash. As he watched the very air seemed to shake and a crescent-shaped piece of rock from the summit of the mountain was blown skywards; at least thirty hardwood trees were rooted to it. It flew vertically until it was lost from view in the spreading cloud of ash. More chunks of mountainside followed it, none smaller than a house. Light flashed on and off inside the cloud assembling itself in the heavens; it widened into a colossal dome, a rain of yellow particles clustered around its outer edge, ready to fall upon the sea. The dome's shadow slithered with crushing speed down the mountain, eager to consume the island that had spawned it, keen to journey beyond its birthing ground, hungry for the mainland.

The noise was immense, the noise was the entire world, yet neither Jonah nor Annie could hear anything at all; Jonah was convinced, if only briefly, that the gates of Hell had opened on this lonely beach, that God had finally caught up with him, had judged him for his sins and found him guilty.

A sand-caked hand grabbed his head and drew it roughly round. Annie stared at him and carefully mouthed three silent syllables that showed that she too had understood their peril.

'Vol . . . kay . . . no!' she mimed, dragging him into the sea. They were waist-deep now. Jonah looked up the beach for his clothes and saw only a rain of ash, a dense yellow mist like a sulphurous curtain. The cloud leaked across the sky, still attached to Krakatoa by its thick, black root. Lumps of the mountain were being launched steadily up into its belly; smaller pieces were beginning to return to earth, crashing into the jungle like meteorites.

We're dead, thought Jonah, casting wildly around him for some means of escape. *Painted into a corner.* Annie turned from him and, holding the box out in front of her like a child's flotation aid, kicked off from the bottom and began to swim out to sea. Jonah was surprised to see that the box floated – he had imagined that the ivory tiles and tubes of paint would have weighed it down beyond the buoyancy of the wood – but he had little time to marvel. The beach was gone; there was no choice but to abandon himself to the waves and pursue her into the darkening ocean.

The sea bed shelved downwards with alarming speed; equally alarming was the growing ferocity of the waves. No sooner had Jonah thrown himself headlong than a pulse of energy – a massive shock wave that moved through the water like a heartbeat – thumped him ten yards beyond the point where Annie was kicking her way out of a deep trough. He tried to turn, swallowed a mouthful of hot, salty water and gagged. The horizon was lost; the sky was alive with spray. This was no sanctuary – if anything it was worse. Annie disappeared briefly then she too was thrown forward. Her shoulder crashed into the small of Jonah's back and he reached for her, grabbing the box, sharing its fragile buoyancy. Yet another swell lifted them practically clear of the water altogether and tossed them like driftwood entirely out of their depth.

Barely thirty seconds had passed since the eruption had begun, yet already the island was invisible behind an expanding wall of black and yellow ash. Mountain-sized fists punched out from this advancing mass, propelling jagged rocks and searing clouds of gas and dust into the atmosphere. With every second the concussions grew more powerful, pumping new, raw energy into the frightful vanguard.

We are already lost, Jonah realised as the wall of ash flowed towards them over a boiling sea. *There is nowhere to go. Even our bones will be turned to powder.*

Miraculously the box continued to support their combined weight. Then the first tendrils of the curtain overtook them. The already dark sky grew black and smouldering ash started to rain down. The water hissed angrily as it was struck by the volcanic downpour.

They ducked beneath the waves, holding their breaths for as long as they could before gasping their way to the surface again. The hellish shower was accompanied by a searing wind that burned their faces and shoulders. Again and again they ducked, rotating their bodies whenever they surfaced so as to present the backs of their heads to the gale. Jonah felt blisters rising on his neck and winced at the sting of salt water against wounded flesh.

Each time they emerged into ever more turbulent air. Breathing was painful. Close by, yet barely visible, floated a vast sheet of pumice, an agglomeration of small, porous rock particles that bobbed on the waves like corks ejected from a million bottles of champagne. The darkness deepened and swallowed the raft up.

They broke the surface together, and their eyes met. All Jonah could see now were her eyes; then the great shadow in the sky fell across them like dark lids. Annie was gone, all light was gone and he was alone in the burning ocean. The volcano, hidden behind its cataclysmic shroud, was a looming presence in his mind, a monster come to pluck his soul and Annie's from the skin of the world.

Here I die, he thought in the void. Somewhere unseen, thunder roared and the monster toppled towards him . . .

Then Annie's eyes suddenly shone out again like twin beacons cutting through the doom. It seemed to Jonah that they reflected a miraculous spark of daylight; the light was strong and blue, the colour of summer sky.

She was looking past him now and Jonah realised that what he could see in her eyes was a reflection not of the sky but of some huge object close by. Behind him. He turned to see what it was that Annie had already seen.

It loomed over them like a mountain, yet it seemed as insubstantial as a dream. It wavered, its outer surface rippling, its inner structure shifting strangely – now here, now gone. The waves fought about its base; however insubstantial it might have appeared it was real enough. It filled their vision, a glowing edifice that shone out under the shadow of the volcanic cloud with an ethereal glow. Cold air wafted down from its dripping heights, repelling the ash and soothing their tortured skin. It was huge; it was beautiful; it was impossible.

It was an iceberg.

Jonah's jaw sank as he watched it solidify before his outraged eyes. Its interior, initially transparent, thickened and clouded until he could barely see more than a few yards into the ice. Behind the blue he fancied he saw something . . . red? Even this degree of transparency was unnatural, he knew, but then the iceberg had no right to be here in the first place. He gaped, uncaring. He had lost all capacity to question; all he could do was marvel.

The iceberg wallowed, throwing off a spray of icy pellets from its flanks and rolling sideways slowly and inexorably. A thin sheet of ice detached itself from somewhere high up on its side and fell, shattering on the ocean surface. Slowly, like a giant turning in its sleep, it righted itself . . . and grew solid. Jonah sensed rather than saw the unimaginable bulk that lay concealed beneath the waves, felt its pressure against his loosely flailing legs.

Then Annie was moving again, striking out towards this exotic lifeboat, locating a shelf of ice that lay barely two feet above the level of the sea. She tugged at the painting box, tearing it from Jonah's grasp and tossing it on to the ice. Then she found purchase in some hidden crevice, pulled herself clear of the water, turning deftly as she swung her legs up on to the ledge, and landed with a slap. She bent forward, reaching out to Jonah with her hands, which he took gratefully. The sea contracted then struck, spitting him out, projecting him upwards so that he knocked Annie backwards.

They slid the width of the ice shelf in each other's arms, and only when they struck the sheer wall at its far side, shaking loose a miniature avalanche of crystal shards that struck the ledge with a brittle tinkling sound, did Jonah realise that his hearing had returned. A massive explosion sounded close by, parting the waters briefly, revealing a view as if into a canyon of water. Then the ocean closed up again, throwing up thirty-foot waves; as they watched the height of the swell increased yet further.

Despite the strength of the swell, the iceberg hardly moved at all. Jonah noticed his kilt had been torn away.

Naked, they continued to cling to each other, Annie's painting box sandwiched between them, the only man-made artefact they had brought with them from the island. Though reason screamed at them that this could not be happening, that icebergs simply did not appear from nowhere – and certainly not within eight degrees of the equator – nothing could deny the hard certainty of the ice beneath their clumsily folded legs. For now there was nothing to do but sit here and listen to the steady artillery of the volcano; the questions would come later.

Ice pillars rose on either side of the ledge that had become their sanctuary, framing their view of the island. Krakatoa threw its fractured self into the heavens with a series of resounding, low-pitched concussions. The cloud sped out over the water, its black and yellow form illuminated from within by fantastic discharges of electricity. It moved fast at the perimeter, fast enough to overtake the flock of parrots fleeing for the mainland. It consumed them, clogging their feathers before sucking them in and baking them, then spewing them out, charred and lifeless. They fell with the ash and pumice, forming floating rafts that mirrored the spread of the cloud above.

Somewhere on the remains of the beach, a Hunter chimed eleven times, then fell silent forever.

Though it was still many months from its final death throes, Krakatoa continued to rip itself apart. This was merely the prelude to the symphony it had been composing for the last few thousand years. After such a long wait it could afford to take its time.

For a long while there was nothing to see. The iceberg and its human cargo were entirely enclosed by the cloud of ash and debris gradually expanding outwards from the shore of the island. There was no way to tell if it were day or night beyond the shroud of cool air that was their only protection against the searing heat. All they could do was wait.

Jonah watched as Annie opened the painting box and sorted through its contents, dabbing at splashes of linseed oil and turpentine, rearranged scattered tiles.

Distraction, he decided. *Like the woman who cleans the house from attic to cellar on the news of her husband's death.*

For were they not dead?

Jonah glanced at the glowing ice walls of their lifeboat. *This does not look like any representation of the afterlife that I have ever encountered.*

The particular tile Annie had been working on, the one bearing the painting of the Javanese coast, had been held in its place by the little brass clips; now she pulled the clips apart and removed it from its plinth. She held it up in the eerie light and Jonah saw for the first time that there was something on its underside – what looked like an abstract pattern of red lines.

Distraction.

'May I?' he ventured, holding out his hand. Annie shrugged and handed the tile over.

'It's still a little wet.'

He looked first at the tiny painting on the upper side. It was truly exquisite: a perfect miniature composition possessing a depth of colour he could almost reach into. 'You're very talented,' he said.

Then he turned it over to study the pattern on the other side. It comprised five red lines and looked a little like a sword:

'Is it Chinese?' he guessed.

'It's a *ma-chong* tile,' answered Annie. 'I've got a complete set in this box. I'm travelling round the world, and as I go I'm painting a different scene on the back of each tile. I reckon by the time I've finished the last tile I'll be back home again. That's the symbol for the Red Dragon, by the way.'

'Ma-chong?'

'It's a game, like a card game or something.'

'I have never heard of it,' said Jonah, turning the tile over in wonderment. 'I thought my father had collected most games in his time, but this is very strange. How many tiles are there altogether?'

'One hundred and forty-four.'

Jonah's jaw dropped as he stared first into the box, then at Annie, with new respect. She returned his stare with the open-eyed honesty he was beginning to find appealing. 'I've only done thirty-one so far – I've got a long way to go, Jonah Lightfoot.'

'So where is home?' Now that they had returned their attention to each other rather than their surroundings Jonah found himself disconcerted all over again by their nudity. His solution was to talk, and Annie seemed grateful for the opportunity.

'Kansas. My folks were among the first settlers out on the plains. I remember them breaking up the sod – those big old steers, six to a plough.' She laughed. '"Drouthy Kansas" they used to call it, because there was no water. Plenty of grasshoppers, mind you. Folks were heading back east in their droves in the early days, but we stuck it out.'

'Until you decided to head west. You said earlier that you sailed from San Francisco.'

'That's true enough.' Another laugh, this one tainted with bitterness. 'It's a lot harder to run west than east, but I managed it somehow.'

'What were you running from?' At first Jonah did not think she was going to answer this, then she sighed and looked away across the sea to Krakatoa.

'Oh . . . no one thing. I guess my man was the main reason, though.'

'Your man?'

'My husband.' That direct stare again, challenging Jonah. 'Are you surprised, just because I've no wedding band? I lost it on that damn prairie! Lost everything, or so it seemed at the time.'

'Did your husband die?'

'No, leastways not in the way you mean. You heard me mention the grasshoppers, Jonah. Do you have any idea what a plague is really like?' He shook his head dumbly. 'Thought not, not many do; not unless they've lived in Kansas, that is. It was in '74; there were other years but that was the worst. They filled the skies like that volcano filled the sky today, only you knew it was no cloud – you knew it was *alive*. The noise is like a buzzing in your head you can't get rid of, no matter how hard you shake it. It's like the end of the world, Jonah. Just like in the bible, only *real*.

'They're in your hair, crawling over your eyes. The sun's gone, just a shiny, metal cloud, as far as the eye can see. The corn's gone in a matter of minutes. A year's food, a whole year. You go inside and they're scratching at the roof; you go out and they're smothering you again. Later, when you think they've gone, you find their bodies filling up the wells, you can taste them in the water, Jonah – you can taste them everywhere. It's hell on earth. They promise you a new world and all you get is grasshoppers and prairie fires and bad men.

'He took to hitting me, my man. We damn near starved that year, and even though it was the grasshoppers were to blame it was me he hit. I was just sixteen.' She paused before going on.

'He breathed one in while they were swarming. He swore he could feel it kicking and squirming in his lungs all the next day. I don't know if that's possible, but he swore it was true. I think it affected him, you know, in his mind. He changed after that, didn't look at me again, just looked through me. Hit me so hard in the belly one day I bled, and I mean I bled a *lot*. Then he got even angrier when I didn't give him children. Took me seven years to pluck up the courage to leave, and another year to reach the coast. This old Chinese took me in, fed me up – I was scrawny as a lizard when I got off the trail.' She fingered the catch at the front of the box. 'He made the box for me, set me on my way.'

Jonah thought for a moment that she was going to cry. Her face started to crumple but she checked herself, hitching in a single, deep breath and . . . again that stare.

Then the world beyond the iceberg changed. The cloud thinned abruptly, revealing the stars. Night had fallen.

'I guess it was the drawing and painting that kept me going . . .' Annie was saying, but the words died on her lips.

'It cannot be night already,' whispered Jonah. 'Barely an hour has passed.'

The stars shone, but they were not the hard, bright points they should have been: they were blurs, their trails curved around the central Pole Star. The sky was spinning like a child's top.

Everything grew bright and the sun exploded into the sky. Dawn arrived, a silent gunshot, and the sun flew up the arch of the heavens like the catch of some great fisher-god. Barely two seconds had passed before it had reached its zenith, whereupon it began its descent into the west.

Clouds whipped past, vague hulks travelling from one horizon to the other in the space of a single breath. The sun winked out and night returned. The stars resumed their dizzy round and then the sun hurtled into view again, moving faster now, a bar of hazy light painted across the celestial sphere. Darkness again, then the sudden dawn, speeding up all the time until day and night were flickering on and off once every second.

'It's like the world just got faster!' gasped Annie. 'And here's us standing still in the middle of it.'

No, we are the ones who have been accelerated, thought Jonah in mute wonder. *We are travellers in time!*

A new dust cloud expanded from Krakatoa across the sky, a near-black shroud that swelled then receded as the days raced past. Except for its lowest peak of Perboewatan, where a little vegetation still clung on, the island had become a grey corpse; the trees on the upper slopes lay flat, blasted into submission by the eruptions. The column of smoke remained at the summit of Rakata however. It looked to Jonah like a giant cauliflower reaching miles up into the sky.

A boat flashed into view, anchored off the shore of the island for a few brief eye-blinks then was gone again. *Explorers,* thought Jonah, *seeking the gates of Hell.* Steam was spurting from fissures on the mountainside. As the darkness of night flicked on and off the crater was revealed as a vast, glowing pit.

Weeks sprinted by.

There was a brief lull in the volcano's activity, during which time the sky cleared completely. Then a tremendous black cloud appeared above it as if materialised by some cosmic conjuror.

Vast mats of pumice rode the sea before vanishing; more ships came and went. For a horrifying instant, Jonah was convinced a ship had sailed right through the iceberg: for a fraction of a second he thought he saw a wall of steel plates, then a churning of machinery and the hot brilliance of a furnace. Then all he could see was Krakatoa again, and he pressed his hands against his chest, trying to reassure himself that he was still alive. He glanced across at Annie: she, like him, was frozen in place, mesmerised.

Another lull, fleeting seconds of true daylight interspersed with brooding clouds of black, others of pink and grey. Krakatoa appeared to be slumping into the sea. It was entirely stripped of its vegetation now. Jonah, who had been counting the flicks of light that indicated the passing days, calculated swiftly: in the outside world it was by now the middle of August.

'There's no sound,' observed Annie, her voice loud and unexpected. As she spoke these very words there was a crash high above them and the iceberg shook. Annie grabbed the painting box, then clutched Jonah's arm as they were pitched forward. They slid together for several feet across the smooth ice shelf before coming to a halt just short of the water's edge. The quality of the light changed, seemed to *relax* somehow, and they rejoined the normal flow of time.

The sun slithered to a halt, high in a perfect sky.

It was 26 August, a Sunday. It was 1.00 p.m.

The first, absurd, thought that Jonah had when the iceberg lifted beneath them was that the sea was getting ready to belch. He began to laugh, a nervous reaction that drew a quizzical look from Annie. What happened next banished their smiles even before they were fully formed.

At last the prelude was over. It was time for the symphony to begin.

The previous, spectacular eruptions that had driven Jonah and Annie from Krakatoa's shore, that had brought ships full of curious seafarers to mount its slopes and peer into its crater, that had blackened the sky and skinned the ocean with floating rock, were mere firecrackers compared to what happened next. The plugs of ancient lava that had kept the island's three cones sealed shut for untold centuries gave way simultaneously; the sister peaks of Perboewatan, Danan and Rakata disintegrated finally and utterly as they unleashed the fire below.

Krakatoa had finished with eruptions; at last, Krakatoa began to explode.

The sound came in a steady rhythm – deep inhalations followed by rich, bass thumps. Steam and rock were discharged into an expanding pillar of debris. It rose up and up, gaining what seemed an impossible altitude, its flanks opening out and assuming a shape that made Jonah think of a pine tree. Its progress was steady, inexorable, and after what he guessed to be about forty-five minutes of constant explosions he tried to estimate its size, based on what he knew of Krakatoa's original dimensions. He thought it was around fifteen miles high.

The sea was becoming choppy, causing the iceberg to lurch from side to side. With sudden horror Jonah realised that they were no longer sitting on smooth ice but in a steadily deepening pool of water.

'Quickly!' he urged, drawing Annie away from the sea. A gully had opened in the wall at the back of the ledge and together they clambered up it. Icy water poured down past them, making the going treacherous, but eventually they found their way to a second ledge rather higher than the first and set well back in the melting iceberg. Several times along the way Annie nearly dropped the box, but despite Jonah's repeated pleas that she be done with it and throw it into the sea she would not let it go.

'It's all I have left!' she protested, shouting over the volcano's artillery.

After an interminable afternoon, night fell as an evil, cloying blackness alive with the never-ending sound of the explosions. Lightning carved the sky into a nightmare mosaic, drawing red faces in the underbelly of the cloud; balls of fire drifted over the swollen, pitching ocean, crackling and spitting with pent-up energy; a sticky rain covered them with hot, grey mud that clung to them insistently.

Some inner sense told Jonah that they were still under some mysterious protection, some cloak with which the iceberg shielded itself from the rest of the world. Certainly no humans could have remained this close to the volcano and survived. Yet, if this was so, why was the force now allowing the iceberg to be destroyed? Of more immediate concern, what would happen to them when the iceberg finally vanished altogether?

He had no idea what brought them through that long, awful

night. The mud remained long after the rains which brought it departed, hardening and cracking on their skins. Their icy haven bucked beneath them like a restless steed, tipping first one way then the other as waves of mounting intensity began to radiate from Krakatoa's shores. The regular breathe-thump of the volcano was occasionally interrupted by ripping sounds from closer at hand: slabs of ice detaching themselves and crashing into the sea.

Dawn came, an ominous, dust-filled affair. The iceberg was lifted high on a massive wave and Annie raised her head with a start. Jonah looked across to the mainland, just visible now through a deep ravine in the side of the failing iceberg. Ash clouds were devouring it. *People are dying over there,* he thought. He wondered how long the island could keep this up.

Perhaps a minute later, his question was answered.

Krakatoa, which for the last nineteen hours had been unloading its guts into the atmosphere, suddenly found that there was nothing left to expel. The mountain no longer had a heart – inside there was a huge void. Its power utterly spent, the mountain simply caved in on itself.

A pulse of sound louder than any sound heard by human ears before swept across the iceberg, on its way to Australia. The sea fell into a deepening crater along with the collapsing mountain, only to be ejected with renewed vigour. It rose, forming a circular wave that expanded from the vacuum where Krakatoa had once existed. One hundred feet in height, the tidal wave bore down on the Javanese coast at over three hundred miles an hour. Soon, thirty-six thousand people would be dead.

Both sound wave and killing wave rolled *through* the disintegrating iceberg, leaving it practically unscathed. Then the iceberg started to spin lazily, affording Jonah a reverse view of the titanic wall of water as it accelerated into the narrow straits, gaining speed and rearing high over the already devastated mainland. It rocked again and they were thrown hard against its flank. Annie's head struck the corner of her painting box. She dropped, senseless, at Jonah's feet.

He reached for her, disorientated. Everything was spinning now, and the world had become suffused with red light. Something tickled his upper lip; reaching up to rub it he found his nose was bleeding. He stumbled, fell on his back, stared up.

The sides of the iceberg had completely melted away, leaving a thin, central spire. He and Annie were lying near its base, on a broad shelf of ice that encircled the spire completely. It towered overhead, a crystal cathedral. It was from inside the spire that the red light was coming.

The spire was almost transparent, and Jonah gradually began to make out a shape inside it. It was flattened, a red sketch of something that looked both alien and eerily familiar. As he watched the ice melted further, narrowing the spire and revealing more and more of its strange prisoner.

Coils appeared at the base, extending into an elegant spiral form that reached its pinnacle at the very top of the spire. Two broad fans extended laterally about halfway up.

Not fans, Jonah thought in terror. *Wings!*

The iceberg was spinning faster now, beginning to whirl like a carousel. Something was pulling it towards the maelstrom that was Krakatoa's grave. Jonah dropped to his knees, leaning over Annie in an instinctive gesture of protection. A whirlpool the size of a small city had opened up in the ocean, but he was only dimly aware of its rapid motion. A steady roaring noise filled his ears, squeezing them as though he had swum to a great depth. Above, the ice spire had all but melted away. Slowly at first, then with increasing speed, the remains of the iceberg descended into the whirlpool.

Everything grew dark as the water climbed above the level of the ledge. Jonah found he was incapable of responding to this latest turn of events. Many years before he had been put into a trance by a stage hypnotist; he felt now much as he had then, fully aware yet quite unconcerned that he had relinquished all control. His eyelids drooped and the ocean swallowed him up.

The last thing he saw before the blackness claimed him was the red shape finally breaking free of the ice tower. It appeared to him now to be a winged skeleton, some primeval ghost which bent its neck towards him even as his own awareness drained away. Its head – if head it was – was long and narrow.

Curious, he thought, drifting. *It has no eyes.*

The sheets of pumice floating on the tortured ocean were joined by a different sort of debris. Wooden houses, blown flat and buckled beyond recognition drifted amid the wreckage of entire towns. Cattle pitched and rolled, their dead and bloated bodies jostling the remains of the men who had harnessed them to their ploughs. Through the ranks of men the exotic corpses of tigers carved their way, their pelts as glorious in death as they had been in life.

The tempest caused by the explosion of Krakatoa travelled a little over seven times round the world before it died; the remnants of the tidal wave, reduced to a height of a few inches, were observed on the opposite side of the globe at Cape Horn.

An area of ocean the size of Australia was covered with ash.

Where Krakatoa had once reared high and proud there was now nothing but barren ocean. Amid the slowly swirling currents that marked the place where the volcano had been bobbed the tattered remnants of a book written nearly twenty-five years previously by a man called Charles Darwin.

Of Jonah Lightfoot and his newly-found companion, no further trace remained.

2

Crusoe

The sunlight showers through the skeleton of iron and glass, describing a grid on the endless floor. Jonah runs ahead of his father and brother, the book held to his chest. His feet kick up dust, which scintillates in the crisscross of light beams. His heart thumps against the cover of the book, against the name of his father's hero; together, Jonah and Darwin run through the Crystal Palace.

'Wait in the doorway!' booms the voice of his father. Outside, the sunlight is unbroken yet somehow the world there is darker. The marching shadows of the transept intensify the process of vision until it becomes unbearable. Though he knows this is no cathedral, Jonah, at eight years of age, knows he is in the presence of God.

Throughout his tour of the Palace his every sense has been assailed. His father's rich prose has conjured for him the myriad sights and smells which once filled this mighty edifice. In the year of Jonah's birth it opened its doors to the world, and although it is by comparison now but an empty shell, still it is home to the ghost of the Great Exhibition of 1851.

'This was the Machinery Court, boys. Imagine the Great Hydraulic Press, its chains and girders pressing against that ceiling of glass. Raw metal went into that press; bridges emerged fully-formed at the far end. Traps and tractors, steam vessels and carriages of iron. A crystal fountain, four tons of glass which drew in the sun and cast it out again in a rainbow of colours. I can remember the sight and sound of it as though it were yesterday.

'And the scents! The Indian Pavilion, an elephant with howdah and battle armour. The spices! My boys, you cannot conceive the rich aroma of the spices brought from the East Indies. The whole world was here, if you can but believe it. Pear wood, fossils from the Americas. The Koh-i-noor. The whole world!'

Hall after hall, empty of exhibits now that the Palace has been dismantled and reassembled at Sydenham. Eight years on it has become a venue for Sunday afternooners, a diversion for visiting dignitaries. A shell filled with the ghosts which justified its creation.

Jonah does not stop. Instead he runs out into the gloom of the afternoon sun. His nostrils are filled with the smells his father has caused to materialise out of the air: pepper and mace, nutmeg and cloves. Phantom smells which bite at his mind. On The Origin of Species *jabs at his ribs and the sudden pain returns him to the physical world.*

'Stop, Jonah!' his father's voice is distant, laboured. He is running. Jonah begins to laugh. 'Albert, see if you can catch him!'

Jonah's legs are pumping hard now. Albert is three years his senior and will easily outpace him. What he needs is a goal, something close enough so that he can win the race. He sees the dinosaur.

The dinosaurs are what brought them here on this sun-filled Sunday afternoon. His father has never forgotten the absurd spectacle of twenty-one scientists squeezing into the hollow, concrete Iguanodon *in 1853, when he reported on the unusual New Year's Eve banquet for the* Evening Chronicle. *As dinosaur enthusiast Professor Richard Owen and his guests dined on Pigeon Pie and Braised Woodcock, so Henry Lightfoot scribbled in his notebook, torn between finishing the assignment and returning home to see in the New Year with his sick wife and their two sons. Now, for the first time since his wife's death, he has taken the opportunity to return to the Palace and view the rest of the dinosaur models scattered about the grounds. The boys have been looking forward to the trip all week, especially young Jonah, who already has an impressive collection of fossils gathered from the Dorset coast during the previous summer.*

It is an Iguanodon *towards which Jonah is now flying – not the same, carved-out creature in which Owen and his colleagues dined but one whose back is solid and whole. It rears on its stocky hind legs, an audacious challenge to the popular view of dinosaurs as slow, creeping lizards. At eighteen feet in height it surpasses the shrubbery in which it has been so artfully placed, a shocking incongruity in this genteel Victorian park.*

Jonah sees why the sunshine appears so dark: a massive cloud has tracked low over the Palace, killing the cloud-light and now beginning to bite into the face of the sun itself. Cold comes, and with it a sudden shadow which speeds up the flank of the Iguanodon *and flees skywards. Skidding, he turns behind the prehistoric beast and hides.*

Rain spots the dusty ground as Albert arrives to shelter under the dinosaur, quickly followed by a panting Henry Lightfoot. They both call for Jonah, who stifles his sniggers; he holds his hand to his mouth as he clambers aboard the Iguanodon*'s prodigious tail, enjoying the sensation of being soaked.*

The rainstorm is brief but intense; the ground turns to mud. The sun starts to burn through the rim of the cloud but not before the single stroke of lightning rips into the ground. The thunder comes simultaneously, inseparable from its electric twin.

The lightning strikes not the dinosaur but an ancient elm some twenty yards distant. Jonah yelps as the tree explodes, showering him with singed bark. In response to his cry, Albert peers round the dinosaur's oversized claws and grins. Henry appears not to have heard. Jonah raises a finger to his lips; Albert shrugs and ducks back out of sight.

The elm tips over, its roots groaning as they are pulled like teeth from the earth. One by one they give way and the elm is suddenly pointing not at the sky but at the Palace. The sunlight breaks through and bathes the scene with incandescence. The tree strikes the Iguanodon*'s shoulder, driving it first down into the mud and then over on to its side. Jonah feels an initial thrill as he is lifted on the rising tail, then shock and pain as he is thrown clear and lands heavily on the ground. He is dazed and does not see the pitiful, incredulous look on his father's face as several tons of iron hoop and moulded concrete topple over and crush both him and his eldest son to death.*

For a long time nobody comes. Jonah sits there, not comprehending. Then an elderly couple approach him and ask him where his parents are. Jonah looks around, shakes his head as though returning from a trance and points dumbly at the stricken dinosaur. At first they look past it, then the old lady sees a pair of small hands protruding from beneath the beast's cracked jaws, raises her own hands to either side of her face – now quite drained of its colour – and begins to shriek.

Soon the police come and Jonah finds himself taken first to his own home, then to that of his uncle and aunt, where he will stay for the next ten years. His sister, Mary, is twenty years old and already married; the sudden death of father and brother turn her heart to ice, at least where her relationship with Jonah is concerned, and he sees little of her until the year he decides to go to Java. They touch, briefly at the funeral, but the touch is cold. Jonah finds he is mourning not two deaths but three.

His uncle is sympathetic – it was he who first sparked Henry's interest in dinosaurs – and attempts to reassure Jonah that he would be happy to die that way himself. Jonah considers it unlikely that the opportunity will present itself to him. His aunt blames first Jonah and then her own husband for the untimely death of her brother. Only the considerable legacy – courtesy of Jonah's late mother and her immensely rich Scottish ancestors – sweetens the pill and allows her to bear the presence of either of these irresponsible males in her house. At the earliest opportunity, Jonah moves out and buys himself a small house in Downe, near to where Darwin lives.

He takes his grief with him, and though the guilt fades with time . . .

Patricide! Fratricide! his aunt's voice rings sometimes still in the dead of the night

. . . he retains his most vivid memories of that day: the geometry of shadows on the floor of the Palace, the ghost-scent of the Spice Islands, the jab of Darwin's book against his ribs, the sudden storm.

He grows and learns to put away his memories. His father and brother he puts away too. Their deaths are not something he gets over: he simply finds a place for them to stay, a place he can still visit when he needs to. His fossil collection grows and he turns from dinosaurs to man. The new and controversial vocation of anthropologist takes him around the country in search of prehistory; at one memorable lecture, shortly before the aged naturalist's death in 1882, he encounters Darwin himself, though he does not find the courage to speak to him. His mother's money has sustained his physical needs but for Jonah mere sustenance is not enough. Ancient bones call to him from the cliffs and caves, their voices dry and rich with the spice of age. They have secrets to tell and he knows they will confide in him, if only he can decipher their language.

It is the smell of the spice which finally draws him to the East Indies. As the end of the century draws perceptibly nearer Jonah senses a great movement out into the world. Ships consume the spaces between the continents and great bridges span the smaller divides. His perception of mankind changes: instead of individuals he sees migrating tribes moving like glaciers across the surface of the globe, and he knows that if he is to unlock the secrets of the past he too must travel beyond his native land.

As to where his search should take him, there is only one answer: the mysterious east, the Spice Islands of Java and Sumatra, the exotic

lands which so captivated his father and which linger still in his own memories, though he has never been there.

The trip proves easy enough to arrange: his father's journalist contacts secure him a berth on the Caroline *and approaching the age of thirty-two Jonah Lightfoot finds himself embarked on an epic quest to the opposite side of the world, with his goal nothing less than the vindication of all that Darwin preaches and the discovery of the true cradle of mankind. His colleagues scoff, for there is little enough evidence of ancient man's existence in the East Indies, but still Jonah is drawn there.*

The scent of the spice spins round him with heady grace, spinning, spinning, pulling him down, down, down . . .

Jonah opened his eyes. His head seemed filled with fighting muscles, each pulling in a different direction, each aching with fatigue. He struggled to focus, gave up; all he could see was a vague, brown blur.

He breathed in and immediately started to choke. Water streamed out of his mouth and nose and as his sinuses emptied the pressure inside his head ebbed away, the muscles relaxed. Again he took a breath and this time he was rewarded by a sudden flow of warm, dry air. As he inhaled he closed his eyes again, concentrating on the revivifying experience of simply breathing.

The air circulated through his lungs, and for an instant it seemed to Jonah that it was moving of its own accord, that instead of being drawn in it was invading under its own power. The sensation was a peculiar one, but not uncomfortable. Dizziness overtook him.

I am bound to be disorientated. After all, I have just . . .

There his thoughts stumbled. What *had* just happened to him? He could remember only snatches: the screaming of a flock of parrots, a rich thumping sound underlying their shrieks, rocks soaring into the night sky like children's balloons, the colossal wave that had left the iceberg unharmed – *the iceberg!* He remembered the whirlpool dragging him down into the ocean . . .

More signals began to arrive from his other senses. A hard surface beneath his body, a thick scent of spice on the air that was flowing so effortlessly in and out of his lungs, a faint scraping sound. Dried blood on his face. Warmth on his skin. Tentatively he flexed his fingers: the ground on which he was lying face-down was firm and pitted with tiny craters; as he moved his right hand across it he felt a deep crack extending beyond his reach. His left hand lingered in a pile of dust.

He tried opening his eyes again. This time he was able to focus on the object lying directly in front of him. He saw dark brown, fine-grained wood and a brass clasp marked with an Oriental symbol. For a moment he could not place this object, then he remembered – everything.

'Annie!' he cried, lifting himself up on to his elbows. The painting box slipped below his field of vision as he peered over its lid; what he saw took his breath away.

Jonah's first impression was that he was inside a huge cave. The floor – black and rough – extended far into a dark haze, turning upwards at both sides until it became a pair of curved walls. The ceiling was a broad arch, dim and distant. A long way ahead he could see a tiny disc of light. Turning his head he saw how the sides of the cave shrank towards the light and realised this was not a cave but a tunnel.

Slowly he clambered to his feet. A thin film of dust sifted off his arms and chest as he did so. As his eyes adjusted to the gloom he saw that he was standing inside a vast, oval corridor – it was easily two hundred yards across – cut from jet black rock. Weird spars spanned its width like fallen masts. Their presence was unsettling; they were like nothing he had ever seen before.

Strewn to his left and rather closer to hand was a bedraggled line of rags and a length of rope – it looked like washing line; the body of a small monkey lay in a piece of tangled red linen. Further away he could see the top half of a palm tree and what looked like a small boat. More debris littered the floor but his eyes skated across it as he searched, turning a slow 180 degrees.

Annie lay directly behind him, not ten yards away, her body stark against the black floor. Her dark hair was spread about her head and seemed almost to have merged with the substance of the tunnel. All around her there was slow, steady movement like the swell of an ocean, and Jonah's first impression was that the floor itself had come alive and was undulating beneath her. Then he discerned individual shapes amid the motion: there were hundreds of creatures crawling slowly around Annie, even over her! Each one was the size of a large dog, many-limbed and clad in a broad, flattened shell. The scraping was the sound of their embossed carapaces colliding and their wavering limbs scraping and feeling. Jonah's amazement grew as he saw that immediately behind Annie's prone form the tunnel came to an abrupt end. A sheer, uncompromising wall rose, blanking off the corridor. The entire wall was thronged with the lumbering creatures, which clung to its sheer face in shocking defiance of gravity.

'Get away from her, you brutes!' Jonah screamed, launching himself towards Annie. He kicked at the creatures, bruising his bare toes against their resilient shells. One of them slipped beneath his foot as hc ran and he felt its underbelly give way on the rock with a soft, wet sound. As he reached her, one of the ungainly monsters crawled up on to her stomach and he kicked it aside; it bounced off the wall with a metallic ring. Ignoring the clumsy probing of countless others, Jonah scooped Annie up – he was relieved to find her body warm against his own – and backtracked, ready to fend off the marauding creatures.

To his surprise they let him go; indeed, it dawned on Jonah that they had really taken little notice of him at all, nor of Annie for that matter. As he stumbled backwards, dragging the warm, exotic air deep into his labouring lungs, it came to him that the creatures might not even have known they were there at all. His feet brushed against something soft, then got hopelessly tangled in the washing line and before he knew it he was sprawled on the ground with Annie lying across his legs. He pulled himself clear, reassured himself that she had not struck her head during the fall, then squatted there, panting, actually taking in the strange creatures for the first time as they performed their stately pavane. With their heavily-ridged shells, thick, leathery limbs, and their ponderous manner Jonah found himself thinking of tortoises, although these creatures, slow-moving as they were, were considerably livelier than their terrestrial equivalents.

Testudo nigra, he mused, thinking of Galapagos, thinking of Darwin. Thinking of Annie's exquisite paintings of volcanic rocks and sun-drenched lizards.

Exhausted, he let his head drop lower and lower until his brow was resting on the ground. He had time to wonder about the wisdom of falling asleep, then darkness took him again.

* * *

Surfacing from a dreamless sea, Jonah Lightfoot found his mouth filled with the taste of the air. He dragged the tip of his tongue forwards across his upper palate and swallowed the soft residue it removed, shivering involuntarily as it brushed against a sensitive nerve. He had no idea how long he had slept – there was no clue as to how fast time was travelling inside this subterranean tract.

Perhaps it is not travelling at all, he mused as he rose and stretched. The soft scrapings of the tortoids (the name came to him unbidden) were distant and unintrusive; much louder was the insistent growling of his stomach. Annie slept still, or else was in some deeper state of unconsciousness. This second possibility Jonah was not ready to contemplate; for now he was more concerned with determining where exactly they were and, more importantly, how they were to get out.

Hungry and alert, he surveyed the tunnel with what he hoped was an explorer's eye.

A flattened, irregular cylinder, it had the appearance of volcanic rock. Had they somehow been swept underwater and into some undersea cavern? Its pitted surface was black and glassy, very like the dark rock that abounded on Krakatoa (*Had abounded,* Jonah corrected himself); the scars and cracks distressing its contours supported this theory very nicely.

Less convenient were the smooth-sided rods which crossed horizontally from one side of the space to the other. Where their ends met the rock there was a clean, featureless junction. As Jonah stared at them he sensed something radiating from them – not heat exactly, but *something.* He was reminded of an experiment in electricity he had observed several years before and cautiously held out his hand towards the nearest of the rods, steeling himself for the lightning strike. Nothing happened. He withdrew without actually touching it.

He regarded the light at the end of the tunnel: oval in shape, it was brilliant white with the merest hint of blue. Its edges were blurred by the haze that filled the tunnel.

The end of the tunnel, thought Jonah with relief. *Daylight!*

The distance was difficult to judge, but Jonah hoped that even carrying Annie, and despite the roughness of the terrain, it would not take him more than a few hours to walk it. But would he need to carry her? Perhaps he should try to wake her instead. He knelt beside her prone form, brushing her hair away from her face and drawing her arm out of the awkward position into which it had fallen. He could not prevent his eyes from straying down her body, and he blushed as they took in the gentle swell of her breasts and the soft lines of her stomach. In an effort to divert himself from what struck him as ungentlemanly voyeurism, Jonah bent forward and was about to listen for a heartbeat when he realised this would bring his head into even closer proximity with Annie's breasts. He held his cheek against her lips instead; her breathing was shallow but detectable. She was alive, of course, as if the warm glow of her flesh had not been enough to tell Jonah this in the first place. He sat up again and relaxed a little, scolding himself for being embarrassed in front of an unconscious woman.

Jonah had never been exactly shy. Both his aunt and sister were strong-willed women (his mother he could barely remember and so between them they comprised the dominant female images of his youth) and he had grown up with a more liberal attitude towards their sex than many of his peers. He had never desired to marry, not until he was much older at least; there was so much for him to do first, it seemed, so much to discover.

One girl had come close to catching his heart, many years before. He had spent several summers on a farm in Kent, giving both himself and his uncle and aunt a break from the storms that constantly clouded the relationship between guardians and orphan. Mr Jackson's daughter, Lily, was two years older than Jonah and fully six inches taller. He adored her, with her hair like autumn and the spray of freckles across her sun-darkened cheeks. They would undress each other in the apple orchard, their forbidden games of discovery somehow innocent, always exciting. Jonah could never imagine doing such things in London; but here, on Jackson's Farm, it was as though he had been transported to another world where ordinary rules did not apply. Here he could forget all that lay in wait for him at the end of the summer, here he could, for a space of time at least, lay aside even the most painful of memories. Lying in Lily's arms, with the sun pressing against his bare skin, he could sleep without dreaming.

They were discovered one day, of course, and after three

perfect summers the trips to the farm ended abruptly. During those years Jonah had grown from twelve to fifteen; on the last day he saw her Lily was seventeen and already a woman, no longer the girl he had loved. He missed her still, but the feeling was one he had become comfortable with, one he still traced occasionally in his memory, like an old scar.

There had been no others since then. Jonah had buried himself in his research, more interested in the shape of primitive women than of those more tangible creatures he met in Covent Garden market or in the museums and galleries. It was the very untouchability of ancient flesh that fascinated him so, its fluid, dreamlike quality. Bones survived, but little else: tissue and tendon, muscle and memory were all consigned to the insatiable jaws of history. Only the human spirit remained after death, if his god-fearing aunt was to be believed, and even then there was considerable doubt as to where exactly such a thing might end up, particularly if its owner had spent too much time dallying with farmer's daughters during his earthly existence. Thus his journeys into the past drew him further and further away from the present in which he increasingly felt trapped, until he decided that physical relocation was the only way to satisfy his quest for knowledge. The Spice Islands were calling him and he could ignore their cry no more than he could rid himself of their scent.

It occurred to Jonah now, as he regarded Annie, that this was the first time he had looked on a woman's naked body since his last time with Lily in the lower orchard. He smiled, filling his lungs with the aromatic air: he felt strong and young, and he began to believe that anything was possible, anything at all.

Jonah got to his feet and went over to the washing line that had tripped him up earlier. It lay in a sprawl, a comically prosaic sight in this outlandish environment. What he had at first taken to be clothing turned out on closer inspection to be a jumbled collection of sheets, all brightly coloured in reds and greens. Gingerly he lifted the body of the monkey from the knot of linen that had enwrapped it – it felt stiff and strangely unreal, like a sculpture or a piece of taxidermy. He was about to lay it aside when he paused, reminded of his hunger. The monkey's eyes, dark brown marbles shrouded by matted fur, stared over his shoulder in an accusatory fashion.

'No matches,' muttered Jonah. 'And I have no desire to be eating you raw, my simian friend.' He placed the body decisively out of sight behind a ridge of broken stone and gathered up the linen. By now, in the warm atmosphere of the cave, it was quite dry, and Jonah was able to tear it into usable strips. After fashioning a new kilt for himself from the red cloth, he improvised a similar garment for Annie, managing to secure it round her waist without scraping her skin on the rock floor. He wound a strip of the green material about her upper body, unsure whether he was doing this for her benefit or for his; whatever his motive he felt that the whole situation was less unseemly now that the more intimate parts of their bodies were tucked away in an appropriate manner.

This time he carried Annie on his shoulder, with her hair trailing down his back and his arm rested in the crook of her knees. He walked with a slow, steady pace, picking his way through the maze of cracks and ridges and ducking beneath the lowest of the spars. The light ahead was a constant call to action, with its promise of daylight and rescue.

And water, he reminded himself. *We will not last more than a day or two in such heat without water.*

He trudged on, trying to ignore the insidious doubts which were beginning to crowd into his mind: the conflict between the glow of the light and the conviction that he was deep underground, the unnatural order of the slick-surfaced rods, the absurd tortoids. The scraping sound made by their shells became fainter as he moved on.

Jonah tired much more quickly than he had anticipated. The oval of light was considerably bigger, but he had covered barely half the distance towards it when he realised that he had left Annie's painting box behind. The realisation struck him like a low punch – he even grunted as he thought of it – and he stopped in his tracks.

The rods were much more densely packed here, stacked almost from floor to ceiling. He tried to ignore them, for something about them continued to unsettle him, but without much success. They seemed to crackle whenever he came too near, and on several occasions he felt the hairs on the backs of his hands and neck stand proud of the skin. Most of them he was able to duck under; a few he had to climb over. He managed to get away without touching any of them at all.

'Storm coming,' he laughed without humour, because that was exactly what it felt like.

It was as good a time as any to take a rest, he supposed. Laying down Annie (who had not so much as twitched during the entire trek) he sat and considered the distance he had travelled. Just as there was light ahead there was only blackness behind, a blackness within which rose invisibly the wall on which the tortoids had been swarming, and beneath which the flotsam and jetsam of the eruption had been scattered, including himself and Annie.

And also including the painting box.

It would be madness to go back for it, he reasoned as he rose stiffly to his feet. But drowning the logic of the thought were Annie's words of the previous night: 'It's all I have left!'

And so it was. He could not leave it behind, it was as simple as that. He took ten steps away from her then turned, suddenly fearful. Would he be able to find her again? After all, the tunnel was big enough to get lost in, and the thicket of horizontal rods made it difficult to navigate. His concern was lessened when he saw how stark her body looked against the dark rock: even though she was heavily tanned her skin still seemed to shine in the gloom, and the gaudy fabric in which he had wrapped her sang out even more strongly. He would see her well enough.

Reassured, he began to retrace his steps.

The march back was easier, but it tired him dreadfully all the same. The urge to urinate came over him when he had gone only a few hundred yards; the relief was tempered by the paucity of the flow and the burning sensation it invoked. When at last he reached the body of the monkey he found himself looking at it with distinct greed, imagining the life-giving water locked away in its flesh, wondering what raw monkey might actually taste like.

He shook the thought away before his stomach rebelled and instead sought out the box. For an awful moment he thought it had gone: the notion that there might be somebody else here was unexpected and horrifying. He crouched, glancing round wildly, convinced that he should not have left Annie alone and at the mercy of whatever predators might be lurking in this subterranean lair.

Do you still think you are underground, Jonah Lightfoot? Do you really *believe that?*

The scraping of the tortoids was louder again now that he was back near the wall. Jonah ignored it as he searched through the dust and debris. He came upon a small, dead rhinoceros (how had he missed *that*?) and then he spied the box, exactly where he had left it. He could even see the imprint of his body where he had lain before first waking. Sitting down, he picked the box up and opened it. As far as he could see the contents were intact: the little painted tiles, the brushes and palettes, the tiny containers of turpentine and linseed oil. He closed it and snapped the clasp shut.

Something snuffled at his ankle. Whirling round in shock, heart like thunder in his chest, Jonah stared at it for several long, stupid seconds before crying out and scrabbling backwards on his hands and knees. The tortoid tracked his movements with two luminous eyes that glowed faintly green from within deep sockets set into its horny, black face. Jonah stared back warily, waiting for its next move.

But the next move did not come: the tortoid simply stood there, short and bow-legged, returning Jonah's gaze.

Jonah studied it, willing his heart to still itself. This particular creature looked a little different to the ones he had seen earlier. It still resembled the giant tortoises Darwin had observed on the many islands of the Galapagos archipelago but this one looked bigger and leaner than its fellows, and its shell was much smaller in proportion to the rest of its body. Its long, mobile neck and four, thick legs were correspondingly much more visible and for the first time Jonah found himself aware that the species possessed a recognisable face.

Each of its pale green, lidless eyes was bisected by a reptilian pupil. Directly beneath each eye was a tiny, horizontal slit; he took this pair of apertures to be nostrils. The tortoid's mouth was wide and seemed to promise considerable mobility, although for the time being it remained resolutely shut. Its shell, an ebony carapace that clad its entire back but stopped some eighteen inches short of the ground, was a lustrous, studded affair. The tortoid was as big as Jonah.

It held his gaze for so long that Jonah became quite unnerved. *Outstared by a tortoise?* he thought. But it *wasn't* a tortoise, was it? In fact, this was no kind of animal he had ever heard of before, let alone seen. Granted there were countless unexplored lands in the world – indeed Java and its thousands of neighbouring islands undoubtedly harboured a treasure of species not yet seen by man – but there was something so insidiously alien about this creature.

Then the tortoid moved and Jonah knew he was very far from home indeed.

It shifted its weight on to first one pair of legs then the other. As it did so it turned so that it presented its broad, shell-encased flank to Jonah's view. There was a marking high up on its shell, an embossed shape. Jonah recognised it at once. His hands shook as he prised open the box again and located the tile bearing Annie's most recent painting. Tentatively he turned it over and held it up so that he could compare the symbols. There was no doubt: the mark on the tortoid's back was the mark of the Red Dragon from the set of *ma-chong* tiles.

Jonah let out a slow, controlled breath.

Abruptly the tortoid folded up the rear half of its shell with an audible creaking sound and extended twin pairs of long, probing limbs from the space within. Concealed until now, these limbs were as slender and articulate as their siblings were thick and supportive. Jonah felt repulsed: reptiles he could deal with but this was unexpectedly insectile. The legs – or arms or feelers or whatever they were – busied themselves about the tortoid's hindquarters, clattering against each other and snicking through the air with curt little whistling noises.

Suddenly Jonah did not want to see any more. He clutched the box to his chest and stood up. He stared into the darkness beyond the tortoid, aware that the scraping of its companions had become very loud now. The wall, still thronged with the climbing, lurching things, seemed very close. As his eyes adjusted he was able to pick out individual creatures – they had *all* grown bigger.

But there was more. The boat he had seen when first awakening here now lay hard against the wall, indeed, it lay half *in* it, as though the wall had suddenly descended on it from above like a guillotine. The broken palm tree that had lain beyond the boat was gone altogether.

The wall is getting nearer!

Claustrophobia gripped Jonah, immediate and uncontrollable. It was a feeling he had never before experienced, as alien to his system as this place had become to his eyes. He turned and ran, while the lone tortoid that had separated itself from the pack specifically to awaken him watched his departure with bright, baleful eyes. He ran headlong, his flight a raw animal response to the terror overwhelming him. Oblivious to the battering he was inflicting on his bare feet, he ran, ignoring the whine of hot air in his lungs, hardly flinching when his shoulder crashed into something. He reached out and grabbed the obstacle, for the first time touching one of the strange rods with his hand.

There was a flash inside his eyes and a jolt of energy threw him backwards. He heard thunder, felt electricity in his skull, saw rivulets of light stream rapidly across the surface of the rod before hissing and evaporating into the air. Shaking his head to clear it of the unpleasant sensation he saw that the tortoid had followed him. It was staring at him with its wide, green eyes.

Jonah ran, and did not stop running until he reached the spot where he had left Annie. All his trust in this place had gone – he fully expected to find her gone too.

'Where am I?' he screamed as he shuddered to a halt before her still-prone form. He continued to clasp the box to his heaving chest, giving it up only when his panic began slowly to subside. As it had for Annie, the painting box with its cargo of ivory tiles had become a talisman, an essential connection to the world he remembered as being his own. *A memory chest,* he thought fearfully. Without it they had nothing; even the colourful rags in which he had clothed them both were foreign to him, perhaps not of his world at all.

He journeyed on towards the light.

His feet were bleeding from the punishment they had taken during his flight across the broken tunnel floor. Yet a kind of numbness had claimed him, a stupor within which Annie seemed to weigh no more than a child and which had narrowed his vision to a literal tunnel, a tight and cloying space where the only thing that mattered was the light at its end. Blinkered like a horse, he trudged on, ducking instinctively beneath the omnipresent spars, conscious only that he must reach the growing oval of brilliant, blue-white incandescence.

He paused, forging a way into the numbness and willing his vision to expand again. Turning to look behind he saw only shadow, an immense maw that pressed against him, rejecting him.

You do not belong here.

Words from the ether.

The light had turned the skin of the tunnel into a mosaic of glistening highlights, as though the rock – if rock was what it was – was wet, though Jonah knew it to be desert-dry. His eyes watered as he stared ahead, unable to compensate after his hours in the gloom. The blue colour had strengthened and again he thought of daylight, although he fancied he could detect a pattern in the glow, a series of irregular, vertical bands. Shaking his head, unable to focus, he returned his gaze to the floor and stumbled on, aware now of the pain in his feet.

Something touched his face and he bit down on a scream.

Wind! Just wind!

He had felt no such movement of air further back in the tunnel. It was cooler here, still warm but without the stifling overtones of the deep place he had left behind. This time he closed his eyes as he paused, enjoying the play of the breeze upon his face and through his hair. There was a sound too, a rushing noise like a waterfall, soothing and inviting at the same time: beckoning. To his amazement Jonah saw that he was barely twenty yards from the end of the tunnel.

The end was defined by a ragged lip like the exit from some gigantic cave. Beyond this lip was nothing but sky. The vertical bands resolved themselves into an array of pure white clouds, as terrestrial in appearance as any he had seen but with one important exception: they striped the reassuringly cobalt sky as though the world outside had been turned entirely on its side.

The rushing noise grew louder as he walked cautiously towards the edge. Ten yards short he could still see nothing but sky. *Am I high up on some cliff or mountainside? Yet the whirlpool dragged me* down!

Five yards short. Jonah stepped over the last of the rods. His heart raced. Fear and fatigue had left him, replaced by a childish excitement. The feeling that he had gained some incredible altitude grew overpoweringly strong, even though the warmth of the air seemed to contradict this supposition. The lip at the end of the tunnel was rounded, distorted by millions of shining bubble-forms as though the substance from which it was made had started to boil then been frozen again before it could turn to gas. It looked slippery and Jonah decided to lay Annie and the precious box down for fear of dropping her over the edge.

Still there was only sky. He dropped to all fours and crawled the last few yards. The final foot he traversed on his stomach, extending his fingers to the very edge of the tunnel and pulling himself forwards across the unearthly, waxy terrain. He extended his head forwards over the edge, whereupon a powerful stream of air – a vertical, falling wind – flattened his hair against the top of his skull. Jonah looked straight ahead into a huge, blue sky laced with straggling clouds that streamed down from above like brilliant white ribbons thrown clear from some immense waterfall, only it was a fall not of water but of vapour. It looked like the sky was the whole world.

Then he looked down.

If claustrophobia had been a new sensation for Jonah then vertigo was more like an old ghost. It had struck him only once before in his life, when Lily had held him by his ankles over the edge of the hay loft, laughing with an uncontrollable cider laugh and shaking with excitement. A pitchfork had lain directly beneath him and for weeks afterwards he had dreamed of those rusty tines rising up to greet him, to pierce his body and release his spirit. He had never experienced that feeling since then. Until now.

The tunnel exit was a microscopic perforation in a wall the size of a world. Like an insect peering out from the highest tower of a mighty palace, Jonah looked down . . . and down . . . and down.

A sheer grey cliff face dropped away into bottomless mist. Its immensity made it at first seem entirely flat, but as he looked markings became apparent: scratches and grooves; pockmarks and trailing strands of what looked like vegetation. Jonah turned his head slowly to the left, where he saw more of the same: an almost smooth surface extending into infinity. A perfectly flat plane inclined ten degrees from the vertical; such a cliff would be scaleable by an experienced mountaineer; that is, if a cliff was what it was.

But it is not a cliff, is it?

Nor was it. It was actually a *wall*. Geometrically perfect, marked off into regular blocks, each at least a mile across.

Nowhere in the depths of the abyss could he see any hint of the ground, nor was there any horizon visible behind the haze of the sky; this was all there was – this mighty wall of stone and the sky it bordered upon. Jonah could hear a thin, shrieking sound; the falling wind carried the noise down into the abyss, breaking it apart into meaningless splinters. He realised it was the sound of his own voice, screaming.

His arms and legs trembling with shock, he retreated several feet into the tunnel. Sweat poured from his face and chest, fluid he could well do without losing but he could do nothing about his body's reaction. The screaming he managed to stop; the shaking proved less easy to control and for long minutes he simply crouched there, bent double with his forehead resting on the hard ground.

Slowly he regained a degree of command over his limbs and tentatively approached the tunnel lip once more. Prepared as he was, he was terrified all over again as he eased himself forward and gazed down into the abyss.

He had never understood the urge that took some men high up seemingly unscalable mountainsides with nothing but ropes and metal spikes and their wits to keep them from dashing themselves on the rocks below. But what lay below *here*? For all he knew, were he to fall from this ledge he might go on falling forever, accelerating until only the force of the air against his body prevented him from falling any faster, bouncing and careering off the cracks and ridges which marked off the miles in their hundreds, thousands, millions . . .

'Stop it, Lightfoot!' he said out loud, his voice hoarse. He repeated the words in a whisper and ran a shaking hand through his sweat-soaked hair and looked again, this time to the right.

The sky was brighter on this side, and behind a thick curtain of cloud there was a circle of white, a glowing sun. Here too the wall ran away into the distance like the very rampart of heaven, except here it was more elaborately marked: a grid of indentations, ledges projecting forwards like huge mantel shelves, their upper surfaces glistening as though wet; several huge, gaping cracks. Further away, flat against the sun, something sprouted from the wall like a bizarre, geometric flower clinging to a cliff. To begin with it seemed a random mass of squares and slopes, but as he squinted into the brightness he began to make out repeating patterns. Its base was an assemblage of thick stanchions rising vertically from the slightly sloping, all-dominating wall. Once these reached an altitude that separated them sufficiently from the wall they fanned out into a series of broad, supporting buttresses. Resting on top of these, cantilevered out over the unimaginable drop, was a castle.

It was the windows that finally locked the scale of the thing into Jonah's mind. While the lower half of the edifice was unadorned and grimy with weathered streaks of muck, the upper parts were studded with relief, both in the form of projecting bastions and ports cut deep into its flanks; there were more than he could count, and it slowly dawned on him that the building was truly colossal. Mediaeval battlements graced its uppermost towers, yet one whole corner of the castle seemed more like a palisade from the American West, replete with wooden spikes and sorry-looking flags. In the vee formed where sloping wall met uprising castle was cradled a forest of tall, straight conifers; the red of their bark shone out strikingly.

A long, straight stairway climbed one angular side, joining two spear-like towers. A complex sculpture of pipes and gutters converged at the apex of a long, black stain running down into the supporting buttresses (Jonah decided that the rivers of dirt which wound down the foundations were more likely the result of the castle's sewage disposal system than the weather). Near the outer edge, set into a mass of stone poised above a seemingly flimsy wooden substructure, was a concentrated pattern of circular windows. Jonah counted twelve or thirteen small apertures arranged symmetrically around a single, larger opening: a vantage point for some ceremony perhaps, or the site for some mighty weapon.

Edge-lit and glorious, the castle presented itself to Jonah in the rich, low light of the afternoon sun. That it *was* the afternoon here came to Jonah suddenly as he observed the sun's disc beginning to slide sideways behind the outermost edge of the castle. Extrapolating on this movement he judged that in no more than an hour it would move entirely behind the line of the great, sloping wall, and then night would fall in this weird, sideways world. Just as the sun he knew followed the track of an invisible arch so, it seemed, did this new one, the only difference being that the horizon here was not horizontal but vertical, with the path of the guardian star consequently tipped on its side.

So it is not a horizon but a vertex, he mused, gazing avidly at the castle and all its festoon of detail. Parts of his mind – hidden, reptilian parts – were already beginning to balk at the impossibility of recent events. Soon he would begin to doubt his sanity, to believe that all this was the landscape of an epic dream, that somewhere close by his real, earthbound body was slowly drowning in the maelstrom that had sucked it down into the warm, eastern ocean. But for now it was enough just to watch, to look out into the minute detail of this vertiginous world and imagine, for a while at least, that this was really happening to him.

Jonah did not hear the soft pad of footsteps approaching him from behind, but he did hear the clunk of the painting box as it was set down on the lip of the tunnel.

'Annie!' he cried. He rolled on to his back, overjoyed.

She towered over him, the red and green of her uncouth garments aflame in the light of the sun. Her legs were set wide, her arms held away from her sides, her chest expanding visibly as she breathed in the rich, scented air. Her dark hair moved like a pennant in the wind. For an instant the sunlight was reflected from her eyes directly into his, dazzling him. He frowned, feeling curiously uneasy as he tried to locate the direction of her gaze. He could not, and as his clarity of vision returned he saw why.

Annie's pupils had gone. Her eyes were featureless, silver mirrors in which he could clearly see both the hard line of the stone from which the world-wall was made and the linear tapestry of the sky. She smiled a thin, inhuman smile and kicked him over the edge.

3

Archan

She looked into the depths of the new sky and mourned the fact that this new body, this temporary host, possessed no wings. She flexed its puny arms experimentally, then ran its blunt claws . . . *fingers* . . . across smooth skin, feeling the fragility of the flesh in which she was encased. The sunlight struck its eyes, which she widened, relishing the small, exquisite pain. Of all the new sensations this body shared with her, sight was the most novel.

For a brief time after she had become immortal, she had forgotten everything, even her name. Now it soared at the front of her mind – or at least, the place she currently inhabited within this borrowed mind – a beacon illuminating her memories as the sun illuminated this strange, vertical world. On her journey south through the Arctic seas she had observed the faeries' iron vessels carving their way through the floes. It was her name, she considered now, that had been her prow as she broke through the icy years of imprisonment. Her memories of the old world were strong; equally strong was her ambition, and at the very tip of her ambition was her name.

Archan.

She came from an ancient time.

Long ago, when the ancestors of men had borne wings and lived aethereal lives, the world had been ruled by very different laws to those that governed it in 1883, a year she plucked easily from the mind she had invaded. Then it was not nature but charm that had reigned supreme, magic had moved in the breeze like a hidden scent and the skies . . . the skies had been filled with dragons.

Archan had been one of those dragons.

For most of her adult life she had yearned for immortality.

Loner, intellectual, telepathic wielder of fire-charm, she held a position of considerable power in the great hierarchy of dragons that existed before the Turning of the World. Her senses were manifold; she even plucked out her own eyes when they at last became useless in comparison to the organs of magic through which she could measure more subtle energies. But all too soon the magic fled, usurped by rude, simple nature. Great storms racked the oceans and the heaving continents, the faeries lost their wings and the dragons fell from the sky.

Like the magic, Archan fled too, fled from the crumbling dragon society in which she had, for a time at least, played an important role. She found a retreat where she might sit out the last days of the dragons and contemplate what it might be like to live forever, to swim against the relentless river of time, perhaps even to escape its flow altogether. It was no coincidence that the place she found to rest was one of the great citadels constructed by the only truly immortal creatures the world had ever known: the basilisks.

Six of these magical creatures there had been, and when they finally came together to seek the death that had eluded them for so long, Archan was on hand to seize the very immortality they were trying to shake off. The violent exchange occurred at the climax of the gathering of the Deathless, when the northern pole was lit up by the spectacular transference of power from the doomed basilisks to Archan. As they died she absorbed the fundamental energy that had sustained them; as the basilisks renounced their deathless state she, at last, became deathless herself.

Thus was Archan's dream fulfilled, but never in her worst nightmares had she imagined the terrible cost of immortality! The destruction of her physical body at the very instant of transference left her a helpless spirit without even the power to move through the world. The polar ice cap, temporarily melted by the fearsome power of the basilisk charm, froze again swiftly, encasing her ghost in clear crystal.

And there she stayed, awake and aware, blind as she had been when mortal, fed now by the countless, stranger senses that the basilisk charm had bestowed upon her. World-spanning threads of magic – among them the dwindling remains of the huge and mysterious trollvein network – brought her news of the burgeoning world of nature. Motionless she remained, unable to sleep, able only to watch, and learn, and wait.

A million years passed, and Archan waited; the glaciers ebbed and flowed, new strains of creature flourished and died, giving rise to new heirs. Archan was witness to it all, to all the myriad currents that vied for supremacy in the uncaring river of time. She sensed every breath of every day of every season of every year. She was the spider at the heart of the invisible web of charm that still stretched across the skin of the world.

She saw the steady drift of the continents, the rise and fall of the oceans, the slow changes in the climate that drew blossoms of algae through the seas, tides of rain forest up steep mountain slopes. The new, natural creatures flocked and migrated, crawling across the globe in defiance of the river that she knew so well, the river that might at any moment snatch them away and dash them against its banks, or suck them under before flowing on, on. Most of them simply survived, eating and hunting and proliferating as creatures had done even when charm had ruled, but one strain in particular caught her attention, a type of creature that seemed to live for more than mere survival.

She had never before paid much attention to faeries, much less their crude, natural heirs, but now it seemed that these hairy beasts were seeking to control their world. They were intelligent, certainly – perhaps even as intelligent as dragons had been – they used tools and language. They were interesting, and Archan duly paid them more attention than most of their primitive peers. Above all she was fascinated by their apparent mastery over a force that had always been the exclusive domain of the charmed: fire.

She watched as they reformed their surroundings, building ever more elaborate structures, manufacturing new and more complex materials with which to challenge the very nature that had spawned them. As they grew to dominate, so the scale of their fire-making grew in proportion, until the atmosphere became choked with the fumes of their industries. Their wars were protracted and dreadful; in them fire again played its wicked part.

Archan knew much about fire, not least the fire that raged inside her. No physical flame this, like the one that had once inhabited her living dragon throat, but a virtual flame of pure anger. A million years' incarceration had infused her with a bitterness that she sweated out through the network of charm. This anger leaked into the natural world sometimes, setting off tiny explosions of charm, leaks from another age; the knowledge that she might yet in some way be bringing havoc to others was one of the few pleasures available to her in her prison.

But such leaks were as nothing compared to the inferno that screamed inside her bleak, dark heart. Dream and nightmare had fused long ago, leaving her in torment. Sometimes the fury seemed the most real part of her; madness would have been a blessed escape, but she would not let herself succumb to its lure. Instead she watched as these fire-wielding faeries swarmed across the world, bore witness as they inherited those lands that were rightly hers. Her jealousy knew no bounds; her wrath was without depth, and as relentless as the river in which she alone lay stationary while all else was swept along.

So perfect, then, that the solution to my predicament should be fire, Archan had thought as the iceberg had materialised before the exploding island.

The iceberg: the very stuff that had held her captive all those aeons she had finally made her saviour. The lingering charm that she had absorbed eventually formed a tight cloak of magic around her ghostly form. At a crucial instant, nearly five years ago now, when the northern pole had been shaken by a subterranean tremor, when the summer had been unusually warm and the pack ice had receded beyond its usual bounds, she had used the magic to separate herself and a mountain-sized chunk of ice from the rest of the floe. More charm had steered her through the protesting debris, pressing her out into clear water. The cloak had become a shield, a subtle, magical fabric that caused most eyes to skid off its surface: that made the iceberg practically invisible.

The charm was weak, of course, as was all charm these days. Sometimes it wavered and Archan was seen. The natural faeries had long since conquered the oceans with vessels made of wood and more lately of iron and their routes divided the seas just as the decaying trollveins enmeshed the underworld.

But such sightings were of little concern to Archan. Twists of magic pushed her steadily on her course. As she drifted into warmer waters the cloak began to exert its secondary influence, keeping the ice frozen despite the rising temperatures. By the time she reached the equator the charm was beginning to drain away with alarming speed and Archan allowed herself several days of anxiety. But she was very close to her ultimate goal and the heat gave her little real concern.

After all, she was headed towards a much greater heat than that of merely the noon sun.

The fire-mountain, which the natural faeries called Krakatoa, the giant stone that lay on the sea bed, allowing only its uppermost tip to protrude from the waves. Hot threads of tropical charm gathered over centuries had told her that it was about to erupt, generating a cataclysm that would send shock waves around the entire globe and killing thousands upon thousands of the feeble creatures.

The gamble paid off. When Krakatoa erupted it sent its energy not only into the world but through it. The deep fires that were unleashed were filled with ancient charm – troll charm, basilisk charm, dragon charm – and they punched a way out of the world altogether. On the day which the natural faeries labelled 27 August 1883, the power of the exploding volcano knocked a hole through the very fabric of creation and opened a route through into another realm.

And Archan was there, ready to cross the threshold, ready to make her escape. After a million years, she was ready for freedom.

Her foot struck hard, driving a sudden wedge of pain into the soft flesh beneath his ribcage, somewhere in the region of his left kidney. Unable to stop himself, he rolled over the lip and for a horrifying second was suspended, weightless, above the appalling drop. Then he fell.

His arm struck out. It was a primal, animal reflex driven by something that had little to do with conscious thought. As his body swivelled so his fingers curled and located a raised wedge of the smooth, resinous material that marked the end of the tunnel. The projection had a pronounced curve and it was into this curve that the ends of his fingers locked. His body continued to swing out on its slow, graceful arc, rotating now about the centre formed by his rigid hand; the momentum took him first out then, as his arm stretched to its limit, down and back on to the almost sheer face of the wall with a heavy thud. His wrist throbbed and the small bones in his hands cracked in protest, but he held on somehow.

Jonah swung there, his entire weight supported by the four fingers of his left hand. His legs scrabbled uselessly; gobbets of the black tunnel material had run down the rougher wall surface here, making it smooth and ungrippable. He swung his body, raising his other arm in an effort to find another handhold, but there was none. After a brief flurry of activity he gave up, preferring to conserve his energy.

Something touched the knuckles of his left hand.

Looking up – the action was painful in the extreme – he saw first the bare toes, then the legs and body of Annie, drastically foreshortened as he stared straight up at her.

'Help me!' he called out in a hot, strangled cry, as if he could deny the fact that it was she who had pushed him off the ledge in the first place. *Perhaps she tripped and fell against me*, he tried to reassure himself.

What she did next did nothing to convince him this had been the case. Her knees bent and Jonah found himself staring straight into her face as she leaned out precariously from the tunnel mouth. Her hair billowed downwards, obscuring her features.

'You have been useful to me.' Annie's voice floated down, except it did not sound exactly like Annie's voice. Jonah was strangely aware of the hot, fluid air as the medium that was carrying her words, could almost *see* her words in fact, writhing clear of her shadowy mouth and pouring themselves down into his waiting ears like tiny wraiths. 'So I find it difficult to dispose of you.'

Her eyes! Never mind the chilling peculiarity of her words, what about her eyes? Blank, without the slightest hint of a human interface in the form of either pupil or iris, they reminded Jonah of the convex mirrors he had seen haunting the backgrounds of Dutch paintings, fish-eyed reflectors in which the true shape of the world was horribly distorted. Instead of Annie, all he could see in those eyes was his own horrified face and the broad sweep of the wall to which he clung.

She stood up abruptly, her mane of dark hair tumbling across her chest as she turned away from the abyss. He heard her soft footfalls receding and screamed her name over and over again.

Long minutes passed, during which time Jonah breathed deeply and deliberately, drawing in as much oxygen as he could. His left arm he held taut – already it was growing numb.

He focused on a small area of the dark resin just inches from his face. It was translucent, filled with bubbles, each bubble like a tiny world trapped in amber. Inside one of the bubbles was an ant-like insect; he counted twelve legs protruding from its frozen thorax. Shutting out the low roar of the wind, denying the pain, he carefully extended his free arm and finger-walked up to the ledge. Smooth and slippery – nothing to grip. But his palm was clammy and it did adhere. Gingerly Jonah transferred a little of his weight, relaxing the muscles of his shoulders as his centre of gravity shifted; he felt friction as a pressure against his sweating palm, the change in tension as an explosion of pins and needles along the length of his strained left arm. He paused, reluctant to test the situation further.

His bare toes found a slender groove in the bulbous stuff against which he was flattened. They crept in like independent beings, soldiers loyal to the army, keen to avoid defeat. He tensed them and relaxed both his arms – just a little – convinced that he was about to fall to his death.

His toes, locked rigid, held the weight he had asked them to. Cursing himself for a fool, Jonah flicked his eyes downwards, absorbing the depths. The abyss yawned, ready to pluck him from his perch, to suck him down. He gave an involuntary moan and jerked his right hand six inches higher, where it located a round knob of resin, a ready-made handhold. He tensed his arms, extended his legs and grunted triumph as he lifted his whole body a complementary six inches towards safety.

But the triumph was short-lived. No sooner had he gained this ground than the very sweat that had made his hands and feet sticky began positively to pour from him. Suddenly his toes were slipping out of the groove, suddenly his right hand was losing its grasp, despite the comfortable solidity of the handhold. He tried to force his aching, protesting left arm to move, but his numbed fingers would not respond and the slow slide of his stomach told him they too were about to fail. Unable to stop himself, he looked down again and screamed. Then both his hands gave way and he fell.

Something grabbed his wrists. His arms felt as though they

were being pulled from their sockets; his shoulder blades seemed ready to explode through his collarbone. He swung outwards, legs flailing, the pain in the muscles of his arms and neck immense. Then he started to rise. His chest struck the lip of the ledge hard and all his breath left him. His vision narrowed to a long, dark tunnel and the sound of the wind rose to an insistent whistle that he knew was coming from inside his own head. Landing heavily, he fell forward, aware that whatever had gripped his wrists had released its hold. He stared at the ground, trying to control the rasp of his breath, before slowly looking up.

Luminous green eyes watched from the shadows beneath the last of the inclined rods. A lone ray of sunlight glanced against the tortoid's shell, confirming to Jonah that this was the same creature he had faced in the tunnel: the red shape was the same, the mark of the red dragon. It had grown a little more.

His wrists were sore, marked with weals and scratches; he was hungry and dreadfully thirsty but his head felt clear. He breathed deeply and felt nourished by the thick, spicy air.

That the tortoid had saved his life he had no doubt, but what he should do now was another matter. He knew everything an English gentleman needed to know about etiquette, but this was no drawing room, and his companion in the tunnel entrance was no titled lady. Nothing in his life had prepared him for this.

'The Voyage of the *Beagle*,' he whispered. It was a curious mantra but it settled his nerves, which were beginning to jostle against his subconscious. And if he was honest he felt anything but unprepared – confused and scared, yes, but something in his heart whispered that he was not yet ready to give up.

The green eyes receded into shadow and the tortoid disappeared.

For long moments Jonah deliberated whether or not to follow his saviour. In the end he decided against it. His main concern had to be Annie, and he had a feeling that the tortoid would find him again if it so wished, regardless of his own efforts.

'Thank you!' he shouted into the tunnel before making his way along the ledge, seeking the way off it that Annie had evidently found.

The sun was partly eclipsed by the castle now, and the air had turned flat and blue. The warm wind still rolled down from on high, a constant buffeting that made Jonah feel as though he was carrying a burden across his shoulders. From somewhere in the distance came a long, whistling sound, the cry of an animal perhaps, or the note of some mighty horn.

He walked straight past the escape route the first time, and it was only when the steepening incline, which was formed as the ledge curved up into the tunnel wall, forced him to retrace his steps that he saw it. There was a crack in the ledge, thin and barely visible, little more than a finger's breadth across at the point where it split the resinous lip. Crouching, he peered down the cliff. The crack ran down the wall, widening swiftly into a cavernous fault, a craggy chimney that descended in a series of ragged tacks until it met a horizontal shelf, several hundred yards down. It was clear to Jonah now, as he traced the broad line of this shelf away to his right, that it was a way of some kind, perhaps even a road, for it led directly to the lowest ramparts of the shadow-filled castle.

On the shelf, moving towards a wide circle of blue that could only be a pool of water lying in the middle of the road, was a tiny ant-figure: Annie.

This time he did not forget the painting box. After hastily improvising a shoulder strap using a strip of fabric torn from his loincloth, Jonah slung it round his neck and began his descent.

Fear seemed to have left him. The confining aspect of the chimney helped him to ignore the immensity of the drop, but all the same he felt braver than he had any right to. He decided it was the prospect of a drink and even a bathe that had brought him this new energy and new confidence. He had already suppressed his memory of what Annie had done to him on the ledge: it was easier to ignore it rather than conjure some explanation . . .

But her eyes! What about her eyes? came a whisper on the cloying air.

The final limb of the crack delivered him on to level ground with no more than a couple of bruises on his shin and scratches on his forearms and back. Here he paused, bent forwards, hands on knees, catching his breath. Then he looked up and the enormity of this world struck him once again.

Had he thought this a wall? It was a *continent,* tipped outrageously on to its side. Here was an entire land, paved and grooved, raised to challenge the heavens. He looked up into the wind, and saw the same haze that claimed the depths. No top, no bottom, neither beginning nor end, just an infinite recession. In that moment Jonah embraced the idea that this wall went on forever.

The shelf too was paved, though the blocks from which it was made were considerably smaller than their upright cousins; this is not to say they were small, however, for each one occupied a plot that could have accommodated an average London town house. The pale brown upper surface of the blocks was heavily weather-beaten; the joints between them were filled with what looked like brilliant yellow moss. Flecks of grit pressed themselves into the soles of Jonah's feet, but the ground was by and large smooth. He gained the impression these materials did not yield readily to the elements.

The sun was nearly gone now and Jonah sensed the hiss of fear return at the back of his mind. He hurried on towards the pool, the surface of which shone in the rays of the dying sun. Falling to his knees he plunged his head into the water, emitting a rich, gargling cry as he immersed his dry and mud-coarse skin. Not even thinking that it might be poison, he turned the cry into a deep draught, gulping down the cool, clear liquid as though it were ambrosia. At once he began to choke. Tossing his head clear he retched and then his stomach threw back everything he had swallowed. He drowned his face again, drinking more cautiously this time; to his relief the water stayed down. He splashed more water across his body, rejoicing in its cleansing touch; he felt baptised.

Annie was on the far side of the lake, no more than ten yards away, seemingly oblivious to his performance. She had divested herself of the garments Jonah had made for her and was dancing naked in the low, sultry light. His thirst slaked for now, he watched, fascinated, as she raised and lowered her feet in an exaggerated tiptoe step. Every movement she made was slow and deliberate; her balance was remarkable, her grace inspiring. Each step took her through a fraction of an arc, a tiny piece of the circumference of the pool, and as she progressed she dipped her upper body like a bird, lowering her head until her long hair trailed over her face and along the ground. Then, just as slowly, she straightened, arching her back and raising her arms as though worshipping the sky.

In this way she moved about a quarter of the way round the lake shore towards Jonah, at which point she suddenly stopped, snapping her body upright and dropping her arms so that her palms were pressed hard against her thighs. She cocked her head to one side – another curiously birdlike gesture.

'Faery!' she called. Her voice was low, full of unexpected humour. 'Are you still here?'

She stepped into the lake, descending rapidly until the water covered her knees. Her pace did not vary as she waded deeper and deeper, not even when the wavelets caused by her passage were lapping just beneath her breasts, nor was her balance upset; her progress was relentless. Jonah was surprised that the pool was so deep – he had expected a virtual puddle, not this obvious crater. There was little time to dwell on this however, as she was already emerging from the water, her dark skin aglow in the fading light. She walked right up to him so that they stood almost nose to nose.

They stared at each other for what seemed to Jonah like an hour, though it must have been only a second or two. He could not drag his gaze away from those alien eyes, those perfect mirrors in which he saw only the distorted shape of his own face. Then she laughed and turned away.

'You have no conception of where you are, do you, faery?'

Still Jonah said nothing. The voice was still Annie's, despite its low, husky note. What could have happened to her? Had her experiences driven her mad? But that did not explain what had happened to her eyes. *Something in the air,* he thought wildly. *Or perhaps the volcano, the result of looking into the fire . . .*

Nothing made sense. All he could do was listen to her, look for clues.

'We have escaped, you and I,' she was saying. Her arms were opened wide as though to embrace the huge, falling sky. 'We are not the first to do so, nor will we be the last.' She spun round, silver eyes shining dully. 'But we are the ones who shall be remembered!'

She advanced on Jonah, scanning his body with a broad sweep of her head.

'I have reconsidered your fate, faery. You might be more useful than I first deemed, therefore you shall live. For the time being. This body –' she stroked her fingertips across her smooth stomach, a languid, sensual gesture '– may hold some surprises for me. With your help I might gain more control of it than I had hoped. Who knows – I may start to like it.'

'Annie . . .' Jonah began, but he stopped as he saw a weird expression pass across her face. It was nothing he could identify, a suspicious, reptilian cast of otherwise familiar features. Whatever emotion it betrayed was utterly inhuman. He took an involuntary step back, shuddering, his mouth dry and hot. Her face changed, like melting wax, and again she looked like Annie.

But you are not Annie, are you?

Annie's face smiled once more. 'You really don't know, do you? You don't know who I am, what I am?' She tossed her head and started to look around as though searching for something. The search took her gaze out into the sky, where she stared long and hard. 'Where are you?' she muttered as she swept her head from side to side. 'Show yourselves and put this poor creature out of its misery.'

Jonah did not have to wait long.

They started to appear just before the final sliver of sun disappeared behind the castle wall. He counted five specks, dark motes of dust floating against the paler bands of cloud. They grew swiftly in size and at first he thought they were birds, giant seagulls perhaps. One was larger, or nearer, than the others.

Four of the five clustered together before veering towards the fifth, which continued doggedly on its course. Then, without warning, the group of four peeled away in tight formation and flew back into the clouds, leaving their solitary companion heading directly towards the castle. Though it was still far away Jonah could pick out features: long, tapering wings beating in a slow, steady rhythm; a lashing tail tipped with barbs; craggy horns erupting from a large, streamlined head. It tucked its wings close against its body and dived towards the wooden fortress supporting one of the castle turrets. What it did then finally convinced Jonah that he had left his own world behind altogether and entered an entirely new realm where none of the mores and few of the truths in which he believed applied. As the stooping behemoth opened its mouth and breathed brilliant orange fire deep into the heart of the fortress, Jonah looked out across the face of this precipitous world and whispered, 'Here be dragons.'

He felt her hand on his shoulder.

'What do you see?' It was Annie's voice, but he no longer believed that it was Annie's spirit that drove it. He looked up through tears.

'A woman I met on a beach. A beautiful woman, whom I wish was with me now.'

Annie's shoulders shrugged. 'She is not gone completely. I have . . . put her away, you might say. Her name is . . . Annya?'

'Annie?'

'My name is not so dissimilar. Perhaps you will learn to love it as you were beginning to love hers.'

'What is your name?'

She spread her arms, but then stopped halfway through the gesture and looked briefly surprised. Amused, she regarded her arms and then lowered them again. 'My name is Archan, and once I was a dragon.'

'And what might you be now?'

'A profound question, faery, and one not even I can answer fully. Superficially, I am now of your species. But you have no concept of what is contained within this primitive form. Your kind have little knowledge of the power of charm, the pull of eternity, the legacy of the Deathless.' She lowered her face to his, glowering now, white teeth bared in a snarl. 'What is your concept of time, faery? How long will you live? Fifty years, sixty? Would you rejoice to even approach one hundred? How can you comprehend what I am now when I know more about you than you do about yourself?

'I saw you crippled by the loss of your wings; I saw you burned by the fire even as you tried to tame it; I saw you die in agony as the glaciers came, whole limbs of your race ripped away. I saw the scars you left on the land, your enslavement of the forests and all the races who inhabited them. I saw you rape the world, faery. Your ancestors would have killed themselves had they known what they would become.

'And I. The last dragon in the world. What power for Archan? None, faery. What chance to set my wing in your air, however stinking you might have made it? None. Only the long, sleepless nightmare of eternity, the endless embrace of the ice.'

She crouched before him, breathing hard, mirror eyes wide. 'And then – escape! To journey here, to the one place left where eternity has any meaning. Two of my kind came here once, long ago when the world turned and the day of creation came. Two dragons slipped across the threshold, leaving behind the world of their birth. Now we have followed, you and I. These creatures you see in the sky, those are their children. Now I have come to rule them. Now, at last, eternity can truly begin.'

She was holding him now, hands gently grasping his shoulders. The touch was warm and gentle, agonisingly human, yet Jonah knew that this was no human being holding him. Annie was gone, and this . . . this reptile had taken her place. Possessed her, as the ghost stories his uncle had read to him as a child had told of dead spirits possessing living people. At that moment, as he gazed upon her smooth features, her slightly parted lips, the soft flaring of her nostrils, Jonah believed he had never seen anything so alien in his life.

Abruptly he shook off her hands and looked away. The dragon had taken up station above the castle, hovering there with slow, heavy beats of its powerful wings. Fires were blazing deep inside the fortress, sending a huge column of black smoke roiling into the sky. Apparently satisfied, the beast slashed its tail through the air, drawing eddies out of the smoke, and flew sedately into the evening mist.

'So,' said Archan casually, 'are you coming with me?'

'Do I have a choice?'

'There is always choice, faery.'

'That is the first time I have agreed with you. But why do you insist upon calling me "faery"?'

Archan raised Annie's eyebrows. 'What would you have me call you?'

'Jonah will suffice.'

'Jonah it is then. Are you coming?'

There! For the briefest instant Jonah saw through the mirrors. Somehow the banter had lowered Archan's guard, revealing a little of what lay beneath – what lay *inside*. Something human, a glimpse of a familiar expression, a face seen screaming silently at a locked window. The face of the condemned prisoner.

Archan saw his eyes widen and snapped her defences shut again immediately. 'Come!' she barked tersely. He fell in obediently behind her, marshalling his reasons for following.

She seemed to know something about this place, and there was much he might learn from her. But that was not why he submitted. *Annie is in there somewhere,* he thought, studying the sway of her hips and shoulders as he plodded in her wake. *And there has to be a way to get her out.*

The prodigious size of the castle became all too apparent the nearer they approached. Jonah knew little about the finer points of architecture but even he could see that it was a mish-mash, a melting pot of styles ranging from Saxon to Gothic, with even a touch of the pioneering American West thrown in for good measure. As darkness descended however it became harder to make out the detail of the stone and wood structures and all he was left with was the whole, an artificial mountain clinging precariously to an almost sheer cliff face; the light from the burning section gave only sporadic illumination. In this light, Jonah felt that the place was somehow Teutonic, that a great palace from the Black Forest had been transplanted here, an impression strengthened by the densely woven conifers bunched into the sharp angle formed where the castle met the wall.

The fire in the wooden palisade continued to blaze. Jonah guessed that much of the higher structure would fall unsupported into the abyss if it burned away completely. There was no other source of animation: none of the many windows was lit and there was no sign of occupation. The place had an air of abandonment and decay.

The road brought them to a pair of doorways set into dark grey stone. The blocks from which the castle had been built were on a satisfyingly human scale, each one measuring no more than three feet across. Slime streaked their exposed faces and strands of lichen were knotted into their joints. To their right, leading into the shadows where the castle intersected the steep line of the dominant wall, rose a narrow flight of stairs carpeted with trailing creepers. It led, Jonah suspected, directly into the forest; it looked wholly uninviting.

Neither of the doorways had a door.

'Will you choose, faery, or shall I?'

Jonah wondered whether Archan was hiding some knowledge, challenging him to make the correct decision. He could not read her expression: the firelight splashed across her metal eyes, her features were set and still.

'In the absence of a doorkeeper,' he proposed, 'I suggest we try the left way.'

'Lead on.'

Presenting his back to Archan made Jonah nervous at first, but as they proceeded into the gloom he found his attention diverted by the strangeness of the decor.

The ceiling was high, almost lost from view. Light filtered down from a high, arched window, revealing a stone wall to their right – the partition separating the two entranceways. The blocks were etched with curious markings that looked to Jonah like Chinese characters. He shuddered and clasped Annie's box close. Were these clues to some hidden mystery? If so, there was something ominously repetitive about them. He searched in vain for the mark of the Red Dragon; if it was here then it was lost in the crowd.

Chains hung from the ceiling. They swayed languorously to and fro, the sound they made like the chink of countless coins. A long wooden bench crouched beneath an overhang extending from the opposite wall; the alcove was barely four feet high, so that no human could possibly have sat on it. The floor was tiled alternately black and white. Jonah felt like a piece on a giant chessboard – which piece he could not say, but the steady motion of Archan behind him assured him that she possessed both the power and the range of a queen.

'Damned if I'll be a pawn,' he muttered.

'What was that?' By God, her ears were sharp!

'I said it's warm.' And it was. The constant wind of the exterior was of course absent here. As a result, the thick, spicy air clung to their bodies like damp clothes. Jonah again had a vision of his words moving visibly through this dense medium, waves of sound carving elaborate patterns as they radiated from his mouth. He looked up at the window, trying to make out the source of the light.

The lintels of the glassless window aperture glowed orange,

but surely the firelight was not coming from the blaze outside – it was in entirely the wrong direction for one thing, and it seemed smaller, more gentle.

'There is a flight of stairs over there.' Archan's voice was loud in his ear and he jumped at the touch of her breath. He could feel her naked body pressing against his back. When she rested her hand upon his shoulder he moved forward sharply, shrugging off the contact.

'Then let us ascend,' he said brusquely.

The staircase turned about the outside of a circular tower bulging from the end of the entrance hall. There seemed to be no other exit, although Jonah would have wagered anything that behind the grey stonework there lurked at least one secret passage. There were no handrails and each step was barely two feet wide, so it was with considerable care that he ascended. Once more he felt Archan's presence as a prickle down his spine: *If she really wants to do away with me this could be the perfect time.*

The staircase took them directly to the window, through which they clambered, emerging into a dimly-lit chamber. The room was circular and immensely tall, like the interior of a vast factory chimney. Around its circumference, more or less on a level with Jonah's eyes, was a series of small, round holes, regularly spaced. At its apex, impossibly high, was a tiny disc of twilight; a shadow moved briefly across it, like a branch beyond a distant window. In the middle of the floor lay a rough wooden torch, its rag-bound end burning fiercely. Beside it was sprawled the body of a man, face down. As they watched, the flames jumped across the gap between the torch and the man's motionless foot and suddenly his whole leg was ablaze.

Uttering a shocked cry Jonah jumped forward and slapped at the flames with his hands. Then, realising the futility of this, he shoved the man away from the torch and rolled him over and over across the dusty floor, bending and heaving until the flames were extinguished. In the sudden silence he thought he heard a faint chattering noise.

Archan watched all this with amused interest, stepping forward herself only when Jonah had finished and was stood panting, hands on hips, looking down at the body.

'He was already dead, of course,' she commented, prodding the man with a disdainful toe.

'He might not have been,' gasped Jonah. 'Besides, we might learn something from him. We could not have done that if he had gone up in smoke.'

Archan afforded him a gracious nod and turned her attention to the hole in the ceiling.

Jonah knelt down and examined the corpse. He could see now that a long, dreadful wound had opened the man's chest from the base of his ribs practically up to his collarbone. His hair was long, blonde and knotted, and a coarse beard covered his cheeks and chin, though not his upper lip. He wore a cloth knotted about his waist, some kind of animal fur Jonah could not identify beyond the fact that it smelt foul, and leather boots. It was one of these that had caught fire so spectacularly; now it was black and ruined. The man had a large leather pouch slung about his neck, the contents of which had spilled across the floor, and it was these things that really caught Jonah's eye.

A dozen stones had been scattered. Most of them were fist-sized or slightly bigger, rounded at one end and sharpened at the other. The sharp edges were notched in a way that was instantly recognisable to Jonah. He bent down and picked up the nearest of them, turning it over and over in his hands, feeling the familiar, cool touch of the flint.

'Do you know what this is?' he called to Archan, who was now examining a decorative border set into the curved wall.

'A stone,' she replied without looking round.

'A stone tool,' he corrected. 'This is a hand-axe, thousands of years old – in fact, I would venture to say it is late Neolithic. You can tell by the way it has been cut, do you see? But what is it doing here?'

'A faery tool.' Archan turned and shrugged. 'Your race's obsession with such things is something I have never understood.'

'Why do you call us faeries?' Jonah's heart was pounding. The find had both excited and confused him. Archan's dismissive attitude angered him too. What right had she to treat him with such contempt?

'Because that is what you were.'

'Call me a man, if you must call me anything other than my name, for that is what I am.'

Archan considered this, flexing Annie's face into a frown. 'Very well, *man*. What do these stones tell you?'

'These are polished flints. A man called Lord Avebury has isolated two key divisions within what we call the Stone Age: the Palaeolithic, or Old Stone Age, and the Neolithic or New. The smoothing of these axes tells me these belong to the latter category. The Stone Age itself is merely the first of three recognised time periods, the second two of which are the Bronze and Iron. Human beings developed over tens of thousands of years, if not much longer, during which time they learned to work first stone, then metal. I am the end result of that process.'

'A dubious honour. And what fuelled this process, *man*?'

Jonah was warming to his subject now. The flint was heavy in his hand, solidly real; it seemed to lend him strength. 'Ah, now that is still under debate. I side with Darwin and the evolutionists, who suggest a process of natural selection, whereby characteristics favouring survival are passed directly to each succeeding generation; societies pass through increasingly sophisticated phases in an ordered manner. Worsaae is an evolutionist too, but his followers would have us believe in their theory of diffusionism, which promotes the idea of local changes spreading outwards to stimulate global ones.'

'Most enlightening. But tell me, what was man *before* he was man?'

Here Jonah paused. This was the question that normally caused him to blush when it was asked of him at a dinner party, for it was the one guaranteed to generate the greatest controversy. 'An ape,' he said, his voice measured.

'And before that?'

'An early primate. We are still discovering fossils. The science is in its infancy.' He felt defensive, as he usually did, but Archan did not laugh at him. She did produce a smile however, one full of pity.

'And this is your proof?' She turned over one of the flints with her foot. 'A few broken stones? What else? Oh yes, these fossils of yours. Old bones sunk into the ground.'

'They tell us a great deal—'

'But do they tell you the truth, *man*?'

Abruptly Archan broke off the conversation and marched to the window via which they had entered the chamber. 'Come, faery. There is no more to be seen here and no way to reach the hole in the ceiling. Not without wings.'

Jonah scrambled after her, forming a makeshift pocket in his loincloth into which he stuffed the axe. The torch was still burning where it lay; he picked it up, taking care not to spill the fuel in which it was soaked on to his skin. By the time he reached the aperture Archan was already at the foot of the stairs. By God, she was fast! He took a last look back at the dead man.

Neolithic hand axes stored in a leather pouch that would not have looked out of place in King Arthur's court; a Stone Age man's skirt matched with mediaeval boots. Just where did you come from?

There was no time to wonder. She had started to walk towards the entrance and he could not risk losing her. He heard the chattering noise again and happened to glance up at the nearest of the holes that circumnavigated the chamber. Two pairs of shining eyes, tiny and intense like a rodent's, stared back at him.

He descended the stone steps two at a time.

Outside it was dark. There were no visible stars. The second doorway led not into a hall but a long, straight corridor. The torch illuminated damp stone walls and undecorated flagstones; the place was dank and forbidding, dungeon-like.

Jonah led the way, nursing his fury. Eventually he could contain it no further. 'Why do you mock me?' he exploded, rounding on Archan and brandishing the torch in her face. Silver eyes shattered the firelight, sucking away its warmth. 'Is it not enough that I have to believe you have stolen away my companion? Why do you taunt me so? Who are you to make me question what is real?'

She waited as he ranted on then, when he stopped to draw breath, she spoke to him almost gently. 'The past you construct is valid for you but it is just that: a construction. You must remember that I am immortal. Your memories begin with your birth but mine extend to the beginning of eternity. These are the memories I inherited from the Deathless Ones, from whom I claimed the gift of immortality. I remember the world as it was before it turned, and as it was before that and before even that. In my memory your race sprang not from the ape but from a being as alien to you now as the fish or the fowl.

'Your ancestors did not grub about in the soil and hack at rocks. They were invisible, aethereal beings, charmed elementals who became corporeal only once every hundred years. They were faeries. Like the dragons, they flew, though their wings were not made for flight but to store the magic that raised them aloft.' She reached out her hand tenderly and stroked Jonah's cheek. 'Those are the beings I remember, the Old Earth Dwellers, the Gentle Ones. They were your fathers, man, not the crude apes you find buried in stone.'

'What *are* you?' whispered Jonah, his eyes filling with sudden tears.

'More than I was.' She kissed him, once, on the lips.

A noise intruded over the crackle of the torch. It retreated briefly then swelled, the unmistakable sound of human voices singing. Or chanting, Jonah decided. He edged forward, holding out the fire as much to ward off attack as to light his way. Annie's feet padded silently behind him, the dragon who guided them inscrutable behind her metal eyes.

The chanting grew deep and rich as they rounded a curve in the corridor. The change in direction was accompanied by a warm, orange glow that spilled across their bodies; up ahead Jonah could see a square of light.

He searched for his anger as they advanced and found it replaced by the same confusion he had felt upon finding the flints in the round chamber. His mouth felt dry again – he had drunk deeply from the pool on the road but his body still demanded fluid. And his hunger had grown monstrous, a deep ache in his belly accompanied by a dreadful weariness. He stumbled and Archan smoothly took the torch from him before he dropped it. She took his hand and led him to the end of the corridor.

I'm not here, thought Jonah, unsure of whether or not to be grateful that all this was a dream. *I am floating face down in the Straits of Sunda. What is left of my body is taking its last, dying breath, but my mind has already escaped from the world into a Purgatory inhabited by dragon ghosts and Neolithic men. There is one thing more it has escaped from too: sanity.*

His eyelids fluttered and he found time to wonder if he would stay here for all eternity.

Before he collapsed he took in the view.

They had exited the corridor into a long, narrow hall. A huge fire burned at the near end, throwing vigorous light across a roof crisscrossed with huge beams, a tattered array of hanging banners and a long wooden table supported on massive trestles. Shiny metal platters and jugs cast reflections over the table's rough surface; bones and strips of meat were scattered everywhere.

Around the fire was clustered a group of perhaps sixty people, men and women, dressed in a bewildering array of skins, metal helmets and leather garments of wildly varying style. Many of the men appeared to be wearing chain mail. And they were singing.

The song sounded old, its harmonies strange to Jonah's Victorian ears. He could not make out the scale they were using, but the sound, dominated by the voices of the men, was powerful and inevitably primeval. It was as exotic as the spicy air that seemed to be clustering around his face, forcing its way into his nose and mouth, his mind . . . The song became a ringing bell, a victorious bass clamour and the hall grew dark. The last thing he was aware of was the press of Annie's body against his as Archan caught him and plucked him clear of the floor as though he were no more than a single feather afloat on the ocean.

4

Annie on the Inside – 1

Fire surrounded her. The pain was immense and she withdrew inside herself, seeking out the secret place she had used whenever Rance decided to spend the evening taking pot shots at her with his fists. Oblivion beckoned but she refused to allow herself to drift into its tempting embrace. Suspended within a red and livid dreamscape, she tried to understand where the pain was coming from.

It was not, as she had first suspected, coming from outside. Instinct told her the volcano was far away now but what had replaced it she could not tell. Something was blocking her senses, a fog that muffled all input and left her blind and deaf, aware only of the fire.

Adrift inside her own mind, Annie realised something had gone very wrong.

Panic swelled up, overwhelming the pain. Years ago, on the trail, an uncle of her father's had fallen from a wagon and broken his neck. He had lived for six more days, during which time he had been completely paralysed, utterly unresponsive and sustained only by the patient ministrations of his wife. Nobody knew if he was still aware inside the shell his body had become, if he could hear, if his wide and motionless eyes could see, if he could feel the touch of loving fingers upon his skin. Annie had been allowed to see him only once, just before he died, and she had run from his bedside screaming, unable to contemplate the notion that he might be locked away in there, silently screaming . . .

Had that happened to her? Had she been injured by flying debris, paralysed even? Was she even now floating in the warm sea, or lying in some sanatorium ashore?

She pressed the panic firmly back down. She would not scream. As the panic subsided so the fire reared up again; she turned towards it.

There! The fire was in here with her: a blaze of anger burning inside her own heart. But it was not her anger. The realisation was shattering, incomprehensible.

Someone else is in here with me.

She had no idea how long it took to piece herself back together. Time itself was cut loose, meaningless.

She levered thoughts and feelings with imaginary muscles about her own, caged mind, assembling a phantom duplicate of herself in her secret place. Perhaps Rance had helped her in the end, for without his cruelty she would never have found her way in here at all.

Step by step, thought by thought, Annie rebuilt herself in her own image.

Even before the process was complete she knew she was right: she had been invaded. This secret part of her mind was just a small part of her overall consciousness, the equivalent of the uppermost tower room of a castle keep.

Rapunzel, she thought as she visualised her prison cell, *let down thy hair*.

Annie too had been locked away, and she even knew the name of the enchantress who had done it: Archan.

Where Archan had come from she could not determine, for the witch kept herself securely hidden behind a pair of veil-like wings. But the infiltrator could not conceal the anger that drove her on, that had, indeed, driven her in here: it burned like a furnace. Archan's anger was the fire that had driven Annie into hiding, but it was also the light by which she could see the interior of her own mind.

So alien was Archan's presence, so utterly inhuman, that Annie at once discarded any notion that she herself had become insane. The precise state of her earthly body she could not judge, but of one thing she was certain: she was as sound in her thoughts as she had ever been. This conviction enabled her to focus on what was more immediately important: evicting the intruder and escaping the prison her mind had become.

* * *

Annie soon discovered that the imaginary self she had created needed no sleep. She paced to and fro behind the barricades of fire Archan had erected, wondering why the witch had not completed the task and done away with her altogether. The most logical and attractive explanation was that Archan still needed Annie, or her essential spirit at least. Annie was beginning to suspect that her body was not comatose at all, that it was in fact entirely awake and alert, operating quite normally, but under Archan's control.

I am possessed!

She reviewed her sources of information and was distressed to discover that she was relying almost exclusively on intuition. Just as she had fabricated a virtual self in an equally tenuous prison, so her assessment of the situation was based on nothing but speculation.

Not a tower but a house of cards.

A picture materialised before her, outlined against Archan's fire. A house not of cards but of tiles. Glowing Oriental symbols chased up its walls, wrapping the precarious structure in an inscrutable web of line and light. One symbol stood out against all the others: a long, vertical stroke capped by the hilt of a sword, the sign of the Red Dragon. The house of tiles was large, large enough for Annie's spirit-self to enter. This she did.

The light was subdued inside the house and this soothed Annie. The tiles were turned inwards, presenting their playing faces outwards to the fire. As she passed through the tall, oblong doorway she entered a broad entrance hall, the walls of which were lined with paintings. They looked familiar, and with good reason: they were the miniatures she had painted during her long voyage from America – images of the Rockies, of the great Pacific, of Galapagos. They were grown large now and looked to her like windows through which she might extend her arms, her head, through which she might step . . .

One of the paintings did not look familiar. At first she thought the tile had been laid on its side, but as she approached it for a closer look she saw that the landscape it represented was tilted in itself. A tremendous cliff face receded into haze; white clouds trailed like banners down a rich cobalt sky; a broad ledge projecting from the cliff shone in brilliant sunlight, pools of water reflecting the cloud-skein.

She looked up and around. The tiles wavered briefly, betraying their unreality, but by closing her eyes and reopening them she was able to recover her belief in their stability, and she had no doubt it was her belief that was keeping them upright.

A spiral of tiles was lying horizontally, forming a winding staircase that led to a series of openings in the upper walls. Shadows loomed up there and Annie decided she would not climb the stairs without good reason. Besides, this painting intrigued her. The closer she got to it the more detail it released; indeed, now it did seem like a window, revealing more and more of itself as she drew near. The clouds were moving fast, she noted, streaming downwards. There was something bulky lying on the ledge, perhaps a hundred yards beyond the plane of the tile's surface – except the tile no longer had a surface. She looked to the side and saw a thin line of ivory blending seamlessly into the rough surface of the cliff face.

Not a cliff, she thought, registering the regular blocks from which it was constructed. *A wall. God damn!*

She stepped across the threshold and entered the world inside the painting.

There was a grainy texture, a sense of reality being stretched to its limit, and Annie was reminded that this place was nothing but a dream within a dream. Nevertheless there was also a taste of spice that lent the vision credibility; the feeling of wind on her face and head, blowing her hair down across her shoulders, was the final convincing detail.

This place may not be real, but it sure does exist somewhere.

The thing on the ledge was moving, unfolding like a Chinese puzzle. She saw without surprise that it bore the familiar mark of the Red Dragon on its side and she risked a glance behind. The *ma-chong* house remained at her back, revealed through an oblong window floating impossibly in the air just an arm's length behind her. The thing unfolded itself further, revealing a black carapace and long, mobile limbs. It stood up on its hind legs and waved her forward with what she presumed to be its arms, though at their ends they bore not claws or fingers but pincers. Its face – what she could see of it from this distance – was wide and flat; green eyes glowed, staring directly at her. She blinked, and suddenly she was face to face with it.

It smiled, an expression that looked uncomfortable on its soft, reptilian face. It looked down at Annie through vertically slitted pupils; tiny teeth lined its wide mouth. Then it spoke.

'Welcome to Amara.'

'What is this place?'

'This is not a place; this is Amara.' The creature's smile was infuriating. Though it was bipedal and stood a good seven feet tall, Annie could not help thinking of the giant tortoises she had seen on James and Chatham Islands.

'Is this real? I mean, I know this is a vision, but is it a real place?'

The creature nodded, once.

'And are you real?'

It nodded again. Annie looked around, thinking, thinking . . .

'But I've made this, haven't I? And I've made you? In my mind?'

'You have enabled me to contact you,' the creature agreed.

'And you can help me?'

'We can help each other.'

Annie suddenly caught her breath. 'Jonah! Is he all right? Is he here?'

'He lives. He is here. He is with the dragon.'

'The drag—' Suddenly she understood. The fire, the taste of the alien presence. 'Archan! My God, I've been possessed by a damned lizard!' Again there was a sensation of this fragile reality wavering. Flames licked at the periphery of her vision and her strange, tall companion seemed to shudder, tiny holes opening briefly through its skin to reveal the fire beyond. 'I've got to believe this, haven't I?' she grated and it nodded again.

'What you are experiencing is a fabrication. Your ability to sustain this level of detail is remarkable in humans of your level of sophistication. It develops upStone, of course, and indeed is used more widely in what you would term your past – your own time is one of appalling introspection. Your imagination may be your salvation, Annie.'

'How come you know my name?'

'Forgive me. I am called Esh. Now I no longer have the advantage over you.'

'I didn't understand what you were saying, Esh. Care to try again?'

'When there is more time, Annie, I will explain as much as

I am able, that I promise you. But you have less energy than you believe and it must be conserved. You have far to travel and little enough time. Trust me.'

Annie gazed into the creature's green eyes. 'Do I have a choice? So I'll ask you again, Esh or whatever your name is, what in the name of Hell is this topsy-turvy place?'

Again the weird, reptilian smile.

'If you ask again I will say again: welcome to Amara.'

5

Castle

To Jonah's relief, Archan quickly decided it would be wise to clothe Annie's body again; several of the glances she received from the Late Neolithic men were less than respectful. The garments she chose were loose-fitting, leather tied with crude thongs and toggles of bone; her feet she left bare. Jonah found it easier to look at her and, as before, found her more attractive now that most of her skin was concealed.

Archan's view on the subject was characteristically forthright: 'I may yet explore the sensual possibilities of this body, but the choice of partner will be mine and mine alone.'

Jonah too had taken the opportunity to acquire more substantial clothing, settling for a short cloth robe that he tied around his waist with a belt of rope. The robe's hood hung loosely behind him; he felt like a mediaeval monk. A pair of ill-fitting moccasins completed the ensemble. Like them, the Neolithics were arrayed in a variety of contradictory garments, a mélange of cultures settled into an alien world.

'It is incredible,' he said to Archan as they observed the tribe's morning rituals from the seclusion of the upper gallery. 'I cannot be precise, but if those stone tools were anything to go by, these people are from a time at least four thousand years before Christ, possibly much earlier. All the metalwork and most of their clothing is much later of course, as is this hall.' He chuckled. 'They come from a turning point in history, you might say, since there are many Christians who would have you believe the world was actually created in 4004 BC . . . October, if I remember rightly. Darwin has proved them wrong, of course, and our friends here are the living proof of his assertions.'

'Do not be so quick to prove and disprove, faery. You may find both histories to be true.'

The night had begun with a brief and awkward dialogue with the Neolithics. The first surprise had come when their apparent leader – a short, lean man whose face was entirely hidden by a bull's-head mask – had spoken to them in perfect English. Belatedly, Jonah found himself wondering how Archan, a million-year old reptile, knew his language too; some function of her having adopted a human body, perhaps.

The man, whose name was Frey, coolly welcomed them to the feast and bade them eat whatever they could find remaining on the table. The polite and formal welcome seemed grudging, and was, Jonah felt, performed more for the benefit of the onlookers than themselves. They both attracted their share of suspicious looks, not least Archan: lust vied with fear as the men appraised first her nudity, then the inhuman sheen of her mirrored eyes. There was also a brief fascination with their hair: both Jonah's reddish thatch and Archan's dark mane aroused curiosity among the largely blond Neolithics. Following this scrutiny they accepted Frey's invitation and tore into the meat with relish, washing it down with cupfuls of warm, weak ale, while the Neolithics sang an increasingly melancholy series of chants and rounds. Eventually the party, if that was what it was, began to break up and Jonah and Archan retired to the gallery where they slept the night. Jonah commented on the casual way they had been examined then dismissed.

'Perhaps they get a lot of people passing through,' was Archan's unhelpful reply.

The Neolithics had constructed a ramshackle village of tents and shacks within the great hall. Once-beautiful hanging fabrics had been ripped from the walls and draped over upturned tables to form a series of covered sleeping areas: now the rich cloth had darkened and decayed, revealing only a hint of its former splendour. Litter was piled waist high around the hall's perimeter, bones and debris banked up against the stone walls; the smell drifting over the gallery was truly awful. A series of rough stone hearths surrounded the huge fireplace; beyond these a slit in the high end wall led to what Jonah presumed to be a latrine, if the regular comings and goings of the tribespeople through it were anything to go by. Above the fireplace there was a gaping hole in the ceiling. It revealed not the sky but the outlines of more roof beams: another storey of the castle. This upper level clearly boasted windows, for it was brilliantly lit; the stolen daylight filtered down through the hole into the hall below.

Two things struck him above all. The first was the blend of squalor and decay: these people were not simply primitive, they were on the edge of extinction. The second was the obvious mismatch between them and their surroundings. The most prominent of the surviving banners showed three deer leaping over a barred gate; the animals were finely portrayed, their outlines drawn with tremendous sensitivity. By contrast, Jonah could clearly see one of the Neolithics' attempts at art – a crude scratching on one of the walls that was evidently intended to represent a hunting scene, with stick figures chasing a rough ox-shape. The latter drawing had a kind of primitive beauty but there was no comparison between the two. On the other hand, the Neolithics seemed happy to use metal knives and plates, though they had surely not manufactured such implements themselves.

Smoke drifted up from one of the hearths; several of the women were hunched there, busily starting a fire. A large section of unidentifiable carcass was dragged out from behind a toppled table and a heavily-built man, stripped naked, started to carve at it with a jewel-encrusted sword. A metal hatchet lay on the floor beside him, and periodically he used this to hack at the tougher pieces of meat. Nowhere could Jonah see anything resembling the stone knives and axes that the dead man had been carrying. Nor, he remarked, could he see any children.

His view was blocked when a pair of antlers rose above the parapet, swiftly followed by the stocky figure of Frey. He had exchanged his bull-mask for a light headdress; beneath a low frill of fur his face was lean and pale. He, like most of his tribe, looked vaguely Scandinavian, though it was hard to tell the true colour of either skin or hair, so caked were both in dirt. Jonah had already taken this man to be the leader and he bowed his head in deference as Frey approached; if he could gain the trust of the chief he might learn plenty.

'Good morning,' he said cheerfully. 'At least, it feels like morning, though there is no daylight in here.'

'The time has not yet come when we may return to the light,' responded Frey. Blue eyes bored into Jonah's. With the confidence of authority, Frey reached for Annie's painting box, which Jonah still bore slung around his shoulder. Without knowing why, Jonah turned slightly away to shield the box from his touch. Frey frowned and withdrew, then turned his attention to Archan, who was sitting on the floor with her back against the parapet, arms resting lightly on drawn-up knees. Raising his right hand, he made a fist and then extended his first and fourth fingers towards her. Jonah shivered.

A modern Italian man might use such a gesture to ward off evil. How many thousands of years old are these imaginary horns?

'You have eyes of magic, woman,' Frey intoned. 'You are not welcome here.'

'You have changed your opinion,' Archan answered smoothly.

Frey suddenly squatted, a smooth movement. He was broad-chested, Jonah noted, a formidable character. How old was he? Thirty, forty? It was hard to guess.

About the Neolithic's waist was a thin belt on which were hung a variety of bones. Most were small, threaded into little circlets that rattled as he moved – the bones of small rodents, most likely. Several were larger however; one of these, hanging down the outside of his leg, looked suspiciously like a human femur. Frey opened a pouch, drew out a handful of loose bones and scattered them on the stone floor. Having appraised them for a moment, he gathered them up again and returned them to the pouch. Then he stood and addressed himself to Archan.

'Last night we were at feast. There was much magic in the song, and I would not have seen it broken. Now morning has come and I must speak plainly. You, at least, must go. The man may stay if he wishes.' His casual air sounded false to Jonah – underneath he sounded angry, even furious.

Archan rose with a silent, graceful motion. For an instant she seemed to tower over Frey. 'Tell us about your king and we will consider our position here.'

Again Frey frowned. This time Jonah joined him.

'You know much, wise-woman. Have you been sent or are all your spells your own?'

'Oh, I have come here very much for my own purpose, isn't

that right, Jonah? Now tell me, how long does your king have to live?'

Frey considered the unexpected question for a long time. Finally he let out his breath. 'No man can say. If I could see the sky I might read the clouds but I have only bones and ox-hearts.'

'How long?'

He shrugged. 'Perhaps a month, perhaps a little longer.'

'And who will take his place?'

Frey's bright blue eyes shone in the stolen light of the upper storey. 'He has a son.'

Archan nodded as if she had known this too. She lifted her hand and traced outstretched fingers down the Neolithic's bare chest. 'Tell me more.'

It did not take long to establish that the Neolithics, like Jonah and Archan, were not native to this place. They too had travelled here in the wake of a terrible event Frey referred to as the 'darkening'. He knew nothing of the nature of this cataclysm, only that it had happened many generations before.

'How many generations?' Jonah pressed. 'Ten? Twenty?'

But Frey would not be drawn. 'Many fathers,' was all he would commit himself to.

As far as Frey knew, the tribe – which called itself the Denneth – had always lived in the castle, although in earlier times they had occupied the sunlit upper levels. More recently they had been forced to retreat into the deeper chambers by the dragons that had taken up residence nearby.

'They came suddenly,' Frey muttered grimly, his eyes cast down to the floor, 'and since that day our people have not been safe. They burn everything they see. They would have killed our king had I not intervened. They are killing us all slowly.'

'What of the people who built the castle? Do any of those remain?'

Frey grew more evasive. There were no others, he explained, and to wonder who had built the castle was to wonder who had built Stone itself.

'Stone?' demanded Archan sharply.

'That is where we are,' stated Frey. 'On Stone.'

They questioned him further, but he either knew little or was reluctant to say too much. Soon he tired of talking and ended the interrogation with a curt wave of his hands.

'You are not Denneth,' he concluded as he returned to the stairs leading back down to the hall. 'And I must repeat my request that you leave. You must go today, upStone or downStone, I do not care.' With that he departed.

Jonah waited until he was out of earshot then rounded on Archan excitedly. 'How did you know he wasn't the chief?' he demanded. 'And what did he mean about magic? Are you working it here? Is there really such a thing?'

'I am wielding no charm, faery. What I discovered I did so by simple observation. Did you not notice the central dwelling as we passed it last night?' She indicated it now, a slender tepee standing proud of the rest of the huts and tents. Four women sat cross-legged at its entrance, heads bent in conversation. Its interior was dark. 'A man lies inside, tended by servants. The tent is full of metal ornaments. I made a supposition with which I challenged the shaman; it proved to be correct.'

'Is that what you think he is, a shaman? A medicine man?'

'Certainly. And one who is more keen to see his king's bones than he would have us believe.'

'Yes, I got that impression too. Do you think it was a volcanic eruption that threw them here, just like Krakatoa did to us? Is that how the doorways are opened to, what did he call it, the Stone?'

'Stone . . .' mused Archan, tasting the name. 'Fire may be the key, faery, but that is of little concern to me now.'

'And those *were* dragons we saw yesterday. By God, what a place this is!'

'Dragons. Indeed.'

'He seems to see you as a threat, Archan. Mind you, with those eyes it's no wonder you put people on their guard.'

'Are you hungry, faery?'

Jonah considered this. He ought to be hungry, and his stomach certainly felt empty, but he was not convinced he really needed food. Archan described a similar sensation.

'However, I am as yet unused to this creature's metabolism. I will take food if only as a precautionary measure.'

As she marched down the stairs Jonah shivered, reminded

of the horror of Annie's predicament, the appalling nature of Archan's crime.

A small group of women clustered round them as they crossed the hall to the banqueting table. Food was still strewn over the table's planked surface; there seemed little shortage of meat. Jonah picked up a handful of dried pink flower petals from an earthenware bowl and sniffed them cautiously. One of the women, blond-haired with blue eyes just as piercing as those of the shaman, snatched some from his grasp and stuffed them into her mouth. Laughing boisterously she led her companions away.

'Does safe for them mean safe for us?' Jonah wondered. He nibbled at one of the petals; it had a sweet, musty taste. He consumed the rest of the petal but left it at that for now, reasoning that one alone might at worst upset his stomach; if he suffered no ill-effects he could always eat more later. Again he remarked on the fact that, though he should have been ravenous, he felt nothing more than a vague emptiness inside.

'Must be the air,' he joked, but Archan did not laugh. She was engrossed in watching Frey, who had gathered together several of the men beneath an overhanging drape and was talking to them quietly. As Jonah followed her gaze he saw one of the men turn and look directly at them before returning his attention to the shaman; he was dark-haired, heavily tanned unlike his kinsmen. 'Is he stirring up trouble, do you think?'

'Have no doubt about it. I have seen enough of this place. Do you wish to join me or will you stay with your kin?'

Jonah found her constant changes of direction unnerving. 'They are not my kin,' he blustered. 'Where are you going?'

Mirror eyes peered at him as though he were an insect. 'Who am I, faery?'

'Archan.'

'What am I?'

He shook his head, not understanding at first. Then he saw it. 'You want to be with your kin. Don't you, dragon?'

'You will come.'

Archan had found a low doorway set into the rear wall of the gallery. Beyond was a spiral staircase leading up into milky light.

Their first priority, she reasoned, was to gain access to the castle roof. From there they would be able to see what lay beyond it and, perhaps, in which direction the home of the dragons lay.

Jonah followed obediently. If he could help Archan find a dragon body to inhabit then there was a chance Annie would be freed. But there was more, because he too wanted to explore: immense though the castle interiors were he was experiencing a perverse kind of claustrophobia, a yearning to see again the impossible breadth of the wall to which the castle clung – to see the majesty of Stone. Already he felt changed, *expanded* by his experiences; he suspected his own world, were he ever to regain it, would feel stiflingly small.

The stairs wound clockwise up through a tower of pale marble. This tower was built in startling contrast to the hall below, its walls clean and smooth with no hint of slab or block, no line of mortar or mark of mason. In fact, it seemed to Jonah that it had not been made by men at all.

Neither window nor door provided view or exit from the tower. Soon they emerged around a curved balustrade of marble into the upper chamber. It was high and bright; light flooded in through countless slits in its ceiling, though Jonah could not make out any detail beyond, only a vague brilliance that may or may not have been sky. The ceiling itself was plain and quite flat, unsupported across its entire span. Some distance away a hole gaped in the floor. Smoke billowed through: here was the Neolithics' chimney. The chamber, as big as a cathedral, was completely empty.

They explored in silence. The antechambers were equally deserted, as was the long, looping corridor that extended with no obvious purpose from one corner round to the next. They did not approach the hole in the floor – its edges looked weak and ragged and neither of them wanted to risk their weight. The final chamber proved to be the only other exit, a short passage leading to another flight of steps, this one progressing steeply upwards into darkness. Jonah counted fifty steps before they encountered an abrupt half-turn; thereafter they ascended towards the unmistakable glow of daylight. A steep draught blew against them, redolent with the familiar scent of spice.

Screwing up his eyes against the brilliant sunlight, Jonah

stepped up over the lip of the final step and set his foot deep into damp grass.

The roof of the castle looked like the plains of the American West.

A vast expanse of green receded into the low, early light. Behind them loomed the uncompromising cliff wall that was Stone; ahead, beyond a distant line of turrets and tiled roofs that rose from the grassland like the foothills of some artificial mountain range, was the blue, cloud-streaked sky. A huge plume of thick, black smoke rose behind the roofs: the fire set by the dragon the night before, still burning even now.

Kneeling, Jonah pushed his fingers through the grass and into the soil, then withdrew them. He reached into the leather pouch he had brought from the lower chamber and retrieved a long knife. Nobody had challenged him when he had taken the weapon from where it had been lying, half-buried, in one of the heaps of debris lining the chamber. The pouch also held a generous supply of dried meat. Several of the Neolithics had laughed when he had requested this; he still did not understand the source of their mirth.

Taking the knife, he excavated to a depth of about twelve inches before striking a smooth, grey slab. The wind pressed against his back; he had forgotten about the wind – did it blow constantly on Stone? His ears quickly tuned out its gentle roar, already growing accustomed to this world and its traits. Behind it he could hear a rumbling sound, like thunder.

'Look over there,' said Archan sharply. He rose, putting the knife away and brushing his hands together, scattering the moist, dark soil.

Archan was pointing to a cloud of dust to their left. Beneath it, hugging the resplendent green of the plain, was a jostling band of deep brown. It grew larger as they watched, resolving itself into a moving sea of heads and glittering eyes. Pointed shapes that could only be horns thrust themselves up and down like pistons pulled from some titanic steam engine. Jonah felt Annie's body suddenly grow stiff at his side.

Her eyelids were fluttering, giving only sporadic glimpses of her polished eyes. He nudged her but there was no response. Scared, he pinched the flesh of her upper arm, whereupon her eyes flicked open again and she grabbed his wrist with a painful grip. 'This mind has no memory of such creatures,' she intoned, the toneless ring of her words making Jonah shudder. 'Does yours?'

Shaking his arm free he regarded the oncoming herd, which mercifully appeared to be slowing down. It was clear they were cattle of some kind, but of remarkable size. Their shoulders were disproportionately large and swathed in black, matted fur, reminding Jonah of pictures of buffalo he had seen, but their horns were straight and long, much longer than those of any extant beast he knew.

Not extant, he thought. *Extinct!*

'Apart from those huge shoulders,' he said firmly, 'those animals could almost be aurochs.'

'Aurochs?'

'*Bos urus,* the wild ox, extinct in Europe now, though I imagine there may still be similar beasts in some remote corner of the world.' The dust was slowly settling: the herd had stopped and was grazing peacefully about a hundred yards distant. 'They were hunted out in the Middle Ages. This must be where the Neolithics get their meat from.'

Archan was regarding Annie's body with distaste. 'Am I to assume this body will offer me little protection against such creatures?' she said with a primness that almost made Jonah laugh. Then she confounded him by running her hands over Annie's breasts and arching her back in obvious pleasure. He looked away and saw, in the opposite direction to the herd of aurochs, a row of small buildings set into the grass.

'Come on,' he said. 'We can reach those huts in ten minutes, then we might feel a little safer.'

They had covered only half the distance to the line of buildings when the herd began to move again, this time at greater speed. Jonah broke into a trot, then a run as he realised the giant aurochs had already reached the hole in the ground through which they emerged – no escape that way, not for the time being at least. They ran faster but the herd responded by increasing its speed too; now it was clearly a stampede. Relieved though he was to see that the huts were stone-built and looked very strong, he started to panic when he looked round again to see one of the aurochs break free of the rest of the herd and accelerate like a gazelle directly towards them. The sunlight glared off its lowered horns and the sound of its hooves was like an earthquake.

What must this roof be made of, he thought wildly, *that it can support the weight of these beasts?*

Archan accelerated past him, leaving him floundering in grass that was by now knee-deep and seriously impeding his progress. He hitched the habit-like cloak up around his waist; Annie's box bounced painfully against his pelvis and he fell forward, splashing into grass like a child into water. He heard the heavy thud of the knife flying out of the pouch and hitting the ground. With no time to search for it he rolled completely over and flung himself forward again, imagining he could feel the breath of the aurochs on his back.

Already Archan was at the door of the nearest hut, shouldering it open and disappearing into the darkness within. He cried out as the plain wooden door swung slowly shut. Behind him the lone aurochs emitted a long, mournful bellow. He did not dare risk another glance back. Its hoofbeats drowned out all sound, even that of his own laboured breathing.

'Archan!' he screamed, hurling himself at the door, which remained resolutely closed. 'Damn you, let me in!'

The aurochs bellowed again, as if replying to his outburst. Something really did brush against his neck and he surged forwards, thrashing through the grass with one final burst of speed. He jumped, half-turning and lowering his shoulder into the door, hoping to smash it open. He was close enough to see the grain of the wood – it looked like oak, solid.

The breath of the aurochs caressed the back of his neck, then Archan opened the door.

I should have joined the circus! Jonah thought as he glanced off the door frame and rolled across the floor of the hut, fetching up against the far wall in a tangle of limbs and an explosion of dust. The jolt knocked all the air from his lungs – all he could do was lie there with his back against the wall, wheezing the thick, hot atmosphere of Stone and watching the aurochs bearing down on him.

He regarded its face with a detached air as it covered the final few yards to the hut. Pale brown eyes with small, intense pupils glowering from beneath a heavy brow sprouting coarse, tan-coloured fur; truly gigantic horns balanced either side of an equally huge skull, as thick at their base as Jonah's thigh; muscles gliding beneath a thick pelt; its huge inertia.

With one last bellow it tossed its head to the side, the mass of those horns shifting its centre of gravity so that as it dug in its hooves it slewed not through the doorway but against the wall of the hut. The building shook with the impact, as the aurochs rebounded and careered out of sight down the outside of the wall; Jonah wondered calmly if it felt as winded as he did. The thunder of its passage died, only to be replaced by the greater thunder of the rest of the herd looming in its wake. Archan crossed in front of Jonah's vision and stood in the doorway for a moment, a leather-clad Valkyrie, dark against the sky.

Then she simply shut the door.

The thunder continued, drifted past the building, then receded. Presently it stopped altogether.

'Why did you shut the door?' asked Jonah quietly.

'To keep out the aurochs.'

'No, I mean the first time. Why did you shut the door the first time, while I was still outside?'

Archan, her back still turned to him, shrugged. 'I didn't,' she said casually. Then she pointed into the corner. 'He did.'

His name, they learned, was Gerent. His companion was called Malya, though she did not speak to them directly for some time, preferring to loiter sullenly behind him, scowling at the intruders.

Gerent, by contrast, was candid and willing to talk, if a little nervous. It was obvious to Jonah that he was from the same Neolithic tribe they had already encountered – both his hair and skin were pale and his voice rang with the same deep timbre. The girl was pretty, blonde with startlingly white teeth and a retroussé nose. After a moment's scrutiny, Jonah decided she was almost certainly Frey's daughter.

As Gerent talked, Jonah was suddenly struck by the *normality* of their appearance. Though he had studied ancient history for many years, and even though he had already placed these people at less than 5000 years before Christ – not a terribly long interval in the span of the history of the world if the stories the fossils told were to be believed – he was overwhelmed by the realisation that *they were just the same as him*. No grunting cavemen these, though they belonged well and truly to the era known to the more liberal thinkers of his time as the Stone Age – these were real people, with features no less human than his own and brains just as able. If they had been translocated to his own, enlightened age of electricity and Empire they would not have looked out of place: take away their primitive clothes and unkempt appearance, wash away the grime of the millennia and what you had left was simply Man.

Could the same be said of me? Jonah asked them silently. *Were I to journey back to your time would I be incorporated so easily? Can you ever go back?*

The first surprise was that Gerent was none other than the king's son. He was, they learned, on a quest to challenge the dragon that had been ravaging the castle. At this Jonah had to turn away, the strangeness of the situation boiling into absurdity. How had he come to be in conversation with a Stone Age Saint George?

There was a window, a narrow slit in the wall to his left. Through it he could see the near-vertical line of Stone, a blurred slash through the clean blue of the endless sky. The urge to laugh abandoned him, leaving him feeling heavy, devoid of energy.

Contrary to what Frey had told them, Gerent claimed it was a solitary dragon that was responsible for the attacks, not a whole flock. Moreover, he said it was because of the shaman that it had come in the first place.

'The dragons of Stone are peace-loving creatures. We have known this for many generations – it is part of our lore.'

'So what changed?' Jonah asked.

He glanced at the girl, Malya. She looked away, pouting. 'Many years ago the shaman Frey was outcast from the Denneth. My father had learned that his magic was mere trickery, a pretence. Frey had no power in the spirit world, though he came from a great line of magic men. He left in dishonour, never to return.

'But he did return. Five years later, Frey crawled on his belly into the great hall and begged an audience with my father.' Here the young Neolithic grimaced and spat on the floor. 'Like a fool the king agreed. The next day he proclaimed that Frey had discovered true magic. The day after he began to grow sick; the day after that the dragon attacked the halls for the first time. Since then we have been forced to move deeper and deeper into the castle as the dragon's assaults have grown more frequent. Our people have grown despondent and Frey's power has grown as my father has grown weak. Now Frey rules in all but name.'

'So, allow me to guess,' said Jonah, unable to resist the temptation. 'The names of all the young people were put into a golden chalice, Frey drew one out and, to everyone's surprise, the one chosen to face the beast was the king's own son.'

Gerent looked puzzled. 'The decision to undertake the quest was my own. Everyone, including Frey, cautioned me against it.'

'Why don't you expose Frey for what he is, if you believe he is behind this? You are the king's son after all.'

'I have no right to power until my father is dead. Only then will I do what is required of me.'

Archan interrupted sharply. 'You will take us to the abode of the dragons. We will leave now, before the aurochs grow restless again.'

Gerent raised one eyebrow imperiously and Jonah saw a hint of the king to be. 'And who are you?'

'I am Archan, and . . .'

'Well, Archan. I have not yet decided whether I shall complete my quest.'

Jonah found he was holding his breath. The Neolithic had dared to interrupt her!

'You have no choice, *man*.' Archan's temper was rising.

'I think any choice in the matter is mine, don't you?' The prince stared boldly into Archan's fathomless eyes, challenging their inhumanity.

'No,' replied Archan flatly. 'I do not.'

'She has magic eyes,' whispered Malya, speaking for the first time. She pressed her hands against Gerent's shoulders. 'We cannot trust her.'

Gerent continued to stare at Archan for a moment, then something gave way and he relinquished his gaze. 'It no longer matters,' he said quietly. 'Sauth is dead. We cannot possibly succeed. Frey has won.'

'Sauth?' said Jonah, his mind racing. 'Was he a friend? Tell me, did he carry a pouch full of stone tools?' The Neolithic couple looked up sharply.

'He was my servant. You have seen him?' demanded Gerent. 'You must tell me!'

Jonah glanced at Archan. 'We saw him,' he nodded.

They had been three when they set out from the hall, explained Gerent, following the same route Jonah and Archan would take the next day.

'We planned to cross the roof by night,' his eyes were wide as he remembered, 'to avoid the gaze of the aurochs. They have only to look on a man and they grow restless.'

'How do you hunt them?' interrupted Jonah.

'We have ways.' The prince waved his hand dismissively. 'The night was falling and we made good progress, but then the dragon came, lighting up the sky. The aurochs were terrified, then they saw us and charged. We fled. Sauth fell – Malya and I ran on. One of the beasts took him up on its horns and threw him into the air. He landed hard and rolled. We watched as he dropped through the roof.'

'A round hole,' murmured Jonah, 'and a very long drop.'

'The whole roof is riddled with such holes. The aurochs know their way through the maze, even by night. Sauth was not so lucky.'

Jonah recalled his headlong dash through the grass and shuddered. How close had he been to following Sauth by plummeting through some unseen aperture?

'As soon as the aurochs had settled we went to the hole and I held my torch down to see if I could see him. But I was clumsy – the torch burned me and I dropped it. Then the aurochs came again and we ran here.' He sighed and looked up at the window. 'We have been here ever since.'

'I saw you,' breathed Jonah, remembering, 'or your shadow at least.' He looked around the hut. A single weapon, a long-hafted spear capped with a straight, double-edged blade, was propped in the corner; apart from this, and the four of them, the building was empty. 'What happened to your supplies? Did you not bring food? Can you truly kill a dragon with just a spear?'

'If he needs to, yes!' snapped Malya, stepping into the shaft of light admitted by the narrow window.

'With a spear we might hope to scratch a dragon,' went on

Gerent, glaring at his companion, who looked back at him with a fiery gaze. 'But there may be another way. We had brought an offering – a gift from another world.'

'The stone axes?' exclaimed Jonah. 'Do you think you can bribe a dragon with a handful of flint?'

Gerent stared at his bare feet. 'The king rarely wakes now. It was easy to replace them with valueless pieces of rock, chips from the castle walls. He lies with them beneath his head, you see, underneath a pillow stuffed with animal fur. They are more than sacred, our forefathers brought them here from the home-world. The art of stone-working has long been lost to our people. The Denneth would rather scavenge the metal remnants of those who built the castle than tire their hands making tools of their own. Our crime will not be discovered for some days, by which time we will have either succeeded . . . or failed.'

'They must be like the Crown Jewels to your people. But I don't see what value they would be to a dragon.'

Before Gerent could reply Archan thrust herself between them. 'I grow tired of this. Retrieve your precious stones, if they mean that much to you. Then lead us to the home of the dragons.'

'We can't go back now,' replied Gerent in a small, child-like voice.

'They would kill us,' elaborated Malya.

'Then leave the stones and be done with it!' Archan shouted. Her voice echoed loud in the confined space. 'Jonah – come! I grow weary of these creatures! We will find our own way, as we originally intended.'

She called me Jonah, he thought, unsure of what this meant.

The aurochs herd was grazing in a peaceful semicircle on the other side of the buildings from the rising face of Stone. Jonah realised he needed a new vocabulary of direction to deal with the tilted geometry of this unearthly place.

I know the names of two directions already – upStone and downStone. But which way are they?

He jumped as he felt a tap between his shoulder blades.

'You wish to know whence the dragons come,' said Gerent.

'That way, I think.' Jonah pointed in the direction he was coming to think of as west: facing the wall, his instinct was to assign north straight ahead, to root the fundamental direction in the solidity of Stone itself. Therefore east was right, west was left and south was behind him, out in the direction of the open sky. Gerent followed his gaze to Jonah's 'west'.

'DownStone. You are right . . . ?'

'Jonah. Jonah Lightfoot.'

'That name I like. I am pleased to accompany you, Lightfoot.'

'But what about your stone axes? I could go back for them, your people might be less suspicious of me.'

Gerent smiled, then beckoned Malya out of the shadow of the hut. She came bearing the spear, which was taller than her by a good three feet. 'Thank you, Jonah, but they belong to the past now. Perhaps they are best left where they are. They will be found again, sooner or later.'

'What about the dragon?'

'It is a futile quest, with or without the offering.' The Neolithic prince surveyed the aurochs. 'We must hurry – as soon as enough of them notice us they will start to move again.'

Jonah was struck by the despondency in the young man's voice. Malya was looking up at Gerent with a mixture of love and awe; what his feelings were towards her Jonah could not yet gauge.

They made good progress through the thick grass. Given the colossal size of the aurochs herd and their apparently voracious appetites Jonah was amazed the growth was as abundant as it was. The falling wind pressed against the tall stalks, gusts rolling through the grass like waves in the ocean; the rustling sound was rich and pleasing. He could not take his eyes off the aurochs, their tremendous horns, their lowered heads and busy mouths. His stomach growled and he drew a strip of meat from his pouch, feeling as he did so for the knife he knew was gone, regretting its loss. Gerent and Malya both refused the food he offered them; Archan took a piece and chewed it distractedly, her attention captured by the sky on their left, the huge vista of Stone on their right hand, rising into infinity.

'There's not a great deal of food, not really enough for the four of us, I'm afraid,' Jonah apologised. 'Is it possible we might find more along the way? Do you farm? I thought your people might have been farmers.'

'Stories tell of times past, in the home-world, when men planted seeds and harvested their crop. In those times the Denneth lived in a land of cold earth and ice, and there were still hunters among us, even though we tilled the land. One day a fire bit through the ice and those of our people who were not killed were thrown out on to Stone.

'The survivors journeyed many days upStone until they found the castle. Others were there, a dying, black-haired clan who had lived a long time in the castle. They fought for a while, but they were weary and at last the Denneth took pity on them, accepting them in to their tribe. This was many generations ago and now the two peoples are as one.

'But to answer you, no. We do not farm. On Stone there is no need.'

'"Cold earth and ice",' repeated Jonah. 'It may very well be that your people came from Scandinavia, Gerent. And the others you found, with the dark hair – they could have been an ancient Welsh clan, which would account for your name. I wonder where the aurochs came from. Do you hunt them? Surely it would be easier to tend a field of wheat, or plant a few potatoes.'

'The hunt is a challenge for our young men, a demonstration of prowess. And one carcass can last a hundred days.'

Jonah stopped and thought about this. The breeze was warm on his face and neck and he loosened the robe, exposing his shoulders. 'A hundred days?' he asked doubtfully.

Gerent shrugged. 'As I said, there is no need to eat on Stone.'

No need to eat?

'Then you mean . . .' Jonah faltered, remembering the strange sensation of feeling hungry yet not really wanting food. 'But no man can survive without food.'

'A man can on Stone,' answered Gerent casually, the assertion of little apparent interest. 'We must plan our route carefully – I think the aurochs are beginning to gather.'

'Wait!' Jonah rounded on the Neolithic. 'You eat, and the rest of your people eat, I saw them. So what do you mean? What else is there to nourish you?'

Malya laughed. 'A man likes the feel of food in his belly, whether he needs it or not. And, despite the miracles of Stone, a man needs to shit. A woman, too!'

'But what else can provide nourishment?' repeated Jonah. Archan, he noticed, was listening with interest.

Gerent lifted his arms and turned both his face and palms up towards the heavens. 'Breathe in, Lightfoot, and you will know.'

So Jonah did, and as the hooves of the aurochs began to beat their thunder into the plain, he tasted afresh the rich spice of the air of Stone, felt the vibrant thrust of its particles forcing their way into his mouth and throat, into his lungs, into his system. Felt the energy it brought him, felt its power, its magic.

'Oh dear God,' he whispered as tears painted his cheeks.

In contrast to their earlier stampede, this time the aurochs moved slowly and deliberately. Jonah and Archan allowed Gerent to lead them into a region where the grass was higher than ever: now it reached their waists, high enough to seriously impede their progress. The sky had transformed itself into a curtain of brilliant blue almost entirely free of cloud; Stone cut through it like a fantastic tapestry, an upturned world studded with a mass of detail – slender projecting fins, long vertical indentations, countless unidentifiable structures adhering to the sheer slope. The view beyond the castle revealed a richer, more complex world than had been hinted at by Jonah's first view from the tunnel exit. *I must have emerged in Stone's equivalent of a desert,* he thought, absorbed by the dazzling fretwork revealed as they moved further downStone. *All I saw there was blocks and lines, but here . . .*

Here a line of stiletto spires stabbed out into the open sky, tiny square windows marking off their varying lengths; higher up a delicately scrolled disc of what looked like silver spun lazily in the sunlight, its diameter prodigious – motionless at its centre was an edifice that looked like St Paul's Cathedral turned sideways; there a smooth, unmarked slab protruded like an architectural tongue. Structure and unfathomable purpose, conspiring between them to quell the mind and dwarf the soul.

The huge blocks still assaulted Jonah's sense of scale – his provincial mind protested that they were mere bricks, that Stone was simply a gigantic wall marking the perimeter of some greater kingdom. But perhaps each block was its own castle, and Stone itself *was* the greater kingdom, he mused.

Wading through the grass behind the Neolithic couple, breathing in the life-giving air with new respect, Jonah found himself weighing the alternative perils with which he was faced. Confronting a dragon had seemed fearsome enough, but now it seemed he might be pounded into the dirt by a herd of extinct cattle before he even reached the dragons' home. The aurochs' patient stalking of them had convinced him that the animals were simply biding their time, that the herd was doing its own herding. *We might as well be a flock of sheep, chaperoned by the biggest, nastiest looking sheepdogs that ever lived.*

With their goal tantalisingly near – the downStone edge of the roof was clearly visible as a firm horizontal line in the middle distance, a powerful counterpoint to the dominant verticals – they entered an area where the grass was much shorter again; the coarse cropping of the stems announced that this patch had been recently grazed, not to mention the mounds of sweet-smelling dung. The ground ahead looked uneven to Jonah in a way that made him uncomfortable, though he could not put his finger on why. Then, as the herd split into two distinct groups, he saw the first of the holes.

It was a long, narrow slit in the ground to their left. Beyond it, quite close now, the castle threw up a series of high-level ramparts. Slim towers supporting external stairways rose above the line of the roof, access ways to the outermost turrets and battlements. The sight was reassuring with its promise of safety – and frustrating because the promise was one it could not keep. The slit was quickly revealed to be a gaping abyss at least thirty feet wide opening into a dark, unlit space; it lay directly between them and the sanctuary of the castle towers, an unswimmable moat defying them to cross.

'There is no sense in us returning within,' announced Gerent as Jonah peered nervously into the crevasse. 'Look – the fire burns still. Perhaps this time the beast will truly drive us out.' The prince pointed to the broad smoke trail still billowing into the sky. The fire had evidently taken firm hold of the wooden parts of the castle and was now burning out of control. 'We must go on, the edge is close at hand.'

Indeed it was, but they had advanced only a further hundred yards before a second hole barred their way. It intersected with the first slit, forming an uncompromising 'T' across which there was no passage. Jonah noted with concern that one half of the aurochs herd remained with them on this side of the slit, while the others, having found some other way round, were tracking them on the opposite side. Their behaviour was too considered for his peace of mind, too *intelligent*.

'I don't like this,' he announced suddenly. 'They seem to be forcing us into a corner.'

Gerent shrugged. 'They are many and we are few. We have little choice but to carry on. Perhaps there is a way down into the Cleft Forest.'

Jonah could not offer a better proposal and so continue they did, turning right now so that they walked directly towards the glowering face of Stone. Treetops were just visible beyond a low parapet marking the inner boundary of the castle roof. This was surprisingly near; Jonah was finding that his sense of both distance and direction was more shaken up than he had realised.

'What is in the forest?' he asked Gerent, keeping one eye firmly on the aurochs.

'Trees!' scowled Malya, thumping the haft of the spear into the soil. 'We have to run, Gerent, or they will have us in their trap!'

'We are in it already,' Gerent sighed. His shoulders were stooped, his feet dragged. Jonah was beginning to regard the prince as something of a pessimist.

You are no dragon slayer. So why did you come on such a quest?

'The female is right,' said Archan calmly. 'We should run. Now.'

They sprinted towards the parapet. The grass had diminished to a coarse scrub, pale and bleached. A dark line drew near, grew large: another hole, huge and square, blocking their way to the parapet and the forest canopy beyond. Malya led them left, downStone once more. Gerent slipped and fell as they veered; she stopped and ran back to help him up. On they ran.

More cavities opened up in the ground and they were forced to dodge between them, following a tortuous course through the lethal maze. Behind them and to each side the aurochs swarmed, raising dust from the flattened earth, picking their way between the openings with unerring accuracy. Squares of pale grass stood out sharply against black and yawning chasms.

To his amazement Jonah found an image of his father bright in his mind, his father leaning towards him over a small wooden table. Marquetry tiles – a regular array of sixty-four squares – patterned the table-top. Two opposing armies of ivory and ebony faced each other across the battlefield, Jonah's in ruins, that of his father hunting down his exposed king with ruthless calm. His father's queen stood proud and tall above her subjects; all but one of Jonah's pawns had been taken, the rest squandered in a series of rash offensive manoeuvres. Henry Lightfoot's creased face was alive with humour as he watched his son struggle to work out the move that would deflect the checkmate.

'If chess teaches you one thing, Jo,' he laughed as his younger son finally turned his ailing king on its side, 'let it teach you the power of the pawn.'

Next time Jonah heeded this advice and treated each pawn with as much reverence as he did his king, finally securing a draw, the best he had ever done against his father. Soon after that had come the visit to the Crystal Palace, the sudden storm and the awful judgement that had fallen on Henry and Albert. He had never once beaten his father at chess, nor would he ever have the chance to again.

Wooden squares, light and dark, defining the parameters of the game.

A dark chasm loomed. Before he knew what he was doing Jonah leaped high, landing heavily on the other side and jarring his ankle. Suddenly Malya's hand was there, pulling him on, thumping Gerent in the back with the spear, urging her men. Ahead of them all was Archan, sprinting soundlessly, weaving and jumping, consuming the distance to the edge of the roof. Individual aurochs began to feed themselves along narrow bridges spanning the holes, massing ahead of them, cutting them off, closing in, all the time closing in.

A patchwork of holes, squares of ruined grass suspended impossibly over bottomless pits, pieces of ground like tiles floating unsupported in the air. The castle roof was broken up like an ice floe at the turn of the season. They were no longer running on solid ground but springing from one island to the next. They were surrounded by aurochs now, their only way forward blocked by a wall of massive heads, all possible routes back disappearing one by one. Heedless of the danger Malya threw herself across a seemingly impossible gap. She barely made it; her upper body crashed into the thin side of the grass tile and she had to haul herself up over the edge. The spear fell from her hand, bouncing once against the tile before tumbling into the gloom; their only weapon was gone.

Jonah looked around wildly, having lost sight of Archan. Beside him Gerent had fallen to his knees and seemed to have given up. Jonah glanced at the gap Malya had just jumped, trying to gauge the distance – it really did look impossible. Directly behind him came an all-too-familiar snorting sound. He turned to look at the aurochs.

It was inches from his face. All he could see was a mountain of black fur, a thick pelt alive with squirming ticks. Large brown eyes regarded him solemnly and a surprisingly small jaw worked from side to side with an incongruously casual air. The aurochs's horns extended out of his peripheral vision, massive and curved, ready to embrace him.

Then the air shrieked. Jonah had time to see the eyes of the aurochs widen briefly before suddenly the beast was in motion. But it was not coming for him – it was moving *sideways*, some massive inertia punching it not towards Jonah but away. An instant later there was a sound like a prizefighter thumping a sack of straw, but amplified to suit the grandeur of the location, a huge, air-filled thud. Grass-stained saliva sprayed from the aurochs's mouth; a thick trail of blood splashed through the air in its wake as it gained speed. It began to ascend, and Jonah was afforded a better view of its fate. What he saw stopped the breath in his throat.

Red scales striped with black filled the sky, a curved serpent shape sliding through the air like a whip. The shape was connected to the aurochs by a pair of taut legs sleek with muscle. Curved talons as big as canoes pierced the hapless creature's flank, drawing gouts of blood that sprayed down on to the scant grass, into the gaping roof holes. On it barrelled, carrying the screaming aurochs steadily higher, revealing more of itself as it receded skywards.

Its striped underbelly flowed smoothly into a long, spreading tail. Feathery spines rippled on either side, bright red fins through which movement cascaded like running water. A deep breastbone, massed with muscle, held scaly skin tight against the thrust of the two enormous wings eclipsing the sun; their downdraught, immense and unforgiving, pressed Jonah to his knees. The aurochs was much smaller now, a distant shape limp in the grip of those colossal claws, yet still its captor spanned the sky.

Wingtips and tail-tip came into view simultaneously: the former were barbed and shone gold in the revealed sunlight, the latter bore a stiff triangular vane that slashed at the ground, raising a trail of dust in its wake.

Then at last it dipped and swerved, climbing into the sun and Jonah was afforded his first view of the dragon's head.

It was sleek and beautiful, black and white stripes coursing from snout to brow across a mosaic of tiny red scales. Four coarsely-textured horns flared from the back of its skull, their movement echoing the line of its gaze. Black, whiteless eyes glared from deep within bony sockets; flames spurted loosely from between its tightly closed lips. It was terrible, a magnificent angel of death, and it had just saved Jonah's life.

The dragon accelerated with a speed that belied its size, diminishing downStone until it was a mere seagull speck beating its rhythm against the blue. Jonah remained on his knees, vaguely aware that the rest of the aurochs herd was in disarray, fleeing in all directions and leaving their would-be prey alone on a grassy archipelago. Something touched his leg and he turned, unable to summon the energy to react. It was Gerent.

'It . . .' stammered Jonah, his voice barely a gasp. 'I didn't think . . . these dragons are so *big*.'

'They are not . . .' began Gerent, but then Archan's call cut through his words. Following the departure of the aurochs she had found a way through the maze to the parapet; she led them there now, pointing out the least difficult jumps, grabbing at Jonah's arm when he misjudged a leap, standing back as they gathered at the edge of the roof and looked out across the falling landscape of Stone.

Falling, thought Jonah. *That is the fundamental truth of this place, and its underlying peril.* The outer wall of the castle fell away beneath them; Stone itself fell, down, down into infinity.

He looked round at Annie's body, trying to associate the being that inhabited it with the beast that had taken the aurochs. *There is a dragon inside that woman's body.* But the thought was not sufficient: he simply could not equate that giant serpent with the creature called Archan whom, against his every effort, he was beginning to regard as his companion.

Annie, are you still there? Archan caught his gaze, stared back at him with eyes like mirrors, eyes that drank in and threw back the infinity of Stone. Were he to look too deep into those eyes, he would start to fall and never stop.

6
Ledge

Archan was exploring the memories harboured inside Annie's mind.

By far the smallest volume was occupied by the memories belonging to the faery host. Annie's personality, her essential spirit, had been compressed into the tiniest gap, a mousehole in the mansion of her mind. In contrast, Archan was a vast, swollen presence, a huge and ancient dragon persona squeezed into this cramped space.

Images of light – the brilliance of birth, raw sunlight piercing the cracking egg. Images of darkness – the fast eroticism of sharing thoughts across the span of the world, telepathy, the miraculous scent of instantaneous contact. The myriad thrills of charm, the touch of magic in all its forms. Dragon memoirs.

Yet Archan's memories were more than those of a mere dragon: they were those of a dragon who had inherited the blessed curse of immortality. They were the memories of the Deathless. In stealing the immortality of the basilisks Archan had also absorbed their endless past. She recalled times so far distant they had no meaning to her, aeons so far adrift on the currents of eternity they held no point of reference for her dragon sensibilities.

Afloat on that primitive ocean she perceived an age when the world was made of metal, when mercury creatures crept through sponges of gold, their rudimentary intelligence part of a thinking hive; infinitely further back, in a place where time did not simply flow but danced, she perceived a world in which there was no form, only fluidity, no cause, only ceaseless change for no sake but its own. In that dusty past the concept of life had no meaning; in that different reality, even the Deathless existed by different rules.

Yet exist they did, as they existed throughout eternity, storing, recording, recalling . . . *remembering*.

And now their memories were hers to command.

Yet her frustration was immense. Even given this infinite store she was powerless to exploit it to its full. Her limited dragon perception understood only a fraction of what she had access to, and there were so many gaps! Despite their tremendous power, the basilisks forgot much. Moreover, her transfer to this faery mind had resulted in colossal damage, swathes of memories sloughed away like dead scales. Gone? Archan did not think so, not entirely, but she had no idea how they might be resurrected.

There was so much she did not know, so much already forgotten. This place, for example, this Stone. Something called to her from within its blocks, words she could not interpret spoken by a voice she could not hear. Her frustration increased but the voice was pulled away by the falling wind. The sound of a memory not her own.

I know this place. I belong here. But why?

Enough. The mystery would resolve itself in time. And she, like the Deathless before her, had all the time in the world.

More immediately exciting was the prospect of returning to the body of a dragon. The sight of the striped male taking the aurochs had stimulated her almost to the point of madness. That was the body she wanted! Not for over a million years had she felt so vigorous, so potent. Even this temporary faery carcass seemed filled with energy, sensual and full-blooded. The prospect of becoming male held no fear for her – had she not transcended such petty distinctions? Nevertheless, it seemed a pity to waste what little time was left for her in female form, however crude the incarnation.

Annie's flesh slid smoothly beneath the hot leather garments, the feel of its perspiration endlessly fascinating.

Vertigo returned to Jonah as he looked down from the parapet. Here was the westernmost point of the castle roof (his mind still insisted on maintaining that Earthly frame of reference), and, for now, the end of their journey downStone. Unlike the steep slope of Stone, the castle wall was perfectly vertical; the prospect was a sheer cliff edge, challenging and utterly useless, with neither stair nor shaft by which they might move down and on.

They were thwarted equally by the inaccessibility of the outer battlements. There surely lay within those towers a way back down to the surface of Stone, but the holes in the ground conspired to bar all routes across to them. Even here, at the very edge of the roof, the way was cut through by a bleak slit, a shadow-filled gorge they could neither bridge nor infiltrate. Further peril was added by the increasingly dense pillar of smoke issuing from just beyond the line of towers; how long would it be before the flames set by the rampaging dragon reached these upper levels? No, only one direction remained open to them: Jonah's north, towards the wall of Stone, where the crowns of gigantic trees peered over the rough flank of the castle. Towards the forest.

Once they reached the inner parapet Malya found the ladder almost immediately. It was wide enough for two, a heavy lattice supported by paired lugs of stone projecting clear of the wall. These were spaced vertically at regular intervals, not so far apart as to make negotiating the ladder impossible but far enough to make it awkward. Hunks of timber spanned the gaps between the lugs to form crude rungs; they were held in place with filth-covered knots of twine, many of which creaked ominously when weight was brought to bear. Archan went first, barely hesitating before swinging Annie's body over the edge of the parapet and guiding it smoothly on to the first rung. She began to climb downwards, moving her shoulders and hips swiftly and economically. Jonah followed hurriedly, anxious not to let her get too far ahead.

On this side of the castle the wall was flat and unremarkable. Once they passed tantalisingly close to a patchwork of small, square windows, none of which was near enough for them to see in. Otherwise the wall just went on, block after block, carrying them down into the gloom.

Quickly the forest wrapped itself around them. The trees, huge and red-trunked, spread broad coniferous fronds across their path and soon they were fighting the foliage, kicking branches away from the rungs and brushing aside fans of fat needles. At the same time the trees drank up the light, drawing them deep into a strange green twilight, a shadowless ocean in which they lost all sense of depth and scale.

How long the descent lasted Jonah could not tell, and he wondered later if he had not dozed during the latter part. Suddenly his foot struck something flat and hard, a solid surface less yielding than the timber rungs. Rubbing his face he half-turned, supporting his body with one hand and swinging round to take in the view.

'Faery,' called Archan, her voice flat and dry, 'you look like an ape.'

'I am an ape,' answered Jonah, grinning despite himself as he dropped to the ground. He bent forward, rubbing his palms against the backs of his calves, then straightened and examined his spine. 'But I think I may have become rather too civilised for all of this.'

Their Neolithic companions alighted, both adopting almost identical crouches that Jonah found vaguely amusing: primitive man and primitive woman, tense on the edge of the unknown, teeth bared.

'The way ahead is clear,' Archan announced, indicating a narrow platform hugging the wall, a paved way leading downStone, at the far end of which glowed a welcome patch of daylight. Less than two yards wide, this ledge bore no balustrade, no means of security to prevent unwary travellers falling into the clutches of the trees; for, as Jonah peered over the edge, he saw they were by no means at the bottom of the castle wall but barely two-thirds of the way down it. The colossal trunks, now wearing thick lianas and waistcoats of moss, continued down into unwelcoming darkness.

He recalled the way the castle was attached to Stone: they had descended into a V-shaped notch, an acutely-angled valley formed by the intersection of the castle's vertical wall with Stone's greater one inclined at around ten degrees. This ledge permitted travel along the length of the notch – clearly whoever had built it did not regard it necessary, nor perhaps prudent, to continue the journey all the way to the bottom. Jonah wondered what lay down there, in that sharp vale.

'Is there a floor to this forest?' he asked Malya as they walked. Prince Gerent trudged behind them in silence, having retreated into himself. 'Surely there is a depth of soil into which the trees are rooted, and the leaf litter must increase year by year.'

Malya shrugged, uncaring. 'Once my people hunted in the

forest. Then it grew dangerous and they did not go there any more.'

'Dangerous? Why, what lives there?'

But Malya did not know, or would not say.

Jonah could not resist looking down into the gloom whenever he got the opportunity, though Archan had set a punishing pace and there was little enough time for sightseeing. There was nothing to be seen down there, not even anything in the way of undergrowth. At this lower altitude the trees' foliage was relatively thin and further down it was almost nonexistent, the trunks naked but for their parasitic costumes of vine and moss. Eventually he gave up, but not before the notion of *altitude* had lodged itself in his thoughts like a shred of chicken caught between his teeth.

If Stone does indeed go on forever, upwards and downwards as well as from side to side, then what happens to the air?

Jonah found himself wishing he had more detailed knowledge of the physical sciences. The study of life, both extant and extinct, was what had always captured his imagination. Sometimes it seemed the more time he spent looking backwards the more detached he became from the modern Victorian way of thinking – no matter how skilled he became at deciphering the puzzles of prehistory, how deeply he explored the revolutionary ideas of Darwin, he remained at heart a savage. Perhaps he had to remain so, in order to empathise with the past.

Like most of his peers, he was gripped with the excitement of the century's end; it seemed that hardly a day went by without a new discovery or revolutionary theory. Men were communicating over great distances by means of a simple electrical wire; electricity brought light to the world from the heart of matter itself; the Russian Mendeleyev had catalogued the fundamental atoms, his periodic table reducing the whole of creation to a set of simple building blocks. Far from scorning God's work scientific discovery glorified it: by dismantling the watch one could begin to perceive the skill of the watchmaker. But although he was aware of the ideas being spawned by this age of enlightenment still their intricacies eluded him. His father on the other hand had been an avid reader of the latest scientific papers, and had speculated enthusiastically on the possibilities they raised. Jonah had attended as well as a boy of eight was able but much of it had gone over his head. Not the excitement though – that was transmitted via a kind of visceral telegraph, a language of body and expression rather than of mere word.

When it came to ancient history, Jonah could hold his own with the best thinkers of the day, but he wished now he had paid more attention to his father's zealous scientific lectures. Their frequent games of chess had often been played against one of Henry's background monologues: Bessel, Pasteur, Maxwell, an eclectic mix. But it was reliable Newton he craved now as he stared into the dismal forest, trying to gauge the true dimension of Stone.

How far down does it go? he pondered, considering not just this tremendous cleft but the even greater abyss into which Stone plunged. *Surely, the further down a man travels, the more he is pulled at by gravity and the heavier he gets. And does the air not become rarefied at higher altitudes?*

He thought of the constant, falling wind, wondered at the unimaginable pressure the weight of Stone must be exerting on the blocks near its base – if it had a base. *What force keeps it up? Who in God's name built it? And why?*

None of the old thinkers could offer him any insight; nor for that matter was he able to apply anything useful from the indistinct, modern realm of atoms and magnets. Darwin alone travelled with him, in memory only since his books had been lost during the death throes of Krakatoa, and on the subject of gravitation Darwin had little to say.

Prising a large flake of rock from the castle wall, Jonah dropped briefly to his knees and gingerly leant out over the chasm. He dropped it, hearing it skitter against the branches long after it had disappeared from view. The surrounding silence amplified the clumsy sound of its descent, and even after he was sure he could no longer hear it it echoed in his head, falling still.

They found a door set into the castle wall, a rusted iron affair bound with long hinges. Chains crisscrossed it, their extremities pegged firmly into the deep metal frame. Jonah and Malya put some effort into trying to lever it open while their companions looked on unimpressed, but despite their efforts it moved not a single inch. Jonah ran his fingers along a line of studs embossed down the door's central line – each one was moulded in the form of a tiny gargoyle; the detail of the sculpting was exquisite and quite out of keeping with the crudity with which the rest of the door had been fashioned. Another puzzle to walk away from, another mystery to leave unsolved.

Once Jonah fancied he heard a noise from the trees, a pale, whistling cry high in the forest canopy. A bird? He had seen none since his arrival here; indeed, he had seen no native fauna apart from the tortoids and the aurochs, and a variety of insects. The cry came and went in a matter of seconds; it left him feeling cold and alone.

Jonah sat and waited for Gerent to catch up. His legs dangled over the ledge. Not for the first time he wished he had chosen tougher footwear than the flimsy moccasins: the soles of his feet were aching and the bottoms of the shoes were beginning to feel decidedly thin. All the same, he took care not to lose them to the chasm.

Archan and Malya were just visible at the far end of the path, twinned stick-figures all but engulfed by the glare of the sky. They had stopped walking and were waiting for their male companions. As far as Jonah could tell they were still keeping their distance from one another, not talking, companions by chance rather than choice.

Gerent's bare feet approached soundlessly. The prince's head was still down when Jonah stood in front of him and he might have continued on his way without stopping had Jonah not barred his way, arms spread theatrically.

'Forgive me,' the Neolithic man mumbled. 'I would not hold you back.'

'Nor I you. But tell me . . .' Jonah paused, searching Gerent's bleak and downcast eyes. 'God damn it, man! What on Earth is wrong with you?'

Instead of recoiling Gerent simply nodded, as though this was just what he had expected. Then he sat down. Jonah exhaled noisily, exasperated. 'You are a very frustrating young man, king's son or no king's son.'

'Pah! "King's son", indeed. My father might not agree with your judgement. Do not waste your care on me. I am of little enough value to my king and my people, and can be of even less concern to you.'

'On the contrary, I am very much concerned with your welfare. I have few enough companions in this strange land and I am not about to give up those I do quite so easily.' Unaware of the indignant tone he had adopted, Jonah frowned as Gerent first smiled, then laughed at him.

'You are a pompous man. You remind me of my father, a little.' Jonah blustered briefly but it seemed the prince's tongue, once loosened, would not readily still itself. 'Do you know what it is to be a disappointment, Lightfoot?'

Jonah thought carefully about this, divining his meaning. Had his own father been disappointed in him? He believed not – Henry had always taught his sons patiently, never allowing his fearsome intellect to overwhelm his compassion. Jonah, younger than Albert, had been the favourite, but Albert had never seemed to mind. But at the end? Had his father turned against him then, when the foot-race Jonah had forced through the grounds of the Crystal Palace had become an absurd tragedy?

'I don't know,' he answered quietly. 'I really don't know.'

Jonah's uneasiness was quite lost on Gerent, who continued, gazing up into the oppressive forest canopy as he spoke. 'Do you understand the importance of lineage? Perhaps you do not. For my people, the Denneth, the line of the king is everything. All my fathers were warriors. But I am not a warrior. Therefore, although I am my father's only son, I am not his heir.'

'Not in your father's eyes, perhaps.'

'Not in any eyes. Least of all my own.'

'But surely . . .'

'No. Please, if you wish to understand my misery then hear me out. My father was the last man to hunt in this forest. There are boar down there, and a breed of aurochs, much smaller than the beasts you saw on the roof plain. Every ten days he would lead five men down into the forest; none would return until each had gained a kill. Days of feast followed, then it would be time for the next hunt. An endless cycle of sport.'

'It doesn't sound as if there was very much time left for anything else.'

'That is true,' Gerent snorted. 'And so I would advise the king, though he did not hear me. Then came the day of my manhood, the day when my father led me alone into the forest.

We stalked a mighty boar, a huge, silver-backed monster with tusks like swords, and I killed it with a single blow. I think he was surprised – I think he had expected me to fail. Perhaps I had expected that, too. We returned triumphant, or rather my father did: I would not attend the feast, nor would I accompany him on the next hunt.' His eyes grew cloudy. 'It was shortly after that day that Frey returned from his exile. The king hunted only once more after that before he became sick. Nor has he spoken a single word to me since. Much else has changed since then.'

A shiver ran through the body of the Neolithic prince and he dragged a hand across his sparse beard. Then he thumped his fist on the path. 'He is such a fool! Do you know, there is a chamber adjoining the one in which you found us. Its single door seems impenetrable, but I found a slot that lifted aside, allowing me at least to look inside. It is full of such wonders! There is a great bowl, big enough for a man to curl up in, suspended from the ceiling by enormous beams. It looks made to turn, to tip its burden across the floor. The floor harbours pits of sand in which are pressed the shapes of tools. I looked on it and I knew its purpose at once! It is an apparatus to shape metal!' Suddenly, Gerent's eyes were shining. Some of his excitement penetrated Jonah: he had not seen the man so agitated before. 'To think – behind a closed door lies a secret knowledge my people has never owned. Instead of being slaves to metal we might become its masters.'

'You are beachcombers. You make nothing – you use only what you find.'

'But it should not be so! The only things my people possess that they can truly claim as their own are the stone tools you saw. They were crafted by the hands of our ancient fathers, and there is great power in them. But what does *my* father do? The same as his father and his father before him – he sleeps with his head buried in our history and dreams only of the hunt.'

A faint sound carried through the thick air: the cry of a woman. Both men turned their heads and saw only a single silhouette at the end of the path. Whether it was Archan or Malya they could not tell. Jonah felt suddenly chilled. 'We should go,' he muttered.

They walked quickly, matching each other stride for stride. Gradually the trees to their right thinned, admitting more and more of the heavy, liquid light of Stone. 'Tell me,' said Jonah, 'when you say those stone tools have power, what is it that you mean precisely?' He was remembering first the importance Gerent had placed on the artefacts with regard to his quest to challenge the dragon; second his curious reticence to recover them once they had been lost.

'The stones of the Denneth were my weapon against the great dragon. But the stones are lost and I must go on unarmed.'

'But *why* were they so vital, and if they were so vital then why did you leave them at the bottom of that well?'

Gerent rounded on him. His eyes were no longer merely shining – they were ablaze. 'The stones are charmed! Do you have charm in your world, Lightfoot? Well, we brought ours with us when we crossed over, locked into a handful of axes and arrowheads. And that is the only way the dragon can be defeated, by the use of charm.'

'Then go back and get the stones,' said Jonah quietly.

Gerent's lips trembled. 'I cannot,' he blurted after an agonised delay. 'I . . . I am afraid.'

'Of your people? But you are the son of the king.'

'There is more. The chamber into which Sauth fell . . .'

'The round room, yes. We went in there and . . .'

'You went in there?' Gerent's eyes grew very wide. 'But, the rat-horde! To enter the Chimney is certain death to any man!'

Jonah remembered the strange chattering sound, the gleam of rodent eyes in the darkness. 'Not to me, apparently,' he murmured. 'Nor Archan,' he added thoughtfully.

'You think I am retelling some tall story, but let me tell you a *true* story. The last man to enter the Chimney did so as a wager. He and a group of his friends had become intoxicated and he had hoped to earn the right to another man's wife by braving the rat-horde. They goaded him, urging him on until finally he crawled in there on his hands and knees, hoping perhaps to avoid the gaze of the rats. They live in a network of tunnels with exits all around the chamber, and have excellent vision.'

'I know,' shivered Jonah.

'It was night, and the Chimney was quite dark. The other three men heard nothing for a breath or two, then they heard a loud chattering and a tremendous tearing sound. By the time they managed to bring a torch and hold it inside the doorway there was nothing left of their friend but a tangle of bones. No blood, no meat – just bones.'

'We must have been lucky.'

'There is no luck when it comes to the rat-horde. They are many bodies but one mind, and that mind knows only one thing: how to eat. They do not eat very often, so when they do . . .' He let the thought hang in the air. 'You and your companion were not lucky, Lightfoot, *you were charmed*.'

They were close enough to their goal now to see that it was Archan who stood alone beyond the trees. 'This woman,' said Gerent, pointing ahead. 'She has strange eyes, magical eyes. Clearly it was her magic that kept the rat-horde at bay. What is it that she wants with the dragons? Might she be of some use to us?'

Jonah almost told him everything then, that Archan was the shell of a woman empowered with the spirit of a dragon, that he had no real idea what her desires or motivations were, that he was at once entranced and terrified by her beauty, her intelligence, her sheer unpredictability. That she was immortal. But as he opened his mouth to speak he saw Malya emerge from beneath an overhanging bough, saw that she had been there all along and that his fears had been unfounded. He noted the trace of fear that crossed Gerent's face as he too saw her reappear and wondered again what held them together.

'If you really needed those stones you would have gone back for them,' he said abruptly. 'So what is really going on here, Gerent? Will you tell me?'

The Neolithic prince closed his eyes and pressed his palms into their sockets, a gesture that seemed to Jonah curiously modern. The gulf of time between them was, he realised, no more significant than that between members of successive generations. The language of the body transcended history; temporal colloquialisms aside, the raw text of man was the same. An Australian aboriginal would smile a welcome in just the same way as a Cockney barrow boy; with the same primary language this ancient man now displayed his fatigue, his quiet desperation, his futile effort to quell the rising tide of his thoughts.

'I am simply afraid to go back, Lightfoot.'

'Yet you are ready to face a dragon.'

'That is different. But, Lightfoot, you must remember what

I said to you just now, for it is the truth: *I am not a warrior*. I cannot fight, and I could no more confront the terror of the Chimney than the wrath of my father.'

With that, he moved ahead, leaving Jonah to pursue him along the final hundred yards of the forest path. The prince's head was lowered, his gait little more than a fast shamble; a more dejected figure he could not have presented.

Yet there is more to you than you would have me believe, Jonah pondered as he advanced out of the shadow of the canopy and into the glare of Stone's vibrant afternoon.

He was aware of a humming sound, a faraway noise that swelled and receded with irregular rhythm. There was movement too, erratic movement in the depths of the forest. More sounds descended; his ears had by now learned to suppress the steady whisper of the wind and now he could hear a virtual orchestra of tiny instruments – the chirping of insects, the steady thump of some distant machinery, the rustle of foliage, a faint, crackling roar. And the humming.

It grew louder, accompanied now by a frenzied motion amid the conifers immediately behind them. He took a step back and then, seeing that the others were regarding him somewhat querulously, stood his ground. Seconds later a stream of tiny birds, their wings invisible blurs, erupted from the trees. At once Jonah was transported back to Krakatoa, to the moment when the parrots burst from the jungle, and he could not help but flinch. Out of the corner of his eye he saw Malya nudge Gerent and chuckle. The hummingbirds flew over their heads, ascending in a tight curve before plunging back into the forest once more, but not before one of their number simply dropped from the flock, falling lifeless on to the path before Jonah's feet.

He picked it up and turned it over. Feathers like brushstrokes from a rainbow pressed warm against the skin of his palm; its head lolled, golden beak polished to a gleam. It was so small – no bigger than the first joint of Jonah's thumb. *Bird of paradise*, he pondered, *made by Fabergé*.

He looked around at his companions, embarrassed again: they all seemed to be looking at him. Carefully he placed the little corpse at the side of the path, tucking it beneath a skirt of lichen. Of the rest of the flock there was no further sign.

As his earlier view from the edge of the roof had suggested, this side of the castle the realm of Stone was teeming with life. Long-legged insects, somewhat resembling craneflies but exhibiting brilliant, jade-coloured wings, fluttered valiantly against the falling wind. Small black birds – not as small as the humming-birds but smaller than the terrestrial swift which they resembled greatly – darted through the denser swarms of these insects, yellow beaks wide and hungry. It was only when he looked more closely that Jonah realised they had not one pair of wings but two.

High above the flight paths of the swifts prowled a bird of prey that was, Jonah guessed, at least twice the size of the Andean condor.

So much that seemed familiar but on closer inspection proved to be quite alien.

The face of Stone was still made from the same, enormous blocks but here, downStone from the castle, their joints were thick with vegetation of an astonishing variety. One of these main horizontal junctions ran barely two feet above eye level, and Jonah found himself wishing he were a botanist as he reached up to pluck a large, blue flower from a tangle of bramble-like creepers. Its petals were wide and slightly sticky; its odour was decidedly pungent. He cast it aside, moving on to a clump of bright red berries adhering to a long, straight stalk, curved over at the end like a walking stick. Thin juice dripped steadily from the berries; the path immediately beneath them was stained the colour of wine. More blooms, small white ones these, a little like the wood anemones he remembered from barefoot walks with Lily in another world. And these purple ones that grew seemingly everywhere, reaching out from this astonishing hedgerow in a broad fan of purple that dwindled into the middle distance, what were they? Jonah searched his memory and came up with *prince's feather*; though he was uncertain of the identification, a glance at Gerent somehow made up his mind and he decided that was what it was. *Prince's feather . . . now what was the proper name for it?*

At length he drew his attention away from the blanket of purple and green and glanced behind him. The others, like him, were staring at the castle with undisguised amazement.

The entire outer half of the castle was ablaze. The wooden

palisade extending around and beneath the whole of the overhanging section was burning ferociously. The downward wind fanned the flames back into the structure, creating violent eddies of hot air that sent sparks exploding far out into the sky. The upper part of the overhang, the complex of stone towers that the roof maze had prevented them from reaching, was sagging visibly, giant cracks opening its flanks like a wounded beast.

Built on sand, thought Jonah, his heart racing, *and now the tide is coming in!*

Smoke was pouring from the black holes of the high-level windows, dispersing erratically as the superheated air tried to rise against the constant pressure of the falling wind. Eddies knotted the smoke into elaborate signatures. Behind the castle, in the forest-filled cleft from which the travellers had emerged, more birds were taking anxious flight, among them a cloud of hummingbirds ten times the size of the one they had first seen; they swarmed like dazzling bees.

'It cannot stay up much longer,' he whispered, gripped again by vertigo. He tried to imagine something that size simply *falling,* dropping like a *stone* into the abyss . . . but he could not. It was just too big; castles were just not meant to fall anywhere.

'There is nothing we can do,' said Malya, her tone quite free of any emotion. 'Let us move on.'

They moved on.

Perhaps two miles ahead the narrow path – which was still really a ledge, this time adhering to the ten-degree slope of Stone instead of the vertical inner castle wall – widened into what looked like a stairway. The steps – if that was what they were – led up into the shadow behind the silver disc they had seen from the roof, which was spinning slowly, held a little away from the face of Stone by some vast apparatus. Its size he could not accurately judge: distances to objects he was beginning to develop a sense of (such measurements were dependent on the deep atmospheric haze, and that seemed to remain constant throughout the day) but their size, the sheer scale of Stone, was something he had not yet absorbed; perhaps he never would.

Motionless at the centre of the disc was a palace constructed from what looked like the same silver material. Except *constructed* was not the correct word, Jonah considered as he picked his way carefully along the narrow ledge: in fact, the edifice looked more as though it had been extruded from a single, seamless piece of metal. A bizarre thought struck him, that in fact it was not solid at all but liquid, a palace of quicksilver somehow frozen in space and time and held in stasis while the disc revolved in stately fashion at its root. Its towers, extending horizontally towards the open sky, were smooth and organic, unmarked by weave or window; the buttresses flaring at its base were swollen pods, like fruits ready to burst, but smooth, so smooth.

Of one thing he was certain: no man had built it.

There was a thundering sound from just above his head and he ducked instinctively. Archan, who preceded him, stopped so suddenly that he nearly collided with her; when he looked round he saw that the two Neolithics were pressed against the moss-covered stonework, heads raised, eyes seeking.

'Here they come!' called Malya.

A pair of hooves descended through what Jonah had come to think of as the *hedgerow* mere yards ahead of them, scattering the purple flowers out into the air, where they were sucked away by a sudden downdraught. He saw pale grey fur, long, curving horns and then the creature was gone, his impression of it an incomplete jigsaw in his mind's eye.

No sooner had it vanished over the precipice than a second appeared. This one crashed unceremoniously to its knees in front of them before picking itself up, shaking its head in an absurdly human gesture and then launching itself in pursuit of its companion. This time Jonah got a good look before the animal disappeared: it resembled nothing so much as a mountain goat, though it was quite small – the size of a beagle, perhaps. Its chipped horns were as high again as its body at the shoulder, and they curved through two complete circles before reaching a pair of rough points. He cried out, an involuntary yelp, as it launched itself into space, then dropped to his knees and hugged the edge of the path to watch it fall.

But it did not fall. It dropped lightly on to an outcropping of Stone material, a broken mass of rubble supported on what looked like a mountain of compressed foliage, a veritable squashed jungle. The two goats pranced to the side, descending all the while, taking prodigious leaps across timbers that looked too rotten to support their weight. One such trunk projected far out into space; the goats bounded to the end of it and hurled themselves into the chasm. Seconds later the sound of hoofbeats rose again, testament to their survival.

'What do you call it?' asked Jonah suddenly, pointing towards the sky. 'I mean, what is the name for that direction? I know downStone and upStone, but which way is the sky?'

'Out,' answered Malya tersely, as though it were obvious, which, Jonah reflected, it probably was.

'And this way?' he smiled, indicating the looming face of Stone behind them.

'In.'

'And "up" and "down", of course.' He gestured accordingly. She gave him a withering look.

'We must make faster progress!' Archan's voice cut through their exchange. 'The sun moves quickly in this world.'

Jonah looked up and saw that she was right. Though his Hunter still lay buried on what was left of Krakatoa (or, more likely was either foundering beneath the sea or circling in microscopic pieces high in the atmosphere), the clock that ticked inside his body told him that the days here were shorter than they were back home. The sun, speeding downStone along its subverted, horizontal track, was rich orange in colour and cruising close to the tips of the longest spires. He guessed they had as little as an hour before sunset; already long, blue shadows were reaching out to them, the greatest of them the shadow of the rotating disc that now filled half their world.

Beside him, Malya was reaching into her pouch. He looked back down over the edge, trying to see more clearly what appeared to be a split in the surface of Stone, just above the rubble. When he looked up again he saw she had retrieved a thin, coiled rope which she was swinging lightly in her hand as she cast about on the path for something.

'Are you coming, faery?' Archan was already several paces downStone, striding purposefully towards the steps which were clearly visible through the orange-tinted haze. Gerent hesitated, then pursued her without even glancing at Malya.

'We'll catch up,' called Jonah impulsively. A secret voice warned him that it was folly to split their group, but he was intrigued by Malya's sudden and decisive action; already she had chosen a fist-sized chunk of broken rock around which she was securely tying the end of the rope.

But was there not more? Was there not another voice calling to him? Something down below, something drawing him down like iron to a magnet, as undeniable as gravity or the open arms of a child.

Malya was searching amid the foliage at the back of the ledge. At length she found what she was looking for – a small, round hole piercing the ledge from top to bottom; peering down through it over her shoulder Jonah could clearly see the rubble and a little of the yawning chasm below.

'A drain,' she explained tersely. Jonah felt a modicum of pride that he had worked this out for himself, that he had not been forced to ask another foolish question; Malya had a way of making him feel quite inadequate.

The ledge sloped slightly inwards, towards Stone, presumably to make it safer for travellers. Clearly this presented a drainage problem, one solved simply and neatly by a series of holes set at regular intervals along the inner edge. Most, like this, were covered or even blocked by the rampant vegetation; clearly whoever had built Stone had not placed maintenance terribly high on the agenda.

That question: *who built Stone?* It stuck in Jonah's thoughts like a knife.

Having cleared the vegetation away, Malya carefully dangled the stone over the hole and fed it through like an improvised plumb bob. Jonah heard it thump against the wall beneath the hole's exit point and looked over the outer edge of the ledge once more to see it rattle down towards the rubble. Was she fishing for something?

That voice again, calling . . . down, down.

'Hold this,' she demanded, handing him the middle coils of the rope. Obediently he complied. While he held the plumb bob rock in place, she fashioned a lasso from the rope's other end. Then, like a cowboy, she stood on the very lip of the precipice, swinging the lasso around her head twice before dropping it lazily over the edge. It struck Stone with a faint slap; at once Jonah felt the tension in the part of the rope he was holding change. 'Let go,' she barked.

He joined her, and saw that she had lassoed the rock she had just lowered through the hole. He was about to ask why she wanted it back when she had only just got rid of it, but decided that of the character traits he had noted in the Neolithics so far a sense of humour was not the most prominent. So he watched in silence as she drew the rock, still tied to the rope's other end, back into her hands. Then she untied the rock, cast it aside, and fed the free end back through the loop of the lasso. At last Jonah saw what she was doing.

'You've just tied a slip knot around the entire ledge, haven't you?'

'Are you coming, faery?' Malya asked, mimicking Archan's tone with uncanny accuracy. 'Why does she call you that?'

'It is a long story, and yes, I will come with you.'

With the rope now tied securely around the ledge, Malya was able to shin down it to the rubble. She alighted gingerly, testing the ability of the scree to support her weight. Jonah followed with care, cursing once as the slender rope slipped through his palms, burning them. He landed with less grace than she, disturbing a few loose pebbles which went tumbling out into space.

All around them broken tree boughs pointed upwards, framing the rubble as though it lay in the clutches of some arboreal giant. Above them, perhaps fifteen feet away, the underside of the ledge was a dark blue shadow; the hole through which Malya had fed the rope was a disc of pale grey light.

Directly in front of them was a crack in the skin of Stone.

It was as high as a man and about as wide. He thought of the enormous tunnel from which he had first emerged and wondered if this was the same phenomenon, if somewhere at the end of this miniature tunnel there lay a doorway back to his world.

Do not be so fanciful, he scolded himself. *This is a crack and nothing more, caused by weathering or frost or some similar action.*

But it was no such thing, and he knew it.

He observed Malya while she probed the crack. She was agile, completely at home in this perilous world. Well, of course she was – she was a *native* of this world, perhaps even on her way to becoming an entirely new strain of the human species. *Homo verticalis,* he chuckled to himself, noting her perfect poise. *Evolution in action.* No grunting primitive this, but a young and pretty woman. Her blonde hair and pale skin were completely at odds with Jonah's preconceptions of Stone Age humans as swarthy and leather-skinned. Yet again he felt the narrowness of the gulf between them, the minuscule scratch those few thousand years of evolution made in the entire sweep of history.

Or eternity, he shuddered, looking around at the enormity of Stone.

There was a soft *clink* as Malya drew a metal object out of the hole – a weapon that looked to Jonah like a Roman *gladius*, a short, stabbing sword. It was pristine, gleaming in the late light, the blade no more than a foot long, the pommel surmounted by a bronze-coloured sphere. She produced a thin leather belt from nowhere and lashed the sword triumphantly round her waist.

'Come,' she said defiantly. 'I don't trust your friend.'

But Jonah was not really listening to her, he was listening to the gentle scraping sounds coming from inside the crack. Bending to peer in, he was unsurprised to see one of the tortoids working patiently in the darkness. The rear of its shell was open, exposing an armoury of spindly limbs working with dark threads; he was reminded of nothing so much as a spider building a web, except this creature was not spinning silk but exuding the very stuff with which the interior of the crack was lined. Sticky black paste emerged from the tortoid's abdomen to be moulded by those busy limbs and applied in thick layers to the smooth wall at the rear of the crack. Quite simply, it was healing the wound.

He had to stifle a gasp as he saw a human arm protruding limply from the wall: the unfortunate owner of the sword, entombed now in resin.

The tortoid had nearly completed its task – it was only two yards short of the opening. It was much smaller than the others Jonah had seen, and it looked cruder somehow, less nimble, less *formed*. He was about to remark on this to Malya when he saw the rod.

It was just like those he had seen in the big tunnel. Sleek and black, an ebony cylinder running straight through the crack and into the wall on either side, part of Stone yet not part of it. The more he gazed upon it the more he seemed to fall into it, and the louder became the voice that had called him down here. He reached towards it, heedless of Malya's warning cry . . .

His hand touched it, gripped it. It was narrow enough that his thumbs met the tips of his middle fingers on the other side. It was warm, it throbbed. Something like electricity jolted the muscles in his arms but he retained his grip and was not afraid. He had thought it might feel like metal, and it did, a little, but it also felt like flesh. There was movement beneath its outer surface, something flowing slick and strong, a liquid energy that urged him to drink from it.

Part of his mind fell into the current. He saw a cone of rock, heard a sudden explosion like a thousand cannons fired simultaneously, saw a white-walled house buried beneath a wave of mud, a soldier thrown against the flank of a screaming horse . . . then he pulled back. His mind grew detached and he saw the rod through physical eyes again, only this time he saw thousands more of them, millions more, a great skein of rods threaded through Stone like the bars of metal that gave concrete its strength. The vision was unbearably vivid, like a scene lit by a lightning flash that would not fade. The colours were electric, the air filled with the scent of peril, like smelling salts.

He snatched his hands away from the rod, gasping and crying out. His palms felt as though the skin had been flayed from them, but when he turned them over he saw they were unmarked; the pain fled, leaving them momentarily numb. He was panting, sweating, and when he looked he saw the rod was sweating too: beads of clear liquid trembled on its glossy surface. They evaporated as he watched, hissing quietly.

Malya stared at him wide-eyed as he clambered unsteadily to his feet. He could not tear his eyes from the rod – was Stone really pierced through with such things? If so it was *riddled* with power! But to what end? And what exactly had he experienced?

'What did you see?' asked Malya. Her former aloofness had completely gone; now she seemed afraid, a little awestruck even. 'Did you see what has been?'

Jonah rubbed his forehead. 'I saw . . . I don't know.' He could still taste the fear on his lips; it made him feel very small.

'What you did was foolish. The Rods can kill a man. We dare not go near them.'

'I seem to have survived.'

He sat down heavily, exhausted, and watched without interest as she loosened the rope and paid it back through the hole until she held both ends in her hands. Then she found a thick branch, tied it to one end and hauled it back up so that the branch lodged against the underside of the hole, allowing them to shin directly up to the edge of the ledge. Once they were both safe (the climb was something Jonah did not even recall doing once he was back on the path) she discarded the branch and stowed the rope efficiently in her pouch.

'Are you all right?' she asked. She sounded uncomfortable, but her concern was genuine enough.

'I think so. I can't really remember a great deal except a curious sensation of speed.'

'We should catch up with the others. We should not have left them alone together.'

Malya's sense of urgency was infectious and he joined her march without question; besides, he was all too keen to explain away his strange experience. He had heard of the potential of the electric shock to addle a man's brains – perhaps the rod had delivered just such a jolt to him. Perhaps Stone was shot through not by mystical energy but by ordinary Volts. Some small part of him, the tip of the iceberg, was convinced, but underneath . . . *iron ribs, the strands of continuity that hold together the fabric of the world* . . . he felt very uncertain.

Malya was like an entirely different woman as they hurried to catch up with Archan and Gerent. Her former antagonistic manner was gone, replaced by an eagerness to communicate that Jonah found strangely endearing. It was as if she suddenly regarded him as an equal, whereas before he had felt a little like something she had trodden in.

'What did Gerent tell you of our mission?' she asked. They were walking in single file – Malya in front, Jonah behind. Though he tried, he could not get the image of the rod out of his mind.

'Less than he might have done. I gained the distinct impression he was holding information back.' He let the words float ahead, testing the ground.

She stopped suddenly and turned, lowering her voice. 'Gerent sees enemies everywhere – part of being a king's son, I suppose. I perceive things a little differently.'

'And how is that?'

'You know we have embarked on a quest to kill a dragon.'

'A noble undertaking.'

'Has Gerent told you how we plan to defeat the beast?'

'With magic,' replied Jonah uncomfortably. He shivered; stray pulses of energy lingered in his system, making his muscles twitch.

'With magic,' she echoed. 'Oh yes, with magic. But do you know who wields the magic of the Denneth? It isn't me, and it certainly isn't Gerent.'

'Frey? The medicine man.'

'My father,' agreed Malya. Again Jonah noted the family resemblance: the striking blue eyes, the confident, almost arrogant posture. 'Frey is the shaman of our tribe, and he alone possesses the secret knowledge necessary to wield charm. You asked if we could kill a dragon with a spear: not this dragon, Lightfoot! The only weapon that counts for anything against this particular dragon is the man who made it the monster it is: Frey. My father!'

'So that is the real reason you brought the magic stones. You think Frey will want to get them back. You're luring him out so you can use his magic to kill the beast.'

'The stones were the bait,' Malya agreed. 'But we decided we needed an alternative plan.'

'In case you lost the stones – which you did.' The weird electricity seemed to be dispersing, leaving him curiously refreshed.

'Or in case they were not enough. So we brought another kind of bait with us too.'

'And that was?'

'Me.'

The sky was by now the purple of twilight; night fell as swiftly as the day passed on Stone. Not far ahead was the enormous flight of steps into which the path widened and Jonah was tempted by the safety it promised, both in terms of the broadness of its treads (safer than this perilously narrow ledge) and by the fact that it led into the lee of the revolving disc, which he had for some reason come to regard as a sanctuary. *Just a basic instinct to be under cover by nightfall,* he decided.

Still, he was intrigued by Malya and her new-found willingness to speak.

She seemed to have lost her sense of urgency, for the time being at least. Jonah scanned the staircase, seeking human shapes amid the dense blue shadows and finding none. The others had already reached the disc – would they wait?

'Very well then, Malya,' he sighed. 'Tell me about your father, and how he comes to be connected with this dragon you are so eager to see defeated. But I hope it's not too long a story, because I don't think we should stay out here alone for one minute longer than we have to.'

'It is not a long story,' she replied, her voice soft and quiet.

Just before she started to speak Jonah's thoughts darted back to the crack, and he wondered if the lone tortoid had finished its job of sealing it up. *If so, what has happened to it?*

And what of the tortoid he had come to regard as somehow *his*? Was it out there still, following Jonah's progress as he inched his painful way across the vast expanse of Stone like a fly crawling over a window pane?

Absently he scratched an Oriental symbol in the dust on the ledge: a sword-shape, the sign of the Red Dragon. Then Malya began.

7
Malya

The magic had never been real.

At least, not in the home-world.

Frey, shaman to the tribe of the Denneth, man of medicine with a lineage to rival even that of the king, was the first of his line to recognise that here on Stone the magic was *real. More real, in fact, than any of his predecessors had dared to believe magic could be.*

Like many shamans before him, Frey had been well trained in the art of guile. His hands moved fast, deceiving willing eyes and working miracles by simple fakery; he read faces with uncanny insight, perceiving moods and sometimes even thoughts by the flick of an eyebrow; he could contort his body into extraordinary positions, arching his back over until his feet dangled above his head; he was fleet of both foot and mind. Whether or not he believed in the magic was irrelevant – he made others believe, that was all that mattered.

The first shaman of Stone had also been called Frey, and he too had been full of guile. It was his king, Sabor, who found the deserted castle with its wealth of treasures, having trekked many miles upStone from the tunnel through which they had emerged. There they settled, there they stayed. Food was plentiful, although they soon realised they no longer really needed to eat; the hunting was good, thanks to the sheltered forest and its boar and miniature aurochs; the dark-haired people were pathetically eager to join their tribe. Tools made from wondrous new materials lay everywhere. There was no need to make things or plant crops or do anything very much except live and love and grow lazy.

So, for nine generations the people of the Denneth grew stagnant, and their shamans grew stagnant with them, working their traditional guiles while all around them, unseen and unimagined, the real magic flowed.

So it went on, until Malya's father Frey was born and, in time, became shaman.

Frey looked deeper than his forefathers; in particular he looked out into the sky. As a young man he would often wander alone through the empty outer halls of the castle, seeking out new windows from which he might observe the ever-flowing clouds as they cut through the magnificent blue. He watched the dragons at play, marvelled at their aerobatics, considered the way they could hover without moving their wings.

They remain still without so much as breathing, *he would think.* Yet the wind blows ever downwards. What trickery is this?

And soon he began to realise that it was no trick: it was magic. So he caught himself a dragon.

'He did what?' exclaimed Jonah.

'A dragon,' Malya repeated. 'One flew too close to the big round window – my father's favourite lookout spot – and he captured it with a net.'

'A *net*?'

'Must you repeat everything?' She laughed, a light sound quite at odds with her usual aggressive manner. 'Be quiet and let me tell the story.'

'Oh, very well then, I apologise. But I must admit to being curious about how . . .'

'Shut up!'

Frey had a secret place, a dungeon deep in the roots of the castle. He alone held the metal shapes necessary to open the doors to the dungeon – not that he had any real fear of intruders, so indolent were the tribespeople.

He drugged the dragon with a strong poison and dragged it down the many flights of steps to his lair. Here he laid it out on a great stone table, pinning its wings and legs so that it could not escape. Then he began his experiments.

'Experiments?' asked Jonah nervously.

'Lightfoot!' warned Malya. 'You're doing it again!'

He kept the wretched serpent drugged to keep it quiet and pierced several of its veins to drain samples of its blood. He collected its spit and piss, scraped the corners of its eyes and drew mucus from its throat. Soon the dungeon was filled with vessels of glass and metal that he had gathered from all over the castle, vessels that were in turn filled with these ghastly fluids. For many days he worked, ignoring the bleating of the helpless creature.

Once he allowed the drug to wear off and the dragon reared up, tearing one of its wings free from the metal spike with a spray of blood and throwing him against the wall. He struck back with a wooden club, knocking the beast unconscious. Its tattered wing flopped pathetically on the altar-like table; Frey took the opportunity to dissect it, drawing out tendons and clipping sections of its translucent flight membrane to store in yet more jars.

The dissection fuelled his drive for knowledge. He pulled out several of the dragon's teeth and removed all the claws from one of its hind legs – it was a four-limbed beast, a little like a bat, with its wings formed from long, tapering arms powered by massive shoulder muscles; its hind limbs were relatively underdeveloped. He plucked scales from its hide: coarse bony ones from its back, smooth flexible ones from its throat and underbelly. He broke the tip from one of its horns and delved into the cavity within.

He was looking for its magic. He did not know if it was focused within an organ, like a second heart, perhaps, or if the power permeated its whole body. By dissecting the beast he believed he could locate the magic he was convinced it possessed.

He almost succeeded.

After fourteen days of this torture the dragon finally spoke. Frey was astonished – dragons had never before been heard to speak, even when they had flown close to the castle walls; they had always been assumed to be as dumb as the birds with whom they shared the sky.

It said, 'Let me go, or I will kill you.'

Once he had recovered from his surprise, Frey laughed. Then the dragon blew a jet of flame from its mouth that started a fire in the corner of the dungeon. The fire took hold swiftly; Frey began to gather his jars and boxes in panic when the dragon blew out a second jet. This was a strange phenomenon, a kind of cold fire *that fell over the original flames and extinguished them instantly. Frey stopped, amazed.*

'Why did you not try to kill me earlier?' he demanded, trying to regain control of the situation.

'If you knew anything about the true nature of charm then you would understand the efficiency of the prison you have chosen for me.'

'Go on,' said Frey.

'The magic is in the air, isn't it?' cried Jonah triumphantly. 'That's what the dragon meant! And by shutting it away from the sky, away from the *wind*, Frey had severely reduced its magical powers, including its ability to breathe fire. I am right, am I not?'

'Indeed you are, Lightfoot,' answered Malya, clearly impressed.

'Gerent told me about the air,' he said modestly. 'So what happened next – did Frey set the dragon free?' He thought for a moment, then touched her cautiously on the shoulder. 'Did your father really do those terrible things to a living, thinking creature?'

'Yes, he did. And I hate him for it. He says he would never have done such things had he known the creature was aware, but I know he's lying. I can read faces, too, you know.'

They entered a period of fragile alliance, during which time Frey kept the dragon more heavily drugged than he had previously, so suspicious was he of deceit.

In return for Frey's promise of freedom, the dragon told the shaman some of the secrets of charm.

It told him how the falling wind of Stone is saturated with magic. It told him how any creature can reach out into the invisible rain of charm and fashion a spell – literally – from thin air. It also explained that some creatures are more adept than others, and that dragons, here on Stone at least, are among the most adept. On the skill of men to wield charm it would not comment, but it did not see any reason why a man like Frey could not acquire at least a little of the gift.

Frey listened and believed, and then demanded instructions, which the dragon duly gave. Frey returned to his windows and held his hands out into the wind to practise his new-found skills. He wove spells and worked charm. He became the first shaman of the tribe of the Denneth truly to perform magic.

Then came the day of the dragon's long-promised release. Frey had already fashioned the spell that would, he claimed, restore the dragon's strength and break the bonds he had placed it under.

He descended the gloomy steps and approached the prostrate beast, a glowing sphere of pure charm cradled in his palms.

'Do you know what this is, dragon?' he whispered. The dragon said

nothing, merely nodded its heavy, drugged head. 'There is more of you in these jars than there is on the table, dragon.' The beast blinked its glazed eyes dopily. Shiny metallic blood dripped from a dozen unhealed wounds. 'This is the end of misery for you.'

The dragon leaped up and roared. Flames erupted from its mouth in a torrent.

Shrieking, Frey jumped backwards and hurled the ball of charm into the serpent's gaping throat. It lodged there, a spell not of release but of death, the shaman's final blow, his broken promise. The charm expanded, swelling into a writhing mass of tentacles that started to bore their way into the dragon's flesh.

But, predicting betrayal, the dragon had been preparing itself for this day. Silently it had gathered what little charm it could, inhaling draughts from beneath the dungeon door and between the minute cracks in the stonework. Now it unleashed its own magic against Frey's attack, its intention being not to deflect the shaman's spell – it was still too weak for that – but to absorb it and change it into something it could use.

It swallowed the attacking charm and altered it, turning it from a means of destruction into a changing charm with prodigious power. Instead of wrecking its body the charm became a part of it, flowing through veins and across sinews, into muscles and swelling . . .

The dragon grew. When Frey had brought it into the dungeon its body had been typical of its kind: only slightly larger than that of a man yet weighing perhaps half as much, with long wings trailing like gossamer behind it.

Now it was twice the size, hunching against the ceiling, doubling again, the black and red stripes that marked its underbelly rippling like waves. By the time the dragon stopped growing it was a veritable giant, dwarfing Frey in the tiny dungeon. Charm continued to boil like foam from the corners of its mouth, spilling out on to the floor where it hissed and danced. It loomed over him, drawing up its wings, but it was clumsy, uncomfortable with its new body. From behind it there came an ominous cracking sound.

Frey threw himself up the stairs as the outer wall of the dungeon fell away. Cracks raced across the floor as the sudden weight of the beast took its toll on the ancient foundations. The wall vanished into black mist as a rush of wind billowed out of the darkness, and then the dragon fell too, sucked out into the night sky, wings flailing, unable to control its plunge into the abyss. Frey rushed forward again, peering over the edge of the ruined floor just in time to see black eyes glaring *back up at him, two translucent wings struggling to find a grip in the treacherous air.*

He was alone in the dungeon, left only with the pathetic dragon parts he had carved from the beast.

And the charm, of course. That belonged to him now.

'The rest you can probably guess,' Malya concluded. 'As soon as my father began to perform real magic the king grew frightened and Frey was outcast; the Denneth have come to mistrust change, you see. He lurked in the dark recesses of the castle for years, practising his new-found skills until at last he had honed a spell by which he could control the king, keeping him drugged as he had the dragon, except now the drug was not a poisonous leaf but some trickery of charm, undetectable by even the king's advisers.'

'But he told you about it?'

'Of course, he thought I was like him.' Malya laughed, bitterly this time. 'He was wrong – for once in his life he misjudged someone. His own flesh and blood too.'

'Was there nobody you could tell?'

She shrugged. 'Shaman's daughter or not I am only a woman, and my father had even the king believing his tales. He blamed the dragon, you see. Coincidentally – or not, perhaps – the dragon's attacks began shortly after my father's return. It must have fallen a long way before it learned how to control its new body. When it finally found its way back it wanted only one thing.'

'Revenge against the man who had tortured it almost to death.'

'Exactly. So it began systematically to drive the Denneth back into the castle. Then, when it had them hemmed into a corner, it began to destroy the castle itself.'

Jonah looked back at the blazing castle, now a dazzling wall of flame lighting up the night-dark face of Stone for miles around. 'It certainly looks as though it has succeeded. What hope is there for your people, Malya?'

'They will die,' she said coldly, 'if they are not dead already.'

'Do you not care about their fate?'

'Of course I do!' she snapped. 'But they have chosen it for themselves. The Denneth chose their fate the day they walked out on to Stone and decided to shut themselves away in that damned castle. They deserve to burn, every one of them!'

'Even the king?'

'Especially him!' She was weeping now. 'Look at this world.' She snuffled, wiping tears away with one grimy hand. 'Look how much there is to see, look at its wonders. Yet there they stayed – and me too, fool that I was! But not any more. I want to see all that there is to see. This is *my* world, Lightfoot, and I want it. I want it more badly than you can know!'

'What about your father?'

'I hope he burns too, damn his miserable skin!'

Jonah thought for a moment, contemplating the heady glow of the flames; remembering Frey's eyes. 'But he will not burn, will he, Malya? He will follow us.'

She nodded, her tears drying now.

Something scratched against the stonework above Jonah's head and suddenly Malya was alert. In the flickering flame-light she looked to Jonah like a cat poised to leap, legs wide, nose twitching as she scented the air. Her fingers clutched at emptiness as if seeking prey; her eyes roved the heights.

'What is it?' he said, his voice unexpectedly loud in the ensuing silence.

'Be quiet, damn you to hell!' she hissed. Shocked by her vehemence Jonah took a step backwards and shut his mouth with a snap. That step probably saved his life.

A metal claw slashed through the air before his astonished face and ricocheted off Stone with a hard ringing sound. He barely caught a glimpse of it – a tangled grapnel shape with five or six razor tines swinging wildly on the end of a thin black thread – before it was snatched back up into the darkness.

'That would have torn my face away!' he exclaimed indignantly, then Malya was running bent double and knocking him to the ground. Again the sound came, a whirring that parted his hair. They rolled and then she was dragging him upright.

'Come on!' she yelled. 'Run with me!'

They ran between black sky and dim, orange-lit stone, gaining the wider part of the ledge within a few leaps and then bounding up the staircase two steps at a time. Some other light glowed ahead, green and welcoming, but for now Jonah could not make out its source; he was only aware of Malya jostling immediately in front of him, tugging at his arm and tossing her head about wildly.

'We need cover!' she gasped, but already Jonah was aware of a dark shape moving above them and a little ahead. It was moving lower, swinging like the pendulum of some gigantic clock, impossible to pin down in the weird light. It reached the limit of its arc, swung back towards them and Jonah saw that it was a man, descending on an invisible wire. A heavy metal cuirass reflected the light of the burning castle; a broadsword flashed yellow and then Malya was pushing Jonah aside, sending him reeling against Stone and ducking beneath their attacker's first, wild stroke. She rose as the sword struck sparks from the stonework and knocked the man down just as she had knocked Jonah down a moment before. He landed heavily against the angle of the step and grunted in surprise and pain. His sword swerved back abruptly, cracking her kneecap with the flat of its blade; if he had struck with the sharp edge she would have lost the lower half of her leg.

Crying out in agony, Malya collapsed on top of the Neolithic, scratching at his eyes with one hand while reaching for the sword at her waist with the other. This left her dangerously off-balance and her assailant took full advantage, bucking her off and lifting his weapon high over his head ready to plunge it into her breast. Jonah belatedly realised he was weaponless; his hands groped about his person in a vain effort to find a blade he knew he did not have. His fingers found a corner of wood – Annie's painting box! Yanking it up over his neck he wound his hand rapidly about its leather strap and shouted at the top of his voice, 'I say!'

Malya's attacker glanced up, momentarily discomposed. Still yelling, Jonah let fly with the wooden box. It hit the man squarely on the temple and he heard the dreadful crack of splintering bone. The man, more clearly visible now in a sudden flare of yellow light from the distant fire, was from the same tribe as Malya and Gerent but he was not Frey. He fell heavily, blood spraying from his ruined skull, and pitched over the edge of the stairs and into oblivion. Jonah was about to help Malya to her feet when he heard the footsteps of a second Neolithic ascending the stairs behind him.

He was garbed more elaborately than his cohort: though the

breastplate he wore was similar he also bore a metal helm boasting a feather of absurd size and improbable rainbow colours. Leather epaulets and what looked to Jonah like a bright blue Samurai skirt completed the ensemble. His face was partly covered by a nose-guard but Jonah recognised him as one of Frey's men – the dark-faced individual with whom he had shared a glance just before leaving the castle hall.

Malya was struggling to her feet, her left hand clasped around her injured knee. She had drawn her Roman sword and was holding it straight out ahead of her, elbow locked; Jonah noticed that the tip of the sword was absolutely still.

'Get behind me,' she grimaced, her teeth drawn back in pain. 'Get up the stairs and find the others. I'll hold this one off.'

'I don't really think that's a terribly good idea,' he replied, hefting the box. His hand touched one corner and came away slick with what had to be blood. His bravado left him in a sudden, cold rush, leaving him feeling naked. The Neolithic continued to advance, grinning wildly now as he drew a long, shining blade from its scabbard.

'Get back, Tamon,' called Malya, struggling to keep her voice steady. 'You have no quarrel with us.'

Tamon said nothing, merely widened his grin. His teeth were small and yellow, dirty little ivory tiles in a bleak, black mouth. He was by now only ten steps beneath them. He slowed a fraction, perhaps conscious of his foes' superior position in terms of elevation, though he showed no sign of fear, just a calm analysis of the battlefield.

'Which of you is to die first?' he asked, his voice a deep rumble emerging from that unpleasant mouth. 'Frey is not pleased with either of you, so it makes little difference to me.'

'I say again, you have no quarrel with us,' Malya repeated. The tip of her sword was trembling now and as she inched forward, trying to put herself between Jonah and Tamon, her injured knee buckled slightly, causing her to drop unwillingly on to the next step down.

'You took the sacred stones!' snarled Tamon. There was real fury in his voice; Frey might have instructed him to do this deed but it was a cause he believed in passionately. At last Jonah understood something of the magnitude of Gerent's crime, and of his fear ever to return to the castle and face his people.

He always knew this was a one-way journey, he realised. *And so did Malya. A suicide mission, perhaps.*

Tamon had paused and Jonah suddenly noticed how heavily he was breathing. The air had turned decidedly cold since sundown and the Neolithic's breath was a veritable fog gathering about his head before being whipped downwards by the constant wind. If it was not for Malya's knee he was sure they could outrun him up the stairs, especially given the weight of armour he was carrying. He looked at her: she was standing again, a sheen of sweat on her face, which was set with characteristic determination.

'Give me your sword,' Jonah whispered. She gave him a quizzical glance then, to his amazement, obeyed. Jonah felt a rush of affection: she had moved from her original position of contempt for him to one of trust in such a short space of time.

Since he had touched the rod – that was when she had changed her mind about him. The thought of it made the skin of his palms throb; for an instant it was as if it was preparing to absorb the sword's hilt somehow, to blend flesh with metal. He raised the sword and said conversationally, 'Run.'

She needed no coercion. Limping badly but moving faster than he had dared to hope, she hobbled up the staircase without once looking back.

Now it was just the two of them, weapons extended, eyes locked. The Neolithic was a dark shape cut from the glare of the castle, which was burning ever more fiercely. Flames prowled across its rooftop plain; Jonah imagined terror sweeping through the aurochs herd, driving them over the edge to their deaths. He could no longer hear Malya's footsteps.

Tamon climbed three steps in a single lunge and brought his sword back. Firelight struck it, almost blinding Jonah. He drew his own arm back and threw the Roman sword directly at Tamon's face.

The Neolithic, clearly expecting his adversary to stand and fight, was caught off-guard. He modified his blow, using it to fend off the flying blade and send it ringing over the precipice. Jonah used the precious seconds to turn and start his own headlong dash up the stairs. He half-expected to see Malya's silhouette limping ahead of him but he could see nothing either within or beyond the glowing green halo of light. Tamon cried out in surprise and rage before beginning his pursuit. Jonah did not dare look back but the sound of his pursuer's laboured breathing and the heavy crash of his footfalls reassured him that his hunch was sound: the man was both too tired and too heavy to match his pace. What awaited at the top he did not know, nor did he have any idea what he might do if he reached an impasse or dead end.

'But the others will be there,' he gasped, the sound of his own, breathless voice spurring him on.

In fact, Tamon fell behind quite quickly; soon the thud of his boots on the ever-widening stone steps grew faint in Jonah's ears. At last he dared to stop and look back down the risers: the man still came on but steadily now, head lifted high, sword jostling at his waist, alert for signs of a trap. Jonah felt a little foolish at having fled so frantically. It had worked though, and the gap he had opened between them was useful.

But it had not stopped the warrior, and it had surely served only to intensify his anger.

'Jonah!' The shout penetrated his thoughts, making him jump. He heard a rumbling noise and turned to see indistinct shapes moving against the green glow. He saw too that he had reached the perimeter of the huge, spinning disc: the gap between the disc's rear face and Stone created a slot into which the staircase ran. It was like entering a cavity behind an enormous clock-face, the dark side of Big Ben. It was from within this cavity that the green glow issued, marking the point at which the stairs met the machinery fixing the disc to Stone.

The bubble of hope that rose in Jonah's heart at this promise of sanctuary was unceremoniously punctured by the sight of a large object bouncing down the steps towards him. He could not make out what it was – it looked too regular to be a boulder, with straight sides and awkward corners – but he had no doubt that it was heavy and lethal. He threw himself against Stone, pressing his face into a curtain of lichen as the thing first approached and then thundered past him. Immediately beside him, fortuitously, was a squat pillar projecting from the face of Stone: protection against the object careering too close to the wall.

Turning his gaze downwards he saw Tamon perform the same act of self-preservation, except there was no pillar to protect him. Jonah held his breath as the cartwheeling object, which looked to him now like nothing so much as a fire-blackened stove or range, all glossy black angles and bevelled edges, bounced close to the man . . . then lurched over his head and fell on until finally it struck the narrow path at the foot of the stairs and flew with lazy momentum out into the dark void that seemed ready to claim anything that grew too clumsy on the face of this uncompromising world.

Jonah stayed where he was and watched the Neolithic remove himself cautiously from his defensive sprawl. He could not make out the man's face but fancied there must be a glower of utter fury painted across it by now. He was about to move himself when he heard a new sound, a pattering of . . . hail?

Seconds later a torrent of small stones and chunks of metal cascaded down the steps, crackling against Jonah's harbour wall, which deflected them safely. Tamon, however, was not so fortunate. He stopped dead in the middle of a step some twenty feet below Jonah and simply stared at the onrushing stream. The first rock struck him in the leg and he bent double; then he seemed to realise his peril and knelt right down, tucking his head under clasped hands and offering his armoured back to the storm. He weathered it for longer than Jonah would have thought possible: the smaller stones flayed his exposed hands and the larger pieces – sharp metallic fragments that looked as though they had been torn from some giant industrial apparatus – struck great dents in his gleaming armour.

The end came when a particularly large boulder cannoned against his hands, driving his head into the step. He fell limp then, and the steady rain did the rest, even though it was diminishing now. Stones that were little more than pebbles, mixed with otherwise harmless flakes of steel, flowed beneath his body, lifting it and carrying it down as if on a magic carpet before ejecting it into the darkness. His sword followed him down, clanging like a bell and landing sonorously on the path where it lay glittering in the firelight. Jonah waited for the deadly rain to stop altogether, then padded down the steps, picking his way through the debris, to fetch it. He felt guilty about throwing Malya's hard-won weapon away, even though it had probably saved their lives: he hoped this would be a suitable substitute.

She was waiting for him at the top, sitting under a tall arch of stone that marked the entrance to the large and complex structure rooting the disc to Stone. Here behind the disc, the sky was blotted out – all they could see of Stone was what lay directly behind them: the litter-strewn stairs, the castle, almost completely engulfed by the flames now.

'I feel like a church mouse,' commented Jonah as he watched the back of the disc revolving in stately fashion just yards from his face. 'Oh, I brought you his sword, by the way.'

Malya took it and nodded gratefully. 'I'm sorry about the avalanche,' she said, 'but I let go sooner than I'd intended. I could see you'd be able to take shelter, though.'

Jonah shrugged. 'What on earth was it that you threw down at us?' She smiled – he was starting to like the recurrence of that expression on her face – and beckoned him forward.

'Come on, I'll show you.'

Immediately beyond the archway, which reminded Jonah of the Great West Door leading into Westminster Abbey, was a tangle of odd-looking equipment. Bits of what might have been furnaces were piled alongside long sections of pipe and small, elaborate instruments that brought to mind sextants and theodolites. A random heap of apparatus, clearly abandoned, with no clue as to why or how it had been deposited here other than a gaping hole in the side wall high above it; had it been ejected from some gigantic rubbish chute? Ahead a long, green-lit corridor invited them to investigate further; it, unlike the debris-strewn entrance, was quite bare.

'I don't know what all this junk is,' said Malya, her voice echoing as though they were indeed inside a cathedral. 'But I'm glad it was here.'

Jonah half-supported her as she limped with him down the corridor. 'I have a feeling it's not the first of Stone's little mysteries that will have to remain unsolved,' he commented. He felt odd now that he was 'indoors' again – Stone was having the most curious effect on his mind, swinging him from vertigo to claustrophobia seemingly without pause. He regarded Malya, entirely at home here, and wondered if he would ever adapt to this vertical kingdom. 'Have you been here before?' he asked. 'Do you know what this place is, or what that giant disc is for?'

She shook her head. 'I have never been beyond the castle,' she admitted, 'to my shame. But things are different now.'

They found footsteps in the dust. The floor was tiled with a repeating pattern of green and yellow diamonds; this mosaic was dulled by a thin layer of pale grey dust. Gerent's boot-marks and the impressions left by Archan's bare feet were clearly visible. Jonah relaxed a fraction when he saw them, but remained puzzled as to why they had walked ahead so far without waiting for them. He feared some betrayal of Archan – and Gerent, what of him? He decided that first appearances were deceptive, that Malya, to whom he had not at first warmed, was proving to be a more reliable companion.

The trail led them round a sharp bend to the left, whereupon the ceiling dropped considerably. They proceeded with caution, ducking their heads occasionally when a mass of pipework descended from above. The walls grew dark and dripped moisture; the floor had become an open grille bleeding dim green light up around their feet; Jonah felt as though they were penetrating some great industrial machine. There was a steady throbbing sound that became gradually louder the further they went in.

Once he grasped a rail jutting from the wall to steady himself – his hand touched the shell of a long, ebony beetle with too many legs that chittered rapidly away into a small hatchway. Looking closer he saw large numbers of these beetles squatting behind the pipes; he did not reach out his hand again.

Abruptly, their way was barred. A smooth wall cut through the damp, metal-lined tunnel. It moved.

The effect was most unsettling: the wall, a flawless, glossy silver, was sliding from right to left, appearing from a barely-visible slot on one side of the tunnel and disappearing into a second, opposite. At first Jonah imagined it might be a sliding door of some kind, perhaps activating automatically by some apparatus they had not noticed – but the door, if door it was, just kept on sliding as if it were without end, able to extrude itself *ad infinitum*.

Then he had it, and he laughed at his own foolishness. 'Of course! It is the disc itself! We have turned away from Stone – "out", I should say – and our course cannot help but bring us right up to the disc's rear face. Being so close to it here, we are not aware of its rotation at all, simply of an overall lateral movement.'

He beamed at Malya in the eerie light, pleased with his deductions, then felt deflated as he saw that familiar contempt, though now it was tempered with humour. *Did it really take you this long to figure it out?* that expression said.

'So,' he grunted testily, 'do we go back?' She pointed to the grille on which they stood. It too was layered with dust and, though less distinct, the footprints were still discernible: they led right up to, and seemingly disappeared through, the moving disc.

Malya glanced over her shoulder suddenly and Jonah started nervously. 'What is it? Is it Frey?' She listened carefully for a moment then shook her head. 'But he will come after us, won't he?' Jonah pressed. 'He will be even more determined once he finds out what happened to his henchmen.'

'He will think hard before leaving the castle himself,' Malya sighed. 'All his work is there, and much of his magic. That's one reason he sent them.'

They did not have to wait long for an answer to the riddle of the disappearing footprints. Without warning the disc revealed an edge, an aperture that wiped out of the slot and opened a way through to the other side. Suddenly they were faced not with a sliding wall but a large gap in the tunnel, a slot cutting through not just the walls but the floor and ceiling as well. It was about eight feet wide – the thickness of the disc; not a difficult jump, but Jonah gave himself a long run-up nevertheless.

As he jumped he felt sudden, brief panic as he wondered how big the aperture in the disc was, and what would happen if it closed on him in mid-leap. He landed heavily, panting, his back slick with sudden sweat. Malya followed close on his heels; three seconds later the aperture closed.

'Still,' gasped Jonah, 'I suppose it is a little like a London cab: if you miss one there will be another along in a minute.'

'You're a strange man, Lightfoot.'

The tunnel continued in sombre mood for another hundred yards or so. If anything it grew lower and narrower, so that at one point they had to crawl. Jonah still could not imagine why the others had not waited for them.

'Have they abandoned us, do you think?' he asked quietly as they paused on the other side of the crawl-space.

'Your friend I cannot speak for, but Gerent would not leave me behind, whatever he thinks of me.'

'What do you mean – what does he think of you?'

She regarded him thoughtfully. 'I love him,' she said finally. 'But he does not love me.' With that said she led a thoughtful Jonah through the last stretch of the tunnel and out into a palace.

He saw at once where they were: they had emerged into the interior of the quicksilver cathedral adhering to the outside of the disc. This first chamber was filled with flickering light. Looking to his left he saw a smooth, silver floor rising in a tight curve to meld into a wide, oval window. The window opened on to a view of the castle; the flickering light, of course, was coming from the fire.

The firelight transformed the silver lining of the chamber into a tapestry of moving colour. Like the exterior, the interior of this palace looked as though it had flowed into place rather than been constructed. The far wall was rippled in a series of concentric circles, the ripples imbued with motion by the light, as though a stone had been dropped into a pond of mercury. Several passages opened from this wall – ways through into the rest of the interior. Blunt spears were suspended from the ceiling like metal stalactites. Hundreds of tiny bodies were lodged among them: long-eared bats, looking exactly like their terrestrial cousins except they were pure white. A thousand reflections stared back at Jonah, flexing like those in a circus Hall of Mirrors, making it hard to delineate the forms.

His eyes were drawn back to the window; the light had dimmed suddenly – was the fire going out at last? What he saw held him rooted to the spot, unable to speak.

A tremendous cloud of smoke had issued from the base of the castle, temporarily obscuring their view. As it cleared a new pyre erupted in the forest behind the castle; Jonah thought of the hummingbirds, of the panic of the animals. Then the upper half of the castle started to tip downwards.

It was slow at first, incredibly slow. Countless tiny explosions, tiny only because they were so far away, blasted blackened timbers from the ruined palisades into the night sky. The entire supporting structure, it seemed, had been made from wood. *What insane architect developed that technique?* Jonah wondered.

As the wooden substructure was squirted out so the heavy upper storeys folded down. The superficial stonework began to slither away like skin drooping from burned flesh, revealing the dense, smoke-filled interior. Timber floors, timber walls, everywhere wood, crumbling now as the battlements they had once held aloft crushed them to powder.

Jonah's uncle had once made a replica of the Palace of Westminster entirely from matchwood. He thought of it now as the once-mighty castle sloughed away from Stone, disintegrating into its component pieces, exposing its heart – matchwood and stone splinters, falling into oblivion.

The rate of collapse increased as gravity sucked at the debris. Now the inner storeys, those backing on to the forest, were shearing away, ripping up blazing trees and adding their own huge momentum to the disaster. Nothing could prevent the destruction – it was unstoppable. Ever more quickly the castle, almost entirely fragmented now, peeled itself away from Stone and tumbled into the night. The fire had become a million minuscule fires, then each individual fire became a descending streak of light, a falling star painting brief orange light across the night sky. The noise arrived, a sad rumbling that went on and on, breaking apart gradually as the castle had broken apart, reducing itself at last to a faint and dwindling crash as the last vestiges fell out of both sight and earshot. Only a few shattered piers remained, poking like broken teeth from the smouldering remains of the forest.

When will it stop? Jonah wondered. *Will it keep falling forever?*

He grew aware again of Malya at his side and put his hand tentatively on her shoulder. 'Your home,' he said gently. 'Your people . . .'

She wiped a single tear from her cheek. 'They were stupid, to the last.'

It was very dark in the chamber now, with only a few fires still burning in the distant forest. Then, one by one, the stalactites began to glow with clean, silver light. The bats detached themselves in eerie silence and flew swiftly through a narrow opening into whatever room lay beyond, a white cloud of wings fleeing the growing brightness.

Malya was pointing at the window and at first Jonah could not see what she was looking at. Then he perceived what looked like a bird outlined against the brightest of the fires. It slipped aside and he could no longer see it. The next time it moved in front of the flames it was a little nearer, and looked now more like the dragon that had attacked the aurochs. The third time it dropped into sight it remained visible for some time, during which he was able properly to make out its shape: it was a man, clearly. A man with wings.

'Faery,' he breathed.

'My father,' Malya announced without emotion. 'He is coming to find us.'

A man from whose back sprang a pair of long, tapering wings. They cycled rhythmically, bringing him forward with a smooth, unhurried motion. Magic.

There was further movement, this time in the nearest of the openings in the far wall. They approached cautiously, discovering as they did so that the floor was slightly concave, an unsettling bowl-shape so smooth it was hard to walk on. There were two figures in the shadow there and he was about to call out in relief when he heard Malya take a sharp breath.

Archan and Gerent were sitting naked together, locked in an elaborate embrace; their clothes lay in a tangle beside them. While Malya trembled with rage beside him, Jonah felt similar anger rise within him. Was it jealousy? He hoped it was more noble – pure anger that Archan should have exploited Annie's captured body in this degrading way. Fear, too, for this act seemed filled with a power he could not identify, something that made Archan more than she had been.

Archan looked round sharply, and Jonah believed that she had not heard them at all, that some sixth sense had alerted her to their presence. She pushed Gerent angrily away and stood abruptly. While he scrambled to dress himself, clearly horrified at having been found, Archan marched straight across the curved floor until she was face to face with Jonah.

Those eyes, he thought tremulously as he stared at his own reflection. *I will never get used to those eyes.*

'How dare you!' she growled, the voice barely human.

She was breathing hard, her whole body was slick with sweat. Those eyes . . . Jonah stared into their mirrors and saw something moving within. Behind the reflections, like bodies trapped beneath ice, swam the twin ghosts of Annie's human eyes. Archan's defences had slipped momentarily and here was all the proof Jonah needed that Annie was still alive.

'You bitch!' screamed Malya, breaking the spell. She hurled herself at Archan.

Archan bent double and raised one arm, driving her elbow into Malya's stomach and then standing suddenly erect, lifting her high. Malya *flew*, landing with a solid thump several yards away. She lay there for some time, her hands straying now to her injured knee, now to her chest, which heaved as she tried to regain her wind.

When Archan turned back her eyes were opaque again. Had Jonah's expression betrayed his discovery? He had no way of knowing.

Frey was much closer now, close enough for the dim light of the stalactites to play across the fabric of his astonishing wings. His face was a pale moon, unreadable. If Archan was surprised she did not show it and, despite himself, Jonah found himself admiring her.

'If we are to receive a guest,' she said smoothly, 'then perhaps I should dress myself. What do you think, Jonah?'

He watched her retreat, trying to ignore Archan and remember Annie, fighting to keep the two identities separate in his mind. It was not easy.

8

Annie on the Inside – 2

'Come,' said the strange, shelled creature that called itself Esh. 'Walk with me and I will tell you of Amara.'

So Annie walked, glancing frequently back over her shoulder to assure herself that the floating window, her way in and out of this dream-world, was still there. In fact, it followed her like a loyal dog. The surface of the ledge felt hard beneath her feet, and she could feel the breath of warm wind across her head and shoulders – dream or not, this place felt real enough.

'Amara, or Stone as it is known colloquially, exists far beyond the parameters of the world you know. Yet the two are inextricably linked.' Esh spoke swiftly and clearly as they walked. Clouds streamed past them; ahead there loomed a great spinning disc that looked to Annie like a gigantic clock-face. 'The physical links are usually flimsy. However, occasionally a stronger connection is forged. This takes tremendous energy.'

'Like from a volcano?'

'That is one possibility.'

They stopped at what seemed to Annie an arbitrary point on the ledge. Without warning, Esh stepped over the edge and into thin air; it hovered there, one arm outstretched to Annie.

'It is quite safe. This is your dream after all.' Was that a smile creasing its alien face?

Gingerly she extended one foot into space. Her stomach lifted as she descended through the air, one hand held lightly by the dry shells of the creature's pincers. She laughed nervously, feeling like a child.

'How come I can understand every word you're saying?' she asked suddenly. Giant blocks of stone rose in her vision, caked with lichen.

'Open your mouth and drink,' said Esh, gesturing expansively with its free arm.

Confused by the apparent *non sequitur,* Annie simply inhaled. 'The air is spicy. And hot.'

'The air of Amara is many things. It will sustain you and nourish you; it will cleanse your body and liberate your mind. It knows much and hides more. It is alive with charm and paints the words you speak into the minds of others. When it rains on Amara, it rains magic.'

Annie thought about this. 'Are you telling me that the air is translating for me?'

'Yes,' said Esh. 'Now, we are here. Steel yourself. There is nothing to fear, but you will be afraid.'

She had no time to quail at its words. The stone block before them bulged, then shattered into a million tiny fragments. She flinched instinctively, covering her face and turning away as the avalanche cascaded across her body, yet she felt nothing. Cautiously she looked back and into a stream of fire.

Flames were pouring out of a hole in the stonework, splashing past their floating bodies but somehow leaving them unharmed. Gradually the flow subsided, to be followed by a tremendous cloud of ash that reminded her all too accurately of the death throes of Krakatoa. It billowed into the sky, where it was quickly shredded by the falling wind, carried into the abyss.

'There!' cried Esh suddenly. It snatched a chunk of rock from the air. The rock was black and porous, hissing violently. It pressed it into her hand and she screamed . . . but it did her no harm, though she felt it searing her skin. Esh closed Annie's fingers tightly over the rock and propelled her straight into the steaming hole in the wall.

There is screaming.

Above a low skyline of red-tiled roofs, the flattened cone of the volcano rises into the night sky. From its broken tip spreads a column of black ash. The rest of the summit is indistinct, and every second that passes sees the lower slopes disappear step by step behind a dark, descending veil of cloud. Something is coming down the mountain towards what looks like a Roman town.

The Roman resort is filled with terrified people. A small child wails inconsolably, her back pressed against the wall of the basilica. Someone snatches her up, cradling her head; parent or passer-by, it is impossible to tell. There is a great crash as a salesman's stock of amphorae is overturned; pottery shards are ground into the road surface by running feet. Nobody cares; death is coming down the mountain.

Annie floats through the crowd, sharing their panic though she is merely a ghost here. Torchlight reveals the child again, bobbing on her saviour's shoulder; her arms are clutched round the man's neck. Annie hopes it is her father. The child's eyes meet Annie's and widen momentarily – has the girl seen her? Annie pursues the man, flitting through unseen spaces in the throng, a spirit-woman eavesdropping on disaster.

The side streets are awakening to the catastrophe. Slaves are slamming doors and crying to each other; women stare in bemusement from upper storey windows. Annie follows a torrent of fleeing people into a boathouse near the waterfront. Mud cakes the floor; nobody cares. A man, tall and elegant, waves them down a set of steps into a dark place.

The little girl's face appears again, briefly, a tiny star disappearing into the gloom. She is calling out something, but all Annie can hear is the screaming. She is about to descend with them when she hears the thunder.

She cannot resist its call. Rising through the roof she emerges above the town.

The mountain has gone. All she can see, from horizon to horizon, is a billowing wall of black ash. It careers through the trees towards the town; the instant it touches the trees they snap and burn away. The speed at which the cloud moves is breathtaking: deadly beauty. It reaches the outskirts and buildings begin to disintegrate.

Annie drops again, her ghost-body penetrating the darkness until she is huddled with the people in the boathouse. The space is packed with bodies. Nobody is screaming any more; the silence is a solid presence, like death.

There is an incongruous animal noise and something big moves in the corner: somebody has brought a horse down here. A man – a soldier – pushes through and tries to placate the terrified beast. Annie plunges forward, seeking the little girl.

Outside there is a single scream, cut off abruptly.

A cloud of ash as hot as a furnace drives its way into the boathouse. The people die quickly, all except the soldier, who has been pressed against the wall by the horse. The horse's body protects him. Annie watches him with ghastly curiosity as he struggles to breathe.

Then a weird, new light enters the chamber. The wall peels apart beside the soldier's twitching feet, admitting clean, blue air. He falls to his knees and scrabbles at the dirt on the floor. An opening has formed just big enough for him to squeeze through; this he does, neither asking nor comprehending what has delivered this salvation.

His whole upper body is through now but there is a metallic thud as his sword catches against the side of the aperture. His hand snakes back and draws the sword – a short, stabbing weapon – out through the hole. Before he can wriggle the last three feet a fresh load of ash collapses on to his legs, searing the flesh from them in an instant. He does not even have time to scream.

The chamber is filled to the ceiling with ash and Annie can see nothing. There is a muffled sound near the hole in the wall. She slips through *the wall and is dazzled by the brilliant light of Amara.*

Looking back she saw the dead soldier's head and torso, his outstretched arm. The sword lay just short of the opening. A small, black creature was at work in the hole, extruding a thick, glutinous substance from beneath its carapace and smearing it across the rear wall of the cavity.

'What the hell is that?' she demanded, waving at the tortoise-like animal.

'We are Ypoth – the caretakers of Amara, you might say. Whenever a threshold is made between Stone and the world you think of as your own, we repair the damage.'

'That's an Ypoth?' Annie asked. Esh nodded. She frowned. 'And you're an Ypoth too?' Again it nodded; was it smiling again? 'Well, forgive me, but you don't exactly look like brothers!' Her anger felt very real. She could not erase the image of the little girl's face from her mind.

'When a breach is made in the fabric of Stone – as you have witnessed here – a passage is opened between worlds. Such breaches – with a few important exceptions – must be repaired immediately. At such a site, one or more Ypoth appear and work to fill the hole. We excrete a resin that is identical to the structure of Stone itself – the bond is perfect.'

'Wait a second: "appear"? What does that mean?'

'We ourselves are . . . excreted by Stone.'

'What are you saying? You're saying the wall shits you out and then you shit out new bits of the wall?'

'That is a fair metaphor.'

Annie whistled through her teeth. 'Now I've heard everything. So how come you look so different to that thing?'

'Different events create thresholds of different sizes. The one through which you came,' here Esh bowed its head, 'and which I had the honour to be born into, was of unusual size.'

Annie remembered Krakatoa. 'Yeah, right.'

'And so it will take a correspondingly long time to repair. The longer the Ypoth live the more they evolve. I am the result of several days of evolution – this creature here, born alone into a relatively small breach, will not develop much beyond its current level before it is reabsorbed.'

They were still floating before the hard, black mouth of the hole. Annie watched the tortoise-beast labouring mindlessly, considering its unenviable destiny.

'I reckon that stinks, Esh, if you don't mind me saying. You do all that good work and then this Stone or Amara, or whatever it's called, just sucks you back in again.' She regarded Esh shrewdly. 'No wonder you rebelled.'

If the creature was surprised it did not show it. 'It is uncommon for the Ypoth to live outside the confines of the thresholds that spawn them. Some might even say it is forbidden. As long as I remain on the outside I will not be subject to the ultimate degeneration that awaits my siblings. Indeed, I may continue to evolve, though slowly now that I have abandoned the interior of Amara.'

'Forbidden? So you really are a rebel then – I like that in a tortoise, Esh. Do I get to know why you're taking such a risk? I guess it is a risk?'

Esh looked grave – if she was reading its expression correctly. It drew her gently back up to the level of the ledge. When they alighted it faced her and rested its arms lightly on her shoulders, an intimate and strangely human posture. She gazed into liquid green eyes.

'Your arrival, and that of your companions, on to Amara was a remarkable event, not just because of the magnitude of the eruption that brought you here. Your presence here gives us much to hope for . . . and much to fear. Both Jonah

Lightfoot and Archan possess the power to change Amara, and not necessarily for the better.' The green eyes seemed to glow, to penetrate hers. 'And you, Annie West. I think perhaps you will be a part of it all too. Yes, I do.

'I have abandoned my brethren to act as guide to you and Jonah Lightfoot and, if need be, the dragon Archan. In doing so I have taken a great risk, for no Ypoth has ever spent so long beyond its birthplace; it may kill me, or I may thrive, there is no way of knowing. The risk is great; the potential reward for all Amara is immeasurable.

'Your coming here is the single most important event since the creation of Amara. I witnessed it, and I have been chosen to guide it forward as best I can. I hope I am up to the task.' Esh bowed its head.

Annie shivered, unable to unlock her gaze from Esh's.

'When will I see Jonah again?' she managed to ask weakly. 'When will I be free again?'

'Soon, I hope, if all goes well. Your time here with me now is valuable, Annie West, do not forget that. One day you will be required to use what you learn here. Remember all that you see, remember it.' Its voice was growing hypnotic and she felt her eyelids drooping. 'As a result of your coming here, Amara will change. And if Amara changes, everything changes; everything you have ever known, everything you have ever been. Its connections with the world you know are not limited to the merely physical . . .'

She was drifting now, listening but not heeding. Something else was intruding – she felt simultaneously hot and cold, feverish.

Suddenly she wanted to be away from here, away from this alien creature who spoke in riddles. Turning her back on Esh she blundered through the window that still loitered behind her; a degree of calm returned as she entered her hall of *ma-chong* tiles once more, but all too soon the heat started to race again.

Excited now, she mounted the winding staircase and peered out from a gap in the upper level of tiles. It was still hot here in the interior of her mind, hot with dragon flames, but the flames were moving erratically, leaping up and drawing back, revealing gaps. She felt for Archan's presence and found it there but remote, distracted. Beyond the gaps in the fire was emptiness at first, then an image.

Eyes, staring back at her own. The outline of a human face – Jonah's face!

'Jonah!' she screamed. 'I'm here! I'm in here! Help me!'

She strained at the tiles but they would not budge.

Rapunzel, let down thy hair . . .

Jonah disappeared in a flurry of motion and there was a glimpse of another face, a woman she did not recognise. Then the fire reared up and Archan was back.

Flames lashed up the sides of her *ma-chong* tower, which disintegrated at once, leaving her naked and alone, a prisoner with no cell now but the walls of her own mind. She cowered as the fire seared her thoughts, retreating again into that tiny, primal place where, she hoped, the dragon could not reach her.

Her window on the miraculous world of Amara was gone, as was the sanctuary of her imaginary tower. All that remained was the minute nugget of her consciousness, adrift on a sea of flame.

9

DownStone

They slept alone, each of them. As soon as it became obvious that Frey had bypassed the palace altogether, and that they would receive no visitors that night, they drifted one by one into different corners of the chamber and settled down to rest as best they could.

Before he found his own retreat, Jonah stood at the window on the downStone side, watching as the winged man flew off into the starless night. Stone was an uncompromising slab dotted with lights – fires or furnaces or phosphorescence, he could not tell. Whatever their source, it seemed the further he travelled the more there was to see. Were there cities this way? Settlements of people drawn from his world as he had been, as the Neolithic tribe had been? He thought of the Roman sword; were there Egyptians here, and Sumerians, *homo Neandertalis*, men from the distant past?

There was too much to consider. Exhausted – in a single day he had outrun a herd of aurochs, climbed down a castle wall and fought with a vengeful Neolithic knight – he selected a small alcove near the window and curled himself into it. Less than a minute later he was asleep.

Malya and Gerent had already left when Jonah woke up. Archan was standing like a statue before him. He rose and stretched, his back stiff; the floor was hard.

Behind Archan the upStone window revealed the dawn. The sun – a fat, orange disc – slid out sideways from behind the still-smouldering roots of the castle. Searching beams of light cast elongated forest-shadows across the surface of Stone. Orange turned rapidly to yellow and then bright white, a dust-rich glow filling the chamber with ethereal light.

Jonah felt ferociously hungry. He tried to reassure himself that the air was delivering all the nutrients he needed, but his stomach was not easily convinced.

'This body yearns for food too,' announced Archan, eyeing Jonah as he rubbed his belly absently.

'What? Oh, I see. Where are the others?'

'In the next chamber.'

The next chamber proved to be considerably smaller than the entrance hall. Its curved inner surfaces were lined with the same silvery metal, but on the floor was inlaid an abstract coloured pattern: a swirl of blues and greens that made Jonah think of a sea-battle, Trafalgar perhaps. A single glowing stalactite illuminated the windowless space. Several low doorways spaced around the walls led into similar rooms, which in turn led to a larger array further on – Jonah sensed a maze expanding before them and cautioned Archan against venturing too far.

'They went this way,' she replied confidently, and he had little choice but to follow her into the honeycomb.

The only obvious difference between each room was the picture on the floor. A few were recognisable – here was a clear representation of a pitcher pouring red liquid (blood?) into a shallow bowl – but most were abstract. All of them seemed concerned with violence in some way, and this disturbed Jonah.

'Why did you behave so improperly?' he asked abruptly. They had paused in a room whose floor was a mass of broken yellow scales, tightening into a whirlpool at the centre.

'That is an impertinent question, faery. Especially for one of your sensibilities.'

'What do you know of my sensibilities?' He felt cross and embarrassed and wished he had not spoken. Intrigued though: was Archan learning to read his human ways at last or was this Annie coming through again?

She looked down, considering the picture set into the floor. 'Very like the scales of a dragon, do you not think, faery? When I was a dragon I had little enough time for love. But a million years is a long time – a million years deprived of all physical contact.'

'Do not pretend that your actions had anything to do with love.'

'Jealous, faery? There are words in here.' She tapped Annie's head. '"Agape" is among them – do you know what that means?'

'Christian love. Brotherly love, if you like. Don't pretend that you . . .'

'In contrast there is "erotic",' she interrupted. 'I was a beautiful dragon, faery – and terrible. Male dragons considered me strange, but they could not resist me. All the love I experienced was what you would consider to be "erotic". Eroticism is what I do best, you might say.'

Jonah really was embarrassed now. Archan was holding Annie's body quite still before him now, hands held loosely at her side, fully clothed and superficially quite proper. But underneath, behind the formal stance, behind the mirrors of her eyes . . . there was such a fire! He felt himself flushing.

'You deny the erotic in favour of agape, faery. Hence you are repressed. I am not like you.'

She turned on her heel and moved towards the next doorway.

'Are you telling me that, in your own way, you love Gerent?'

In the shadow beneath the doorway she paused, her head cocked. 'As a dragon I would say "yes", but bearing in mind a gap of understanding between us that spans a million years, I will answer that in terms you can understand: *I have never loved anything in my life.*'

Seven rooms further on they caught up with the others. How Archan had found her way through the labyrinth Jonah could not begin to guess. But then, she was not human.

He felt clear-headed, able to separate the dragon from the woman again. He had come to a realisation too: *part of him actually enjoyed the company of the dragon.* It was hard to admit this to himself, so entangled was the admission with feelings of guilt, but this morning he felt particularly rational; he was, for the time being at least, willing to believe that Archan's actions were more to do with self-preservation than malice. That Annie had simply been in the wrong place at the wrong time.

That it could have been me and not Annie! The thought made him shudder.

He could not say that he liked Archan, but equally he did not hate her. 'A gap of understanding', she had said and he supposed that was fair. A million years was a long time, after all.

'I will not hate her,' he resolved quietly to himself. 'When she finds a dragon host she will transfer her spirit out of Annie's body again and all will be well.'

Nasty questions rose then, questions he did not much like and which he pressed back down again. Questions like: 'What of the unfortunate dragon whose body she chooses?' And: 'How much of Annie will be left behind?'

How much of her was left even now?

Round and round the debate whirled in his head until soon his thinking was not so clear as it had been. It was with relief that he joined the others at the single exit to this final room, a wide arch opening into a long corridor leading both out and in. Tall windows perforated the corridor's wall, affording a spectacular view across sunlit Stone.

Malya was already talking when he arrived; her voice was flat and toneless. Gerent stood with his back to her, staring out at the sky.

'We have no reason to explore this building further,' she was saying. 'We must head in again. Once we regain the surface we can continue downStone.'

Jonah looked back only once as they followed Malya along the corridor. He wondered what marvels they had left unseen within the greater bulk of the palace.

They proceeded in silence until the corridor looped to the right. Here the ceiling lowered again and the smooth floor was replaced by the familiar grillework. Insects chirped softly in the wall pipes. A tight switchback led them to a moving wall which, as they now knew, was the revolving disc; they waited for a slot to open then jumped through one by one. Archan was last to jump, a split-second before the aperture closed – it scissored shut just behind her, almost catching her foot in its jaws, and Jonah had to stifle a cry. She regarded him balefully and they moved on.

The light was that of a cool, crisp morning but the air remained warm and humid. They were sheltered from the wind by a canopy covering the ledge leading out from behind the disc. Here, on the downStone side of the palace, was a similar pathway to the one they had travelled the previous day – a ledge about three yards wide adhering to the side of Stone like some gigantic mantel shelf.

Machinery littered the ledge, forcing them to pick their way between valves and cogs and unidentifiable pieces of industrial wreckage. This linear wasteland was overgrown with moss and lichen, and everywhere grew the same purple flowers, *prince's feather*.

Then, not a hundred yards beyond the outer edge of the spinning disc, the ledge came to an abrupt end.

It was a clean break, clearly intentional. Malya and Gerent had already examined it when Jonah caught them up and were now squinting into the distance, trying to make out details in the haze. Archan stood back from the edge, arms crossed, eyes closed as if meditating. Presently Gerent grunted and trotted back towards the palace.

'Where is he going?' asked Jonah. Malya shrugged and mumbled something that might have been, 'Good riddance,' though Jonah could not be sure.

Lowering himself on to his stomach, he extended his head out over the edge of the shelf and peered downwards. Stone plunged with what was becoming a familiar spectacle, though it still took his breath away. He was interested in something below, a mile or so down, as near as he could judge. It was another ledge, much wider than the one on which he lay, and on it was what looked like a small town.

A patchwork of pale brown buildings was arrayed around a central complex, some kind of forum, Jonah guessed. The radial pattern was divided by several main thoroughfares and many smaller streets. Tiny dots moved along these ways, their shadows long and mobile: people!

The upStone area bore few buildings; here instead were massed fields of familiar purple, entire meadows of *prince's feather*. Larger dots were in motion in the middle of one of the meadows – beasts of burden, perhaps tamed aurochs. From a long, narrow building at the edge of the meadow a plume of smoke drifted out into the sky before plunging down into the soft, white mist.

Only a mile away, thought Jonah wistfully, wondering what people it was that inhabited that village on the edge of the sky. *Yet so far*.

Indeed, there was no obvious way down to the settlement,

nor was it near enough to send any kind of signal. *Were I to drop a message, it would undoubtedly hit some poor soul on the head and kill them!* Tantalised, frustrated, Jonah lifted himself up again.

Immediately beyond the end of the ledge something had been attached to Stone. It looked to Jonah like a single railway track, turned on its side and bolted into the stonework. It sloped downwards, but as he followed its line downStone he saw that it was in fact following a curve, that some considerable distance further on it flattened out before rising again. It occurred to him that, if he were to view this rail from some vantage point out in the sky – a dragon's-eye view, as it were – then it would look rather like a smiling mouth.

The far end of the rail was almost lost in the thickening atmospheric haze, although he could just make out a shape that might have been a continuation of the ledge on which they now stood. Visibility was poor today, and getting steadily worse; the air felt clammy, laden with moisture.

'Does it ever rain here?' he asked Malya, wiping the sweat from his face, to little avail.

'Occasionally,' she replied absently.

Gerent returned holding a long metal rod. Jonah saw Archan open one, silvery eye as he passed, then close it again and return to her trance. Malya studiously ignored the prince as he dropped to his knees and swept a layer of dust from the ground. Soon he found what he was searching for – an oblong indentation in the upper surface of the ledge, like a depressed flagstone. In the centre of the depression was a black sphere, half-buried, with a circular hole in the top. With some effort he inserted the end of the rod into the hole and pulled.

Malya watched contemptuously as the slightly-built Gerent tried to haul the rod over like a lever. He managed to pull it partway (this feat was accompanied by a series of grinding screeches from the dust-locked sphere) before losing his grip and falling awkwardly to the ground. She snorted, spat on her hands and grasped the lever herself. The muscles in her arms bulged as she threw her weight behind it then, with a shriek of protest the rod moved all the way over, dumping her into Gerent's lap.

So keen was she to break contact with him that she kicked him back down to the ground in her hurry to get up. He scowled at her in turn, righting himself with quiet dignity. Jonah found the whole sideshow absurd in the extreme: it seemed clear to him that, far from despising her, Gerent was besotted with Malya. Why she could not see this, and why he would not admit it, was quite beyond him.

At first nothing happened, then a faint whine penetrated the air. Jonah eventually pinpointed the sound to the metal rail bolted to Stone: it was vibrating. There was a deeper sound too, a rumbling sound . . .

'There,' said Archan quietly. She had joined them beside the lever. 'In the distance.'

A line had resolved itself within the haze, a slender column sliding towards them with increasing speed. It grew as it approached, flashed briefly gold as it caught the morning sun then turned brilliant yellow. Its lower end was running along the curved rail; its upper part was hidden in cloud. The rumbling became very loud as it neared.

'It is like a pendulum!' exclaimed Jonah, suddenly seeing it for what it was. 'Its pivot is attached to Stone somewhere high above us, out of sight, and its bob is free to slide along this rail! Why, what Foucault would not have given to see such a thing!'

'Who is Foucault?' asked Archan sharply.

'Oh, a famous physicist. He demonstrated the rotation of the earth in Paris – in 1851, I think it was.' *The same year as the Great Exhibition*, he thought absently.

'That's as may be,' barked Malya, herding them back from the edge, 'but that pendulum, or whatever-it-is, is getting too close for my liking!'

The rail was squealing like a fingernail drawn across a blackboard. And the pendulum, looming like a ship in the mist, was getting awfully close.

But it was slowing visibly, and by the time it reached the ledge it was moving at no more than a normal man's walking pace. It struck the ledge with a solid thump; immediately there came a new sound, a complex mechanical chord that reminded Jonah of a key being turned in a lock. The pendulum stopped dead, and it seemed fair to assume that a lock had indeed been activated, that hidden beneath the ledge was some giant latch on to which it had attached itself.

They looked at the pendulum in the ensuing silence. It was truly enormous, as wide as the ledge, but so tall! It rose up the face of Stone like a slender tower of Babel, piercing the heavens, its top quite invisible. Its surface was smooth gold, slightly tarnished. A series of rungs led up the near side to a square hole just above Jonah's eye level; this hole had been bored all the way through the pendulum, and looked big enough to house them all.

They all seemed to understand the purpose of the strange apparatus without needing to discuss it. Archan climbed up first, seating herself at the far end of the square cave and grasping a convenient rail with both hands. Gerent went next, followed by Jonah.

'Do you want some help?' Jonah called down to Malya, who was bracing herself against the lever again. She did not even look up.

At first it looked as though the lever had stuck fast. Then, her face bright scarlet with the effort, Malya heaved it back in the downStone direction. Immediately the pendulum unlatched itself and started to swing.

'Malya!' shouted Gerent, the first word he had spoken to her all day. She half-fell, clearly dizzy, then lunged for the nearest rung. Her sweat-slicked fingers slipped free and she fell to her knees. The gap between the ledge and the accelerating pendulum widened. Then, with a hearty roar, she jumped.

She jumped up as well as across, and that was probably what saved her. Gerent was already leaning out from the hole, so far that Jonah was forced to throw himself across his legs to stop him sliding out. Malya's fingers contacted not the rung but the prince's outstretched hand, which clamped around hers. A split-second later his other hand was around her wrist and he was hauling her up. Jonah felt his stomach lurch as the pendulum's bob plummeted along the downward slope of its curved path, and helped Gerent scramble her fully aboard. They all managed to grab one of the handrails that some thoughtful manufacturer had positioned all around the interior of the open-ended cabin; after that it was simply a matter of hanging on grimly until they reached the end of the orbit.

Throughout the short journey the rail emitted its high-pitched whine. Whatever system of wheels or pulleys it was that connected pendulum to track, it was Jonah's considered opinion that a quantity of oil was required.

The pendulum passed through the lowest part of its arc then began to ascend. The centrifugal effect that had kept them firmly pressed against the cabin floor began to release them as it decelerated towards its rest position. Presently, having slowed to a crawl, it thudded gently into its downStone latch and came to a halt. They had arrived.

A matching set of rungs on the other side of the pendulum delivered them on to yet another ledge, this one much wider, as wide as a London street in fact. Jonah stretched his arms out and turned round slowly, luxuriating in the feeling of security this extra space gave him. He could almost forget the abyss skulking beneath the road.

Malya was already marching on, with Archan striding elegantly in her footsteps. Jonah touched Gerent's arm before he too made off.

'How did you know about the pendulum?' he demanded. 'And how did you know where to find that lever?'

'I just thought about it,' the prince replied dismissively. Then he relented. 'If you must know, when I saw the break in the ledge I remembered one of the floor-pictures back in the palace. It showed the curved track, and what looked like a lever sticking out of the ground. I had seen a metal rod lying amongst all the junk behind the disc, so I went and fetched it. The rest was just common sense. I didn't know what the lever would do, but it seemed logical to suppose it had something to do with a way across the gap.'

'Well, with your brains and Malya's brawn you make a good team.'

'I'm not smart,' Gerent muttered. 'I just remember things.'

'That makes you smart in my book, Prince Gerent.'

They travelled along the road for the rest of the day, watching their shadows swing round behind them as the sun overtook them on its own journey downStone. Towards dusk, they came upon a ramshackle collection of tents pitched close to Stone's sheer wall. A fire was burning near the entrance of the largest. Cautiously they approached.

A strikingly tall, black-skinned woman – seven feet tall if she was an inch – emerged from one of the smaller tents, reacting to their presence with an almost comical jump before ducking back inside. A moment later she emerged again, this time with a companion, another woman fully a head taller still. They loitered beside the campfire, whispering and clasping each other's hands.

'We will share your fire,' said Archan without preamble, seating herself cross-legged before the blaze. The taller of the women hissed and reached beneath her robe, a bright blue sari-like garment that covered her body from neck to ankle.

'Forgive our companion,' said Gerent swiftly and smoothly. 'She is simple-minded, and does not know when she offends.' Archan graced him with a smile that was somehow ferocious, like a big cat's.

'She has enchanted eyes,' said the shorter woman, regarding Archan warily. Her voice was cracked but her words, thanks to the translating power of the air, were clear enough.

'Go on your way,' added the other, her face hard.

'We have a little food,' Gerent went on doggedly, reaching into his pouch. 'We will gladly share it with you.'

'Begone!' A third voice shouted from the large tent. A third woman was peering out, her face old and wrinkled; the firelight sparkled off bared teeth sharpened to needle points. 'Take your magic, dragon-people. Take your trouble to the serpents – we do not want it here.'

'What does she mean, "dragon-people"?' Jonah whispered to Malya, who had circled round behind him, hand at her hip as if to draw Tamon's sword. She did not reply, instead creeping towards the tent. The women hissed again but did not try to stop her. She bent and lifted something from the ground, something long and white: a bone.

'My father has come this way already,' she hissed in reply, pointing to more bones scattered on the ground.

The taller woman was looking closely at Malya. 'You have the face of the dragon-man!' she wailed. 'Go before the serpents fall upon us!'

'What did he do to you?' asked Malya softly. 'We will not hurt you. Please, just tell us what he did.'

In the end there was little enough the women could tell them. They were nomads, they explained, sisters wandering the ledges of Stone in search of a way back to their home.

'We remember fields of green,' said the taller of the two by the fire. Their elderly sibling, still huddled inside the tent, scolded her for being so free with her tongue but the others shrugged off her protests. 'We remember the hunting, and the way the sun rose high and bright. We moved with the herds, and we move still, though the herds are gone. This falling world is not our home.'

'There were men,' elaborated the shorter woman. They were from Africa, Jonah had decided, but from what age in the history of the world he had no idea. 'But we alone came through. Five sisters.'

'Now three,' whispered the taller.

'What did my father do?' repeated Malya.

'He killed Rass!' howled the woman in the tent. 'Can you not see her bones before you, ignorant girl? He killed Rass and took Shafan, took her off into the sky, no doubt to have his way with her and then kill her as he killed our sister! A thousand curses be on you all if you know this dragon-man. Go now, and leave us to our grief.'

And though they tried to coax them the women would say no more. In the end they retreated inside the tent again and would not be drawn out. After a brief discussion the travellers left a small pile of dried meat beside the fire before moving off into the night.

Looking back, Jonah saw the firelight illuminating the bones, and thought the payment quite insufficient.

Jonah could not get the sisters out of his mind. Were they typical of the castaways this place attracted, lost souls desperate to see their homeland again? He tried to quiz Malya on how the Denneth had perceived their place on Stone, but she was absorbed in Gerent's company. She and the prince had taken to walking hand in hand, and when they finally stopped for the night the two of them disappeared into the silent darkness, leaving him to huddle alone against the bare wall of Stone.

Archan stood for the entire night, as near as Jonah could judge. Leastways, each time he awoke from a fitful sleep she was standing nearby, staring out into the void.

The next day saw a great fog descend. The formerly poor visibility was reduced almost to nothing, and the temperature of the air seemed to have soared even higher. It was like being in a Roman *caldarium*, Jonah decided, a giant steam-bath in which it was impossible to cool oneself. Sweat refused to evaporate into the already saturated air; it was like being boiled alive.

Fortunately Stone ran freely with its version of streams here: narrow channels etched into the wall surface containing miniature torrents of icy water. They stopped frequently to drink and duck their heads, splashing their feet in the gutters along which the water flowed briefly before plunging through drainage holes on its constant journey downwards.

Gerent and Malya continued to walk together, talking constantly and occasionally laughing out loud, sharing some secret joke. It warmed Jonah's heart to see them reconciled at last. It increased his sense of loneliness too.

New landscape began to rise out of the fog. They journeyed into a region where the surface of Stone was swollen and distorted. Great lumps of rock spilled out across the road, pushing them out towards the edge and several times forcing them to climb over outcrops and scale small cliffs. Though his sense of direction was lost, the ache in Jonah's legs told him they were steadily ascending.

A rounded hilltop blessed with a scattering of soil and even a few blades of wiry grass led them on to a wide, wooden bridge. The contrast was sudden and jarring, solid land giving way to rickety human construction. Ropes, their anchor points unseen in the fog, creaked as they stepped out across the bridge and the planked deck swayed ominously.

'What lies down there, I wonder?' said Jonah to himself as he glanced down. The fog parted momentarily, affording him a glimpse of the depths through a narrow chimney of almost clear air.

'Shit!' Malya's voice called back; she was a formless grey blur some way ahead.

'Are you all right?' he called.

'We're fine. I was answering your question.'

'What? Oh, I see. But what do you mean . . . er, what you said?'

Malya and Gerent solidified as he drew near to them. Archan was some way behind them all. 'Just that,' said Malya. 'Some say that what's down there is a huge sea of shit.'

Jonah shook his head, confused.

'Think about it,' she said with a theatrical sigh. 'What do you do with something you don't want? – you throw it over the edge. Where do you take a crap? – over the edge. Imagine all the rubbish that gets hurled over the edge, all the sewage pipes that run down the surface of Stone, all the corpses that find their way into the pit. Everything heading down. It's got to stop somewhere, that's what I say.'

Gerent was grinning. 'Is that what you think?' Jonah asked him.

'I don't have a better answer,' the prince shrugged.

They walked on.

On the other side of the bridge the road was narrower but the rocky outcrops were less intrusive. They made good progress and by the afternoon the air had begun to clear a little.

Jonah was squinting into the drifting fog, trying to identify a looming shape that was, he guessed, some hundred yards distant, when he heard what he thought at first to be human voices chattering somewhere above his head.

'Is someone there?' he called nervously, remembering Tamon's attack.

The ensuing silence was worse than the chattering. Then a dark shape scurried past, followed by another and then another. He thought at first they were more mountain goats, until he looked up and saw a group of monkeys swinging exuberantly from a wooden structure resembling the bridge they had crossed earlier that day, though on a much smaller scale.

They were black and white, very like Colobus monkeys, except their arms were extraordinarily long and seemed to have too many joints. Looking closely, Jonah saw that the bones of their hands were grossly elongated and, he surmised, fused together. Thus their wrists had in effect become secondary elbows. The hands at the ends of these extended limbs were necessarily simplified, lacking as they did the metacarpal bones that had fused to form the additional levers, but the monkeys did not appear to lack dexterity. On the contrary, they leaped and clambered with all the skill of their terrestrial counterparts, grabbing ropes and spars with agile fingers and swooping in complex, triple-jointed manoeuvres as the troop performed for the human wanderers.

The process of evolution, wondered Jonah. *Natural selection moulding the physical form into infinite variety. How many generations did it take for these monkeys to develop as they have? Fifty? A hundred? A thousand?*

Through another break in the mist, near the cavorting monkeys, he saw there was indeed a group of the large-horned mountain goats grazing on a grass-covered slope leading down to the high-level bridge. He tried to recall a tale from childhood that scratched, half-remembered, at the corner of his memory. *Prince's feather* grew amid the grass; brightly-coloured hummingbirds floated like butterflies between the small, purple blooms.

The shape in the distance proved to be another cliff, this one quite high. They scaled it with care, using Malya's rope. Jonah noticed two new weapons hanging from her belt as she helped him over the last overhang – another short sword and a metal-handled axe. Where did she find such things, this strange scavenger-warrior?

Atop the cliff the road continued after a fashion, although now it was reduced to a narrow, winding track. The rock outcrops were back with a vengeance, strident towers carved by runnels of water, turning the landscape into one of mountain pass and sudden drop. The going was slow and difficult.

It took two more days for the dense fog to clear; even then a heavy haze remained. Not that they could see very far ahead anyway, so labyrinthine had the landscape become. On the morning of the third day Gerent called them together.

'It cannot be far to the dragons' home,' he announced. He was seated comfortably on a natural throne of rock at the end of the narrow pass in which they had spent the night. Malya squatted between his feet, one arm resting lightly on his thigh.

'Are you tired, little faery?' Archan asked her scornfully. She had said little to any of them during the journey through the mountainous terrain; now, it seemed, she was ready to make up for it. 'Shall I go on alone now?'

'You'd like that, wouldn't you, bitch?' said Malya mildly.

'We can at least be civil to each other,' began Jonah, trying to keep his tone good-natured.

'I agree,' answered Archan, surprising them all. She levelled her unearthly gaze on Gerent. 'I apologise for seducing you, faery.' Then, looking at Malya, she added, 'and I apologise for taking him from you.'

The jaws of both Gerent and Malya dropped open in slow synchronisation. Before either of them could compose a suitable reply, Archan was going on. 'I have not been a suitable companion. I ask you now to forgive me, and to understand that I am very different from you all.'

'Who are you?' whispered Gerent.

And so she told them. Jonah knew most of it, but to the Neolithics it came as a complete surprise to learn that their strange companion was not the human female she appeared to be, but a dragon passenger in a human body. Archan spoke eloquently, if vaguely, about her life before the event she called the *turning of the world,* about how she absorbed the magic of the mysterious *basilisks* and became immortal. About how she waited for a million years before riding on a wave of volcanic fire into the world of Stone on a mission to find a dragon host whose body she might steal to make her own.

Here she paused and cast her shining eyes down. 'You may consider this a dishonourable quest, concerned as it is with the taking of another creature's life. But the dragon I have chosen is the very beast you wish dead. Can we not work together to achieve our common goal?'

'What about Annie?' interjected Jonah.

Archan turned towards him. 'I give you my solemn vow that there is no reason for this host to be harmed in any way, if I am able to perform the final transfer successfully.'

Jonah considered this promise and found it wanting, but decided not to pursue the matter further for the time being. He was more concerned with Archan's sudden change in attitude, her uncharacteristic humility. She was being *pleasant,* for heaven's sake!

And the Neolithics seemed to be accepting it. Malya still looked wary but she had relaxed visibly; Gerent's face was open, with even the trace of a smile skirting the corners of his mouth. She was winning them over, and Jonah had no idea why she was doing it.

She talked further as Gerent led them forward through the precarious rock formations, drawing out from the Neolithic couple what little information they had regarding the dragon settlement.

'Is it a fortress?' she asked. 'Dragons were great builders in the days of charm, and this place of stone and sky is the perfect site for a dragon stronghold.'

Gerent shrugged. 'Nobody knows – except Frey perhaps.' A sideways glance at Malya, whose expression did not change at the mention of her father's name.

'It *is* a fortress,' Archan said under her breath. 'A place of great power, great charm. Can you not feel it?' She cried out these last words, spinning round suddenly with her arms spread wide and her head lifted to the sky. 'It is near, so near!'

Jonah found himself gradually being excluded from the group. Gerent and Malya were by now inseparable, clinging to each other, helping each other through the narrow passages and over the higher obstacles. Archan was shadowing them like an obedient dog, asking them questions constantly, even when it had become obvious she had drained them of information. With the exception of a moment when he fell, bruising his shin, and Malya trotted back to ask if he was all right, Jonah was effectively alone.

The rocky terrain ended abruptly. The way ahead was reduced to a precarious wooden deck, comprising a series of thin planks set into Stone, each one spaced some distance from its neighbour. The planks retreated into the ubiquitous haze like a set of railway sleepers from which the track had been removed, providing not so much a path as a series of stepping stones.

The individual 'sleepers' (each had one end embedded in Stone, the other thrust into empty sky) were reassuringly wide, and close enough together that they did not need to jump from one to the next, only stride. Still, it was disconcerting; more than once Jonah found himself hypnotised by the strobing of the light-coloured mist visible through the gaps and was forced to pause and retime his steps.

Not a place where you want to step on a crack, he decided with some apprehension.

Eventually they reached a stretch where the sleepers closed together to form an unbroken bridge. A little further on still they came up against a sheer wall made from a weird crystalline material. Brilliant red, it threw back their reflections as distorted and bloodied echoes of their real selves. The junction of this new stuff with the surface of Stone was strangely blurred, hard to see in a way Jonah found impossible to describe. When he tried to touch the seam his fingers skated elsewhere as though they were magnets repelled by an opposing field.

The crystal wall was immense, extending out well beyond the edge of the wooden bridge and climbing high into the tumbling mist. At first Jonah imagined it was simply another barrier, as effective in its way as the spikes with their lethal skirts, but then Archan spoke.

'I think we have arrived, my faery friends.' She reached out Annie's hand and delicately touched the crystal. 'I think this is the fortress of the dragons of Stone.'

Jonah gulped, unable to prevent a shudder travelling the length of his spine. Despite the heat, he felt suddenly cold.

'It is too slippery to climb,' observed Gerent. 'We have reached another dead end.'

'Not necessarily,' murmured Archan, caressing the crystal with both hands. She pressed the side of Annie's head against it as though listening for something.

'What do you hear?' Jonah asked.

'I hear nothing. I feel much . . . vibrations, the beating of dragon wings. There are tunnels inside this crystal wall, many of them. I can feel the motion of dragons through the tunnels they have cut for themselves. There must be a way inside.'

'There is no door,' ventured Jonah.

Like a doctor probing a patient's chest Archan continued to listen at the wall, now crouching, now stretching on tiptoe, now spreading herself quite flat as if to absorb whatever it was she felt through the whole of Annie's borrowed skin. Her movements were staccato, reminding Jonah not so much of the reptile he knew to be hiding within, but of a bird. He noticed that her hands were trembling.

He turned away, turned out to face the sky, and found himself looking straight into the eyes of Malya's father, Frey, shaman to the Neolithic tribe known as the Denneth.

Malya saw him at the same instant; she hissed and gripped Gerent's arm tight enough to make him flinch. She took a step forward, hesitated, then stepped back again, pressing her back into the prince's belly. Her hand hovered over the weapons on her belt.

The shaman was hovering about ten feet beyond the edge of the wooden bridge. Long wings tapered to either side, beating a slow, precise rhythm through the vaporous air. This close, the illusion that the man was a faery was quite destroyed, for it was obvious that the wings were not his own.

They were attached to a leather harness strapped tightly around his chest and shoulders. Each wing was long as the man was tall. Built from shining, metallic scales, they seemed to be powered by a network of sinews bunched behind Frey's back. Light scintillated around the point where all the sinews met to form a knot of motion, a focal point for the energy that kept the wings moving and the man aloft. Jonah had little doubt that what he was seeing was nothing less than magic at work.

Apart from the leather harness and several strings of bones suspended around his waist, wrists and ankles, the shaman was naked. His skin was caked with pale mud. Dark red pigment underscored his cheekbones; on his belly was painted a blue five-pointed star. Jonah thought he looked fearsome.

'So,' Frey announced, 'you have decided to trespass after all. How clever of you to come this far with . . .' he regarded Gerent contemptuously, '. . . such a feeble guide.'

'Say what you will,' Gerent threw back through clenched teeth. 'We are here to stop you once and for all.'

Frey ignored him. 'Come, daughter,' he went on abruptly. 'Leave these addle-headed fools and join me in the sky. We are all that remains of the Denneth – it is time for you to accept your destiny.'

Jonah felt Archan press against him from behind, felt her grip his hand tightly. 'Do not move,' she whispered in his ear, 'not yet.'

'What quarrel did you have with the nomad women?' demanded Gerent, eyeing Frey as though he were no more than a bug. 'Do you kill for sport now?'

The shaman reached down to his belt of bones and raised a tiny human skeleton in the palm of his hand. Bleached white and held together by some means they could not determine, it might have been the skeleton of a doll. But it was not.

'An experiment, you might say,' he explained conversationally. 'You know how I like to experiment, dear daughter. A pleasing result, do you not think?' He caressed the miniaturised skull, running his thumb along the exquisitely-filed teeth.

'It's obscene!' exploded Jonah. Archan gripped his hand even tighter and placed a hand on his shoulder, preventing him from lunging forward as he might have done.

Frey regarded him balefully. 'Have a care, little man, or you will be smaller than you already are.'

'What do you want of me, father?' demanded Malya. She had composed herself and stood free of Gerent now, her hands dangling loosely at her side. Frey bobbed nearer, the harness creaking as the dragon-scale wings slapped at the air. The sounds revealed to Jonah the crudity of the device – suddenly it seemed not so much miraculous as laughable, a desperate attempt by an earthbound (*Stonebound,* he corrected himself) human to emulate the freedom of the dragon.

Still, it functions, he thought, and when he looked again at the fountain of charm spraying from the shaman's back he grew sober. There was power here indeed, power far beyond his knowledge or experience.

'I want only what I have always wanted, Malya: for you to fulfil your role as heiress to the charm of the Denneth. You are all that remains of my bloodline now – you are the one who will wield the magic when I am gone. Join me now, and united we will weave such spells as have never been woven before!'

He swayed in the air and it occurred to Jonah that he was intoxicated.

'You're drunk, father!' shouted Malya, picking up on Jonah's thoughts with uncanny accuracy.

'On the contrary,' he spat back. 'I am *alive*!'

'The magic is eating you up! Men were not meant to work charm like the dragons. What you've done is evil – you've stolen and tortured and for what purpose? To pump yourself up? You're so proud of what you've done, aren't you, father? So proud, and still you can't see what a little man *you* really are!'

Malya's words struck home: the shaman bared his teeth at her and lunged forward, lashing his arms through the air in a gesture of rage. Just as swiftly he retreated, clearly keen to maintain a safe distance between himself and the bridge. Was he scared? Or just cautious?

'Stay with me, Jonah,' Archan whispered. She too sounded scared, much to Jonah's surprise.

'You are not the magic-maker you think you are, Frey!' Now it was Gerent's turn to speak, and he did so in the voice not of an indecisive prince but a king: his words rang off the crystal like the tolling of some mighty bell, demanding silence in their presence. 'You have come here as I knew you would. The stones of power are gone, as are my father the king and the rest of our people. We are indeed all that remains of the Denneth. We have lost everything now but ourselves and our futures . . . those of us who deserve a future, that is.

'Justice demands that you pay for the havoc you brought upon our people, Frey. I am your king now – will you bow before me and accept your punishment?'

In the absence of his words only the silence remained. Frey looked at first thoughtful, then amused.

'My punishment?' he mused. 'You speak to me of punishment, little king? Do you believe you have any power over me? So what if I brought down the wrath of the dragon – does that not prove my superiority?' He paused, inhaled sharply. 'Can you fly, little king? Can you fly like me?'

Jonah could not prevent himself from crying out again. 'You were as scared of the dragon as the rest of them! Why else did you skulk in that castle?'

'Silence!' roared Frey. He brandished the miniature skeleton at Jonah. A small cloud of vapour drew itself around the skull and poured into the empty eye sockets. Light flared briefly, illuminating the skull from within and Jonah felt his legs go numb and buckle beneath him. Archan caught him as he sagged and lowered him gently to the ground.

'Have a care!' she berated him, then called to Frey, 'Enough – he is of no consequence.'

But the shaman had already forgotten Jonah and was redirecting his attention towards Malya. This time his voice was low and full of threat. 'This is your last chance, daughter. The dragon still wants my blood. If it kills me it will then come searching for you, for your blood is my blood and the beast will not rest until it is all spilt. Together we might defeat it. Do not delude yourself that you can choose your fate: join me, or we both shall die.'

His words seemed to strike a chord in the young woman. She looked round plaintively at Gerent, then shook herself and marched to the edge of the wooden platform.

'That's right,' murmured Frey, bobbing nearer, staring all the while over Malya's shoulder and into the fiery eyes of Gerent, who stood motionless against the sheer face of Stone. 'That's right, dearest daughter, come with me, come and join me now.'

They faced each other. The miniature skeleton was dangling from Frey's waist again and both his arms were outstretched, ready to embrace her. She hung her head, dropped her shoulders. Jonah saw the fingers of her right hand twitch, just once.

Then she was crouching, reaching down with both hands, curling her lips back in an animal snarl. There was a soft tearing sound as she ripped the sword from its improvised sheath and whipping it out and up with an agonised, primal scream. The blade slashed through one of the straps supporting Frey's fabricated wings before drawing a narrow gash across his chest. Malya let go of the sword the instant it cleared her father's flesh, letting it fly at colossal speed through the air until it struck the crystal wall with a sonorous clang. It fell to the floor scant feet in front of Jonah, its tip embedding itself in a wooden plank, the blade and hilt humming like a tuning fork. Before Frey could react she was lunging forward, the axe held out in her left hand. She cut him again, this time painting a line of blood down one arm from elbow to wrist. He howled in pain, wings and limbs thrashing the air. Malya tossed the axe into her right hand and held it high, ready to cut his throat.

She never struck the final blow. The shaman turned, and at first Jonah thought he was preparing to flee. Then he saw a line of fire chase down one of the artificial wings; it looked like a jet of water, a flood of translucent energy spraying tiny droplets of light into the sky. It reached the wingtip and darted across the gap between dragon scale and axe-head. The metal glowed first red then white-hot, then it simply ignited. Noxious vapour exploded across Malya's forearm, eating into the flesh like acid. She screamed: already her hand was gone, and now the destructive cloud was washing across her upper arm, though its virulence was dissipating as it spread. By the time it reached her shoulder, having eaten away most of her right arm, its power was spent.

Malya swayed, flailing with her remaining arm for balance. Jonah looked on in horror, Archan still gripping his hand with almost unbearable tension. Gerent was moving his mouth silently, rooted to the spot.

Frey cocked his head on one side, a cold, contemplative gesture. The pigment daubed on his cheeks looked very much like the blood coating his chest and arm; there was no blood on Malya, the cloud of charm having cauterised the appalling wound it had inflicted as efficiently as fire. Then the shaman grasped a long, white bone and threw it at his daughter's breast.

Even though it was blunt, the bone penetrated her ribcage as easily as the most finely-honed spear. Jonah felt his throat fill with gorge as he saw its white, rounded form emerge from her back. Still there was no sign of blood, but there was no doubt that the charm-laden bone had pierced her heart; her eyes rolled up white and she pitched forward, crashing against the edge of the wooden platform. For an instant it looked as if she would remain there, poised on the brink, but momentum carried her forward and her lifeless body slithered unceremoniously over the edge and into the waiting jaws of the endless abyss.

Dazed, Jonah felt as though he were awakening from a vivid dream to the sound of knocking. Then he realised the knocking was Gerent's footfalls on the wooden floor. Soundless, his mouth a grim, white line, the young Neolithic man had pushed himself away from the unyielding surface of Stone and was accelerating towards the shaman, who was bending to tend his wounds. At the edge Gerent launched himself across the clear space between the platform and the flying man, grappling his arms around Frey's neck as he collided with him. One of the shaman's necklaces broke, showering bone fragments into the abyss.

Gerent manoeuvred himself behind Frey, all the time tightening his grip around the medicine man's throat. The dragon-scale wings faltered, sparks sprayed out from the knot of energy giving them their power and that was now partly squashed beneath Gerent's leather-clad chest. Frey scrabbled behind himself spastically, trying to dislodge the prince; his face grew purple beneath its coating of pale mud.

There was a brief, electrical thump and the wings folded up like a butterfly's at rest. At the same time Frey managed somehow to rotate his body through a half-turn so that he was facing his antagonist. Gerent lost his grip and Frey, choking and rolling his eyes, grabbed him around the waist, squeezing him with blood-caked arms. Then gravity took hold and they fell together.

The last Jonah saw of their struggle was an unidentifiable flurry of limbs as they disappeared into a dense bank of cloud some twenty storeys below. After that they, like Malya's body, were completely gone from view.

Archan offered Jonah her embrace almost immediately, but it was a long time before he allowed himself to accept it. When he did so however he felt all control leave him and he wept long and hard for his lost companions.

Later, huddled together in the lee of the gigantic red crystal, they talked.

'The way ahead for us is simple now, Jonah Lightfoot,' said Archan, her breath laboured. She was tired, exhausted in fact, in a way he had never seen before. Jonah closed his eyes, squeezing out the tears and imagining it was Annie to whom he was listening; until now, the dragon-woman had seemed invincible. 'I had hoped the charm of the faeries – of the shaman and his magical daughter – was the means by which I would transfer my immortal spirit into the body of the dragon giant. But now we are all that remains, you and I. It is your help I need now, Jonah, more than ever.'

'Why should I help you?' he said dully. He was certain of nothing now; all he wanted to do was sleep, perhaps never to wake up . . . at least not if it meant waking up here, in this vertical and alien realm.

'Because it is your only hope of seeing Annie alive again.'

At this he opened his eyes and paid attention. 'What do you mean?'

Archan lifted Annie's hands: both were trembling violently.

'This body is rejecting me, slowly but surely. The faery metabolism does not like the dragon intruder. But I cannot leave it until I have access to the host I need. If I were to do so, I would be condemned as I was before – immortal yet incorporeal, a powerless spirit adrift in a world in which I can have no influence, a world in which I am unable to *live*. Would you wish that on anyone, Jonah?'

He started to consider whether she was using his name merely to gain his trust, but was too exhausted to reach any conclusion. *Annie*, he thought, trying to focus on what was important. 'No,' he whispered, 'I would not wish such a fate upon my worst enemy.'

'So. Here is the truth of it. If I remain in this body for many more days, both it and the faery who rides it will die and I will be condemned. Help me to capture the flesh of the dragon giant, Jonah, and Annie will be free again; I will be free again. That is all I ask of you.'

'But how can I help?'

'This body is growing weak. I need you to bring it into the presence of the dragon so that I may confront it and, if the charm is willing, perform the transfer.'

'And where is this dragon?'

'Where all dragons belong, and where the charm is at its strongest. We have already begun to explore Stone, Jonah Lightfoot. Now it is time to explore the sky.'

10
Truths

Within it all there had been truths and there had been lies.

This faery body was indeed rejecting her – that was the first and most crucial truth. Archan's greatest fear was that it would expire before she was able to make the ultimate transfer, and so it was also true that she needed the other faery, the male who called himself Jonah, to remain at her side. It would surely be some days before time and circumstance permitted the transfer to take place and this frail body would undoubtedly need nursing in the meantime.

Archan knew that the simplest way to make the male loyal to her was to promise him the female when all this was over. Love, or the delusion of its existence, was a most powerful incentive. She was unconcerned about whether or not she could deliver on the promise; it did not matter one way or the other, since she planned to dispose of both of the faeries as soon as she was secure inside a dragon body once more.

She despised these meagre, grubbing creatures who skulked on the surfaces of whatever worlds their race was flung across. Devoid of nobility, utterly without charm, they were the ones who had thrived while she had languished. A million years of life, of growth, of evolving ideas – an entire faery history expanding while she had lain trapped in the ice. A long time for bitterness to bury itself deep, and for dreams of revenge to grow sharp.

That she actually needed the male faery's help was a constant source of revulsion. But Archan was nothing if not disciplined, and she consoled herself with the knowledge that each day spent in his company honed her anger yet further, making the prospect of her ultimate revenge ever sweeter.

As long as she rode this faery mind the male would not harm her, that much was guaranteed. But what of Annie?

The female had nearly broken out in the aftermath of Archan's seduction of Gerent (a curious experience, a dazzling mixture of ecstasy and repugnance . . . and a fascinating insight into the crude rituals of these natural abominations). Archan could not even be sure that she had not communicated with the male, if only briefly. No matter – if she had made contact it had been brief and she had been well punished. Archan had destroyed the walls of the faery's mental sanctuary and sent her naked spirit cowering into the deepest recesses of her mind. And there she remained still, silent and still.

Is she dead already? wondered Archan momentarily.

But no, that could not be so. If the native faery spirit were destroyed then the body would fail soon after. This body was failing, to be sure, but slowly and predictably, the inevitable result of the million-year void between captor and captive, of Archan's ancient immortal thoughts and Annie's living finite mind.

She sought out that spirit now, delving through the wreckage of the bizarre tile temple, sweeping its remains into the fire. It was like travelling back through time, chasing elusive faery thoughts back through spiralling channels of meat and memory until she reached a deep, dark place. It was cold down here and Archan noted with interest that, unlike the rest of this warm mammalian cave, it held a familiar scent. Something old and reptilian, something even of the dragon . . .

There she lay, the female, a twisted scrap of consciousness, pared to its most basic form. Senseless, it clung to the core of its mind, this early reptilian version of itself, not breathing, not thinking, barely even aware. It simply was.

Archan shuddered and turned back towards the warm light of the fire; down here, in the icy well of Annie's mind, she was reminded all too vividly of her own incarceration. Here was the fate that awaited her were she to fail in her quest to claim a suitable dragon host: to be without power, without mind, a mere pebble sunk to the bottom of an ocean of memory, a future fragment of the strata to come. A prisoner without influence in this or any world. Immortal, impotent.

She regained the light of the upper mind at the equivalent of a run. Probing out into the world through faery eyes she again bemoaned the feeble senses with which these creatures stumbled through their lives. Though she had improvised a crude version of her former charm-sense she missed the subtle perceptions of the charmed dragon. And what greater glory it would have been to own the ten million senses of the original immortals: the basilisks! What might she not have seen, swimming against the river of time with the power to see beyond the edges of creation?

I will build such senses anew, when I am a dragon once more!

But this body's fatigue was immense and the river of time would have to flow on regardless. Lowering herself briefly to interact with the male faery she implored him to watch over her while she slept. He nodded his rough, flat face and helped her settle this strange flesh back into a groove in the crystal.

Just before darkness overwhelmed her she cast a glance back into the recesses where the female's mind lay in its stupor. Tiny pillars of fire – the booby traps she had laid along the trail – would warn her should the faery awake.

She did not think it was likely, not ever again.

Jonah watched Archan as she slept, secure inside Annie's body, his mind a storm preventing him from sleeping himself.

Malya was dead, Gerent . . . gone, almost certainly dead too along with the evil shaman. The Neolithics, all gone, claimed in one way or another by the immensity of Stone. Fallen.

And now, as he looked down on what was left of his one contact with the sane, human world he had left behind, he felt despair. How he hoped that when she opened her eyes he would see not those cold, blind mirrors but wide, dark pupils, complex irises, shining whites. He reached forward and touched her outstretched foot; her leg twitched and she half-turned, pressing into the unyielding crystal wall. Human lips parted, exhaling human breath. Yet he knew that whatever dreams were unravelling inside that mind, they were not the dreams of a woman.

She will not yield, he thought. *The dragon will take what she needs and then move on, regardless of what chaos she leaves in her wake.*

He believed Archan, for better or worse, when she said that Annie would be free again. But he had no idea in what state Annie would be when she was finally released. Try as he might, he could not imagine what torture she was experiencing inside the prison of her own mind.

The twin ghosts of her human eyes swimming like bodies trapped beneath ice.

How much to trust the dragon?

'Not at all,' he whispered to himself as he held the painting box tight against his belly.

He wandered around the chamber, a large irregular cavern scooped from red crystal. It was strange in here, very strange. He remembered only a little about Archan's discovery of the entrance in the crystal wall. She had pulled him back from the edge, he remembered that much, when he had teetered there, perversely attracted by the rich tapestry of the infinite drop. Then he had wept and they had talked. After that he had just sat there, staring dumbly as she had pored over the wall, poking fingertips into hidden crevices, sniffing at the crystal.

Something came back to him now as he loitered in the vast, red interior, his footsteps hollow. A memory of the dragon-woman somehow *stroking* the crystal. A vision of Annie's familiar face, cheek flattened against the translucent wall, a scattering of glowing dust motes scintillating around her hair. A curious smell, a rippling in the air, and a brief spray of icy water, gone as soon as it had come. Magic?

Charm.

Then, with no sense of movement, no ceremony of opening or parting, there had been an entrance. Archan stood before it, sweat pouring from a face suddenly haggard, a body suddenly limp and exhausted. He had helped her into the passage, a cool, tall slot that took them deep into the crystal, supporting her at first then finally carrying her the last few yards as he had once carried her unconscious through that darker tunnel, the tunnel that had first led them out on to Stone . . .

Clearly the act of magic she had used to open a way into the dragon stronghold had left her weak and disorientated. Moreover, she had already said that Annie's body was rejecting her – he had no reason to doubt her word in this respect, why should she lie?

'If only I could see more clearly,' he groaned aloud as Archan slept. 'If only I could find a way to get ahead of her, a way to help Annie when the time comes.'

The question was rhetorical, but it received an answer nevertheless.

'There may be a way, and I may be able to assist you in its discovery.'

Jonah turned slowly, trying to place the voice which, though he had never heard it before, seemed familiar. Luminous green eyes gazed down at him and he looked up into the face of the tortoid.

'I . . . know you,' he said slowly, though the creature looked very different to when he had last seen it. Much about it was familiar, however: the soft sheen of its carapace, the mobility of its generous mouth. He peered round its flank; yes, the same symbol was there, the unlikely mark of the Red Dragon. He gulped, not exactly afraid but overwhelmed. 'You saved my life.'

'It was a simple deed. I trust I did not hurt you.'

Rubbing his wrists reflexively, Jonah smiled wryly. 'If you did I didn't notice. Thank you.'

'I heard you the first time.'

That seemed to conclude the formalities. The creature – Esh, it said its name was – sat down with a complicated folding gesture, inviting Jonah to join it, which he did. Further developed, Esh looked more like a bipedal insect than a tortoise now. Its skin, where exposed, was a rich, African black; the armoured plates protecting the backs of its thin, bony limbs and shoulders was likewise the deepest ebony. Only its face betrayed the reptile within, a vaguely scaly blend of human and, yes, tortoise, with bright green eyes fluorescing above that remarkable mouth.

Galapagos, thought Jonah, making the connection. 'You're evolving, are you not? Before my eyes, very nearly!'

Esh nodded graciously. 'You share your companion's insight, Jonah Lightfoot.'

'My companion? Do you mean . . . ?'

'I have been able to communicate with Annie, yes, though on a comparatively crude level. You will no doubt be concerned as to her welfare; let me reassure you that she is alive and aware in every sense that has meaning, though since the dragon's latest outburst her mobility is severely reduced. I hope she will survive this ordeal – she has the strength and the will, but as for the fortune, that is out of even my control.'

'W-who are you?'

So Esh told Jonah as it had told Annie. Jonah learned of the ways through from his world to the world of Stone – or *Amara*, as it was also called – and of the role of Esh and the rest of the Ypoth in repairing the damage caused whenever some new catastrophe breached the wall between the worlds, learned that Archan was more than just another intruder, that she was a threat, though what sort of threat he could not divine. Learned that he, Jonah, was one of the few who could make things right.

'"Make things right"?' He repeated Esh's words. 'Do you mean I have power here?' A flash of memory, of Malya's reaction when he had touched the rod in the hole through which the Roman soldier had so nearly come. *The ribs holding the cement together*.

'Come with me now,' said Esh, unfolding itself again. It towered over Jonah, a good eight feet tall, slender and dense. 'I will explain what I am able to in the short time we have.' It saw Jonah cast a nervous glance back at the sleeping Archan. 'Do not fret – the dragon will sleep for many hours. You will not break your promise.'

Esh led him through a red-walled maze. The tunnels were wide and high, but so convoluted that despite his best efforts Jonah quickly became disorientated. It did not help that the walls – and the floors and ceilings for that matter – were partly transparent, so that at any one time he was aware not only of the particular tunnel through which they were pacing but of others, great curving ways spiralling away into vermilion fog, neat burrows bisecting these and others, an intricate network like vessels knitted into a living body. Light filtered its way in from hidden sources, or perhaps it was just captured daylight, refracted over and over again as it recirculated these depths even though it was surely night outside.

Moreover he was hungry, desperately hungry. The initial thrill of knowing that the air of Stone would supply him with all the nutrients he needed had given way to a deep, hollow hunger that would not go away. As Malya (oh, poor Malya!) had suggested, a man could not deny his bodily needs, whatever magic might be at work.

'Oh, for a pocketful of breadcrumbs,' he sighed. Esh regarded him with what might have been a frown. 'Well, what I could not eat, which would not be much, I'll warrant, I could scatter behind me.'

The alien creature nodded sagely. 'A trail, I see. You will not need it, Jonah Lightfoot: there are many ways through the hearts of Amara, and the Ypoth know most of them.'

Amara. The name had lodged itself in Jonah's thoughts like a burr. This world, called Amara, but also called Stone. A vision sprang before him of a field of purple flowers . . .

'We must bow our heads.' The flowers scattered as if on a breeze. Bent almost double, he let Esh lead him along a very low passage, much smaller than any of the others, until they emerged into a dark chamber. Here Jonah could stand upright again, though his red hair brushed the ceiling. Esh was forced to crouch, chitinous legs folded in long double-joints.

'You will think me foolish for asking this, and I hope the question does not offend,' began Jonah, as much to break the eerie silence as anything, 'but are you male or female?'

'The Ypoth are without sex as you understand it. We are spawned by the stuff of Amara itself. We do not mate, nor do we generate offspring of our own by any other means. However, within our race there are certain roles that are determined by the particular balance of an individual's metabolism. Those of us spawned with ability in combat you might consider male; others whose task is to ensure the maintenance of communication within the group you might consider female. The divisions are subtle and many, and there are not enough words in your mind to define them all.

'As for myself, I am in many ways a rogue. As I have already explained to you, it is unheard-of for an Ypoth to abandon its work at a breach or threshold. By doing so I have cut myself off from the rest of my race; I have, to all intents and purposes, made myself an outcast. You are one reason I have done this, Jonah Lightfoot; Archan is another.

'So, to answer your question, I am really neither one thing nor the other, not in any sense that has meaning to you. However, I understand that it is hard for you to consider me as a neutral being, so let us elect to define me as female. This seems appropriate, since my particular skills lie in the field of love and memory. Am I right in believing that as a representative of your race you would consider these as generally female attributes?'

Jonah took a breath before answering. He found himself considering another of the miracles of the air of Stone: its ability to translate language. All through Esh's speech he had sensed that ability being stretched to its limit. It was hard, it seemed, to squeeze the grand perceptions of the Ypoth into the pint-pot of the human mind.

Love and memory. Within the phrase a sense of circularity, continuity, of inevitability that radiated heat, the heat of far-distant stars. An endless spiral, an ascending mirror, a point so sharp it could not be seen.

Strange ideas, difficult to conceptualise, impossible to communicate.

A field of prince's feather, the shadow of each tiny flower defining its position in space. At one end of the field the shadows are short; at the other they stretch into infinity.

'Learn slowly, Jonah Lightfoot, so that we all might understand.' The merest whisper.

As his eyes grew accustomed to the dimness, Jonah saw that he was standing on yet another ledge. For a moment he imagined Esh had led him all the way through the thickness of Stone's wall and *out the other side*. But did that direction – *in* – not lead back to the world he had left behind? He could not resolve the geometry of it all.

The ledge was situated at what might have been considered a gallery level, looking down into a large, dark space, a black-walled cavity scooped out of the structure of Stone. Behind them the walls were made of shining crystal; this clearly was the junction between dragon stronghold and supporting Stone.

Like the other breaches he had seen, this one was spanned by the familiar rods. Thin as a woman's wrist, part of Stone yet not part of it, smooth ebony, horizontally aligned. In this calm, light-starved place they looked to Jonah like the pipes of a fallen church organ, silent yet filled with grace and strength. Silent? He fancied he could hear them humming, whispering to him.

He realised Esh was scrutinising him intently.

'Yes,' she whispered. 'Tell me what you feel.'

He gulped. 'What I felt before. Power, energy. Electricity? A feeling that . . . that something is *stored* here . . .' His voice trailed away. He wondered what his words meant to the Ypoth, what interpretation the air of Amara imposed upon his stifled syllables.

'You have touched one of the rods?'

'I wish I had not. It took me away, like a dream, but it was very real. I saw a soldier dying . . . a volcano . . .'

Esh's voice was low and awed. 'Show me the hand with which you touched the rod.' He did so; she stroked it, cooing strangely. Then she sighed, a long, dry sound like desert wind. 'I will tell you what the Ypoth know about the rods. We know much, more than most, but we do not know all. It may be that your coming to Amara will change that.'

She bent forward then, suddenly excited, grasping his hand between smooth, slightly yielding pincers. 'The rods are made of memories! That is all, it is as simple as that, Jonah Lightfoot! You have already begun to surmise this, I think, from your encounters with them. This is the literal truth, and this is the continuity running through the many hearts of Amara.

'Your world, that which you consider to be the "real world", is a vessel from within which consciousness shines. Life shines, Jonah Lightfoot, and with it shines love and especially *memory*. Consider your own life, your own loves. They have power only because they exist in your memory. Memory makes them eternal; memory *is* eternity. And whatever other eternities may exist, there is one place where memory is certain to survive: here, on Amara.

'These rods are made of memories, you see. Literally. In them is condensed the first breath of every newborn baby, the touch of the autumn leaf on the tree's exposed root, the shout of the storm behind the predator's triumphant cry. Footfalls behind the stalked, moments of ecstasy and insight, the patient sorting of dream and insensibility, years of grief, invention, love, remorse, ornate lists, fruitless investigations, layer upon layer of moment after moment, the endless strata of experience. As lives unfurl in your world, so the memories they create connect to the rods inside Amara. The worth of the memory rods cannot be calculated: they are beyond all valuation. That is one reason the labour of the Ypoth is so important, for every breach leaves the rods exposed and vulnerable. They are strong, reinforced with the might of aeons, but they are not unbreakable. For if even one is broken then the continuity is lost and all is jeopardised. All.'

'"As lives unfurl",' repeated Jonah, receiving the idea with an inevitable, horrific delight, like seeing a lost friend rise from the grave, 'so the memory rods are made.'

'No,' said Esh gently. Green eyes glowed, phosphorescent in the gloom. 'Those are not the words I used, Jonah Lightfoot.' She paused to gain his full attention. 'Listen closely. By travelling downStone we are moving into the past. But if we chose to travel upStone we would journey into what you consider to be the future. There are memory rods there, too, Jonah Lightfoot. Memories of the future, just as here are memories of the past.

'*The memories are here already*, past and future, all of them that ever were and ever shall be. They respond neither to cause nor effect, only mind. You are beyond the river of time now, Jonah Lightfoot, looking down on it as if you were a bird instead of caught up in its flow like a fish. On Amara you can choose to fly upstream or downstream, whichever you prefer. And wherever you journey the memories will be there with you, the echoes of all the lives that were ever lived and ever shall be lived in what you used to imagine was the one, real world.

'For there are many worlds. Yours is just one of them. Amara is the single thread that binds the worlds together, the one strand of continuity, order within chaos. And running through Amara itself: the memories of all those worlds past and future, near and far. The memory rods.'

He listened hard as Esh spoke on. It did not cross his mind to challenge what she told him – it chimed in his head with the clear tone of truth, as if she was not informing him but reminding him, evoking a memory of something he already knew, had always known.

'So we come to you, Jonah Lightfoot. As you have discovered, even to touch one of the memory rods is perilous. Would it surprise you to learn that for most creatures – the Ypoth are an exception – to touch a rod is certain death?' He shook his head. 'So. You are different, very different. There are a few, a very few, who are able to touch the rods and survive. A small proportion of those are able actually to read the information stored within, to experience the memories if you will. You are among that number.

'Furthermore, it is said that chance will occasionally bring forth one who can not only read the rods, but *change* them.'

Esh paused to let the full effect of this sink in. 'Do you see?' she whispered. 'Do you see?'

'You think I might be such a one?' Somehow he could not bring himself to share her obvious sense of wonder. The conversation had entered an abstract realm that had little to do with him, his movement through this world, his insistent, animal hunger.

'I do not know. I hope, for the sake of Amara, that you may be, and that you may have the wisdom to control whatever power you may have.'

'Why? Why do you hope it, Esh?'

'Because Archan *is* such a one, a memory-changer. She does not know it yet, indeed she knows less than you about the nature of Amara, and nothing at all about the rods. But that will change; she is beginning to suspect, I think. That is one reason she has kept you alive for so long, so that she might learn what she believes you have already learned.'

'She says she needs me.'

'In more ways than one, I am sure.'

'If she finds out what she can do here will she cause trouble?'

'It is not a question of "if" but "when", and yes, she will undoubtedly cause what you whimsically term "trouble". She is a bitter soul, angry with her world and all that connects to it, and she will cause great mischief when she learns what she can do. But the real reason she is so dreadful is not simply her ability to distort or even break the memory rods but the fact that she can do all that *and is immortal.*

'What would she care if she sent Amara and all the worlds it embraces crashing into the void? She will live on. And if new worlds and new memories should arise? Still she will prevail.'

Jonah thought about Archan, her anger. 'Would she do such a thing? Destroy worlds? What would be her purpose?'

'To satisfy her thirst for revenge. And because she can. Eternity is a long time, Jonah Lightfoot. The basilisks knew this only too well, and now Archan is just beginning to learn it for herself. Across the span of eternity the river of time is the merest scratch. Worlds come and go in the merest eye-blink; only memories linger. To be immortal is to hear the heartbeat of the cosmos and worse – to count it, and to remember the count. A rising, neverending shriek of numbers, a tide of memories that will rise and rise and never ebb. Archan's anger is only just beginning for, unlike the basilisks who were six, she is alone in eternity. She will scream and lay waste until nothing remains, then she will wait in madness until worlds arise again and so the cycle will continue into oblivion, an eternal round of revenge whose engine was once a dragon, but which has long since become something far greater and more terrible, a depraved goddess adrift in the emptiness, lashing out at everything that threatens the solitude she despises so much.

'Through the mind of your friend Annie I have glimpsed the ice in Archan's fiery heart, so I know all this to be true. Soon she will know her abilities here. Before that happens you must make her gone.'

'K-kill her?'

'Make her gone. It is far more than death. If even her memory remains she will retain the power to destroy Amara. You alone can do this, Jonah Lightfoot. Find the place in the rods where Archan's heart burns brightest and make her gone.'

'How can you trust me with such a task? How do I know that I can even trust what you tell me? You say Amara is in jeopardy, and therefore that my world is in jeopardy. But what hope is there that I should ever return to my world, now that I have been washed up on this distant shore? You claim I can walk into the future but what does the future hold for me here, or anywhere? I am just a man, just a man . . .'

'And therein lies your strength.' Esh tried to console Jonah, who was weeping silently, ignorant of why the tears were flowing or from where. 'Yours is a hard fate, Jonah Lightfoot, and a perilous drop lies beneath you should you fall. You wonder why it should fall to you, and why you should answer the call. Do you remember how I spoke of memory and love? These are not mere words but elemental forces, like magic and the phases of your moon. Tell me something from your past – now!' She snapped this unexpected demand out like a slap and before he knew what he was doing Jonah responded.

'Barley! A field of barley!'

'Its colour?'

'Orange, the setting sun.'

'Were you alone?'

He dipped his head, smiling despite himself. 'Nobody could see us. It was close to harvest.'

'So. Do you have a storm in your mind?'

He regarded those pale, deep eyes. 'The day my father and brother died there was a great storm. That is something I shall never forget.'

Esh nodded, as if she had been expecting this. 'So. Remember your moments of love, Jonah Lightfoot, and remember your moments of anger. When Archan unleashes her anger on to Amara, when she extends her claws into its veins, these memories of yours will be among those she destroys or changes or distorts or consumes. A moment of passion before the setting sun . . . the death of your kin. Would you have them die again, this time forever? Would you consign all those whom you love to the shapeless maw of eternity, never to live again? Worse – never to have lived at all!' She hesitated, breath rasping in her long throat. 'Would you allow her to kill Annie not merely in the flesh but in memory, too? Would you have it that you had never met her, that she had never painted the Galapagos, never been hit by her man, that her mother had never screamed at the agony of pressing her out into the warm embrace of your world? This is not about Amara, nor the many worlds it flanks. This is about you, Jonah Lightfoot, about your past and your future and all that you hold dear, all that you understand and love. All that you are prepared to fight for.'

'I'm hungry,' Jonah said dismally, the horizontal lines of the memory rods looking to him not like organ pipes but a sheet of paper ruled with blank staves, not the instrument but the unwritten score. The music of the future.

'Yes,' sighed Esh. 'So. You have needs. I will tend you. You are not expected to be fearless. I am here to guide you, I am here for you. I will help you in your task, Jonah Lightfoot. I am,' she bowed awkwardly, striking her head on the ceiling as she arose, 'your humble servant.'

At this, Jonah could not help but laugh. A fresh mood of dizzy humour swept away the despair, the emptiness, with startling speed. There was something so courtly about this alien ambassador, something so appropriate considering the nature of the quest into which he had been seconded. The slaying of the dragon who threatened to overturn the kingdom, the rescue of the princess locked away in a high and impenetrable tower. *The wyrm . . . Rapunzel, let down thy hair . . .* And here before him the gentle knight, clad in hard black armour, blessed with secret knowledge.

'If I could only eat something,' he went on, the laughter subsiding as quickly as it had come, replaced by a tiredness, a lingering sense that he was adrift in someone else's dream. 'Then perhaps I might think more clearly. And sleep, yes, I think I could sleep.'

They left the chamber of the memory rods; even before they had exited the low corridor into the wider dragon ways Jonah fancied he heard a familiar skittering sound behind him. Ypoth, he supposed, repairing the breach that had opened up the chamber in the first place.

Esh must have told them to wait. The thought was like a yawn. *Now they can get on with their business.*

Halfway back, as near as he could judge, Esh stopped at a slender crack in the crystal wall. It ran from floor to ceiling, a narrow pinched oval like a reptile's pupil. At her instruction Jonah pushed his hand into it. At once he was rewarded by a gush of clear, sticky liquid on to his palm. It was warm and slippery, and he pulled his hand away with a short yelp.

Embarrassed by his reaction, he gingerly licked his fingers: the fluid was sweet and wholesome, textured with soft grains like porridge, though to look at it was clear as honey. Before his hand was fully clean he thrust it into the crack again, this time scooping up mouthfuls of the stuff and wolfing it. His stomach growled appreciatively; vaguely aware of his ape-like performance he was unable to control his urge to feed and fill his belly.

Presently Esh tugged him gently away. 'You do not need much of it. It will swell to fill you, and its effects will last some time.'

'What is it?' he demanded, savouring its clean, sweet taste, its invisible texture.

'The dragons call it *amboroth*. It is a substance that used to be found in your world, long before the age in which your race prevailed. It has little of its early power in the form it now takes on Amara but it serves the dragons well enough as a mouth-sweetener and belly-filler. They collect it and store it; it is part of what makes this place their home.'

'*Amboroth.* Like *ambrosia,* of course! *Ambrotos,* "not mortal". And like Amara.' That green gaze managed to be both soft and piercing. 'Amaranthus! That's it! That is what was eluding me. The genus Amaranthus, to which the plant known as prince's feather belongs! And in legend the amaranth was meant never to fade. A flower blessed with immortality. There is another too . . . oh yes.' He paused, feeling the dragons' nectar swelling inside his body. 'Oh yes: love-lies-bleeding.'

He looked into the Ypoth's eyes. 'Is that how Amara acquired its name? From the flowers – I have seen them here, very many of them, in meadows and hedgerows.'

'Who can say which came first? But there is power in names, Jonah Lightfoot, great power.'

Archan woke when a fractured beam of light exploded into the red chamber. Rising slowly, rubbing at the small of Annie's back with an agonisingly human gesture, she gave Jonah a cursory glance and announced, 'We must work hard today. This body is failing me. Come now.'

They found a tunnel leading upwards. Light bloomed somewhere indefinable beyond the many corners obscuring the distance. Along the way Jonah, pretending he was exploring, 'happened' upon another of the dragon drinking wells. Archan joined him and drank greedily, glad of any additional energy she could pour into the body that was unravelling ever more rapidly around her.

'Amboroth!' she gasped. 'It must be! Such a delicacy has not been known for many aeons, not since the time of the golden age of charmed dragons, long before my time and long before the turning of the world! And yet . . .' She smacked Annie's lips, ran a human tongue around the inside of a human mouth. 'There is little charm in it. Once this nectar would have radiated charm, faery. It is a poor substitute.'

'If it fills our bellies it is welcome enough.'

'Perhaps.' She eyed him thoughtfully. 'You did well to find it, faery.'

'I was lucky,' he shrugged, regretting his 'discovery'. He should be doing nothing to attract attention to himself, nothing at all. And certainly nothing that might imply possession of secret knowledge. 'Well, are we ready to go on?'

'After you, faery. Indeed, it seems that you are the one who knows where he is going.'

His face burning, Jonah took the lead.

The air was moving again, the scent of spice was strong. Jonah wondered why it was they had seen no dragons in these tunnels – why, if this was indeed their stronghold, it appeared to be deserted. Were they shy, or simply few in number? Light bloomed in all directions, as if crimson fire had blossomed on every side. He was suddenly, powerfully convinced that they were emerging from inside a tiny gem set in a ring on the finger of a giantess, miniature angels rising through the layers of a ruby showstone.

Then they were outside, raising their hands against the morning sunlight, gasping as hot wind crashed against their necks and shoulders, sucking in great draughts of life-giving air, aware that *this* was the sustenance their bodies now needed, not some reptilian broth. Looking out on Stone again.

Amara . . . Esh's voice whispered in his head and Jonah shivered, praying that he would not let the hidden name slip out in Archan's presence.

Haze, naturally; the indomitable cliff face ascending forever. A barren landscape of red crystal, sharp growths and stellated spires inhibiting the view. Islands of crystal beyond the edge of this, towers receding into the sky. Jonah was reminded of the Needles viewed from a cliff-top, slender chalk stacks trailing into the English Channel, pointing the way to America. The image sprang unbidden and he shivered a second time, wondering where behind the skin of Stone that particular memory was located, where ran the rod in which that childhood visit to England's south coast was kept.

'You are cold, faery?' said Archan.

'It's nothing,' he said, too quickly. 'A footstep on my grave, that's all.'

The dragons began to fly soon after they broke surface, lifting smoothly out of tunnels further out. Most of them came from the second tower-top of the five Jonah could make out. They were of variegated colour, much smaller than he had expected, even though he knew the one example of their race he had encountered so far to be a giant. He guessed their body size to be only slightly more than his own, though their wings were very long – a typical span might have been as much as thirty feet. Like bats and birds, they were four-limbed; when they touched down occasionally he saw that they moved on the ground rather like the former, using both wings and legs in an ungainly crawl rather than adopting the bipedal gait of the avian.

They flew lazily, with no obvious purpose other than pure recreation. Well, they had no reason to hunt – perhaps they practised aerial combat. Perhaps they flew for the sheer pleasure of flying. Jonah could believe such a thing to be true, he who had been born in an age when heavier-than-air manned flight was still a miracle waiting to happen. The Montgolfiers' achievement aside – good God, they had first flown a balloon exactly one hundred years ago, in 1783! – man had done precious little to challenge the skies.

Frey had achieved it here though, what no man on Earth had yet done. *Ah, but he was using magic.* So, had there been magic in Jonah's world once, too? What had Archan said – *in a time before the turning of the world* . . . just what did that mean?

One of the dragons was approaching. The rest – he counted twenty-six – continued their play unconcerned by the alien presence on the roof of their citadel.

The dragon halted just short of the place where they stood, hovering in the thick, flowing air with steady beats of its long, tapering wings. Too slowly those wings were beating, too slowly to keep it aloft, especially in the constant downdraught. Tiny stars scintillated along bony blades projecting from the wings' leading edges – magic, he supposed, or rather *charm*. Of course.

Its face was long, utterly unlike that of any earthly creature Jonah could think of. It was primarily reptilian, yet its scales looked very soft; more amphibian, perhaps, with delicately-patterned skin. Something of the lizard, something of the horse. Colours ran like blended brushstrokes: yellow ochre and raw sienna, the names of the pigments Jonah had seen in Annie's painting box, a rich canvas. Black eyes, with the whites almost completely obscured; round pupils, like a human's.

The dragon's mouth opened, revealing a crimson tongue and small, sharp teeth.

'You are welcome here, faeries,' it said in a deep, melodious voice. A strand of light dripped from one of its wingtips like honey.

'Th-thank you,' stammered Jonah. He was hypnotised by the steady thrust of the dragon's wings. 'Um, I imagined we might be considered to be trespassing. Please forgive us if we have taken undue liberty.'

Archan threw him a scornful glance. 'There is one among you,' she said without preamble. 'A giant. Where does he live?'

To his surprise Jonah found he could read the dragon's face quite well. Black eyes widened, swivelling slightly: surprise, a little disdain. 'Torus is no longer part of our company. If you want to see him you must look for yourselves.'

A second dragon had flown up behind the first and was dallying in the air, bobbing uncertainly and peering around its companion's wings like a child looking through its mother's skirts. 'Have they come to counsel us, Master Pax?' Its voice was higher – a female?

'You may leave us be, Kythe. Return to where it is safe.'

'I shan't! It's not fair! The first faeries I've ever seen, and you too, Master Pax, for that matter. You can't stop me talking to them, I won't let you.' She dipped, flattening pale orange wings and peeping beneath Pax's body. 'Hello,' she added, parting her mouth in what Jonah took to be a smile.

'Good morning,' he responded, bowing slightly. Kythe's mouth stayed open, her eyes wide. An awestruck child, he decided, amazed in the presence of . . . well, of faeries. 'It may reassure you to learn that you are the first dragons I have ever spoken to.' This was not true, he realised – there was Archan. Would they realise his apparently human companion was not as she seemed?

'You are free to explore the crystal,' Pax went on smoothly, ignoring Kythe's eager darting motions. 'But if it is Torus you seek I am afraid your presence here is not as welcome as it might have been.'

With that he swivelled his body, flicked his tail and flew back towards the distant circling group. Kythe loitered, curling and uncurling her tail. 'Do not linger, child Kythe,' he called as he went. 'Remain in sight.'

'Your friend seems uneasy,' ventured Jonah.

'Oh, don't mind old Pax! He's just trying to do the right thing. Trouble is, he doesn't know what the right thing is! He's still got his eyesight, mind you. Doesn't hear as well as he used to. He's a good sort, old Pax.'

'I thought you might not like us intruding.'

The young dragon's eyes grew large. 'Intruding? Faeries? Gosh no! This is the most exciting thing that's ever happened to me, and that's the truth! Just a moment.' She tucked in her wings and dropped smartly to the ground. Polished claws sounded xylophone notes on the hard crystal. 'That's better, easier to talk. There's enough charm to fly with but not enough to make it easy, if you know what I mean. Oh, but of course you do – you're faeries!' She craned her neck, frowning as she tried to see behind their backs.

'We don't fly, in case that is what you were wondering.'

'Oh.' Kythe sounded disappointed. 'Oh well. Never mind.'

She was smaller than Pax. Her markings were similar to his, though her colours were more vivid: yellow and orange, fading to near-white beneath her belly. Jonah could see now that she was much younger – her skin was smoother, the scales less heavily embossed, her eyes brighter, more alert.

'Enough,' snapped Archan. 'If you will not take us to this Torus we shall find our own way!'

'I can't take you, I'm afraid,' Kythe replied uncertainly. She hesitated. 'I could tell you where to find him, though.'

'You are willing to help us?' asked Jonah.

Kythe blinked at him. 'You're faeries,' she answered, as if that explained everything.

Kythe led them upStone. Her gait on the ground was awkward and lurching. Her long arms, hampered by the cumbersome membranes stretched between what in a human would have been termed the knuckles and the shoulder (her 'hands' were greatly elongated, their bones almost as thick as those of the forearm), heaved her forwards rather like the flippers of a seal – or, as Jonah had already noted, like a grounded bat.

They passed through a field of crystal spines and out of sight of the other circling dragons. The shiny red ground – a little slippery but not dangerously so – sloped gradually away but Kythe turned to the right before there was any risk of losing their footing. Soon they reached a horizontal groove cut into the crystal, a track leading out towards the open sky.

'This way should lead us to the end of the Flank,' the dragon whispered. 'If we're lucky we won't be seen. I'm probably in trouble already – they're terribly protective, you know.'

'The Flank?' enquired Jonah.

'Yes.' She was cheerful despite her obvious nerves, and still eager to please. 'This part of the crystal that we're on is called the Flank, and the other pieces out there are called the Backbones. Torus lives on the outermost of those, which we sometimes call the Tip; that's where you'll need to go.'

'Tell me how you make the amboroth, dragon,' demanded Archan, interrupting them.

Kythe jumped, a little scared. 'We – we don't really make it,' she babbled. 'It just sort of flows out of the crystal. No one knows where it comes from – it's just there when we need it.'

'Pathetic!' Archan growled. 'And the charm with which you enhance your flight? Do you absorb it from the air?'

'I-I don't know. I mean, I suppose so. Flying is very difficult on Stone – the wind, you see. A dragon can fly unaided but we try to use whatever charm we can to make it easier.'

'What about further downStone,' snapped Archan. 'Is it not easier to fly there? Or upStone: what magic lies that way?'

'I don't know.'

'Think!'

'No, really, I mean *we* don't know. We stay near the crystal, all of us. We don't go far. Especially me.'

Archan stopped dead and gave the dragon a withering glare. 'You don't go far! But you are *dragons*!'

Kythe looked self-consciously from Archan to Jonah, then back again. 'Well . . . we just don't, I'm afraid.'

Under Archan's interrogation she described the factors that prevented the dragons of the red crystal from venturing too far from their stronghold. UpStone, she explained, there were very many faeries.

'It's said that the further you go upStone the more faeries there are. We are . . . uncomfortable in the presence of your kind, so we like to keep our distance.' Jonah was curious as to why the dragons should feel this way, but decided to keep that question until later. 'The surface of Stone is covered with your constructions, none of which we understand. Some of them even think and move of their own accord, so it's said. Moving castles – can you imagine?'

On this Archan did not comment. 'And downStone?'

'It's even harder. You only have to go a short way from here before you reach the Dead Calm.'

'Which is . . . ?'

'The Dead Calm is as flat as upStone is textured. There Stone is as smooth as ice; it's impossible to climb it, or even hold a grip on it at all. All you can do is fall.'

'Or fly,' suggested Jonah.

'But the wind is stronger there, much stronger, like a hurricane. Flight is impossible, even with charm. There is no way for anyone, charmed or natural, flier or climber, to pass beyond the Dead Calm.'

Archan seemed to consider this, then went on. 'Very well. Tell me what lies in the direction known as "out". What secrets does the sky hold?'

Kythe laughed, much to Archan's irritation. 'Oh, every dragon knows what happens when you fly out.'

'But I do not,' Archan grated from between Annie's clenched teeth.

'It's very strange. No sooner do you fly far enough away from Stone for it to be hidden in the mist than suddenly you find yourself flying back towards it again . . .' She broke off, regarding them both curiously. 'Are you sure you're faeries? You don't seem to know very much.'

'Humour us,' was Archan's acidic response. 'Up and down?'

Kythe shuddered. 'Oh no. You must know the perils those ways hold.'

Archan was exasperated. 'So you are as much prisoners here as those short-sighted primitives were in their borrowed castle! Is there no creature here with the breadth of vision this world deserves? Have I come all this way only to find myself imprisoned all over again?' She paused, checking her temper. 'It shall not be so,' she added under her breath. 'All worlds can be conquered in time.'

'Time is short,' murmured Jonah. The glare she had directed on Kythe was turned on him, briefly.

They moved on and before long were negotiating a series of cracks, narrow splits in the crystal path that forced them to dodge and hop their way forward. Kythe took briefly to the air then rejoined them as they reached the end of the Flank.

Jonah gasped as they emerged from behind a translucent red pillar and into the full glare of the sunlight; the wind howled ominously, twisted by the broken contours of the crystal.

For broken it was. Here, far from the surface of Stone, poised on the outermost end of this city-sized ruby outcrop, was a gulf of air. Some unimaginable cataclysm had once shattered the ruby and hurled the severed pieces out into the sky where they floated still, defying gravity like Swift's floating island of Laputa. These were Jonah's Needles, these crystal islands which Kythe had called the Backbones.

'The view is notable,' said Archan evenly. 'But there is no way of reaching the outer crystals. I assume that is where we must go in order to find the giant?'

'Well, yes, of course. Torus lives on the Tip, as I said. You'll have to fly to get there, naturally.'

'Fly,' Archan repeated.

'Yes, fly.'

Kythe looked up sharply. A shadow passed over her and there was Pax, accompanied this time by two other grim-looking dragons. She cowered down, glancing around as if for an escape route, then smiled wistfully at Jonah.

'I'm sorry,' she whispered. 'But I've brought you most of the way, I suppose. The Tip is the last of the floating shards; it's hidden behind the others so you can't see it from here. There's nothing more I can do but his lair is easy enough to find once you get there. Good luck! He's dangerous!'

With that she pumped her wings twice, generating a thin line of what looked like electricity along their leading edges, then joined her elders in the whistling wind. They said nothing, nor did they even look down at Jonah and Archan as they shepherded Kythe away and over the top edge of the fractured crystal face.

'Fly,' repeated Archan once more. She spat over the precipice; Jonah watched Annie's spittle fall into the empty haze like a single drop of rain lost in a vast, unwelcome sky.

'Annie,' he whispered, craving moonlight so that he might see more clearly.

Her eyelids were barely parted; they fluttered like a moth's wings. He could not see the colour of her eyes, whether they were human white or alien silver. Breath slipped in short gasps past her lips, in and out, and he could not tell by whom it was being drawn.

Archan had slipped into unconsciousness during the afternoon, turning what had begun as a brief period of rest into an out-and-out halt. Jonah did not see how they could go any further, and if Archan was as weak as she seemed then she was not going anywhere.

The sky, black and starless, was draped like a silent challenge before them.

Leaning close, picking out her features by the eerie glow emanating from the crystal wall at his back, he spoke her name again.

'Annie, can you hear me?'

Had her eyelids fluttered a little more rapidly? Surely it was just his imagination.

Gingerly he took her chin in his hand and tilted it towards the faint red light. Something spilled out from beneath her lashes, an aura, a reflection too intense. A glint inside, a metallic sheen that betrayed the true nature of who lay within. What lay within. Disheartened he let go; her head did not move, did not loll as it might have done.

'Where are you, Annie?' he murmured. 'Have you left me alone in this strange world?'

Cold and lonely, unwarmed even by the fever-heat of the woman's body lying beside him, Jonah Lightfoot waited for the sunrise.

He was woken by a sharp pain in his back – during the night he had slipped down against the crystal, wedging his shoulder in a narrow niche at the back of the ledge (*Is this world all ledges?* he asked himself). Standing, he stretched, then jumped as he heard a sigh.

'Annie!' he blurted, for the sound had been so heartfelt, so human, he could not imagine it being made by anyone else. He turned to see her raising her body slowly but elegantly from the ledge, lifting her arms languidly above her head and luxuriating in the early sunshine. She looked tired but poised; half-turned from him, her face was hidden. 'Are you all right?'

Annie's head swivelled, revealing tanned features, dry lips.

She opened her eyes.

They were silver, still.

'The will to live is strong,' said Archan, her voice as cracked as the lips through which it was despatched. The body she wore was erect though, and seemed stronger than it had the day before. 'But the river of time flows on. Today is the last day I shall be strong enough to do this deed, faery. See to it that I succeed.'

Jonah was crushed by the disappointment. Now he turned his head, ashamed of his tears, which he wiped hurriedly with one woollen sleeve. The cloak he had worn since leaving the Neolithics' castle was filthy and malodorous and it was as much as he could do not to pull it over his head and hurl it into the abyss. His whole spirit felt in need of cleansing; to be this close to the demon he now considered Archan to be was almost unbearable. Somehow she tainted him.

Almost unbearable, but not quite. Not as long as Annie was there.

'"The will to live".' He looked out at the nearest of the Backbones, floating in the haze. 'Are you not immortal, Archan?'

'Yes, but not omnipotent!' she snapped. 'Not in this inadequate skin at least!'

'But it is better than no skin at all.'

'Of course! Do not waste time on what I already know! We must reach the giant's lair before sunset or I will be condemned and your precious Annie will be no more!'

'But how . . . ?'

'We must convince a dragon to take us across. There is no other way!'

But there were no dragons flying that morning, and they wasted what Jonah guessed to be a full hour retracing their steps and scouring the upper surface of the crystal stronghold. Tunnels beckoned but neither of them wanted to re-enter what was after all a labyrinth – it seemed to Jonah now that they had been remarkably fortunate not to have got hopelessly lost on the previous day. Archan betrayed no emotion as she paced the cliff edge, staring out across the sky towards the massive floating shards of crystal so tantalisingly near, so impossibly far.

By the time the sun passed behind the Backbones, at the Stone equivalent of high noon, both Jonah and Archan were growing decidedly tense.

It was then that they saw Torus.

The dragon giant flew suddenly into view, just visible as a thin, dark shadow against the glare of the sky. Ribbons of cloud were beginning to descend from the heights and he slipped in and out of them, trailing vapour in his wake. They watched excitedly – perhaps he would come to them – but all too soon he slipped out of sight. They waited for him to appear from behind the crystals but in vain. Torus had evidently returned to his lair and there was no way of knowing when he might emerge again.

A dreadful sound cut the air. Jonah flinched at the banshee wail, only slowly realising it came from Annie's throat.

Her mouth was agape, the tendons stood proud of her neck like thick cords; her borrowed eyes were wide and sightless. The sound was utterly inhuman, a raw, primeval screech which, though lacking words, carried on it some ancient anger, a sense of injustice and dreadful, dreadful pain. It went on for longer than he thought possible and for a moment he wondered if this was in fact not a sound at all but Archan's spirit finally leaving Annie's body.

He stepped forward, ready to catch her as she fell. But the sound stopped and she did not fall. Instead she pointed down. 'Look,' Archan said.

Wings were rising towards them, rising through streamers of cloud.

'Frey!' blurted Jonah, but then he looked again.

The wings were long and shiny, Frey's artificial wings without a doubt. But the man slung beneath them was not Frey.

It was Gerent.

Where had it gone so wrong?

The plan had been sound enough. Gerent had believed, and believed still, that the only way to rid his people of the dragon was to lure Frey into its presence. And with both a willing Malya and the precious stone axes as bait, Frey was sure to come. Had come. If fortune smiled on the Denneth then dragon and shaman would destroy each other. There was even a chance the king would recover.

But now all was lost. The stone axes were gone. Malya was gone!

And Gerent was falling, falling . . .

Frey was a mud-encrusted presence surrounding his body. The shaman's arms were locked about his waist, pulling tight, drawing him close with dreadful, fatal intimacy. He could not breathe. Air spilled from between his lips, fleeing his dying body.

Stone whipped past, sprinting upwards, a dazzling tapestry.

Gerent decided to fight.

Somehow he got one arm free and the pressure about his ribs lessened momentarily, enough time for him to take a single, scalding breath. Then those arms clamped tight again and restored the lethal embrace.

With his free arm – so delirious was he that he had no understanding of whether it was his right or left – he hammered at the shaman's neck, knocking his head sharply to one side. Dried mud flaked off, torn away by eddies in the air. Frey yelped and relaxed his grip again; another breath, this one even more painful.

Malya!

The thought was like the entry of a clean-bladed knife into his heart. With a roar he hauled his other arm clear and punched the shaman's face. There was a sharp crack as his nose broke; blood joined the pale mud in a shower of crimson. Abruptly Frey loosened his grip, drawing his knees up to push his foe away.

But Gerent was not ready to fall. Frey was naked and slippery, but he was strung about with belts and loops. Tearing at a necklace of tiny bones Gerent gained purchase on the shaman's upper body and scrambled round until he could reach the strange wings which were still folded, ineffective against the tug of gravity. His ears sang; the air was growing syrupy and something inside his mind was beginning to fold. He recalled childhood tales of those who had journeyed too far down, and the monstrous effects the depths of Stone had had on their minds and bodies.

Is this happening to me now? Has it happened to me already? Can I ever go back?

Now he held a wing in each hand. Frey's face was pressed into his stomach; his own legs were clamped about the shaman's chest, allowing him to reach over his back. Raw charm flared before his startled eyes, the knot of magic by which the wings were attached to Frey's back. He felt teeth biting at the flesh of his belly.

They struck a cloud, a pocket of cooler air enveloped them and they turned over. Visibility fell almost to nothing. In the fog, Gerent fumbled and found the little skull within which Frey's magic had been focused. Was it there still? He had no way of knowing.

Acting instinctively, with no clue as to what his actions might do (but then he was dead anyway, if he did nothing) Gerent drew the skull back, tiny inside his fist, and drove it straight into the minute sun shining on Frey's back. He felt the interlocked bones shatter to dust, felt the magic swarm up his fingers and over his wrist before he could snatch his hand back. Frey screamed into Gerent's belly, his back arching, his arms writhing behind him in vain as they tried to tear away the agony.

Holding on was almost impossible, but the alternative was unthinkable. He found purchase on the lowest part of the wings – which were beating again, slowly but powerfully; their rate of descent was slowing. As his fingers sank into the soft scales Gerent watched incredulously while Frey's tortured body shrank beneath him.

It happened quickly, almost too quickly for the eye to perceive. The knot of charm seemed to suck Frey in, diminishing him in a series of swift, painful jerks. Arms and legs grew short, for an instant his head bulged disproportionately large then it too wasted away until it was no bigger than the shrunken skull with which Gerent had unwittingly worked this trickery. Then Frey was a doll, a minute facsimile of a man. As tall now as Gerent's hand was long, he shrank no further.

Still gripping the wings' roots, Gerent stared deep into little Frey's eyes . . . and the shaman stared right back at him.

Something had changed. Though clearly alive, Frey was shrunken in every respect. Gone was the glare, the venom of his gaze, to be replaced by an egg-like emptiness, a dull stupidity that Gerent considered, if only briefly, to be worse than the evil that had preceded it. Then Frey's finger-sized arms opened and his little moron's face nodded and smiled and drooled, and Gerent understood that if he wanted to live he had now to trust this distortion of a man.

This man . . . this thing that killed Malya!

Stone chose that moment to re-emerge from behind the cloud

and Gerent's mind was made up. Death would not take him yet, not while the dragon lived that had destroyed his people. Not while there was vengeance to be had.

Before turning his back he regarded Little Frey. Vengeance for Malya – was there a chance for such a thing?

Shuddering at the damp touch, he allowed Little Frey's hands to grasp the skin on either side of his neck. He felt the warmth of his body against his spine as Little Frey became the harness by which Gerent was attached to the dragon wings. The leather was gone, the bones were gone – all that remained was naked Little Frey and the long, metallic wings he grew from his tiny shoulders. Now, as long as what was left of the shaman was holding on to him, Gerent was the master of those wings.

'Up,' he said quietly, and up they took him.

Gerent told them of his fall, and about how he had heard the voice of death whispering in his ear. Tears trailed through the mud and grime on his cheeks.

'They say that when you fall on Stone,' he said hoarsely, 'you can only ever go down. Well, I have been there, and I have returned.'

'What lies down there?' asked Jonah gently, but the prince could only shake his head and weep some more.

As soon as he had landed on the crystal cliff edge Gerent had ripped the wings from his back and hurled them to one side. Jonah gave the prince his full attention as he blurted out his story, but Archan was more interested in the wings themselves. As soon as it became clear what had happened – as clear as it could be given Gerent's confused recollection and his assertion that as he had fallen he had been less and less able to track the flow of events – she wandered over to where they lay and squatted to examine them.

'It was as if,' Gerent said slowly, his brow fiercely creased, 'it was not me in motion but the world around me, as if Stone itself were bending like a blade of grass in the breeze . . .' He stared into the sky. 'He killed Malya.'

'Then she fell,' said Jonah helplessly. 'There was nothing we could do.'

'Perhaps she falls still.'

He could not measure the prince's grief, could not even

remember how they had seemed together, the two Neolithics, before Frey's untimely arrival. It seemed to him that they had reconciled their differences and were exploring the first boundaries of true companionship, maybe even the shores of love. Gerent was all cold anger now, whatever warmth he had felt towards Malya drowned for the time being by a thirst for revenge.

'I will send the wings back to you!'

Alarmed, they looked up to see Archan flying clear of the cliff edge, suspended from the dragon wings and moving rapidly out towards the first of the Backbones.

'Treacherous bitch!' shouted Gerent, almost hurling himself into space in his futile lunge after her.

'Let her go!' cried Jonah, grabbing at his arm. 'She will not abandon us here – she needs us.'

Growling, Gerent shrugged off his grip and scowled at Archan's receding faery form.

There was no argument when the wings returned of their own accord some ten minutes later; Gerent donned them and launched himself in pursuit of Archan. Jonah's wait was agonising but sure enough, when another ten minutes or so had passed, the disembodied wings reached the cliff once more and hovered lightly in the air before him.

But they are not disembodied, he thought with a shiver as he stepped towards them.

And indeed, there suspended between them was the smiling face of Little Frey.

Jonah recalled the doll's house that had consumed so much of his sister Mary's early years, and into which she had retreated again as an adult when Henry and Albert had died. Sometimes, he knew, she had wished herself a doll, to be without care or responsibility, to smile without needing the luggage of feeling. He imagined Little Frey placed inside that elaborately decorated house, a grinning golem with wide, stupid eyes.

Stupid? Frey was anything but stupid. Is this creature still him on the inside, however changed it might appear on the outside?

But Gerent appeared to trust it, he who had least reason to trust it, and it had allowed neither Archan nor the Neolithic to drop into the abyss.

Cringing at the touch of those warm, damp doll's hands on

the nape of his neck, he ducked into Little Frey's embrace and felt his body settle into an invisible holster of magic. With the remains of the shaman splayed across his shoulders, he allowed himself to be pulled into the sky.

Try as he might he could not generate any sense of wonder, despite the fact that he had achieved one of man's greatest dreams: the freedom of flight. All he knew was abject fear, and for most of the short trip he kept his eyes tightly shut and covered by his hands. He felt out of control, though some part of him understood that he *could* control the wings if he tried; all he wanted was to feel something solid beneath his feet again. Only when he heard the low breath of the wind against the approaching island did he peek through interlaced fingers to see Gerent's arms outstretched to help him land. Repelled as the prince had been, he yanked the wings from his body, turning away from Little Frey's imbecilic grin as it and the scaly contraption to which it was welded bounced across the red crystal ground.

They did not rest here. Time had become an imperative for all of them and there was nothing here that was different to what they had already seen. The only difference was that from here their ultimate goal was at last visible, a thin red sliver cut like a scar in the hazy sky: the Tip.

Wordlessly Gerent adopted the wings again and set off for this outermost island, bypassing the intermediate Backbones altogether now that the reliability of the wings had been established. The wait was long enough to be tedious; Jonah and Archan retired to opposite sides of the crystal, neither of them receptive to either conversation or company. Archan went next, and by the time Jonah's turn came round again he was tired; a dull pain was pulsing in the front of his head. This time, his eyes remained shut as much to keep the headache at bay as to avoid the dizzying view. One thing he could not ignore however was the inhuman touch of Little Frey's tiny fingers, and the awful way they stroked his skin, busy like ants.

He could not locate the part of his body from which he was suspended. Little Frey's arms were draped loosely around his neck, his legs trailing between Jonah's shoulder blades. Magic, presumably, was doing the real work unseen.

The Tip grew larger, a smooth cone of bright red crystal

hovering motionless against a backdrop of slowly descending cloud. With no other point of reference he could imagine the sky was still and both he and the crystal were ascending into the heavens. The cone was lying on its side like a fallen spinning top. Its apex looked sharp enough to cut thread; the blunt end was ragged and torn, harbouring an area of dense shadow which might have been an opening.

Fighting against the thumping in his head he glanced back towards Stone.

The main body of crystal – the Flank – was transfigured. Brilliant sunshine cascaded across it, enlightening the upper reaches and imbuing the underside with a deep and fiery glow. From here, far out in the sky, it stood proud and clear from the grey complexity of Stone, a glassy sculpture whose form was at last revealed: it was a dragon.

The dragon's body formed the greater part of the Flank; its neck extended vertically up from the junction between crystal and Stone, a tapering drainpipe culminating in a broad, streamlined head. Its posture was confused, its wings reduced to mere spikes and folds – the very formations, he now realised, through which they had picked their way earlier – but it was clear that the Backbones were in fact the shattered remains of the dragon's tail. The Tip was just that: the tip of the broken tail.

A stream of cloud obscured the view momentarily. When it cleared Jonah saw motion against the overwhelming redness of the awesome sculpture: dragon wings – living dragon wings – beating their way towards him. As soon as he saw their orange colour Jonah recognised the individual. It was Kythe herself.

'I'm going to get into such trouble for this!' she panted as she easily overhauled him. 'Your friends are already there – you must be a very slow flier.'

'I am afraid we have only one set of wings between us.'

Kythe looked nonplussed at this, squinting at the bundle of light clumped around Jonah's shoulders. 'Well, I suppose that's faery business,' she decided. 'You're going to need some help.'

'Did you not say it would be dangerous?'

They were over the curve of the Tip now, descending towards the small black motes which were Gerent and Archan. The cone was truly immense.

A crystal palace . . .

'It is,' replied Kythe tersely, and for a moment Jonah could not remember what he had asked her.

From the blunt end there rose a thin trail of dark grey vapour: smoke, rising from the mouth of the dragon's lair.

11
Torus

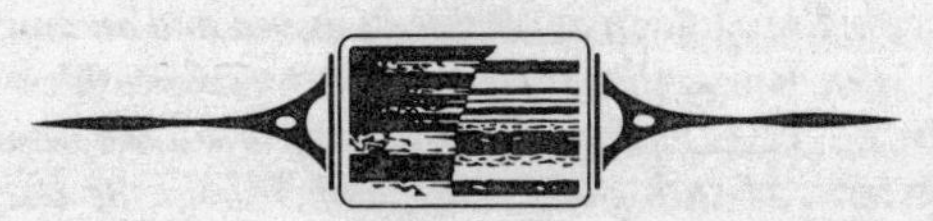

The first dragons to fly in the sky of Stone were called Brace and Ledra.

Back in the other world, which all who live in it call the real world, *dragons once thrived. In the early days that world was ruled by charm. All dragons and all the creatures with which they shared their world were charmed; not a corner of the cosmos was unilluminated by the light of charm; not a single living heart measured its beat but by the steady rhythm of magic.*

For many aeons this Golden Age of charm continued . . . until the world began to turn.

It was noticed by the dragons in small ways at first. An infant born with unusually long wings. Scales losing their metallic lustre towards the end of a dragon's long life. Throats once filled with fire becoming cold.

Magic beginning to lose its power.

Soon there was a new kind of dragon abroad: the natural dragon. Unlike their charmed cousins, these poor creatures were quite unable to make contact with the Realm, primary source of dragon charm, and hence unable to wield magic at all. Charmless, dull of scale, these Naturals survived against the odds and soon outnumbered the charmed overlords, many of whom still looked down on them as an abomination.

Eventually the tensions culminated in war. The great and terrible Wraith led his army of charmed dragons against Shatter and his band of Naturals in a battle that nearly wiped all dragons from the face of the world – and would have done had the world not chosen that moment to turn.

The turning of the world: the moment in time when then *became* to be. *The moment when charm fled, leaving rude nature to take its place. The moment when dragons who had relied solely on their skill with charm to achieve flight fell like stones from the sky.*

The day the magic went away.

A few dragons lived through that moment and emerged into the chaotic time of storms that followed. The skin of the world was wrecked, changed beyond recognition as continents moved and ancient kingdoms were lost. Then it was that the basilisks, the six deathless ones who had survived every *Turning (for preceding this latest cataclysm was an endless series of such cataclysms), gathered up the last shreds of abandoned charm and left the world themselves, giving up their immortality to the one creature who desired it: Archan, the dragon who wanted to live forever.*

The final blow to the old world of charm came with the day of creation. On that fateful day the world acquired a new history, one in which the old ways of charm had never even existed. The rules were rewritten, and in this new world of nature there was no place for dragons.

No longer able to breed, those few who had survived first the Turning and then the gathering of the Deathless stayed on in a world that no longer wanted them, living out the remainder of their days, the last of the dragons.

All except two: Brace and Ledra.

They alone escaped. As their friends looked on they alone made their way through to another world, a world where the sky was vast and blue, with lines of cloud set against its richness in soaring, vertical bands. A world tipped on its side, a world where dragons were more than just a story.

A world where dragons might live forever.

Kythe paused, glancing nervously at the three human faces regarding her solemnly. 'I'm not boring you am I?' she blurted. 'I'd hate to think you were getting bored.'

'Fascinating,' yawned Archan, turning away.

'Please go on,' urged Jonah. 'Ignore her, she is . . . I think she may know some of this already.'

'Oh. Well, we have been here for many generations now – all that was a long time ago. Our ancestors Brace and Ledra are long dead, but here on Stone they managed to have the infants they could never have had in the old world. Dragon eggs became infertile when the world turned, you see.'

'Are there dragons all across Stone now?' Jonah asked. At last he began to understand Esh's reference to the 'turning of the world'. But could all this really be true? Could it be that the battle between Darwin and the Old Testament was irrelevant, that in fact neither hypothesis was true, that the true history was even stranger? Creation working on the past as well as the future. He thought of the memory rods stretching in both directions, both backwards and forwards . . .

'In times past we tried to venture out, and I think a few might have made it. But remember what I told you before, about the Dead Calm and the faery reaches. We don't travel far these days – we're happy enough here on the Flank; it provides us with everything we need. The crystal absorbs the sun's light and heat, so the tunnels inside stay at a constant temperature. And it absorbs charm as well, or at least it seems to. That's how the amboroth is made, we think.'

'You *think*?' spat Archan contemptuously. 'Come, we must move.'

'Yes,' went on Kythe doggedly. 'And we also think the crystal is still connected with the old world somehow. The way it's joined to Stone is very odd: it's as if they're merged together. As if there's something on the other side holding on.'

'A way back?' asked Jonah excitedly, but the dragon shook her long orange head.

'Not in the way you mean, no. But a connection all the same, something . . .'

Gerent interrupted. 'Come on,' he murmured to Jonah, pulling him forward. 'We have to stay together now.'

Jonah saw that Archan had started walking up the shallow slope towards the broken blunt end of the Tip. He also saw that Gerent had fashioned a leash from a thin strip of leather, one end of which he had tied loosely around Little Frey's throat. The charm-laden wings bobbed obediently at his side; when he tugged the leash they followed.

It took them about half an hour to reach the end of the Tip and at least as long to descend the treacherous, slippery angles of the broken crystal. By the time they reached what did indeed turn out to be a large tunnel entrance the sun had moved well beyond its midday position. Archan looked out from a human face made haggard by fatigue; dark circles rimmed her borrowed eyes and the breath in her throat was a thin rasp. Jonah supported her as they entered the shadow of the tunnel, but as soon as they had passed into darkness she shrugged off his arm.

'I have energy yet, faery,' she muttered.

So Jonah Lightfoot, accompanied by a Neolithic prince, his shrunken medicine man and two dragons, one of whom was wearing the skin of a woman, entered the lair of the giant Torus, evidence of whose fire trailed through the air above his head, a skein of dirty smoke thick with the smell of charm.

The smell grew stronger as darkness enfolded them like falling curtains. These walls did not glow like the others they had encountered – here the ruby was dim, admitting only the merest trace of red-filtered light. Ahead all was black as jet.

Parts of the tunnel were porous; Jonah felt at times that they had penetrated a gigantic sponge. Tiny circular holes, none larger than a penny piece, peppered the inner lining of the passageway, the rough texture they created contrasting dramatically with the adjacent stretches of smooth, unbroken crystal. Wind whispered through these minute veins, its sound like a distant lullaby.

This is the lair of a dragon, he told himself, trying to reassure himself that it might not be that bad by seeking out the lumbering form of Kythe, a dragon who was at least friendly.

Then his vision filled with smoke and he was afraid.

The passage, roughly circular in section and high enough so that the ceiling was lost in the gloom, dipped sharply. At the same time the porosity increased so that every visible surface looked as though it had been blasted with lead shot.

Then, without warning, they reached an abrupt turn, a horseshoe twist that took them round a blind corner and into the presence of Torus.

Jonah's first impression was that they were stood at the edge of a vast quarry. The light was a little brighter here; many of the perforations were fist-sized and the chamber was crisscrossed with thin beams of light, clearly demarked in the thick and dust-laden atmosphere. A steep crystal cliff dropped away before them, less sheer and of course much less deep than Stone itself but daunting nonetheless. The quarry was rough-hewn, evidently excavated without concern for either appearance or comfort. It was littered with large bones and curved horns, which covered the floor so comprehensively that nothing of the underlying crystal was visible; it occurred to Jonah that this carpet of skeletons might be many feet deep. After a moment's consideration he judged that these were the remains of aurochs. Hundreds of them.

And on top of the bones lay Torus.

Here rose the stench of decay, the sweet smell of butchery. Suddenly the walls were the colour not of ruby but of blood. Shafts of light merged with the red and black stripes painting the spiny back of the dragon giant, a confusion of line and camouflaged scale that disrupted the contours of the beast, made an enigma of it. Jonah coughed, a loud involuntary outburst that echoed like the blow of a smith around the crystal quarry. He raised his hands to wipe his face and found them trembling, touched fresh sweat on his cheeks. Base terror rose in his throat, threatening to bring with it a scream; biting down on his lip he gulped back the fear, forcing himself to look down on the dragon.

It was even larger than he remembered, though its true bulk was hard to judge, curled as it was around its own, intricate coils. With its limbs hidden and its wings furled it looked truly serpentine, a huge snake sleeping off its latest meal – which looked likely to have been an entire auroch, swallowed whole for all Jonah knew. Its flanks moved in and out rhythmically; its breath sent ripples through the dust, shadows modulating the striated light.

'Are you all right, Lightfoot?' whispered Gerent's voice in his ear. The prince sounded calm, calmer in fact than Jonah had ever heard him.

'Yes . . .' he began. Then he moaned, 'No, I'm not: I confess I am horribly afraid. How can we possibly face this monstrous creature? He would swallow us all in a single gulp!'

'Perhaps,' agreed Gerent. 'And perhaps not.'

Out of the corner of his eye Jonah saw that Archan had crouched at the very edge of the quarry, mirror eyes burning red. With a colossal effort he pressed down his fear and turned his attention to her: she was after all the reason he had come to this dreadful cavern. Here it was that she would finally make her move, whatever it might be.

He heard a pattering sound down in the depths of the quarry. Gerent was pulling up shreds of the perforated crystal floor and throwing the pieces down on to Torus's back. Archan was looking on in interest, Kythe with something that could only have been horror.

'Stop it!' the young dragon cried. 'What do you think you're doing? Torus has such a temper on him!'

'He must be roused,' answered Gerent, his voice still eerily calm. Behind him, still attached by the slender leash, Little Frey and the wings hovered silently.

After the third handful Gerent paused, looking for a sign of movement. When there was none he bent a fourth time, and that was when, with a tremendous cracking of bones and brittle slabs of crystal, the dragon giant raised his head and turned his baleful gaze on the intruders.

Black eyes regarded them solemnly as Torus uncoiled his neck, his head elevating in a single, liquid movement until it was on a level with the top of the quarry walls. Smoke puffed from his nostrils; fluid leaked from them, too, a thin watery substance that had stained the scales round his mouth a dirty tobacco yellow. His jaws were slightly parted, revealing cracked teeth stained the same colour. Smooth though his broader movements had been there was, Jonah noted, a slight tremor in his head, like that of a very old man.

Torus opened his mouth and puffed a ring of vapour over their heads. Jonah noted with unease that he could have lain himself on the beast's livid red tongue and still had more room to spare than on the comfortable mattress he had left behind in London. The fear erupted into his chest and throat again, barely controllable; his skin seemed to contract and legs wanted only to turn and run. Yet he stood his ground, fascinated.

Nobody knew what to do, it appeared, not even the dragon giant who by rights should have swept them from the tunnel mouth with one blow of his snout and gobbled them up even before they hit the floor. In the end it was Gerent who broke the silence.

'You have destroyed my people!' he announced boldly. Only his mouth moved; the rest of his body was like a dark statue, fists clenched against the anger swelling within it.

If the words meant anything to Torus the dragon did not

show it. Huge eyes looked at each of them in turn, lingering the longest on Archan. Then they returned to Kythe, who was cowering in the shadows behind her companions.

'Kythe?' The voice with which a mountain would speak, were it inclined so to do.

'Y-yes?'

A rumble that might have been a sigh. 'Yes, Kythe. I recall your father.'

'H-he died last year, Master Torus.'

'Indeed. You are nearly grown now.'

A long, long silence. Then Torus addressed Gerent. 'You have brought me something.'

'I have brought your doom!' responded Gerent at once. His words were brave but Jonah could hear the fear interleaved with them. He thought the Neolithic prince was very courageous and very foolish. 'You have taken everything from me – my father, my home! Do you doubt my right to confront you?'

Torus lifted a wide, horny brow. 'This is my home. You have no rights here, faery.'

'Please, Master Torus,' wailed Kythe. 'He doesn't mean you any harm. You don't, do you? – tell him you don't.'

Torus's massive head was drawing near, enlarging with frightening speed as it approached them like a ship drawing towards harbour. It stopped just short of where Little Frey was floating. Nostrils the size of sewer pipes flared and snorted.

'You have brought me this?' Torus enquired, swivelling his eyes round to regard Gerent without turning his head. The dragon's presence was overwhelming; now Jonah knew how his Biblical namesake must have felt in the presence of the great fish that had swallowed him whole.

Gerent looked from the disembodied wings to Torus then back to the wings again. His shoulders dropped slightly and he let the leash fall. Little Frey did not alter his position, just continued to smile his idiotic grin, continued to flap those synthetic wings. Wings of red and black, wings constructed from scales taken from this giant, or rather from the dragon this giant had once been, before Frey's cruel magic had made it what it was now.

The great head retreated and Torus turned sideways on. They all gasped, even Archan, as the ruins of his left flank were revealed.

Great swathes of bare skin were exposed where scales had been torn out. Scars and fresh, weeping wounds ran under his belly, raw lines blending with the pattern of red stripes so that it was hard to tell what was decoration and what injury. Having given them a good view of this, Torus unfurled his wings, displaying the many rips through which beams of light played. He tipped his head forward to show the back of his skull, where notched bone was visible. Jonah did not care to imagine what experiment of Frey's had exacted those particular wounds.

Could this be the majestic flying serpent that had snatched the auroch from in front of Jonah's astonished eyes? Surely not! And yet, now he thought about it, Jonah realised that until now he had seen the giant only in brief glimpses, or at a great distance. *This* was the reality, this pitifully scarred creature whose only crime had been to seek revenge for the appalling surgery the evil shaman had seen fit to practise upon it.

But now Gerent was here to seek revenge of his own, and he was not so easily mollified.

'You have suffered indeed,' he called. 'But that does not change what you have done. Will you answer for your crimes?'

Torus growled suddenly and thrust his head alarmingly close. Jonah and Kythe scrambled back but both Gerent and Archan stood their ground. 'Will you answer for *his*?' spat Torus, flicking his grimy snout at Little Frey. 'Give me the evil faery and I will consider the matter finished. Give him to me so that you and your friends may leave here alive.'

'I will not yield to you, dragon. You have murdered my people and you must pay the price!'

At this Torus's eyes widened, and Jonah thought he would incinerate them all there and then. Instead he raised his gigantic head to the ceiling and roared with laughter. Jets of flame spurted from behind his tongue, showering them with sparks. Blast furnace heat washed over them like waves up the shore.

'And what price will you make me pay, little faery?' he demanded when his laughter had subsided enough for him to speak.

With a swift movement Gerent reached out and grasped Little Frey about the midriff. The tiny man grunted, a shrill rodent sound, but the smile never left his moon-like face. 'I will deprive you of your only chance to complete your revenge,' he uttered through clenched teeth. 'I could crush these tiny bones before you could move even a muscle.'

'Then you would both die!' Torus sounded angry, dangerously so.

'But *I* would have taken his life, not you.'

The advantage was too slender. Jonah cowered down, anticipating the fire, but it did not come. Instead Torus sucked air in, generating a high-pitched whistle as it was drawn between his teeth.

'I had considered my work done until you came today, faery. The castle is no more. I had assumed the evil one dead along with the rest of your pitiful clan but it seems I was wrong. Now you have confounded me and I am disadvantaged. What would you have me do?'

Jonah was astonished. He had expected a brute, not a creature blessed with such eloquence. Looking closely at Torus he saw the dragon's whole body was beset by the tremor he had noticed in his head. *He is frail, perhaps he is even dying, and all because of Frey's evil deeds!* He felt, suddenly, desperately sorry for the giant.

'The beast is right, Gerent,' he said quietly, touching the Neolithic man gently on the shoulder. 'It is over between you. As he says, what would you have him do?'

Gerent's throat worked violently; his fingers tightened perceptibly around Little Frey's body. 'Nothing can bring them back. Nothing can bring Malya back.'

'I repeat,' said Torus with surprising softness, 'what would you have me do?'

His face contorting, Gerent flung Little Frey and the flailing wings against the wall behind him; they struck it with a soft thud and dropped to the floor, flapping weakly. Then he turned away, his face covered by his hands, his body heaving with sobs. 'I would have you and he dead and all of this never to have happened. I would have the past wiped clean. I would have Malya back in my arms. I would have . . .' He became incoherent, falling to his knees next to the struggling wings and weeping uncontrollably into his hands.

Torus regarded the weeping man with what might have been pity, then glanced at Archan. 'This business is unfinished,' he announced, 'but you . . . do I know you? You have the eyes of the Deathless.'

'Know me?' purred Archan as though she were trying to seduce him. 'Oh yes, I'm sure you do.'

Torus shook his head like a dog trying to dislodge a flea. 'You are a dragon.' It was not a question. Archan nodded.

'I must know how much charm there is here. How much there really is. I have charm sense but it is dulled by this pitiful body.' She thumped Annie's breastbone, a hard blow that made Jonah wince. 'Will you tell me?'

'I will do better than that,' replied Torus, eyeing her with curiosity. 'I will show you.'

He rocked back on his haunches and closed his eyes. His outstretched wings vibrated and began to sparkle; it was like seeing a thousand fireflies materialising out of nothing. Flashes of red light darted from the walls of the cavern, lines of charm drawn from the crystal sponge. This entire structure was nothing less than a storehouse for magic, Jonah realised, and now Torus was drawing out something from that store to use.

The fireflies, shining vivid red now, swarmed to the dragon's wingtips where they paused, twin centres of jostling energy, crackling with life. Then Torus jerked his wings away and the charm was flying free. It lanced forward in two identical streams, their focus an aurochs skull half-buried amid the remains of its unlucky brethren. The charm struck the skull, illuminating it from within; Jonah thought of Frey's evil spell and shuddered. With a dreamy, fluid motion the skull lifted itself from the surrounding debris and floated beside Torus's claws. More bones followed it: the rest of the skeleton, assembling itself in perfect order behind the levitating skull until the aurochs was remade. This fleshless creation then tossed its head and bent forward as though grazing; Jonah gasped, simultaneously terrified and enchanted.

Torus rang out a peal on the crystal with his claw and the auroch skeleton bolted, the bleached bones of its legs beating perfect time as it surged across the floor of the quarry. It met the far wall with a tremendous explosion, scattering itself and the sparkling charm that had animated it across the full width of the arena. When the remains finally came to rest it was impossible to distinguish them from the other skeletons.

Torus raised his massive head for approval; Archan gave it in the form of a brief nod of Annie's head, which was shaking now in much the same way as that of the dragon giant.

'There is sufficient for my needs. Have you guessed my needs, dragon?'

Torus nodded slowly. 'I have, Archan. Though I have not yet decided whether I shall permit you to take my skin. I may yet have need of it.'

Archan blinked; it might have been an expression of surprise, though those mirror eyes remained as unreadable as ever. 'So, you know my name. Very impressive.'

'Brace and Ledra brought nothing with them but their stories of the world they left behind. Your name rang loud in one of those stories, Archan, very loud indeed.'

'And it shall ring forever, dragon, have no doubt about that.'

'I do not doubt it, Archan, though I question it.'

'Such questions are beyond your concern.'

'I have nothing to lose.'

'Nor I.'

They stared at each other, a long, penetrative glare. Then Torus laughed.

'Your borrowed faery flesh has little capacity for charm, Archan. If I choose not to be taken there is nothing you can do to force your way into my body. What will you say to convince me to sacrifice myself for you?'

'As you say, dragon, you have nothing to lose. Nor do you have anything to live for. Look at yourself: you are dying! With vengeance yours what more reason do you have to suffer? Give yourself over to me and some part of you at least will live forever.'

But Torus only shook his head and laughed again. Jonah could see that Archan was growing angry; she was also breathing hard, as though each breath were painful. Was she feigning weakness, or was she really as much at the mercy of the dragon giant as she seemed?

He saw Torus's ebony eyes flick towards him then past him, felt a touch of air on his cheek and saw Little Frey fly swiftly past, directly towards the dragon giant's head. Torus recoiled, hissing steam, then snapped at the tiny hybrid. Little Frey retreated, grinning silently, arms held rigid at his side; charm poured from his stolen wings in a bright cascade. Once more he darted forward then pulled back, drawing Torus forward, teasing him. As Torus hesitated Little Frey spun round and flew at Jonah, halting just inches from his face.

Jonah looked deep into mad eyes and saw the man trapped inside. Frey was there, buried deep just as Annie was buried deep inside her own, ravaged mind, and clearly visible now as he surfaced briefly, fighting the shackles of lunatic charm that had kept him restrained until now. In those eyes, shining like pins, Jonah saw Frey's evil concentrated, distilled to a pair of tiny droplets and ready to be administered in whatever way he saw fit. He shrank back, holding up his hands to ward off the harpy.

But it was not for him that Frey was making – it was Gerent.

The Neolithic prince looked up at the last moment and understood at once. Frey was riffling searing charm between his fingers like a poker player shuffling cards; he wavered, once, between Jonah and Gerent, a fog of idiocy clouding his eyes briefly, but then he redoubled his speed, clearly anxious to complete his task before his mind was taken from him again. As he lashed the skein of charm about Gerent's neck it seemed that task was simple enough: to throttle the last of the clan of the Denneth.

But Gerent was fast. He ducked beneath the glowing garrotte and rolled clear, leaving the miniaturised Frey to spin clumsily in the air, backtracking now in pursuit of the retreating prince.

'Enough!' roared Torus, his voice deafening in a chamber that seemed suddenly too small to contain it. 'I have had enough!'

In those four words Jonah heard more pain than he could have imagined. Before him stood not a noble dragon but a wrecked and dying monster, a pathetic creature whose life had become an endless round of agony and revenge, a creature entirely divorced from the cares of those around him, divorced even from his own concerns: a creature simply ticking like a clock whose mainspring has almost run down. And it was at that moment that the mainspring burst.

Had he been frightened before? He had not known the meaning of fear! Torus thrashed first backwards then forwards, throwing his mighty body against the side of the quarry; a monster cut loose at last. His tail whipped up, scoring crystal and bringing down great chunks of ceiling, breaking several of his own dorsal spines in the process. Mercifully he kept his head high, spraying flames across the lacerated ceiling rather than the horrified onlookers. Kythe screamed like a human child and flew back into the tunnel, but it was too late for the others. Already the ground was tipping as the quarry walls began to collapse inwards. An avalanche of red fragments sucked them first forwards then down as Torus brought his crystal palace crashing down around himself.

Jonah tucked his head down and clasped his hands around it. He fell heavily on his back and lost all the air from his lungs; a further series of impacts disorientated him completely and convinced him he was suffocating, unable to draw fresh breath for the constant battering. Blurred stars danced in the blackness, then he opened his eyes into a grey cave and found himself staring into the empty orbit of an aurochs skull, for all he knew the very skull Torus had used for his conjuring. He cried out, the reflex breaking the spell that had clamped his lungs shut, then kicked out, scrambling clear of the pile of bones into which he had fallen and gaining slightly higher ground in the form of an outcrop of crystal. There he crouched, gasping, looking up at the underbelly of Torus as it descended to crush him.

At the last possible moment the dragon slewed to the side; red and black scales struck sparks from the bones to Jonah's right, reducing many of them to powder. Then Torus lunged up again, snapping at something small jabbing at his face: Frey, still working those wings, still making mischief.

Jonah looked around for Gerent and Archan. Finally he looked up again and saw them as if frozen in a moment snatched from time.

Both were much higher up the landslide than he; both were leaping into the air, Archan jumping towards Torus's throat, Gerent apparently jumping into nowhere. He tracked Archan, saw her thump into the soft flesh of the dragon giant's neck, saw Annie's fingers lock into the wrinkles. Saw her begin to climb.

Gerent – where was he? Fallen? He looked down but saw nothing. A birdlike movement to his left: Gerent, grappling with Frey's wings, falling swiftly but aided by the open membranes. Charm fountained from their entangled forms; it was impossible to tell what was going on.

A gaping maw plunging towards him: Torus's mouth closing

around Gerent, Frey and the wings but not closing all the way. A giant, scaled head slicing the thick air barely a foot in front of Jonah then hauling its catch up, up into the dust and light. Archan hanging on grimly as the gigantic neck coiled tight then extended.

Light broke through high above. The ceiling had crumbled altogether, admitting clean blue sky-light. Above the crackling of disintegrating bones and the angry bellowing of Torus could now be heard the tearing of the crystal walls themselves.

There was a kind of halo from which a giant dragon profile was etched. Its jaws were parted; inside them rode Gerent and the wings, continuing their battle. Archan was a small, leather-bound fly ascending the tower of Torus's neck.

Why doesn't Torus kill them? Jonah wondered, then he remembered the dragon giant's lust for revenge in its purest form: if Gerent were to despatch the shaman, even in the throes of his own death, Torus would be robbed of victory.

All of which gave Archan the time she needed, and she had other ideas than simply waiting on the outcome of a contest in which she had no interest whatsoever. A new light entered the scene, a twinned beam projecting directly from her mirrored eyes. Jonah recalled a legend about the basilisk – that its gaze was lethal – and wondered if that ancient power had been dormant in Archan all along.

The two lines of light Archan had fired converged on Gerent. Suddenly those giant dragon jaws were illuminated from within by a titanic explosion. Several teeth tore free and cartwheeled through the air accompanied by a fine spray of blood. Within the conflagration Gerent and the thrashing wings continued to move. Then Torus pulled his head back and roared and the light from outside poured in like an avalanche, blinding Jonah. When his vision recovered, Gerent, Frey and the wings were gone.

Blood showered down all around him, fizzing as it struck the bone litter and stinging his skin. To his astonishment the aurochs remains began to dissolve; instinctively he pulled his hands beneath his robe and lowered his head – if it could dissolve bone what might this acid do to him?

Something struck his back and bounced away – a dragon's tooth the size of a beer barrel. He was thrown forward into what had become a sea of bone fragments rapidly melting to dust. Floundering in this weird fluid he felt a sudden current drag him away from the relative safety of the landslide, which now stood proud of the dust like an island jutting from the ocean. Soon he was spinning, caught up in a whirlpool in the shadow of Torus's massive belly, drawn down just as he had been drawn down after the eruption of Krakatoa, except now he felt like a grain of sand caught in a giant's hourglass, a glass that was marking off the last few seconds of his life.

The cone into which he had been sucked grew dark. Motion and pressure increased simultaneously then the latter was released and light flooded across his face. The roaring sounds were gone and his stomach lifted into his throat. Coughing out bone dust, flailing with his arms and legs, Jonah fell through the split in the floor of the chamber and into the empty sky. Beneath him was pure blue haze. He was falling free amid a cloud of debris towards a smooth grey monolith jutting out from Stone like a plank from a pirate's ship. Except this plank just grew and grew, filling his vision as it eclipsed the sky beneath it until it had assumed gargantuan proportions.

So Jonah fell.

12

Annie on the Inside – 3

Cold. Hell was cold.

The Bible was wrong, all the stories of fire and brimstone were wrong. Hell was a place of lonely ice and deep, bitter cold. Annie knew this for certain, because that was where she was.

There had been fire but now that was all but gone. Now she was alone like the ice, with the ice, lost and alone in the bottom of this ancient well. The walls surrounding her were gnarled with scales, as cold as the air sitting heavily inside her motionless lungs. Far above was a star of orange light, the top of the well, an impossible climb.

And yet . . .

She moved her mind and what passed for her body moved with it, struck the cobbled wall and sent flabby echoes skimming up the sides of the well. The star twinkled and it seemed to her that she was higher. Looking down she saw there was no floor; she was suspended above a bottomless pit.

She panicked and fell a lifetime's distance into the abyss before checking herself. She scraped to a halt against the wall. Tentatively she pressed it: it yielded like flesh, or liquid skinned over. Carefully now, feeding her concentration with what little was left of her energies, she ascended once more.

The star grew bigger with agonising slowness. At times the walls seemed to close in on her but she fought her way past their frigid, reptilian embrace. The higher she rose the more she thought she felt fleeting touches of warmth, the more strength she seemed to find. Now the scales were rattling past at dazzling speed, melting as they fell away, liquefying until she was no longer flying but swimming, thrusting against the descending current that was trying so hard to pull her down into its stream. Bubbles cascaded past her, each one containing tiny scenes from her life, sharp jabs of memory.

The star was a flare now, a flickering beacon guiding her ever higher. Its heat was undeniable, a fabulous grail she had to attain; its light melted the scales yet further until the current through which she swam was a free thing, an exposed column of filthy liquid draining itself into the well from which she had nearly broken free. Things were visible beyond that column, things she could not identify but which were achingly familiar: the landscape of her own mind, the shape of herself.

Now the star divided, revealing itself as twins. The liquid that had held her back was thinning rapidly and she found her lungs were working, pulling at air she could not yet locate. Her fingers were suddenly there, tingling; her tongue swelled in her mouth, startlingly big; blood flushed its way past her burgeoning senses, tasting salty and metallic.

The last of the scales fell away and Annie expanded. She felt her whole spirit inflate to fill the empty chambers it had been denied for so long. Screaming with the inexpressible agony of birth, Annie burst free of the prison into which she had been banished. She crashed against the twinned stars, pressed herself against their windows and looked out into the world of Stone with her own eyes once more.

At first she could not tell where she was. All she knew was that she was being tossed around like a boat in a storm. She found her hands were lodged deep into a pair of cracks in what might have been a cliff face, while her knees were clamped tight against a rough, curved surface. She held on desperately, casting around with all her rediscovered senses in an effort to make sense of the situation.

It did not take long, though the discovery was anything but reassuring.

The crevices into which her hands had been thrust were in fact deep notches in the skull of a giant dragon. Four great horns reared backwards, two on each side, flanking her like an honour guard; she was sitting astride the very top of the dragon's neck, her legs protected against its jagged scales by a pair of leather breeches. Briefly assessing her garb to be some curious blend of mediaeval and prehistoric, with a touch of the

Oriental thrown in, she turned her attention to seeking a way out of this predicament.

But there was no time to think. The giant dragon was bucking like a bronco.

'Whoa, you head-shy bastard!' she cried. The dragon responded by tossing its head forward, jerking her arms almost out of their sockets and lifting her buttocks from its neck. It shook its head like a dog but Annie's handholds were located at the very base of its skull and the leverage was poor. She slapped back down into a sitting position and saw stars.

Her brother's voice echoed through her head (and she whispered a silent prayer of thanks as she acknowledged that it was her head again): 'Quit your buckin', you fantail mare!' His broad, deep voice sounded sweet in her head and she missed him with sudden, radiant longing. She saw him – actually saw him – clinging to the bronc saddle with one hand and waving the other deliriously while the low Kansas sun shone from his perfect teeth.

Was he still alive, her brother Luke? Or had the droughts got him too?

There was the briefest of pauses then the dragon flung its head sideways and renewed its vigour. Still Annie held on, though only by virtue of the death-grip her hands had in the crevices notched into the back of its head; her thighs slammed against its craggy neck and the breath blurted from her mouth in short, hard bursts.

She realised that there was more action going on than just the bucking of the dragon. In fact, she appeared to have recovered consciousness in the middle of an earthquake. Confused, wondering momentarily if she really had dreamed her encounters with Esh, her thoughts moved abruptly from Kansas to Krakatoa and then to her strange incarceration.

Rapunzel!

But the dragon beneath her was real enough, and so were the sharp red boulders raining out of the sky.

Fortunately the dragon appeared to consider them a danger too, for as the rain intensified it ceased thrashing about and flew straight up through the widening hole in the ceiling of what Annie now identified as a giant crystal cave. She had little time to marvel at this fabulous structure before it peeled completely in two and collapsed into the ever-ready clutches of gravity. The rain of gems was past them in an instant and they were flying free. Dragon wings, their red and black stripes striking despite their otherwise tattered appearance, cycled back and forth behind her; the muscles of the beast's shoulders made its neck flex each time it beat its wings so that riding it was uncannily like riding a very large horse.

Then she saw Stone, and she knew that nothing had been a dream, nothing at all.

It spanned the full range of her vision, a vast grey plane inclined before her eyes, an infinite wall encrusted with detail. Dominating the space immediately in front was a huge dragon-shape sculpted from the same red crystal she had seen disintegrating around her; it was as big as a mountain. But beyond it in every direction – left and right, up and down – was spread a canvas so immense she could scarcely perceive it.

To the right of the crystal ran a series of ledges or bridges, some of which looked incomplete. Further to the right was what looked for all the world like an enormous pendulum, its upper portion lost in cloud. Beyond that was an upright disc, spinning slowly. Cloud obscured much of the higher levels but lower down, immediately below the crystal in fact, jutted a large, iron-coloured platform. To the left the wall was almost blank, a flat cliff face unmarred by relief but mottled with subtle shades that might have indicated changes of colour or of surface texture. Nothing else was visible in that direction; Annie was reminded of a desert, which it might very well have been.

In amongst these larger features ran endless cables and conduits, the engraved outlines of the gigantic blocks from which Stone was made, elaborate channels, outpourings of water, slender footways and deep undercuts where strange flora lurked in richly-coloured tangles.

'Oh my,' she whispered, weeping. Annie West, who had once looked out across the Kansas plains and wondered what else there was in the world to see, now knew there was far more than she had ever imagined.

Warm wind pressed her hair against her back and shoulders. She sucked it in: it tasted rich and spicy. Her body pulsed about her, making her aware of its every function: the spurt of blood through its arteries, the prick of its nerves, the intense electricity of thought.

'Your tenacity is unparalleled.'

The voice was at once familiar and horribly strange. It came from beneath her and a little in front: the dragon, clearly. Her body jerked, almost pulling her fingers loose.

'What did you say?' she managed to utter.

'I was applauding your remarkable ability to survive,' the voice said again. It was deep and cracked, although as it spoke it changed, growing higher and more controlled. 'You have presented me with a dilemma, for I was convinced I should kill you straight away. However, now there is the opportunity for sport. But I wonder – is the temptation dangerous? Should I simply end it now?'

Annie froze. 'You!' she grated. 'It's you!'

'My name is Archan,' said the voice, coming from the throat that had once belonged to Torus.

'I don't care what your name is,' snarled Annie. 'You raped me and you'll pay. By God, I'll make you pay for what you've done if it's the last thing I do on this Earth!'

'I think you will find this is not your Earth,' replied Archan pleasantly. 'But your attitude has solved the debate: I shall have some sport with you.'

All this time they had been drifting closer and closer to the crystal sculpture. Now Archan, confident in her new dragon body, tucked in her wings and accelerated towards the nearest of the Backbones. Annie shut her eyes and dug in her fingers as a sharp outcrop whistled past just a few feet from her head. She was protected to a degree by the horns that rose on either side of her, but by raising her snout Archan could effectively drop these below the line of her neck, exposing Annie to whatever peril she was able to bring near.

The Backbones thundered past in dizzying succession. Archan looped around the last of them, nearly scraping Annie off against its underside as she flew recklessly close.

She will kill herself too, thought Annie as she clung on, desperately afraid and quite unable to conceive a means of escape.

The Flank loomed ahead, framed by the infinite plane of Stone. Archan sped through a series of spines and columns, rolling sideways and even upside-down in her attempts to dash

Annie's body against the crystal structures, but always Annie managed to duck down, or else Archan drew back at the last minute.

Several times Annie saw other dragon heads – these much smaller – poke up out of partly-concealed holes then swiftly duck down again. She could not help but think of gophers and stifled a hysterical laugh.

She thought it might be over when the onrushing face of Stone forced Archan to turn, but her dragon steed simply retraced her course, flying even closer to the lethal barbs and towers this time, rolling even more swiftly as she tried to throw her rider clear. Annie's fingers throbbed and the insides of her legs felt raw and slicked with blood, despite the leather garments. She grew light-headed and wondered how much longer she could hold on.

Archan cleared the outermost edge of the Flank and was about to turn again when she halted so abruptly that Annie was nearly hurled forward like the driver from a pot-holed wagon.

'There!' sighed Archan, her voice filled with longing. 'Oh, there he is!'

Annie looked through tears of pain and saw a minute speck all but lost in the haze. It was falling some distance below the crumbled remains of the Tip (chunks of crystal tumbling into the emptiness); shortly it would land on the monolithic structure projecting from the surface of Stone.

'Jonah?' she whispered, though the falling mote was barely identifiable even as a human body, let alone a recognisable individual.

But she knew, and Archan knew. The same mighty wings that had once carried Torus through the skies of Stone now took Archan and her human passenger down towards that speck of human dust.

13

Fall

Jonah fell.

Serenity was with him. As he observed the monolith widening and lengthening beneath him, seeming to stretch along its horizontal plane to swallow his view before finally swallowing him, he found time to wonder that he was at peace.

But there was more than that: *he did not believe he would die.* Not here, not now in this way. Where this conviction came from he could not say, but he did know there was much he had not yet done.

'Make her gone,' Esh had said. Well, that was certainly not yet done. Nor did he know Annie's fate, nor Gerent's, nor even that of the dragon-child Kythe. But why such certainty, for he surely *would* die?

By tilting his body he found he could partially control the angle of his descent. Not enough to avoid the huge obstacle towards which he was careering but sufficient to survey the scene around and, in particular, above him.

It was not encouraging.

Scattered across the entire sky were the remains of the Tip, a mosaic of crystal falling perhaps half a mile above Jonah, falling at roughly the same speed and ready (in the highly unlikely event that he should survive hitting the monolith) to crush him to death like a hailstorm from the gods. The sun forged through their turning facets, reflected and refracted in crazy directions so that the cloud of debris resembled a collection of lighthouse beams tainted red and set in wild motion. He could hear nothing but the roar of the air, but he fancied the crystals rumbled as they fell.

Yet still he was not afraid.

Time stretched out, not as it had done on the iceberg, when the world had accelerated past him and Annie, but in his own mind. The monolith loomed but seemed simultaneously to retreat, its threat actually diminishing with every yard he fell. He looked downStone across the smooth, vertical desert lying there, that part of Stone Kythe had described as too slippery to cross, where the wind blew too hard for even a dragon to fly.

What had she called it? *The Dead Calm.*

That was where Jonah was now, in his own Dead Calm, an island of peace in a sea of chaos.

In his mind he sketched a line. The line was Stone, and on it he drew a circle to represent that first threshold – the one that had brought him here. He labelled it '1883': his own present. A few miles downStone had existed the castle, an essentially mediaeval structure (the fact that it had been inhabited by prehistoric men was irrelevant, since they had travelled *upStone* to find it). Yet further downStone he and Malya had found the Roman sword. Now here he was, further on still, among dragons.

The further downStone you travel, the further back in time you go. Only now did the full implications hit home.

Stone was huge, inexpressibly so. Its span was beyond measure, perhaps infinite, and in the few days he had spent here Jonah had covered maybe twenty miles – barely a scratch on its gargantuan hide. He felt like a flea traversing the flank of an elephant. *Yet I have travelled back through the whole of human history and beyond!*

Never had the parks and museums of London seemed so far away. Had he thought his trip to Java the journey of a lifetime? He had not known the half of it! Once he had been surprised to find himself feeling at home on the Spice Islands but now, as he gazed around at the awesome vista of Stone, he was not surprised to find himself entirely at peace here. A clean, clear line connected him with his past in the old world (he chuckled as he realised he no longer thought of it as the 'real world') but it was not into some distant future of man that the line led, nor into the marvel of the new twentieth century but into the hot and spice-laden light of Stone. He belonged here, he knew it in every pore. And there was a job to be done here, a job he alone could do. Fate had ever loomed large in Jonah's life: from the day a concrete-and-steel dinosaur made him an orphan . . .

Again he looked downStone. There was a distant blot in the Dead Calm, a dark mirage. It looked somehow heavy, somehow permanent.

All sense of Stone's verticality was gone now: he might just as well have been falling from a balloon or high tower back in his own world. The surface of the monolith was laid out below him like a colourless county, a tremendous, mottled grey counterpane close enough to create its own horizon. No structures were visible, so it was very hard to tell how near he was; nevertheless the ground it made was bright and sharp and getting bigger with every second. It was close, very close.

Jonah looked up and into the deep black eyes of Kythe.

At first he thought she had lost her wings, then he saw they were tucked tight against her sides, with only six inches of wingtip protruding out into the airstream.

'Hold out . . . hand!' the young dragon yelled, her words buffeted by the shrieking wind.

Jonah's fear returned in a single, devastating wave. He screamed and flailed towards her, rocking on the wind like an unsteady boat. Their shadows suddenly flashed into view, speeding across the surface of the monolith, enlarging to meet them . . .

Kythe's wingtips flicked the tiniest amount and she plunged towards him. He recoiled involuntarily, causing her to crash clumsily into his shoulder. She retreated, cursing.

'Only get . . . one more chance!' she blurted and dived in again.

This time he did not flinch, steeling himself instead against the blow. But Kythe's touch was feather-light: her hind legs wrapped about his torso from behind, claws locked together just below his breastbone. With a guttural cry Kythe stabbed her wings out into the wind's blast and tightened her legs about Jonah's midriff. Without warning he had weight again, seemingly tons of it, hauling at his legs, his stomach and threatening to pull his arms from their sockets. Then Kythe pulled him even closer and started to flap in earnest, the jerky rhythm of her wings transferring itself into Jonah's body and rattling his teeth.

The two shadows had merged into one, a weird chimera with a

man's legs and the long, sweeping wings of a dragon. This hybrid plunged over the grey plain, stretching out its awkward limbs to greet its progenitor . . .

With his feet just five yards clear of the shadow's Jonah felt his downward motion finally stop. Kythe was anything but relaxed however: maintaining this hover in a constant downdraught and with a passenger over three times her body weight was no mean feat. She managed to lower him two of those five yards before her wings crumpled and they fell the last few feet to the ground, their shadows rolling apart again as their bodies separated and they tumbled to an ignominious halt.

Jonah lay there gasping, commanding his lungs to draw in air despite their winded protests. He was alive! He had survived the fall – he had in some small way proven himself worthy to move across the face of Stone; he had defeated the abyss.

Thanks to the dragon, he reminded himself.

Then he rolled on to his back and looked up at the avalanche of crystal that was still falling towards them.

'This way!' cried Kythe in his ear. 'I can't carry you any more – you'll have to run!'

She took off again, flying low to the ground. Drawing painful breath, glancing apprehensively at the oncoming hailstorm, Jonah gathered up his robe and started to run after her.

At first it did not occur to him that they were fleeing anywhere but away from the target area of the falling crystals, but presently he saw a shape up ahead, a slim black line standing straight up from the ground. Before long it resolved itself into a figure. But who? Somehow he managed to increase his speed. Far to his left he could see the shadows of the crystals sprinting across the surface of the monolith just as his and Kythe's had done moments before. The sky was growing dark; there was not much time.

The figure remained quite still, a black cutout from a Japanese shadow-play. Its legs were slender but something was bulking out its torso so that it looked top-heavy, ready to fall over.

Then Jonah saw something else. Beyond the figure was a shape in the sky: the unmistakable profile of Torus. The giant dragon was diving towards them.

Except it did not look altogether like Torus. The body was the same but the dragon carried itself differently, flew more smoothly. Suddenly Jonah's blood was ice water. Archan had made the transition!

But if Archan was a dragon again, where was Annie?

The ground shook; a second later Jonah heard a dull *crump*. Flashing a glance over his shoulder he saw a tremendous cloud of sparkling red dust: the first impact of a crystal shard. He tried to run faster but could not. Sharp pain stabbed him below his ribs and he nearly stumbled. Up ahead Kythe dodged to the side as a shadow clipped her wings and a piece of crystal the size of a house crashed to the ground two hundred yards to their right.

The giant dragon dropped lower then flattened its dive. Had Jonah been born a few decades later he would have been reminded of a warplane swooping low before commencing its bombing run.

How fast can a dragon that size fly? he wondered, considering the speed of a stooping hawk, judged by some to be close to one hundred miles an hour. Accelerating out of such a dive she was surely flying much, much faster than that. Tons of vengeance-laden flesh travelling at hundreds of miles per hour: the prospect was sobering.

At last Jonah could identify the figure towards which they were running. It was tall, glossy black and slender: it was Esh. She was holding something in her arms, a bundle of rags perhaps.

She stood alone on the flat and empty plain. There was no promise of sanctuary whatsoever.

The noise of the falling crystal blocks was becoming more regular, a series of explosive concussions interspersed with light pattering sounds as tiny fragments were showered across the monolith's deck. They had managed to run clear of the centre of the target zone but there were still enough pieces landing nearby to make their position perilous.

Archan was no longer part of the backdrop, she was a real, three-dimensional juggernaut bearing down on Esh's back.

Why are we running towards her? thought Jonah deliriously, trying to imagine whether it would be better to be crushed by the oversized hail or torn apart by ravening claws.

Kythe swerved to a halt and without warning Jonah found himself very close to Esh. He slowed reluctantly, for the remains of Torus's lair were still dropping around them, then stopped abruptly as he saw what it was that Esh held in her long, many-jointed arms.

It was Gerent, lying with his head thrown back and his arms splayed out like some classical hero slain on the battlefield. His face was burned and his left leg was dark with blood, and at first Jonah thought he was indeed dead. Then he saw the prince's chest rise and fall, the movement almost imperceptible. Gathered beneath his body like a clumsily-folded blanket were the artificial wings; Jonah wondered what had happened to Frey.

'We are in some danger here,' said Esh conversationally.

'Well I could have told you that!' blurted Kythe.

'We know,' replied Jonah simultaneously. 'Gerent – is he . . . ?'

'Later,' interrupted Esh. 'First you must lead us to safety.'

'I . . . ?'

'Look closely at the ground and tell me what you see.'

There was a muffled bang and splinters of crystal sprayed against Jonah's legs. 'This is no time for mysteries, Esh,' he protested, noting Kythe's obvious surprise that he knew the name of the Ypoth. 'Just tell me what you mean me to do.'

'The ground, Jonah Lightfoot.'

Puffing with both exhaustion and exasperation he looked down and saw that here the ground was anything but grey: it was patterned with thin red lines, strange marks and sigils whose purpose was impossible to determine. Decoration, he supposed.

The patterning was local to this immediate area – just twenty yards behind Esh the lines faded to the familiar grey. They were standing at the very centre of a rough circle of crosshatched decoration, a tiny focus of detail on the skin of the otherwise bland monolith.

He saw it at once. Amid the vaguely Cyrillic characters one mark stood out, a sweeping Oriental symbol he had seen too many times before for its presence here to be mere coincidence. As if to confirm this, Esh turned her back to display the identical mark she bore on her carapace. Except the mark on the ground was fully six feet long and painted on the marble-like surface of the monolith with what looked like enamel. Without thinking, Jonah reached down and opened his hands as if to grasp it.

It was like reaching into treacle. He saw his fingertips disappear into the ground, saw the hilt of the sword fill out like an inflating bladder, felt its sudden thickness against his palms. Then he was lifting it clear, transporting it from its former two-dimensional realm into the solid world of Stone. He raised it high, six feet of clean and shining blade held on a skeletal hilt of brilliant red. It had no weight at all, and he knew without testing that it was sharp enough to cut steel.

'Excalibur!' he cried, filled with joy.

'Push it into the crack!'

Looking down again Jonah saw that the sword had left an impression in the ground, a negative mould of itself. Inverting the blade he stabbed it down into the depression and hauled back as though trying to pry open an unyielding door. The ground lurched and a fresh pair of cracks opened up on either side of the depression. With a metallic squealing a square section of the ground began to lower itself, forming a ramp.

A way into the interior of the monolith.

'Hurry up!' pleaded Kythe, understanding that here was a possible escape route. But Jonah could do no more. Whatever mechanism he had set in motion had to work at its own speed, however leisurely that might be. He started forward, taking two paces on to the gradually-lowering ramp before pausing. So far there was just a blank grey wall at the lower end, of which more was revealed with every second that passed, but slowly, so slowly.

The rain of crystal was lighter now, although the occasional impact still scattered debris across their feet. Archan on the other hand was dreadfully close: her cruciform outline slipped through the air like liquid, sensual and full of restrained power. And fast, unbelievably fast.

Gradually, its painstaking movement accompanied by ancient grinding sounds and sudden tremors, the ramp descended. Kythe joined Jonah on its inclined plane, as did Esh, still carrying Gerent's unconscious form. At the ramp's lower end there was still no sign of an entrance, even though it had dropped over six feet into the sub-structure of the monolith. Jonah raised the unearthly sword again, peering over the lip of the aperture as he tried to locate Archan again. He did not have to try very hard.

She was on her final approach, silent as an owl seeking prey in the dead of night. Light rippled across red and black stripes; her claws hung low, as long and sharp as scythes; her mouth was slightly open, trailing dense smoke that looped across her dorsal spines only to be torn apart in her slipstream. A dragon, looking exactly like Torus but for one crucial difference, a difference Jonah was now close enough to see: the eyes in this dragon's face were not the dark eyes of a dragon but the perfect mirrors of the Deathless. The soulless, fathomless eyes of Archan.

Now there was no doubt. Jonah flinched, lifting the sword high, convinced she would strike it and tear his arms from their sockets.

'Look!' screamed Kythe, lunging down the ramp.

A slit of darkness had appeared at the base of the far wall. They all rushed towards it, this appearing aperture. It grew with awful slowness, but here at least, with their heads actually below ground level, they were partly protected from Archan's attack. *Is she slowing even now?* wondered Jonah. *Slowing to land and then pounce over the edge of this ramp, to seize us as we cower here and wait for the door to open?*

The ramp shuddered and stopped. They looked at each other aghast: the slit was barely six inches high, nowhere near large enough for any of them to squeeze through. Somewhere beneath their feet something ticked and whistled, then with a reluctant sigh the ramp slid smoothly down the final few degrees of its arc and thumped to a halt. Before them was an opening running the entire width of the generously-proportioned ramp and fully four feet high, big enough to admit them all. *And too small for Archan!* rejoiced Jonah.

They moved as one, heedless of what dangers might lie within, caring only to escape the onrushing dragon. The last thing Jonah saw as he ducked beneath the smooth grey lintel was the sudden eclipse of Archan's shadow as she flashed over their heads. She had not slowed, not the slightest bit; she was there and gone in the blink of an eye.

'That was too close for comfort,' he muttered, his voice echoing as though he were in a cave.

'Do not expect comfort, Jonah Lightfoot,' came Esh's voice from the blackness behind him. 'Simply strive for survival. That is all any of us can do for now.'

'What is this place?' quavered Kythe, her voice eerily like that of a small child.

The darkness was total: he could see nothing at all of his

companions and called their names in fear. 'We must not stray apart. Damnation! I can see nothing at all!'

No sooner had he uttered this than they were surrounded by livid orange light. A fireball exploded through the narrow opening and into their sanctuary. Jonah raised his hands, anticipating the agony . . .

But the fire dulled and thinned before it reached them, washing across his hands and arms like a wave of lukewarm water. Trails of sparks chased its wake, busily evaporating into the returning darkness. A big shape looming outside had blotted out most of the daylight; there was no doubt what it was.

Archan screeched her frustration and spat a second fireball out of her mouth, but this too dissolved before it could do any damage. She shook her head in frustration and lunged forwards, snapping at Jonah with teeth like ploughshares, but her snout was too small to penetrate more than three feet through the opening. Nevertheless Jonah retreated, uncertain of the integrity of the monolith's structure and fearful she might break her way in.

Snarling, she pulled herself free. Her head darted to and fro, seeking a way in but finding none. She was straddling the cutting made by the lowered ramp, wings tented over the top, neck coiled down into the cavity. By degrees she brought her wrath under control and began to breathe slowly and deeply, the sound of the air in her throat like a ship's boiler.

'She's trying to gather charm,' blurted Kythe. 'That's why her fire has failed: transferring herself into Torus's body must have used up enormous amounts of charm, not to mention flapping around at that ridiculous speed. There's only so much to go around, and once you run low there isn't much you can do about it except wait for it to build back up again.'

'How long do we have?' demanded Jonah.

'Not long. We shouldn't stay around here, that's for certain.'

But Jonah *did* want to stay around, for a moment or two at least. Something had caught his eye, a curious lump on the back of Archan's head. He craned his neck as she wove back and forth – what could it be?

The lump moved, unfolded, grew arms and a head – it was a human being.

Annie!

And it was. There, clinging on between Archan's back-swept horns, was Annie. Each movement of Archan's head nearly tossed her clear but somehow she managed to hold on. Archan had to be aware of her presence there – perhaps she was having difficulty shaking her free. *Or perhaps she is just preoccupied with us.*

He took a step forward, just one. At once Archan lunged, teeth clashing with the ring of a hundred blacksmiths' hammers. He stood his ground; if he had raised his arm he would have been able to touch the very tip of her nose. Neither of them moved.

'Archan!' he bellowed. The dragon waited, snout pressed tight into the opening, steam pulsing from her nostrils in short, regular bursts. 'Archan,' he repeated, more softly. He wanted her to strain to hear. 'Archan, who do you want?'

'You know well enough, faery, just as you know that whatever I want I shall get. Step forward and I may choose to show you mercy.'

'Mercy? I thought you preferred a challenge.'

She laughed at this. Threads of flame darted from between her teeth like phosphorescent worms, a grim reminder that all the while he kept her talking she was gathering charm, readying herself for the final onslaught.

Without moving his head Jonah tried to see if Annie was taking advantage of the lull to make her escape, but the angle was bad and most of his view was blocked by Archan's enormous muzzle.

'Do you really believe that one such as yourself is a challenge to the Deathless?' responded Archan when she had stopped laughing.

'If I am no match for you, then why am I not dead on the floor?' The taunt came easily but he cursed himself: he wanted to tease her, not provoke her. But she did not rise, although her nostrils flared wide, spewing steam across his face.

'Your friends have abandoned you,' she said suddenly. Jonah turned to look and Archan pressed forward, gaining an extra six inches of ground. Her teeth snapped delicately, just once.

'We are here,' murmured Esh from the shadows, and he realised that of course she was playing with him just as much as he was with her.

'It occurs to me,' he said, his voice low again so that she would have to strain to hear, 'that you are at a considerable disadvantage.'

'Explain yourself!' Was that confusion in her voice? Irritation?

'Well, we merely *natural* creatures are well sustained by the atmosphere of Stone in terms of nutrition and energy. But as for you poor *charmed* – you are like a steam engine, constantly in need of coal and water. How inferior it must make you feel.'

She was trembling now. In a moment she would lose her temper, regardless of how much magic she had managed to absorb; Jonah suspected that however small the amount it would probably be enough by now to create a fireball big enough to reduce him to ash where he stood.

'You are pitiful, faery.' To his surprise she withdrew her snout and yawned theatrically. To do this she turned her head sideways-on, affording Jonah a clear view of the back of her skull and neck. Annie was gone!

He almost ran forward, then realised Archan was almost certainly watching him out of the corner of her silver eye. Frantically he scanned the ramp, seeking a skulking human form. The shadows cast by Archan's enormous wings were thick, but here and there, where the membranes were split, a shaft of light penetrated. The underside of her jaw floated barely two feet above the floor of the ramp, a roving canopy studded with sharp-edged scales. It passed over an area of deeper shadow . . . and the shadow moved!

'Annie!' he shouted, and the curse he yelled in his head was almost as loud. But Archan had already seen her.

She sprinted beneath the dragon's jaw. Archan's response was simple: she brought her head crashing down on to the ramp. There was a sound like falling masonry. Jonah saw Annie's face, a white oval widening with terror, then her features were erased by Archan's shadow.

Heedless of his own safety he hurried out through the opening, but before he had taken two paces on to the ramp Annie's hands were slapping at his chest, clutching his robe and turning him back towards the interior. She was clambering to her feet, having rolled clear of Archan's pile-driving attack and missed being crushed by a hair's breadth. 'Git going, you're no wiser than a coyote, Jonah Lightfoot!'

The sound of her voice, her Kansas accent broad in adversity, the word *coyote* pronounced *kih-yote,* the crack of her palms on his breastbone, her sheer aggression, all these things lifted Jonah, spun him on his heels and catapulted him back down the slope. His hand floundered behind him then found hers and gripped tight; she gripped back, a hard, human connection.

Archan roared. The noise was big enough to span the million years she had waited for this moment.

The two fleeing humans stumbled into the darkness, nearly tripping over their own feet in their desperation. Behind them the sound of Archan's roar had transformed into a colossal intake of breath; they could almost feel the suction drawing them back out into the sky.

Now they would feel her wrath; now they would feel the fire.

'The sword,' said Esh sharply.

Jonah swore – he had dropped it. How could he have been so stupid?

'Here!' Annie pulled him sideways. His feet skidded and his shoulder struck something soft.

'Ouch!' protested Kythe. 'Watch where you're . . .'

The sword was clearly visible, glowing brilliant red. Still holding on to Annie with his left hand, he extended his right and snatched it up. By the faint glow it cast he could see markings on the floor similar to those on the surface outside. Surely one of them matched, would close the doorway.

They swam before his eyes. The puzzle was made doubly confusing by the paucity of the light. He swung the luminous blade from side to side, seeking a familiar shape.

Outside, beyond the opening, there was a dreadful silence.

'Annie!' he wailed, and she pulled free of his grasp.

'Here!' she barked, kneeling just in front of him and placing her hands on either side of an engraved pattern that looked just like all the rest.

'But what . . . ?'

'It's *here,* damn you!'

The shape coalesced, or his eyes focused. Crying out he thrust the tip of the sword down between her outstretched hands, driving it into the cleft in the very centre of the swirling Oriental symbol.

At the same instant Archan gaped wide. Her tongue was flattened, revealing the interior of her throat. It stretched like a tunnel. Fire engulfed its depths, a blistering, swelling flood of dazzling orange flames rolling over themselves in their eagerness to escape. The fireball raced along the tunnel like a flaming piston, now flooding the back of her mouth, now spilling across her teeth, now mushrooming across the short space between her head and the doorway . . . except the doorway was closing. Jonah prayed it closed more quickly than it had opened.

It did. He ducked, joining Annie on the floor as the fire reached the aperture, but the ramp was already rising, swiftly this time and without the squeaks and whistles that had accompanied its descent. Perhaps the mechanism had loosened – they would never know, nor did Jonah care. By the time Archan's fire reached the aperture there was scarcely an inch of free space left; there was a brief squirt of flame, a harmless orange jet that flew across the space in the blink of an eye, then the ramp was moving on up, closing them off from the outside world altogether. Two seconds later there was a faint thud as it locked into its closed position. They listened, but hard as they tried they could hear nothing more, though Archan was surely venting her fury on the surface of the monolith, and the depth of her rage was impossible to imagine.

Trembling in the blackness, Jonah felt Annie's fingers steal over his.

'H-hi,' she said, her voice unsteady.

'Is it really you?' he asked gently.

'I think so. Oh God, yes, I hope so.'

'It is you.' He reached out and found her arm, then his touch became an embrace. They held each other for a very long time, held each other very hard.

It was Kythe who suggested, somewhat nervously, that they try to explore their pitch-black surroundings.

'There must be a way to make some light in here,' she ventured. 'Or perhaps there are some windows.'

Jonah took the lead, with Annie behind him, holding the tail of his robe with one hand and one of Esh's bony elbows with the other. Esh herself insisted on carrying Gerent; Jonah offered to take a turn but she refused (he was secretly relieved – he suspected the Ypoth was far stronger than he was). Kythe brought up the rear, holding in her jaws a thin strip of leather, the other end of which was tied around Esh's wrist. Thus chained they trailed blindly into the interior of the monolith.

It was silent and cool, a striking change from the hot and windy exterior they had left behind. A thought struck Jonah.

'Kythe,' he called. A distant echo returned his voice. 'Could you make some kind of fire, something safe of course, by which we might see our way? I know we have nothing to make a torch, but . . .'

'I'd already thought of it,' replied the dragon-child enthusiastically, but then her voice dropped, 'but I'm afraid I used up most of my charm flying you down to the ground, and then getting away from the falling crystals. There's no wind in here, so I can't build my store up again. Mind you, there's a whiff of charm in the air, very old and strange. Actually,' she confided, 'I'm not terribly clever with magic yet.'

'Don't worry,' Jonah reassured her, 'neither am I.'

They had not gone far when Jonah remembered something. 'The sword! I left it sticking in the ground back there!'

'It had served its purpose,' said Esh at once. 'You could not have brought it with you.'

'Oh.' Having felt positively Arthurian when he had drawn it from the floor, he was bitterly disappointed.

'Don't worry,' Annie whispered in his ear, 'there'll be other swords.'

'Slow down,' commanded Esh, cutting into Annie's words. 'There is light ahead.'

And so there was. They had been descending steadily but now the floor turned horizontal and there, less than fifty yards away, was a faint pool of light. They approached it cautiously, maintaining contact with each other even when they entered its magical ring, lest it suddenly be extinguished and they be plunged into darkness again.

But it remained, and as they entered its welcoming glow they saw that just beyond it rose a wall. The wall, like the now-illuminated floor, was made of what looked like slate, a dark grey substance striated with faults and sheared-off angles.

It climbed into darkness: the ceiling was invisibly distant. Bitten out of the slate was a ragged aperture framing a door of shining bronze.

'We should rest here now,' said Esh, paying the doorway no attention whatsoever.

'Should we not at least see what lies beyond?' Jonah gestured at the bronze door. He fancied he could hear something on the other side, a low grumbling sound like deep-seated machinery slowly ticking over.

But Esh did not even look round. 'We have all come far today and this is a safe place for us, for the time being at least. Let us rest and tend to our wounds and wounded. Doors can wait.'

So saying she gently deposited Gerent on the floor. Together she and Annie peeled away the clothing from around the injury to his leg; when revealed, although it had bled a great deal, it was clearly a minor cut, perhaps caused by a dragon's tooth or claw. The burns down the right side of his face also looked superficial – there was little they could do for these and only time knew if he would be scarred.

'He is very lucky,' said Jonah with feeling, remembering Gerent stanced in those giant dragon jaws, remembering the bolt of charm Archan had driven into him. 'What about Frey – can we get those wings out from under Gerent?'

Esh looked at him quizzically. 'I do not think you understand, Jonah Lightfoot. These are Gerent's wings now.' And with infinite care she turned the prince over.

The back of Gerent's leather jerkin had been torn open; the ripped edges were charred black, though there was no sign of burning to the skin beneath. The dragon-scale wings, their span approaching twelve feet, were creased and scored with lines of soot. Gingerly Jonah lifted the nearest edge and peered underneath. At first he did not understand what he was seeing: the black and red scales, arranged haphazardly, with no thought of pattern or design, grew smaller the nearer they got to Gerent's shoulders . . . then they simply merged into his skin until they were no longer visible.

He blinked and looked again, giving the wing a tentative waggle in an attempt to betray the illusion this surely was. But it was no illusion – Esh was right.

The wings were growing out of Gerent's back.

'F-Frey?' he mumbled, unable to take it in.

'I cannot explain exactly what happened,' said Esh softly, 'but you will begin to understand when I tell you that most charm is concerned with *exchange*. Nothing is ever created, no more than anything is ever destroyed. The bolt of charm Archan delivered when she was still inside Annie West's body was intended to kill both Gerent and Frey – I suspect simply to remove them from the arena, leaving her free to infiltrate Torus's mind and body.

'The charm cannot have struck either Gerent nor Frey directly however. Had it done so both would surely have perished. It must have struck the core of charm in which all the power of the wings was bound up – you may have noticed a glowing sphere at the place where the wings joined each other?' Jonah nodded. 'So. In some way I do not fully understand, the fusion of the two forces of charm must have destroyed Frey and caused this fusion of his wings with Gerent's own flesh.

'The wings are a part of Gerent now indeed. He has in some small way fulfilled the destiny denied your race – he is now what you might call a faery.'

'I always imagined faeries as being small,' murmured Jonah, transfixed by the blurred boundary between dragon scale and human skin. 'Tell me, Esh, how do you know all this? I didn't see you in Torus's lair.'

'You were otherwise occupied, I suspect. However, you are correct, I was not there. I was down here, waiting for you.'

'Down here . . . but you were miles distant.'

'Close enough to see.'

'I beg your pardon!' Jonah fancied he detected a smile playing at the corners of Esh's wide, expressive mouth, although it was her eyes that captured him: luminous and green. *And as powerful as a telescope!* 'How far can you see, Esh?' he demanded.

'Far enough,' came the unhelpful reply. 'Help me lay your friend back down. He is sleeping now: let us try to make him comfortable.'

Between them they settled him into what they hoped was a position of repose – it was hard to know what to do with the wings, so in the end they lay him on his front, with his head turned to one side. He was breathing steadily; his eyes flickered occasionally beneath the lids, as though he were dreaming.

'So you saw all this going on,' said Jonah, sitting cross-legged and inviting his companions to join him. They did so, huddling close. Kythe tucked herself behind Esh, her long neck extended like a giraffe's over the Ypoth's sleek black head. 'But I do not understand how Gerent got from the dragon's lair to here. Are you telling me that he fell and you *caught* him?'

'No. He flew down. He was thrown clear by the charm that transformed him, and though he was injured he managed to control his descent sufficiently to bring himself to ground here on the monument. I happened to be waiting close to the place where he landed, so I took the opportunity to bring him to safety. He was unconscious by the time I reached him.'

'Did you say "monument"?' Annie butted in. Jonah raised an eyebrow at her – he thought he had heard the word 'monolith' but then, had he been listening properly? 'Then you know what this place is?'

'Not exactly. I believe it to be a monument built by those who built Amara.'

'A monument to what?' pursued Annie, but Esh could not answer.

Jonah became aware of a sniffling sound. He looked up and saw it was Kythe: she was crying quietly. He stood and reached towards her trembling snout; the young dragon pulled away, refusing his touch. 'What is the matter, Kythe?' he asked softly.

'You all talk in riddles,' she blurted, her voice that of a frightened ten-year-old girl. 'I don't understand any of this, and I'm scared of the monster outside. I'm scared,' she repeated, her sharp dragon teeth chattering with a sound like rattling dominoes.

'Archan *is* a monster,' agreed Esh, 'and we are all afraid. Do you wish to return to your kind? To do so may be difficult, given the fact that we may very well be besieged.'

'Back there?' Kythe's eyes widened. 'Oh no . . . I mean, I didn't mean . . .' She broke down then, her deep orange serpentine neck descending in tortured curves to the floor. Esh laid one claw-like hand on the back of her head; Jonah and Annie looked at each other helplessly, devoid of the etiquette they needed to help console a distraught dragon. Her sobs spiralled beyond the envelope of light, invisible trails of sadness evaporating into the mysterious distance.

By and by Kythe composed herself. 'I'm sorry. Please let me stay with you. I don't want to go home – they all boss me around and none of them look any further than their own nests. I want to go with you, I want to explore Stone instead of ignoring it. Will you take me with you, will you, please? Please say you will?'

Her tone was so anguished, so imploring that Jonah could not restrain himself from moving over to where Kythe sat and wrapping his arms around her neck. This time she did not protest; instead she rested her head on his shoulder. He hugged her tighter, conscious of the strange weight against his body, the alien angles of her jaw.

'You saved my life,' he said simply. 'Why should I want otherwise?'

Kythe gulped. 'I'm sorry,' she said, smiling a little now. Jonah ducked as her tail unrolled and coiled through the air just inches from his face. With casual dexterity Kythe used its tip to wipe the tears from her scaly cheeks. 'I suppose I've made a bit of a fool of myself.'

'Not at all,' responded Annie warmly. 'Now hunker down and join us properly, instead of skulking back there in the shadows.'

Disentangling herself from Jonah's embrace, Kythe shuffled round and squatted beside Esh. Jonah returned to his own place at Annie's side, wringing dragon tears from the soaked place on the shoulder of his robe. As he seated himself her hand sought out his and squeezed it.

'You didn't give up on me,' she whispered.

'Never,' he replied. 'I always knew you were there.'

'Thanks. I mean it.'

'Do you want to talk about it?'

'Not yet. Later, Jonah, I promise.'

Esh cleared her throat. 'There is much for us to discuss, but we are all tired; we should rest. Soon we must face Archan afresh, and such hard-won moments of peace will not be afforded to us often. We must make the most of them.' Esh sucked in a slow breath, seemed to consider something briefly, then added, 'Jonah Lightfoot, Annie West – I have spoken a little to you both. You both know me for what I am, and you know more than a little about Amara, which is also called Stone. Before you ask, Jonah Lightfoot, I was able to communicate with Annie West while she was possessed by Archan's spirit, a form of contact you may like to think of as *mental projection.*'

Kythe's eyes widened suddenly. 'You're an Ypoth, aren't you?' she blurted, and when Esh nodded she almost danced up and down. 'I knew it! My father used to talk to me about your kind, about how you only appear when there's a big fault, a crack or something in Stone. You fix things, don't you? Then you go away again.'

Esh smiled at this, and Jonah thought the expression the most spontaneous he had yet seen on the face of this supremely composed creature. 'Yes, Dragon Kythe, you express it well: we fix things, and then we go away again. So. Let us rest now.'

'Then we'll talk about . . . about her?' said Annie, her face like stone.

'Yes. Then we will talk about her.'

Beyond the door of bronze, the barely-audible noise grumbled on.

The floor was hard, and the two humans found it impossible to make themselves comfortable. Jonah regarded Esh with envy: she had gone to sleep only seconds after her final remark to Annie, closing her eyes and resting lobster-claw hands on folded legs. She remained bolt upright, sitting in the centre of the pool of light like an Eastern mystic meditating atop some Himalayan peak; she looked like a statue carved from the deepest ebony.

Kythe too drifted into sleep without much ceremony, curling herself up a few yards away from the slumbering Ypoth. As Jonah and Annie shifted restlessly however she stirred, then sleepily called them over.

'Rest against me,' she murmured, pulling one sleek wing away from her flank. Tentatively they sat down and leaned back against her body. The scales were surprisingly resilient, very comfortable in fact, and invitingly warm.

'This is better than my old Chesterfield,' whispered Jonah. 'Are you all right, Kythe?'

There was no reply, just a faint snoring and the regular swell of her dragon breast behind them, a slow and somehow motherly rhythm that relaxed them still further.

'Leave her be,' murmured Annie. Then she said, 'Hold me.'

Jonah squeezed his right arm between Kythe's scales and

Annie's shoulders, drawing her gently near. She leaned into his body and rested her head on his shoulder. He thought they would fall asleep like that, but sleep evaded them both. Instead they talked.

'What was it like?' As soon as he asked the question he cursed himself, but Annie answered willingly.

'It was . . . very bad. It took me a long time to work out what was going on, and when I did I . . . I kind of made up a story.'

'A story?'

'Yes. I imagined I was a princess in a tower – don't laugh now.'

'I am not laughing,' he replied, smiling.

'I didn't even know what Archan was, not for the whole time she was in me. I knew what she was *doing* well enough, but, well, I figured she was a witch or something. And me – I was in my tower. Trapped. Like Rapunzel.'

'"Let down thy hair,"' whispered Jonah, touching her long, black hair.

'Right.'

'Esh said she came to you. What did she call it now? Oh yes, a *mental projection.*'

Annie shrugged. Her body felt very close to Jonah as it pressed against his own, very *real*. 'It felt real enough to me. Esh took me out along some ledge, then I saw flames coming out of the wall and I was – my God, I think I was in *Rome* or something. No, not Rome, but someplace like that. There was a volcano.' Here she shuddered, her ribs bumping against Jonah's. 'Like Krakatoa. A lot of people died. I watched them . . .

'When I came out again, back again, there was a hole in the wall. Somebody's arm – he was a soldier I think – was sticking out. He was still holding his sword.'

Jonah swallowed, his throat clicking audibly. 'A short sword? A round ball at the end of its hilt?' Annie nodded, wide-eyed. 'A *gladius*, used by the Romans to stab barbarians, and each other on occasions.'

'How . . . ?'

'I saw it too – held it briefly. Malya found it and carried it for a while.'

'Malya.' Annie frowned and put her fingers to her temple as if trying to retrieve some misplaced memory. '"You bitch".

Did I say that? I remember a woman's eyes . . . and your eyes, Jonah!'

'The woman was Malya,' affirmed Jonah cautiously. 'She and Gerent fell in love – well, I think they had always loved each other, but it took them a long time to realise it.'

'Gerent and Malya. And me!' Her hand flew down and clutched his, her nails digging into his flesh. 'And me, Jonah! Archan used me, didn't she? I don't have many memories of what my body was doing while I was trapped inside my head but I can see his face, I can see Gerent's face, Jonah! She – she *used* me to use *him*, didn't she? Tell me the truth, damn you!'

'I do not need to tell you the truth,' Jonah said gently, 'for you already know it. Nor does anyone need to be damned.'

She cried quiet and hard, face pressed into cupped hands, long hair tumbled forward into her lap. He tried to hold her tighter but her body had gone stiff; he tried to withdraw his arm but could not. So he just sat there miserably, unable to console her, unable to imagine what she was feeling, uncertain even of his own feelings. He felt aroused, much more so than he had ever been when they had been naked together on a deserted beach in the East Indies, but he believed this was not the time or the place for such thoughts.

But what is the right time or place? a voice inside protested, fighting against his supremely English sensibilities. *What time is this, Jonah Lightfoot? What place is this? How many of the old rules apply here, in this place where the air is filled with magic and dragons are real?*

The lurch of her body as she wept and the hot press of her ribs against his conspired to blur the boundary where his senses met his physical self. He felt almost ready to fly, not to fall this time but to *fly*. His arm was numb, in fact his whole body felt numb, except for the one part of him that had responded most promptly to the intimate contact. Her hair brushed his cheek and he gasped, watching as tight spiralling shapes reeled into his vision. Oh, how she filled his world! How tiny seemed the immensity of Stone, how irrelevant the strange conflict into which he had been summoned. For that brief moment Jonah's whole world was Annie West, her alone, with even his own existence subordinated to a mere speck of dust dancing in the beam of light she made.

But the old rules were engraved deep into Jonah's heart and would not be disobeyed. As Annie began to relax again he felt himself drawn back into his body as if from a great distance. It came as no surprise to find that he was sweating profusely. That part of his body he usually thought of as his 'loins' ached. Close to panic, he allowed welcome Victorian reserve to push back the flood of emotion that had so nearly swamped him, and succeeded in pulling his arm free, only to find it yanked unceremoniously back into place.

'Just where do you think you're going, Jonah Lightfoot?' Annie said tartly, her voice lighter now. 'Now, isn't there something you've got for me?'

'Something for you?' He was squirming now, embarrassed by the continuing intimacy and nonplussed by her unexpected demand. *It would not be right,* he told himself in a tight little voice which, though he did not believe it, managed to soothe him nonetheless. *I cannot take advantage of her in this way! She is clearly distressed and . . .*

'You bet,' she went on pleasantly, sounding anything but distressed. The tears had given way to a brightness that appeared entirely genuine. Jonah felt his heart turn over as he recognised her innate resilience; she was if nothing else a survivor. 'You've been keeping it all this time – I know you have, I saw it. Are you gonna give it me or do I have to get it myself?'

Suddenly he understood.

'Of course,' he cried in relief. 'The painting box! It's right here!'

So accustomed had he become to having the mahogany box swinging and crashing against his hip that he had laid it down quite unconsciously when he and Annie had snuggled up against Kythe. Now he reached down and retrieved it, dragging it from where it lay half-hidden beneath the dragon's belly. At first glad to have been given a diversion from the confusion in his heart (though if he were honest it was not his heart but his stomach that was folding itself into knots) he was surprised to find a lump in his throat as he raised it up by the strap he had fashioned and lowered it reverently into her lap.

She stared at it for what seemed an age, tears welling but not quite spilling out. With one hand she caressed its battered lid, brushing the brass clasp with her fingertips, tracing the scars wrought upon it by water and ice, sand and stone. Then, with enormous care, she slipped open the clasp and drew up the lid.

The odours of turpentine and linseed oil billowed out like spirits released from long entombment. So familiar was their combined perfume, so *homely*, that it was as much as Jonah could do not to weep himself. He watched in silence as Annie stroked the trays of pigment, the small, slightly stained porcelain cup, the rows of tiles, some blank, some painted by her own hand. *Such beautiful hands*, he thought as they worked their caresses. The middle finger of her left hand brushed across a nugget of paint; when she withdrew it it was smudged with crimson. She stared into the box for a while, her lips moving soundlessly, then turned to him, eyes shining.

'Thank you, Jonah,' she whispered. Then she leaned across and kissed him lightly on the cheek. He felt as if he had been struck by lightning, and did not even flinch.

She picked her way through the tiles for a while. Jonah did not think she was counting them, simply reacquainting herself with them. *Old friends*.

At length she closed the lid, fetching a deep sigh as she did so.

'Why?' she asked. Jonah frowned.

'What do you mean?'

'Why has it come all this way? Why was it not left behind?'

'I – I brought it.' He was puzzled. Ever surprised by the fickleness of the human heart – not least his own – he was mortified to find himself offended by her remark. 'I carried it with me because I thought you'd want me to keep it safe,' he replied tartly. 'Aren't you glad?'

'Oh yes, of course,' she responded dismissively. 'That's not the point, that's not what I mean at all. What I mean is: *why*?'

Jonah shook his head, mystified. Why did they have to talk? Could they not just . . . ?

'Oh, come on – are all Englishmen this slow? You've seen the mark on Esh's shell as well as I have. And what about the symbols on the floor of this damned monument or whatever it is? They're *ma-chong*, Jonah. *This* is a *ma-chong* set. And when Archan had me all roped up in my own skull do you know what I built for myself? A damn *house* of *ma-chong* tiles! That's how I got out for a while, got to see Esh, until Archan tracked me down. That's what I mean when I say "why?". For some reason these tiles have become, oh I don't know – markers on the way or something. And one marker keeps turning up: the Red Dragon.'

She was both scared and intense, and Jonah felt his clumsy desires ebb a little as his mind turned itself to this unlikely reality: not only had the Red Dragon been the tile Annie had been working on when they had met, but it had followed them across the surface of Stone, even to this very spot. It was indeed on Esh's shell, it was the key that had unlocked the way into the monolith. And what was Archan now if not a red dragon, albeit with black stripes?

Annie was nodding at him as his eyes widened. 'Scary, ain't it?'

'Sure is,' he replied, clumsily mimicking her smooth Kansas drawl. 'But – I don't know how much we can read into it. Annie, how much did Esh tell you about what Stone really is – or Amara, as she seems to prefer to call it?'

'Not much. She said it's joined to our world, but she didn't say how. Is that what you're thinking, that we're bound to find connections, just because that's the way it is?'

A sudden image flashed into Jonah's mind, a cylinder spinning round and round. 'It's like a phonograph. Like Edison's phonograph! Everything that happens in our world, Annie, every fall of rain, every baby's cry, it is all recorded and stored here on Stone. It is a store of memories, all the memories that ever were and ever will be. A phonograph of the gods.' He could almost hear the scratch of history as it rubbed its needle against Amara's wax.

'That doesn't explain why the gods that turn it are so crazy about *ma-chong*.'

'No,' he sighed, 'it doesn't. But Esh was right – Stone *is* inextricably linked with our world, so perhaps we need not be surprised to find echoes of what we know here.'

'Anyway,' Annie yawned. 'I'm tired. Let's sleep.' And with that she turned herself a little away from him and closed her eyes; a few moments later Jonah was the only one of their small band still awake.

He rested for a while, feeling sleep beginning to draw him

down into her current. Dozing, he tried to recall the intensity of feeling he had held for Annie only moments before but found he could not. His own body was quite limp now – perhaps his fatigue had finally overwhelmed him. He tried instead to imagine what it must have been like for Annie, to be trapped inside her own mind, to have her body requisitioned by a monster from another age. And to reawaken in a world far removed from her own. He found he could not shake the memory of Annie's eyes from his own drifting mind: Annie's eyes, shocked and wide, punching momentarily through Archan's silver orbs when Malya had found her lying with Gerent.

The last thing he heard as he fell asleep was the soft thunder of the machinery behind the door. It tugged at his thoughts, infiltrated his veins, slithered along the nerves that connected him with the worlds through which he moved. If it penetrated his emotions too, he was not aware of it. He was not aware of anything but its sound, deep and distant like the song of a whale heard from two hundred miles away.

14

Monument

The location is correct but everything else is garbled. To begin with it seems all seasons at once: bluebells peer through new grass while dry leaves tumble on an Arctic wind. Snow falls as swifts dart through clouds of mayflies, beaks agape; the sky is filled with the sound of their chicks, seemingly thousands of them, a bird chorus to fill the palace as if it were a concert hall.

The palace itself is ruined. Icicles of glass dangle amid the vines and creepers that have swarmed up its broken flanks. It lists like a sinking ship; he can hear the creak of metal even over the screaming swiftlets. Where are their nests? He looks around but can see nothing but shattered glass and twisted ironwork.

In rolls the storm, but of his father and brother there is no sign. He runs anyway, following the demands of the dream, runs towards the dinosaur. Except there is *no dinosaur, just a shallow depression in the soil where it ought to be. He stands there as the depression fills with water and becomes first a puddle then a swamp. His head tilted back, he screams into a sky as black as night.*

Lightning forks. Still the snow falls and still the swifts fly, but now they are huge and breathe fire. He turns and runs for the cover of the palace, which has changed: now it is streaked with red, every broken pane and every metal arch bloodied and clawed. It screams as it leans towards him, an iron skeleton folding into the mud even as he skids in a hopeless attempt to reverse his steps again. A cloud of birds bursts through the ruined roof, each one turning into a dragon as it strikes the snow-filled air. The palace's collapsing bones jitter with blue fire, electrical discharges sucked down from the storm. One of them strikes him in the chest and his heart stops beating.

He falls face-down into the mud, watching the shadow of the palace folding across the place where he lies, anticipating the final, crushing impact.

Something floats by on a trickle of water, a small white shape that looks a little like the empty hull of a toy boat. It bobs then sinks and then, impossibly, rises to the surface once more. It shines with an inner light, a hard and brittle glow that is quite unpleasant to look at. As his life ebbs away Jonah watches that light separate into thousands of individual threads, watches those filaments expand before his failing eyes, feels himself slip between their gossamer filaments.

Hears the crash of the palace as it presses him into the mud.

They awoke to the sound of hammering. Gerent was stood before the great door banging his upraised fists repeatedly on its bronze surface. The sound was like that from a badly-cast bell, a thick ringing full of discords and uninvited harmonies.

His wings were spread wide, and with each blow they trembled.

It was Esh who coaxed him away from the door. He regarded her more with curiosity than fear, reaching out a tentative finger to touch the black armour protecting her shoulders and neck and peering quizzically into her eyes. Then he allowed himself to be ushered into the company of the others.

The instant Gerent saw Annie his eyes sprang wide open and he rushed at her, hands clutching forward, lips drawn back in a soundless grimace. Both Annie and Kythe, who was still rubbing sleep from her eyes with the tip of her prehensile tail, blinked in surprise but Jonah and Esh were ready. While the Ypoth restrained Gerent, Jonah hovered protectively before Annie, shouting at him to calm himself.

'This is not Archan!' he yelled. At first his words did not even register. Spittle flew from Gerent's mouth as he thrashed in Esh's powerful grip, and Jonah wondered briefly if he had gone entirely insane. 'Leave her alone, calm yourself down and listen to what I have to say! Archan has relinquished her grip on this woman – her name is Annie. The dragon possessed her but now she is free. Damn it, man, look at her eyes if you will not believe what I tell you!'

Gerent stopped struggling abruptly. 'Let me near her,' he growled.

Esh looked towards Jonah, her soft brow raised inquiringly. He felt strangely touched that the Ypoth, who seemed so certain of everything, should allow the decision to be his. He nodded once, almost imperceptibly, and she released him.

Gerent shrugged his shoulders – the movement sent little ripples down the length of his wings – and took three paces forward. Despite his fear for Annie's safety Jonah found time to notice how haggard the prince looked: even beneath the red swelling of the burn his face was drawn, pierced through by sparse blonde beard.

The prince raised his right hand and grasped Annie's chin roughly, then tilted her head first this way then that. She flinched slightly at the first touch but remained still thereafter, allowing herself to be examined. After a moment's consideration Gerent let his arm drop. Then his shoulders slumped – in fact his whole body seemed to slump – and he looked over his shoulder at Jonah and uttered one word.

'Torus?'

'Is dead,' answered Jonah quietly. 'Archan killed him – or rather she evicted him from his body, which amounts to the same thing I suspect. He is gone, Gerent.'

'Gone,' echoed the prince. He looked down. 'Frey?'

'Dead too,' volunteered Annie. Gerent nodded, then sat heavily on the ground and rubbed his hands across his face, hissing and pulling them back as he touched the raw flesh of the burn.

'It will heal soon enough,' Annie went on. 'You're not badly hurt.' But when he gazed up at her she saw that this was not the case at all.

Jonah stayed with Gerent while the others examined the door. The prince did not want to speak, despite all Jonah's efforts to engage him in conversation. Eventually Jonah subsided into what he hoped was companionable silence.

Except there was no silence. Forgotten during the excitement of Gerent's awakening, the thrum of the machinery had reasserted itself. His eyes were drawn time and again to the huge door from behind which the noise was leaking; his mind in its turn was drawn back to the dream, the distorted memory of the Crystal Palace, and hence to his father.

This was the Machinery Court, boys. Imagine the Great Hydraulic Press, its chains and girders pressing against that ceiling of glass.

He did not have to imagine it now: he could *hear* it.

Nasmyth's steam hammer, eh, Albert? Think of it! The power of the gods was wrapped in that great piston, yet a skilled man could make it tap open his breakfast egg without even spilling the yolk. And the sound of it, oh yes, the sound of it all!

Steam and wheels, the huge sign swinging: *Passage To Machinery*. Every wonder of the modern age of 1851 under a single glass roof. Yet all those things had existed for Jonah only in the words of his father, both those spoken to his sons and those penned, the articles with which he had started his Fleet Street career. Jonah's Crystal Palace had been a shadow of its former self, transported in jigsaw pieces from Hyde Park to Sydenham Hill, as grand as it had ever been but . . . sad. Sad and silent.

This is where they brought the noise, he thought edgily. *This is the noise of the Machinery Court. It's there behind the bronze door, all of it, waiting for me.*

A sudden thump brought him to his senses: Kythe had whacked her tail against the door in frustration. Esh and Annie turned to Jonah and shrugged in unison, the shared gesture comical.

'Perhaps we need a magic word,' he offered, smiling at Gerent, hoping to share a joke. The Neolithic prince's face did not move.

'Perhaps,' agreed Esh without a trace of humour. 'But if that is the case we stand no chance at all of penetrating this door. It would be impossible for us to guess such a thing. Even were we to recite every word we knew of every language we knew it would still . . .'

'All right, all right,' laughed Annie.

'Is it hopeless, then?' asked Jonah, standing up and rubbing cramp from the backs of his calves.

'I don't know about that,' replied Kythe, 'but my tail hurts now.'

'There is no visible seam,' sighed Esh, tapping one of her claws absently against what might have been termed her thigh, had her legs not possessed one joint too many. 'Nor is there any obvious mechanism such as a handle or stud. It does not push open, nor is there anything to hold so that we might pull it.

We cannot slide it. So. We seem to have reached the end of this particular road.'

'Do we have to go through?' asked Annie, looking warily up the door's considerable height. 'I mean, what do you expect to find on the other side?'

But Esh could not say. 'You will quickly learn how little I know of this world, though I am of Amara in every literal sense. However, I fear the only way out of this monument may be the way we came in. Do you wish to try it? Archan is certainly out there still.'

Annie shuddered and did not reply.

'See here,' said Gerent, approaching the door. His voice was level; Jonah had expected the prince to sound . . . broken somehow. 'There is a small channel here, full of dust so it's hard to see.'

Suddenly Gerent was half-running, half-crawling, knees bent and hand outreached to track the line of the channel to the right-hand edge of the door. 'It continues, see?' he called, then he was off again, following the base of the wall. Before any of them thought to follow him he was swallowed up by the blackness.

'Should we go after him?' wondered Kythe.

Esh shook her head. 'Wait.'

They did not have to wait long. Presently a cry floated back from the gloom: 'Stand away from the door.'

They obeyed, and seconds later there came a tremendous grinding sound from beneath the floor. At first the door did not move. Then, as the noise began to climb the scale into a screech the door trembled, resounding like a gong. Finally, with a lurch and a crack like a breaking branch, it juddered to the right, along its dusty track into concealment within the wall. Just as the last foot of bronze disappeared Gerent came sauntering back into the light, smiling broadly.

'It occurred to me that a good way to hide a door handle might be not to put it on the door,' he said. As he spoke he looked deep into Annie's eyes. He seemed jovial – too jovial, Jonah thought, for a man who had lost the woman he loved, lost his people, wrestled with a dragon . . . *But have not we all suffered?* he reminded himself. *And do we all not go on?*

'And is that what you found out there?' laughed Annie. 'A door handle?'

'More or less.'

'Well, it worked!' cried Kythe, bounding forward then checking herself. A flicker of fear crossed her young dragon face. 'Um, who wants to go first?'

'We will all go first,' answered Esh, and she raised both her claw-hands to her companions. Jonah took her right and Annie her left. He thought Gerent would take his free hand, then felt a stab of jealousy as the prince changed his mind at the last minute and darted round to grab Annie's. Something scaly slipped into his palm.

'Will you look after me?' It was Kythe's tail, of course. He turned to her, a mythical beast standing a little taller than he. Each of her teeth was the size of one of his thumbs. Given enough time to prepare she could, he knew, breathe fire.

'Look after you?' he repeated, struck by her sheer beauty. She nodded, a scared child desperate for adult reassurance. His heart settled and softened. 'Of course I will, Kythe,' he said gently. 'I will protect you, that I promise. How could I not?'

The room was a perfect square, an indoor arena as big as a rugby pitch but contained by a low, unsupported ceiling; the ceiling made Jonah feel a little like an autumn leaf waiting for the flower press to descend. Around the perimeter of the square, reaching right up to the white outer walls – and lying therefore directly at their feet as they stood in the doorway – was a moat of milky water. Not a ripple marred its surface; it was like looking down into a flawless yet slightly steamed mirror. It was not wide – they would be able to jump across it easily enough – but its depth they could not determine.

Framed by this pale moat, the inner part of the floor was divided into a chequerboard of smaller squares, nine along each side, coloured alternately white and black. The central square was identical to the others except for its colour: it was vivid red. That was all; there were no structures, no other doors, no clue as to the giant room's function or provenance. Except the sound of machinery, which was now very loud.

'What is this place?' murmured Annie, voicing the question on all their lips. Despite the uncertainty there was an unspoken easing of tension down the line. Jonah felt the extra weight of

Kythe's tail in his right hand as she released the knots in her muscles, and was aware of Esh's lobster-claw opening a little. Annie's shoulders had dropped too, and Gerent was running his free hand through his hair.

'I don't know,' Jonah replied. It was not what he had expected, not at all. Where were the beam engines, the towers of brass and iron, the jets of steam and runnels of oil? Where were the pounding metal pistons and the ticking valves?

'That sound,' said Kythe. 'It worried me when we were on the other side of the door, but now we're in here – it's funny, but even though it's louder I don't mind it so much.' The others nodded agreement.

'It's strange,' came Annie's comment, 'but it's not as threatening. What do you think, Jonah?'

'I think . . .' He was about to say that the noise sounded more organic than mechanical, that the valves they could hear hissing and squeezing might very well be the valves of some gigantic heart, that the creaks and groans might have travelled to them not by way of pipe and lever but sinew and tendon. That the monolith, crisp and geometric though it appeared, sounded very much as though it were alive. He thought all this, but while he thought it his eyes were drawn back to the milky water. 'I think,' he went on, 'that we are all in need of a bath!'

His companions looked at him in astonishment, then Annie laughed uproariously.

'Damn right, Jonah Lightfoot! I smell worse than a mountain man's breechcloth! There's worse things we could do than spend an hour getting cleaned up.' With that she started to unlace her jerkin. When she saw the two men staring at her with their jaws hanging she turned to Esh. 'What do you say, Esh? Shall we girls get ourselves a little privacy? Kythe – you coming?'

Jumping easily over the moat, she led Esh and Kythe to the far corner of the room, where the moat turned its first right-angle against the wall, and continued to disrobe, grinning mischievously at Jonah and Gerent all the time.

Jonah could not stay embarrassed for long. Turning his gaze to the inviting water (he suppressed irritation as he noticed Gerent continuing to stare openly at Annie) he quickly pulled the coarse cloak over his head, dropped the loose cloth he had bound around his lower extremities and put a cautious toe into the water. It was warm, gloriously so, and it was as much as he could do not to simply jump in. But he was more cautious than that: he still did not know the moat's depth, and for all he knew the bottom might be studded with spikes. It occurred to him just then that there might be something *living* in the moat, something with sharp fins and sharper teeth.

'Fortune favours the bold,' he muttered as he sat on the edge and lowered himself gingerly in. His feet touched a smooth floor when the water had reached the level of his collarbone. Warm as a hot tub, smooth as oil, it was perfect.

'Come on in,' he cried to Gerent. 'The water's fine!'

Once the prince had torn his eyes away from Annie he lost no time in undressing himself. He stood on the edge for a moment, tall and pale-skinned, thin but, Jonah noted grudgingly, well-proportioned and lean with muscle. His eyes skated away from Gerent's undeniably handsome form – he did not care to be reminded of what had transpired between this handsome Neolithic man and Annie.

Not Annie, he scolded himself. *Archan.*

Having seen that the water was safe, Gerent extended his arms and plunged in, a perfect dive. Water splashed across Jonah's face and he had to snort it out of his nose.

'Curse you!' he bellowed. Tipping on to his back he kicked his legs out as Gerent surfaced, sending a plume of water right into the prince's own face. Gerent spluttered and launched himself at Jonah and then they were laughing and wrestling, spitting great sprays into the air, dunking each other's heads beneath the surface and racing each other to the far wall. Gerent's weird dolphin-like stroke was superior to Jonah's more sedate paddle and he won the contest with ease.

'Where did you learn to swim?' spluttered Jonah as they rested, chests heaving, in the 'L' of water formed by the corner of the moat. 'Were there pools in the castle?'

'There was a lake in one of the forbidden rooms,' Gerent answered breathlessly. 'We used to go there when we were children.'

'We?'

'Malya and I,' answered Gerent with only the briefest hesitation. 'The first time we were in love.'

'What happened?'

'Family happened.' He shivered despite the warmth. 'My father found us swimming together. Except we were doing more than just swimming. He dragged me from the water and threw me on to the bank – it really *was* a lake, you see, made with earth and clay, and a long beach of stone at one end. There was a waterfall too, and a secret cave behind it.

'Malya fled screaming, making for the cave, trying to hide. But my father ran around the bank and caught her. He pulled her out kicking and screaming, pulled her out by her ankles with not a stitch on her. She was swearing and punching him. She screamed for a long time, and then she screamed a curse I had heard only once before. It was a shaman's curse, one of Frey's very worst: *"Falar take you deep! Othumla's tongue not creep!"* It shocked my father and he slapped her senseless, then picked me up bodily and carried me out of the room.'

'What did the curse mean?'

'To understand it fully you must know our people and how they view the spirit-world, and know the hold the shaman has over that relationship. There is too much to explain to you here and now, but I will tell you the legend from which the curse arises.

'Long ago, before even the old world was made, there was a great river of ice flowing between the stars. One day it flowed too near to the sun and part of it melted, and a frost-giant was formed. He was Ama, and he was the father of all the world's giants, those of frost and those of fire, those of earth and salt and iron. It is said he was even the father of the trolls. Beside Ama was formed a bullock with horns big enough to split the sky. He was called Othumla, and he licked at the ice until he had carved out the shapes of the spirits. The spirits shared the old world with men, and those spirits who knew only evil followed the Denneth to Stone. None of the good spirits came to Stone. None at all.

'The spirits are our damnation. The shaman of our tribe knows the spirits and uses their power for prophecy. But it is a dangerous business, and often the spirits take hold of the shaman. Then *they* start to use *him*. This is what happened to Frey, it might be said.'

'Might it be said by you?' asked Jonah carefully when Gerent paused. 'Do you believe in the spirits?'

'Perhaps, perhaps not. I was raised in their shadow, and it is a long shadow to outrun even in a lifetime, whether it be real or not. So, we get to the curse. By saying what she said, Malya was calling upon Falar – an especially malicious spirit who delights in drowning men in blood and honey – to steal my father away and imprison his soul inside Falar's own. The second part is an invocation to Othumla, to make it so that Falar, and thus my father, never existed in the first place. To make them gone.'

'What?' Jonah felt his voice catch like a barb in his throat.

'To make them gone,' Gerent repeated, looking at Jonah closely. 'If Othumla's tongue never carved out Falar in the first place, then my father would be worse than dead – he would never have been born. It is complicated, I know.'

'No,' said Jonah in wonder. 'It is not complicated at all. Suddenly it seems very clear. Like ice.'

Gerent's eyes grew distant. 'It shocked me, too. To hear such venom, such dreadful thoughts, come from Malya's lips . . . All my love for her seemed to burst like a bubble. I clung to my father and wept like a baby, and for a long time I believed Malya to have inherited not only her father's black magic, but his black heart too.'

'But you loved her through it all, did you not?'

'Yes. Yes, I did. Though I did not rediscover that love until it was too late.'

'Not too late,' said Jonah, grasping the prince's shoulder lightly. 'Not quite.'

Gerent regarded him intently for what seemed an age before pulling his gaze away. 'It may be that you speak true, Lightfoot. But for now I am hurting too much to know what is true and what is false. It is hard enough for me just to breathe.'

And, just as Gerent's love for Malya had burst, so did Jonah's jealousy. How could he have forgotten Gerent's grief? He turned away, feeling ashamed, as all his anger dissipated with a silent rush of acceptance. Gerent and Annie were beautiful, he decided then. As for who loved whom, well, they must all love each other, of course. What mattered was their fellowship, the fellowship of them all, Esh and Kythe included; he resolved to do nothing to endanger its integrity. Nothing whatsoever.

Looking up he saw Gerent's eyes straying to Annie once more, saw her raise a hand and wave to them both – or was it just to Gerent? Jonah waved back.

'Come on, prince,' he cried. 'I hope you remembered to bring some towelling.'

On the other side of the chamber Kythe glided effortlessly through the moat, her neck and tail held clear of the water like the coils of a legendary sea serpent.

Closer inspection of the chequerboard proved it to be nothing more than a pattern on the floor. Not for the first time Jonah imagined himself as a chess piece roaming a giant's board. What piece was he then: the knight? He had felt like one briefly, when he had drawn the sword from the stone; now he just felt like plain Jonah Lightfoot, son of Henry. And what of his companions? Annie was surely the queen, but did that make Gerent the king? And their alien friends . . . ?

'Look,' cried Annie, spilling his thoughts. 'The red square's higher than the others.'

'Be careful,' warned Kythe.

'I do not believe we are in danger here,' announced Esh as they gathered along the red square's nearest edge. 'Nevertheless, caution is wise.'

It had not taken them or their clothes (rinsed through and spread out beside them) long to dry off after their extended bathing session. The air was warm and quite lacking the humidity of Stone's exterior. While they had lain sprawled along the moat's inner bank it had occurred to Jonah that he had not felt so relaxed since that morning on Krakatoa.

With the three humans dressed again, and the scales and shells of their companions gleaming like new, they had quartered the arena, seeking clues as to what this place was – and perhaps why they were here. The closer they approached the central square the louder the sound of machinery had become, until now, within six feet of its slightly upturned edge, it was overwhelming.

'Do you see anything, Gerent?' Jonah had to raise his voice to make himself heard. If the prince had managed to get the door open, maybe he could solve this puzzle too.

Gerent shook his head. 'It is seamless, as far as I can judge. The solution must be a simple one.' So saying, and before anyone could stop him, he took three paces forward and stepped up on to the platform. Abruptly the machinery fell silent.

'Oh dear,' moaned Kythe, her voice shockingly loud in the ensuing silence.

Slowly the platform began to rise from the floor. Gerent dropped to a crouch, hands folded over the edge, looking apprehensively at the approaching ceiling.

'Jump!' called Annie but he motioned her to wait.

'There's time,' he responded. 'But I don't think I will need it.' Nor did he. When it had risen some four feet clear of the rest of the chequerboard the platform came to an easy halt. As soon as it had stopped Gerent leaped nimbly down, dusting his hands in satisfaction.

They were now confronted by a giant red slab, no longer a section of a chessboard but a gigantic version of a child's building block. But the sides of this particular building block were etched with a complex pattern of straight lines, a spider's web of squares and rectangles and long, narrowing triangles. It looked to Jonah a little like a sampler of lacework his aunt had hung on the wall of the parlour, only a thousand times as elaborate and lacking its soft curves. There was a sense of movement too, a feeling that the pattern *flowed* somehow from left to right, drawing the eye along to the far edge and inviting it to explore what lay around the corner.

Jonah reached out his finger and traced the nearest of the lines, half-expecting a jolt of power as he did so. *Like touching one of the memory rods . . .* Mesmerised by the sheer volume of detail (the closer he looked the more he seemed to see, like seeing a thousand more stars for every minute spent staring at the night sky) he found himself following one line in particular as it tracked its way to the corner of the platform; it rose gradually, forcing him to lift his finger a little as it did so. When he reached the corner his hand was almost pulled around to the next side; this side was similar to the first – not identical of course, the pattern was too elaborate ever to repeat itself. On he went, unaware that the others were following him in a kind of daze, not touching the red maze as he was but just as entranced by its beauty.

The third side was if anything even more complex.

In the centre of the fourth side all the strands came together, zigzagging in to a central focus. The effect on the eye was startling: so close and so fine were the engraved lines at this point – much finer than a human hair – that it hurt to look at them. At the focus was a small white shape, a pinched oval, slightly raised from the surface. It looked a little like an eye. It looked very much like a button.

'It looks very . . . pushable,' offered Kythe.

'Should we?' Annie asked. But Jonah was already pressing it. There was a soft 'click' as the button withdrew into the block.

The quality of the light changed. Shadows slipped up the side of the block like dark water flowing magically uphill. The chamber dimmed briefly then brightened, slowly at first then with increasing speed. Annie cried out suddenly, pressing against Gerent as she pointed down at the floor.

Every one of the white squares was turning transparent, including the one on which they all stood. Along with his companions, Jonah looked down to see his feet seemingly unsupported, floating against a ragged blue and white haze. The floor had become a patchwork of enormous windows affording a spectacular if chilling view of the abyss over which the monolith extended. Stone's oblique façade spread downwards into a panorama of cloud, its impossible slope doubly daunting thanks to the impossibility of their viewpoint. Jonah found he was holding his breath; he expelled it slowly, convincing himself that the glass – if indeed it *was* glass – on which he stood was assuredly strong enough to support their weight, and probably that of London Zoo's entire complement of elephants if it came to that.

It was utterly terrifying and quite, quite beautiful.

'Jonah Lightfoot.' Esh's voice infiltrated his reverie like a streamer of cloud.

'What? I'm sorry, I mean, what did you say?'

'Touch the pattern again.'

Reluctantly he tore his eyes away from the cloudscape. He could see shapes down there, just as he had seen shapes in the clouds over the fields of Kent where he had lain basking with Lily. 'Cloudbuilding', they had called it, fashioning sculptures out of the random swarms of vapour: there a dog, there a reclining woman, there a scuttling beetle. He was doing the same here, except all the shapes he made were elongated, carved as they were from the speeding, stretching clouds of Stone: a weeping willow, a rifle, its barrel grossly extended, a church tower. Earthly forms cut from an alien sky.

'Where would you like me to touch it?'

'I do not think it matters.'

A little afraid now, he raised a trembling finger, convinced now that he *would* receive an electric shock, that here above the sky he would be struck by lightning. Closing his eyes he reached forward until his fingertip contacted the grainy, slightly warm skin of the block. There was a tremor, not so much a noise as a change in the texture of the silence. Esh gasped in what might have been wonder; Jonah thought it sounded more like relief.

Floating above the block was a ghost.

Jonah recognised it at once: it was an extinct marine reptile called *Elasmosaurus*, a serpentine swimming beast whose bones had been only recently discovered, in Jonah's time, in Colorado. No fossil relic this though: it loomed above them in semi-transparent splendour, a sinuous giant with a long neck and a great barrel of a body. Its skeleton was clearly visible through its tenuous flesh; less well-defined but undeniably present were its internal organs, and as he looked Jonah began to see more – veins and muscles, tight bunches of ancient anatomy.

His finger slipped a little and the vision changed. The neck shortened and the *Elasmosaurus* became a creature he did not recognise, still an ocean-dweller but much smaller. Before he could take it in it blurred again, only this time it did not settle into a new shape, simply oscillated between this and other, stranger forms. Jonah began to feel dizzy.

'Keep your finger still,' suggested Annie dryly.

He withdrew his finger then pressed it firmly against the block, somewhat to the right of where he had before. The new vision was an *Archeopteryx*, or something that greatly resembled it. This feathered phantom glared down at them balefully, translucent bones shimmering through taut and insubstantial flesh.

He pulled his finger away and immediately the proto-bird was gone.

'You try,' he suggested, touching Annie's arm. She did so. When she touched the slab nothing happened, nor did the apparatus work for any of the others, dragon and Ypoth included.

'It is as I thought,' said Esh. 'This mechanism is linked directly to the memory rods. You alone of our group can make it function, Jonah Lightfoot.'

'But what is it?' Annie demanded. 'I mean, what's it for?'

'It may not be "for" anything in the sense you mean, Annie West, any more than Amara serves a purpose.'

'*Does* it serve a purpose?' interjected Jonah. 'Amara, I mean.'

Esh stared long and hard at him. 'That is not for us to know. As for the purpose of *this* – I believe it to be a kind of well, a means of tapping the collective body of information contained by the memory rods themselves. By making contact with the etched pattern, Jonah Lightfoot, you are in some way making contact with a particular set of memories stored in the body of Amara. This apparatus visualises those memories and presents them to us in a form we can understand. Evidently it is currently calibrated to represent living creatures; undoubtedly it can be adjusted to tap the memories in a different manner, perhaps by depicting geological events, or streams of emotion or other data we cannot imagine. It is wondrous.'

This latter statement Esh made in such a matter-of-fact tone of voice that Jonah nearly missed it; it was uncharacteristic for the Ypoth to express an opinion, he judged, especially one that revealed her feelings.

'Try it again, Jonah!' urged Annie excitedly. 'What else can you conjure up?'

He made contact again, if a little reluctantly. Reluctantly because, although there was no jolt, no shock, touching the etchings made him feel light-headed, as if his blood were being drawn away from his brain and down to his fingertip. He felt that, were he to remain connected to the slab, he would be drained of all energy, even his very life-force. Wondrous, certainly. Dangerous, probably.

A bipedal dinosaur this time, one he had never seen before, huge and menacing with jaws like machinery; massive hind legs, tiny forelegs. He broke contact and touched the pattern further to the right: a wolf-like animal with long tusks jutting from its lower jaw. Another spot: something like a mammoth. Further back again: a tiny shrew.

Something about the shrew caught his attention. This time he slid his finger, maintaining contact as he did so. The result was a dizzying succession of images metamorphosing from one to the next; it was like watching wax flowing into invisible moulds. The further he moved to the right the larger the creature became (he quickly stopped thinking of the image as a series of separate entities but rather as a single organism undergoing accelerated change). Soon it looked more like a lemur than a shrew, then, suddenly, it reared up on its hind legs, adopting a hunched but undoubtedly bipedal stance. Huge eyes shrank beneath precipitous brows, which in turn receded as the animal's face flattened.

Jonah held his breath, slowing the rate of movement of his fingertip, watching Charles Darwin's theory of evolution unveiled before his wondering eyes.

Now the creature's prehensile tail had gone, now it stood erect, now its fur retreated across its back like an ebb tide. He paused, regarding the tall, slim figure of *Homo sapiens*, modern man, the species to which he and Annie and even prehistoric Gerent belonged.

The figure was male, large and well-built. With an intuitive twist of his hand Jonah transformed it into a woman. Her heart and lungs shone from beneath her ribs like hidden jewels; her circulatory system was a web of light.

A muscle twitched in his forearm and he felt an almost overwhelming urge to move his finger even further to the right.

'It's like Stone, isn't it, Esh?' he whispered. 'Left into the past, right into the future.'

'It is so, Jonah Lightfoot.'

There he stood, poised at the limit of the present he had abandoned on Earth, the evolution of his race at his fingertips. Then Annie's hand was on his wrist.

'Not for us to see, Jonah,' she said softly. 'Not yet, anyway.' Trembling, he stepped back, wrapping his own hand around Annie's. Something in the engraved labyrinth tried to pull him back like iron to a magnet but he resisted it. Then she said, 'Look backwards, Jonah. Let's see what's there. I think we need to, don't you?'

And he found he thought so too, though he could not say why.

Backwards, left, *downStone*. Back in time. In that early direction he discovered first a primitive crocodile and then, to his surprise, an elegant mammalian creature that looked very much like a giraffe, except it was much taller and improbably slender. Yet he had commenced his search precisely in the region of the pattern where he had found the dinosaurs. The chronology he had established was abruptly shattered, for this proto-giraffe was surely from a period much later than that of the early reptiles. He moved a short distance to the right again and received another shock.

The ghost floating above the slab was a twelve-headed serpent. Its pale blue flesh enwrapped a skeleton of pure silver. Unidentifiable organs filled its curves. At the tip of its tail was a long, golden spike.

'Hydra,' breathed Jonah. 'But this was never real. Esh, this is not a creature from prehistory – it is a creature from legend.'

'Do you not know by now, Jonah Lightfoot?' replied Esh softly. 'There is no difference.'

'This is where the dragons are, isn't it?' blurted Kythe, lunging forward and nearly knocking Jonah over. 'Isn't it? My ancestors!'

Then she glanced down through the transparent floor and screamed.

Instinctively they followed her gaze. Annie's fingers tightened on Jonah's and she hissed, a sharp reptilian sound.

From out of the haze rose a speeding dragon shape. It grew large with impossible speed; striped wings propelled great scoops of air behind them, hauling the stolen body upwards in a series of ever-accelerating lunges. Archan's mouth was open, huge teeth bared. Her blank, silver eyes reflected the blue and white of the sky and the deep grey shadow of the monument towards which she was speeding.

Esh had time to say, 'Fear not . . .' then Archan was *there*.

At the last instant she furled her wings close and coiled her neck beneath her belly. Suddenly the space beneath the glass floor was filled with rising spines, a gnarled red backbone barbed with hooks and splinters of bone. It flooded their view, darkened and then cut off all sight of the sky beneath. At the last instant Jonah saw the tiniest details: a spine whose tip had broken off, a jagged scar still weeping fresh blood, a small, crablike parasite just vanishing into the crack between two scales.

Then she struck.

Most of the spines shattered on impact. Archan's entire backbone seemed to compress momentarily, absurdly like a child's face pressed against a window pane, then she was literally rebounding, flailing back down and to the side, wings cycling madly as she sought to regain control. One wing swept past the window in a tremendous arc, wiping the view of Stone and sky back into place. Except now it was seen through a ghastly smear of blood and shards of fractured scale and spine adhering to the underside of the glass.

As Archan folded into an effortless hover Jonah realised that, although they had all jumped reflexively, they had neither heard nor felt the collision at all.

Annie was now clutching both his hand and Gerent's. Her face was white and taut, her breathing fast.

'It's all right,' he croaked. 'She cannot get in.'

'I know,' she responded through a mask of fear. 'And we can't get out.'

They watched with fascinated horror as Archan brought her huge striped form close again, but slowly this time. Blood was pouring from a dozen wounds on her back and drizzling down into the sky, but she seemed untroubled. Her mouth was split in a leer; her eyes, as ever, were totally unreadable.

Her mouth moved: she was talking, but of course they could hear nothing. All the while her wings beat in languid rhythm and Jonah found himself thinking: *She cannot possibly be flying like that. No beast that large could beat its wings in so lazy a fashion and remain airborne.*

A closer look revealed the answer to the riddle: threads of light were wriggling across the upper surfaces of her wing membranes, coating them with a shining patina like clinging silk. No sooner had he seen it than Kythe confirmed his theory.

'Charm!' she cried out. 'Oh, by the sky, she's using charm like I've never seen a dragon use it before! This must be what it was like in the old times, before the world turned. But where's she getting it from?'

That too became obvious. Raining from the monument was a curtain of the same diaphanous material that coated Archan's wings: a veritable shower of charm. Clearly Archan was capturing the stuff and drawing it into her body, using it to fly.

As if to prove the point, she slowed the beating of her wings until they were almost still, then calmly folded them and tucked them against her flanks. There she floated, serene on a sparkling bed of charm, while the blood dried on her back and her eyes flashed with the light of the sun in the sky.

'I think this thing just developed a leak,' said Annie dryly. Jonah could still hear the fear in her voice; anger too.

'Is she going to stay there all day?' moaned Kythe. 'Can't we just close these windows up again? I don't like seeing her down there – it scares me, it really does!'

'That is a commendable idea,' agreed Esh. 'Gerent?'

The prince, who had said nothing during the whole encounter, turned wordlessly and lofted himself atop the platform. Nothing happened, and although he scouted around he found no mechanism by which he might lower it again, and thus close the shutters.

'I think we may have started something we are required to finish,' he commented, looking down grimly from his perch. 'Jonah Lightfoot, did it occur to you to wonder why we could hear machinery *before* we set all this in motion, and not after?'

Jonah opened his mouth to speak, then closed it abruptly. The truth was he had not, but now Gerent mentioned it it was strange indeed. The noise of the machines had stopped the instant the prince had activated the platform, and they had heard nothing of it since then.

'It seems clear to me,' Gerent went on, 'that whatever mechanism is enclosed in this structure, its purpose is not to supply power but to restrain it. The Ypoth has told us that this apparatus has all the knowledge of Stone held within it. Can you imagine the energy it takes to hold that back? Of course you cannot, no more than I! By raising the platform we have removed that restraint: in other words we have opened the gates in the dam. All Archan has done is exploit the resulting flood. Now we must find a way to close the gates again before too much damage is done.'

'Or before the dam bursts,' muttered Jonah between gritted teeth. 'By God, Gerent, you are right! Archan must have spotted a flaw in the monument – it is surely many aeons old and perhaps not in the best repair – and she has certainly turned it to her advantage. Magic must be leaking out of this thing like water from a sprung barrel!'

'Yet Gerent has found no way to restart the machinery and shut off the flow again,' interjected Esh. 'So. It is an interesting dilemma.'

'Interesting indeed. Are we in danger, do you think?' asked Jonah.

'Probably,' wailed Kythe, 'and all the time she's lapping up the charm like *amboroth*!' She waggled a dejected wing at Archan's hovering form.

Jonah felt Annie tense at his side. Her eyelids were fluttering; he drew her to him, worried that she was about to faint. Instead she came to and pushed him roughly away, then immediately apologised. 'Oh, Jonah, I'm so sorry! It's just . . . you startled me.'

'Are you all right?'

'Yes. No – I was just thinking, she *is* growing stronger. Kythe is right: I can feel it. Every minute we stand here debating she's sucking up power. If she carries on like this soon she'll be strong enough to do anything. This window,' she stamped emphatically on the glass, 'might be tough enough to keep her out now, but . . .' Her voice trailed off eloquently. 'We've got to get to the bottom of this place, Jonah. You know that, don't you?'

Night proved not to be the relief they all hoped it would be. As daylight failed they found that Archan, far from disappearing into shadow, remained the one beacon of light in the darkness. The falling charm was like a rain of silvery fire falling into a body burning like a furnace. She was impossible to ignore.

Kythe discovered that lights had come on back in the outer hall, beyond the bronze door. Previously the darkness had kept them from exploring out here, but in the end there was little of interest. The hall was proved to be nothing more than a passage, very wide but quite featureless. Even the area around the ramp, where they had first entered the monument, was empty: gone were the markings on the floor, nor was there any sign of Jonah's sword.

None of them remained there for long. It was as if something had come along and cleaned away all evidence of their passing.

The remainder of the day they spent on a somewhat listless survey of the chequerboard room. An air of futility hung over them all, even Gerent, who had begun to display a certain pride in his knack of getting Stone's hidden machines to work: the giant pendulum, for instance, and the red platform. Between searches they swam in the moat, glad to be out of sight of Archan, but as night fell the light she cast invaded the whole space, firing up through the windows and playing across the ceiling like reflections from a hundred bathing pools.

There was a brief surge of interest around dusk when, as if in response to this alien light-show, the raised platform began to glow too. Each line of the elaborate engraving shone with sharp red light, creating a dazzling filigree. But though they all touched it and probed it, fiddled with the still-recessed button, clambered on top of it and traced the seam where it met the floor, still it yielded no new information.

Each time Jonah touched the pattern a different shape sprang into life above it. Once he did this while Gerent was standing in the middle of the platform and the prince was immediately enveloped by a tall, six-legged creature resembling a huge horse, except it wore a straggling set of gills behind its mane and bore a long paddle instead of a tail. He withdrew his finger at once; Gerent stood there for several moments, hands pressed against his chest, eyes closed.

Jonah's curiosity in the visions quickly waned. If he touched the pattern close to where he had begun his study he saw ever more outlandish versions of familiar beasts both from history and legend. He saw a modern swan with bright blue feathers; he saw a worm with a swollen cluster of eyes at one end and a peacock's tail at the other. On one chilling occasion he saw a man, heavily-muscled and bent low; he had the head of a bull, horns as wide as those of an aurochs. The Minotaur, staring back at him across an ocean of myth.

On the few occasions he tested it further afield – on one of the other faces for instance – he saw things he simply did not understand: a long, bronze spear dappled with black shadows; several squat barrel-shapes floating on a cloud of green vapour; what looked like a termite mound, but on closer inspection proved to be made of millions of identical, individual rings like gold wedding bands. There was no sense of whether he was looking into the past or the future, into story or history; as far as he could tell the pattern ate its own tail, with neither beginning nor end, a closed yet infinite maze in which an unwary explorer might lose himself forever.

When he conjured up a vision worthy of Bosch – a squalid heap of flesh whose countless mouths were engaged in the act of self-consumption, entrails stretched like ribbons between sibling jaws – he turned away for the last time, unable to comprehend, unwilling to see.

Esh was standing behind him, and she said, 'You are troubled, Jonah Lightfoot.'

He jumped. 'Oh, Esh. You startled me.'

'Evidently. So. You are troubled.'

'You've said that once already.'

'The tone of your voice proves the accuracy of my observation.' Plaiting her legs into a complicated crouch she settled herself on one of the opaque black squares. 'Come, join me. There is much still to be done.'

Jonah sat down. 'Esh, what on Earth do you mean?' It was useful to have a target for his irritation. If not Esh herself, then the tasks she imposed. 'We've searched this place high and low and found nothing. The only way back out of here is the way we came in, and Archan will be waiting for us the minute we stick our heads outside – if we can even coax the ramp into opening again. Heaven knows what new powers she will have after a night spent drinking magic!'

'Found nothing, you say? Would you call this pattern "nothing"?'

Jonah glared at it; the red trails glared back at him with their baleful, inner light. 'It is an encyclopaedia, nothing more,' he said finally. 'Miraculous, I will allow, but useful? I think not. And it is . . . upsetting.'

'Indeed. I can see you are upset, Jonah Lightfoot.' Esh tilted her dark, reptilian head in an entirely inhuman gesture. It occurred to Jonah that she never blinked. 'Do you wish to talk about what is troubling you?'

Jonah laughed despite himself. Such a human concern spoken by such an alien creature! He lowered his head and pressed his hands against his face.

Perhaps I have gone quite mad. Perhaps I am indeed still drowning beneath the Straits of Sunda. They say one's whole life is paraded before one's eyes at the moment of death – maybe it is possible to live a whole new life in the same instant. Is there any better explanation for all this?

Something hard touched his hand: Esh's claw. 'You are not asleep, Jonah Lightfoot, nor are you insane.'

He shivered. 'There's more to that pattern than meets the eye, Esh, is there not?'

'Jonah Lightfoot, I think you overestimate my faculties. There will come a time – very soon now – when you will know far more than I do about Amara. It is my task to guide you to that moment. After that . . .'

'Yes, Esh? After that?'

'You may find no further advantage in my presence.'

Jonah sighed and shook his head. 'I know I have power here: I've felt it, near the memory rods. And I need to use the rods, do I not, if we're to stand any chance of vanquishing Archan?'

'Yes.'

'Then we must return to the nearest threshold.'

'Again yes, ideally. But there is a problem: Amara's flesh is exposed less frequently than you might think.' Esh frowned briefly, her slitted pupils dilating as she seemed to drift momentarily away. 'There are at present no active thresholds within convenient travelling distance of this monument. The threshold through which you came was unusually large, but even that has already been closed by my kin, as has the minor puncture from which Malya retrieved the sword. The surface of Amara is, in effect, sealed. The rods cannot currently be reached.'

'What about the place you showed me, the chamber at the back of the dragons' crystal?'

'A projection. There *is* a break there, one that is taking an unnaturally long time to repair, but it is not accessible. What you saw was simply a representation of something lying many of your miles beneath the surface.'

'Do the rods represent the only way in which Archan may be defeated?'

'I fear so.'

Jonah slammed his fist into his palm and cursed. 'There must be a way! Can we not simply wait for another threshold to appear? They seem linked to volcanic activity back in my world – there must be a volcano erupting almost every day in some place or other on the globe.'

'Vulcanism is only part of the picture, Jonah Lightfoot. And you must understand that the flow of time on Amara does not echo the flow of time in the world you have abandoned. They are quite rare – we may have to wait for many days.'

'Then what are we to do?!' Anger was bubbling up inside him, matched only by his frustration. He paced back and forth, practically growling as he marched. 'I don't even know what I should do were I to get one of those damned rods in my hand! You tell me what is expected of me, then you tell me it cannot be achieved!'

'I do not have the answers. As I have already told you, I do not know everything there is to know about Amara.'

Jonah could not restrain himself. 'Some guide you've turned out to be! Are we even travelling in the right direction? Kythe says there are plenty of faeries – human beings – upStone. Perhaps we should go that way and petition them for help. Surely the men of the future will be more than a match for a dragon, even a dragon such as Archan! All we've found downStone are a few pitiful encampments – Stone might as well be deserted for all the evidence of civilisation we've seen. And if we travel any further we'll reach this "Dead Calm"! What answers can that possibly hold for us? It's a hole in the wall we need, not an impenetrable desert leading even further back into the past . . .'

He broke off. A memory had surfaced. He recalled his fall from the dragon's lair, recalled stringing moments from history along an imaginary line like beads on an abacus. Now he imagined the line becoming one of many that were interwoven, like the pattern on the platform. No longer a solitary line but a series of skeins, all focused on a single point.

A button shaped like an eye. A dark mirage . . .

'What are the thresholds to you, Esh?' he demanded suddenly.

The Ypoth considered this for some time. 'A threshold is a temporary breach in the structure of Amara . . .' she began.

'Yes!' shouted Jonah. 'Yes! You said "temporary", didn't you?' Esh nodded; her expression might have been one of bemusement. 'In your experience, can a threshold be anything other than temporary?'

'I do not understand the question,' replied Esh.

'No,' he breathed. 'I don't believe you do.' He shut his eyes as if to stop the elusive logic from escaping. 'Esh, what would it mean if there was a *permanent* breach, one the Ypoth couldn't repair?'

Esh froze, regarding him intently.

'A permanent break in the structure of Stone. Not a threshold . . . *the* Threshold. Yes, let us capitalise it! A gateway just like its lesser sisters, but a gateway through to the time of – what was it? – *the turning of the world*! The very instant in history when the laws of nature took over from the laws of magic. Or *charm*, I should say. A wound so great it can never be healed. Esh, might that not be what lies beyond the Dead Calm? It's in exactly the right place on the time-line. And if it has never healed, it must be a place where the Ypoth have never been!'

The expression on Esh's face, often so hard to read, was unmistakable: amazement. 'A permanent breach. I had never imagined such a thing but . . .' A dazzling smile broke across her alien features. 'What if you are right, Jonah Lightfoot? A place where the memory rods are constantly exposed. A permanent Threshold would be such a vulnerable feature that it would need protecting, hence the bounding zone that has been termed the Dead Calm. If true, this knowledge offers the solution to our predicament, but it represents much, much more! Such knowledge may be the first step on the route to understanding what Amara is and why it is here!'

'First things first, Esh. How do we get there? If the Dead Calm really is impassable then all this is of no practical use whether the Threshold exists or not. We'll never know if I'm right.'

Esh's smile did not falter. 'You have solved this much, Jonah Lightfoot. I am confident in your ability to solve the rest.'

He turned away from both Esh and the platform, excited by his theory yet with the fire of his frustration still undamped. He let his eye rove across the chamber, saw Kythe's coils as she swam lazily around the moat. Saw Annie and Gerent lying side by side on the black square nearest the entrance. Their bodies were a little way apart but their hands were touching; he could just hear them talking quietly together, though he could not make out their words.

Without warning Jonah's anger resurfaced, and the jealousy he had so valiantly subdued returned like a stabbing knife.

No longer could he tell himself he did not love Annie: even now that first vision of her on the beach, brown and naked, was vivid in his mind. Had he not carried her for miles through the black tunnel of the threshold? Had he not pursued Archan across this insane, upturned world so that he might set Annie's trapped spirit free?

And this is her gratitude! he cursed silently, watching their breathing, hers and Gerent's, their chests rising and falling in perfect synchrony.

Was he owed her love then? Because he had cast himself in the role of her champion? *She owes you nothing!* clamoured the voice of reason, which in his head was the voice of his father. *What you did you did by choice.* And duty too, of course.

But reason could not quell the rising fury that was the only thing he could find to fill his unfulfilled heart. Nor was that anger focused wholly on Annie, for was she not bewitched by the man who had intruded on their privacy? Gerent, who had once seemed so noble! Who claimed to have loved a girl who had died for him, and yet began to woo the first woman he met afterwards. Who, when he should have been mourning, was courting.

Who even now lay together with Annie when it should have been Jonah with her!

Teeth clenched, face burning, he whirled to face the etched platform. His heart crashed. Raising his arms to the level of his shoulders he reached for it, not merely touching this time but *punching,* slamming his clenched fists square into the mesh of brilliant red lines with a force that should have broken all the bones in his fingers.

Instead his hands slid straight through. It was like thrusting them into warm cheese. As they slipped inside he opened his fingers and grasped, feeling the soft, pliable stuff squeezing out from between them.

Now he was in up to his elbows; his forearms were quite invisible, lost in the apparently solid slab. Where it met his body the mesh grew busy with chasing, pulsing flickers of light. Tiny darts of energy swarmed from all corners of the platform, gathering around his truncated arms like bees.

The mesh expanded, each thread of light thickening in his vision to become a rope, then widening further to become a road; it was like falling towards an illuminated map of some great city – London perhaps, or New York. Roads became rivers, then wide channels and eventually oceans, until there was no gap between them, there was only the red.

15

Jonah on the Inside

He swam in the red. Time did not flow here, not in any meaningful sense, so when the red began to separate again he had no sense of how long an interval had passed since he thrust his hands into the mesh.

Perhaps he was returning to that moment now, travelling backwards through time, watching the bars of light contract from seas to roads to mere threads again.

It was not so. Now, as it shrank and solidified, the mesh of lines was spread out not vertically but horizontally before him. He drifted down and landed lightly on it; it was like standing on an immense, glowing spider's web, the extent of which could not be judged. The distance was deep red fog.

He found familiarity here, and could not understand why. Then it dawned on him: he could see a horizon again, one blurred by infinity but a horizon all the same. Gone was the endless fall of Stone. Alien though this place may have been, nevertheless it held one, small echo of home.

One of the strands of the web started to vibrate beneath his feet. He wondered if he was the spider or the fly.

There was movement in the corner of his eye and he turned towards it. No sooner had he done this than he saw another flicker; he turned again. Spinning anxiously, he began to make out six shapes advancing towards him across the web. Five of them halted before they were anything more than blurred humps, barely visible against the fog. The sixth continued to approach, moving clumsily.

It lurched the final few yards to where he stood and squatted there, staring up at him with its untrackable gaze.

Untrackable because its eyes, like Archan's, were silver.

It was not large – about the size of a small pig. It had two arms, each of which was armed with a ferocious array of claws; these were also metallic, and reminded Jonah of the blades of carving knives. Behind the arms swelled a pale, scaly body tapering into a long, muscular tail. It had no hind limbs at all. Its face was broad and flat and ugly, vaguely reptilian but also in some way Oriental. *Squashed,* Jonah thought, *like a pug-dog's.*

A cloud of evil-smelling vapour floated around a wide mouth. The silver eyes blinked and it cocked its head.

. . . *Welcome.*

It said. The words came not from its mouth, which remained closed, but through the web, entering Jonah's consciousness by way of his feet.

. . . *Bacht is not, of course, real.*

Jonah tried to place this strange, pallid creature but could not. It was from neither natural history nor mythology – it was beyond both, yet at the same time familiar. Salamander, lizard, crocodile and, yes, dog.

He composed a response, tried to speak. His mouth opened, but no sound emerged. Instead his thoughts spurted down through his body and into the shining web. He felt their vibration through the soles of his feet.

. . . *Are you one of the Deathless? A basilisk?*

. . . *Deathless are we. As for the name –* basilisk *is acceptable, as is* Bacht. *Names can be useful, or they can be a distraction from the matter at claw.*

. . . *And what is the matter at claw? Oh, do you mean* hand?

. . . *Your education, faery.*

Jonah found time to wonder if the members of his species were deluded in thinking themselves men at all. The basilisk spoke again.

. . . *You have brought peril with you into the realm of Amara. You alone are responsible for vanquishing it.*

. . . *Archan. Yes, I know.*

. . . *You are gifted, faery. Only one other with the power to move the memory rods has ever come this way. Your coming is – remarkable.*

. . . *One other? Who?*

. . . *Ask not what became of him. Concern yourself only with your own fate and the fate of the red dragon.*

. . . *You* do *mean Archan, don't you?*

. . . If you persist in interrupting you will learn from experience what happened to the other adept. Now listen, faery. You will not forget what Bacht tells you – that is not the way of this place – but you must understand, and understanding is a greater thing than remembering. The Deathless knew this better than most.

Bacht is not real. This much Bacht has already said. No more real than Ocher or Geiss or any of the six you see before you. There is sadness here now, because the presence of the Deathless on this web of light can mean only one thing: the basilisks are dead.

Understand, faery. Listen.

There is immortality in the cosmos. For all eternity, the basilisks were its six guardians, sharing its curse. The Deathless were the rocks against which the river of time dashed and broke itself apart.

But eternity takes its toll. To be immortal is a great curse; to have lived forever *is intolerable. Ever did the Deathless seek ways to end their existence, sometimes in isolation, occasionally collectively. Then, at last, their chance came. Ocher it was who called the last and greatest Gathering of the Deathless, drawing its siblings north to the crest of the world where the last of the abandoned charm was earthing itself. Even Bacht came, though it had grown bitter and evil by then. In that raw moment the basilisks at last succeeded in throwing off the curse of immortality. The Deathless – bar Ocher, which died later – found release.*

But this was possible only because of the presence of Archan. She it was who intervened at the critical moment. Her body it was that provided the empty vessel into which the rejected immortality flowed. As the Deathless died, so she gained the power to live forever. It might be imagined the basilisks have a lot to thank her for.

But never did the Deathless imagine one of Archan's power would find her way to Amara. Her presence here puts in jeopardy all the basilisks strove to do here, for between you – faery and dragon – you represent all that is necessary to bring the great wall of Amara crashing to the ground.

And that cannot be allowed to happen!

Bacht paused, its flanks heaving, vapour swirling from its mouth. Jonah recalled the legendary beast that shared this monster's name, if not its appearance – was the basilisk of myth not reputed to kill with a single breath?

And with a single glance too, *he thought with a shudder*. Just like Medusa.

. . . Then help me, Bacht. If you want me to help you, you have to show me how to get to the Threshold. That is the only place from which I can make contact with the memory rods. It does *exist, doesn't it?*

. . . And when you make contact. What will you do then?

. . . I – oh, I don't know. I have an idea that I will know when I get there. You will have to trust me. But please explain – you tell me that the basilisks are dead and that you are not real. Are you ghosts then, the six of you? Do you haunt Amara?

Bacht seemed to consider this.

. . . Ghosts we may be, but Bacht has already stated that names can be distracting. Tell Bacht why you wish to save Amara.

The question caught Jonah off-guard, and he was answering before he had properly considered his reply. This made his response honest however, which was probably what the basilisk had intended.

. . . To avenge Annie. I mean, well, I feel that Archan must be brought to justice. And Esh tells me that Stone is connected to my world, so I suppose I want to be sure that my world is not placed in jeopardy either.

. . . As Bacht thought. Faery motives.

Silver eyes swivelled like oiled mirrors, reflecting the intricate mesh of the sparkling, red web. Then the ancient ghost, if ghost it was, spoke again.

. . . Archan. Bacht will not bid you welcome here.

A sleek, white shape descended before them. It was a dragon like none of the dragons he had seen before. Even though it was unfamiliar he knew it to be Archan.

This must be what she used to look like, he thought.

Creamy-white – almost identical in colour to the basilisk in fact – her body had been reduced to a slim worm-shape, tapering at both ends to a sharp point. She had no legs, just two enormous wings like the sails of a clipper; her face was featureless but for a wide slit where her mouth was. She had no eyes, but her head turned to appraise both Jonah and Bacht with a sightless gaze that managed somehow to penetrate. The inside of her mouth was silvery, as perfect a mirror as the basilisk's eyes.

. . . Do not imagine we have any secrets from each other now, Jonah. She was floating just above the web, touching it only with the tip of her tail, sufficient contact to transmit her message without abandoning flight. *Go on, Bacht. It was just getting interesting.*

. . . Bacht would say less in your presence, dragon, if it did not believe you had divined the knowledge already. Have you not been basking in the falling charm?

. . . And very informative it has proved.

Archan purred this last response like a satisfied cat. Bacht ignored her and addressed Jonah again.

. . . Bacht repeats the direction to listen, faery. There is little time now.

Amara is a means of storing memories. This much you know from what the Ypoth has told you. Amara was, as you may already have guessed, constructed by the basilisks – you would say long ago, *though the phrase has no meaning in this context.*

Long ago, *the basilisks considered the remote possibility that death might eventually claim them, however strong was the grip of eternity on their spirits. For many aeons they argued the likelihood of such an event, finally agreeing that it was inconceivable.*

But not impossible.

So they built Amara, which you have come to know as Stone.

Yes, Amara is a repository for memories, but its primary purpose goes beyond that simple function of cataloguing and storing.

Inside Amara are stored the basilisks.

. . . Stone is a safety net! Jonah exclaimed. Bacht blinked, clearly not understanding; Jonah elaborated. *If the basilisks were ever to fall from the high wire they had suspended over the abyss of eternity, then Amara would catch them!*

Bacht contemplated this and found it acceptable.

. . . It is a clear image, faery, and accurate enough for the purposes of this discussion. Eternity is *memory. Immortality* is *remembrance. Within the memory rods of Amara is recorded all that ever was and ever shall be. Memories are as real as any of the worlds that spin their way through eternity. Therefore, as long as Amara survives, the Deathless live on. If Amara is brought down, the basilisks are truly gone forever.*

Archan could not keep herself from interrupting.

. . . This is very touching, Bacht, but do you honestly believe you can inspire this primitive, this man, *with such concepts? He cares only for the female whom he considers I defiled. You should think twice before placing your fate in his paws.*

. . . You should let me be the judge of what drives a faery on, responded Jonah quietly. He would save his anger for the

time being; he had a feeling he would need all of it before this was over.

. . . *Then seek your Threshold, Jonah! I will be with you every beat of the way! And I will be there with you right at the end, when you are still fumbling in the ocean of the past and I am closing my jaws on your precious memories. I shall bring Amara down! The eternity of the basilisks was pathetic and inward-looking. They filled it not with wonder and dread but with citadels and follies and tiresome monuments, of which the most tiresome of all is this crumbling edifice – this Stone!*

. . . *Do you believe your eternity will be any different?* asked Bacht dryly. *Do you still believe immortality to be a blessing?*

. . . *It does not matter. It is mine! That is all that is important now. Mine to own, mine to purge of all that has gone before! Beginning with the last stronghold of the basilisks! Beginning with Stone!*

Bacht turned from her then, the movement of its clumsy body strangely eloquent.

. . . *Faery. Look closely at Bacht's claw.*

Jonah did so, noting that the claw this repulsive creature presented to him was one it had kept tucked away until now. It was not a blade like the others; instead it was cone-shaped, very long and slender. It was positioned approximately where the basilisk's thumb ought to be, and projected out sideways. As Bacht rotated what might have been its wrist the claw stuck straight up in the air, and Jonah was reminded of two things.

The first was his father raising his thumb in congratulation to celebrate the very first time Jonah beat him at chequers.

The second was the hand of *Iguanodon,* which bore a stabbing claw almost identical to this in every respect.

. . . *Hold.*

Jonah grasped the claw. It was cold, like steel.

. . . *Where would you go, faery?*

. . . *To the Threshold.*

. . . *The way is prepared. Go now, and do your work.*

Everything was falling away now – Bacht, Archan, the maze-like web. Everything except the claw, which Jonah held still in his hand.

He drifted very close to Archan. Eyeless, she still seemed to regard him with bright hatred as he swept past. She spat; the globule of fire missed him by a fraction. Then she was receding.

Something glinted halfway down her back, between her wings. Silver shone through and at first it looked like a bizarre third eye. Then Jonah saw it was simply a cavity left by a missing scale.

He opened his fingers and the flawless cone of the claw tumbled away into the haze. It was very bright, and dominated his vision right up until the moment it disappeared.

He returned with a jolt, yanking his arms clear of the platform so hard that he fell to the floor. Looking up he saw them all clustered around him: Annie and Gerent, hand in hand; Esh, looming over the two humans, black and glossy; Kythe, panting and dripping having just rushed here from the moat.

'Jonah!' Annie was shouting. 'Jonah, are you all right?'

'Yes,' he said firmly, running his hands through his red hair.

'It's started to move!' cried Kythe. 'This whole thing, this monument or whatever it is! Just after you went into the trance, Esh says. It's *moving*!'

'How long was I gone?' Jonah demanded.

'Not long,' replied Esh quietly. 'One moment, no more. Are we going to the Threshold, Jonah Lightfoot?'

'Yes, we are.'

'What happens when we get to the Threshold?' wailed Kythe. 'Wherever *that* may be.'

Jonah watched Annie huddle against Gerent out of the corner of his eye. Yes, the anger was still there all right. He said: 'The genie escaped from the bottle, Kythe. And we're going to put it back.'

16

Threshold

The discovery that the monument was in motion was joined by the realisation that Archan had vanished. Nobody believed she had gone for good, but they were reassured to see the rain of charm had dried up. With the water gone from the well, Archan had clearly decided to wait elsewhere – or seek out other sources of magical power.

'She won't have gone far,' said Annie with conviction. 'Believe me, she's still out there somewhere.'

Rapunzel, thought Jonah as she ran one hand absently through her long, dark hair. The recurring fairy tale name brought to him not only the image of a castle keep but the unwelcome idea that an occupying army, upon leaving the castle they had plundered, might very well riddle its towers with booby traps. Dreadful though it was to think like this, he decided it might be wise to watch Annie very closely. Especially her eyes.

The monument glided downStone. They had no idea how it was attached to Stone, whether it ran on some mighty set of rails, or slid along within a slot, protruding like a gigantic tongue. Jonah's initial impression was that it was moving quite slowly: the misty view seemed to roll past beneath the windows in stately fashion. Then he saw a large building – a large, elaborate construction even bigger than the Neolithics' doomed castle – and was struck by the speed at which they traversed its upper storeys.

Scale, he mused. *That is what always surprises here.*

The building was a grand, palatial affair. Domes crowded its roof-line, each one decorated with brilliantly-patterned tiles. The domes were encircled by gantries from which steep stair-ways spiralled down into a variety of hatches and shafts. The gantries were deeply overgrown – on one a virtual forest had sprouted up – and the vegetation betrayed the colossal scale of the palace. Each step on those elegant stairways was at least twenty feet high.

Yet it, like so much of Stone, looked utterly deserted.

Esh was talking quietly with Kythe. The dragon was crying.

'What is the matter, Kythe?' Jonah asked when Esh, catching his eye, beckoned him over.

'I have asked Kythe again if she wishes to return to her kin,' answered Esh. 'I believe we may be able to operate the ramp again, and I do not believe Archan will prevent her from leaving.'

'What lies ahead will be dangerous,' agreed Jonah. 'And they will be missing you.'

He had intended his words to be consoling, but they just made the young dragon cry even harder. He looked around foolishly, wondering what one might use to blow a dragon's nose.

'Of . . . c-course they w-will,' snuffled Kythe. 'And I m-miss them too. It's just – oh, it's just so c-complicated!'

'It doesn't need to be,' soothed Jonah. 'You have helped us all, Kythe, me especially. You saved my life, and I will never forget that. But if you want to go back we'll understand. You're really very young.'

'Th-that's the problem!' she blurted, bursting into tears yet again.

Eventually she calmed herself enough to explain.

'When my father died I was very upset. My mother's been wonderful though – they've all been wonderful. Even Master Pax, even though he can be a bit . . . well, you know. And they all love me, I know they do.'

'But?' prompted Annie, sitting down beside the dragon and placing a hand on her claw.

'But they coddle me. They're so over-protective. I can't go anywhere or do anything without some dragon checking up on me – where am I, when will I be coming back to the crystal? "You won't fly far, Kythe, now will you?" That's what they say. "You will stay close to home." I feel trapped all the time. And then there's Dreke.'

'One of the other dragons?'

'Yes, if you can call him a dragon. He's skinny and brash and

I can't bear to be with him. I suppose he's not bad-looking, but he's just so *ghastly*! He makes my scales curl whenever he comes near me. Ugh! Even thinking about him makes me go cold all over!'

'And he likes you.' Annie nodded as if she was beginning to understand.

'Oh, yes. Well I suppose he does, in his own *ghastly* way. But the real point is that we're *supposed* to like each other. We have no choice. Soon Dreke will be of age and then that will be that – he and I will be paired and I'll never get away from him. I couldn't bear it!'

'Your betrothal was arranged against your will,' said Jonah. 'By your parents.'

'Our betrothal was set by the laws of Stone. It is simply the way things must be. And in flying away from it I have certainly brought doom upon my kin. We are the Infants, you see, Dreke and I. If we do not mate there may be no others, and the line of the dragons will be lost forever.'

Jonah glanced at Annie; she shrugged. 'When you say you are the "Infants",' he said, 'there are no other young dragons in your community?'

Gerent interrupted suddenly. 'Must the beast spell it out, Lightfoot? Youth is precious on Stone. Malya and I knew this only too well.'

'No children,' murmured Jonah. 'We saw no children in the castle.' He looked the Neolithic prince in the eye. 'There weren't any, were there? And I'll wager you and Malya were the youngest people in your tribe.'

'Yet our love was forbidden,' added Gerent bitterly. 'And our shame was all the greater.'

'Esh – can you explain this?' Jonah asked the Ypoth.

Esh nodded. 'I believe so. I have some knowledge of the differences in reproductive efficiency between your world and this particular region of Amara. Expressed simply, these differences mean that procreation on Amara is almost prohibitively difficult.'

'Everyone's sterile?' asked Annie, wide-eyed.

'Not quite. The problem stems, I believe, from the large concentrations of charm in this region. In your world, around the time of the turning of the world, the death of charm was associated with a series of plagues, one of which was a plague of sterility affecting all charmed creatures and many natural ones, dragons included. Extinctions occurred. Entire races were lost.

'The charm that leaks through to Amara is thus contaminated. By mixing with the purer charm of Amara itself I would speculate that the plagues' devastating effects are diluted. However, among all the known species that inhabit this region, most suffer similar problems to those of your kin, Gerent, and your kin, Kythe.'

'Youth is venerated,' agreed Gerent, and Kythe nodded. She was looking at the prince with wonder and surprise. Gerent returned her gaze and something passed between them – the affinity of shared experience. 'It is venerated, for it is rare.'

'That's why Stone is so empty!' Jonah stared at Annie. 'Think of how quickly the American West has been tamed. Why, already one can travel by train across the entire width of the continent. Yet only a few years ago the West was the domain of the buffalo and the Indian, unexplored by white men. If one were to set a small colony of men on Stone, after only a few generations they should be swarming across its face, busily taming it and marking it as their own.'

'Someone's been busy enough down there,' commented Annie, indicating the palace, which was just disappearing from view.

'Colonies come and go,' explained Esh. 'There are extinctions here, just as there are in your world. The difference is that on Amara it takes only the opening of a new threshold to bring a new wave of immigrants, perhaps from a very different time to their predecessors. But survival is not guaranteed. Species, like individuals, are only mortal.'

Annie had stood up and was rubbing the side of Kythe's face as one might stroke a horse. 'Now I see why you're so upset, Kythe dear,' she said, managing to sound like a mother reassuring a small child. 'But you needn't feel guilty about leaving. It's not fair to load that responsibility on your shoulders.'

'I wouldn't mind if I *fancied* Dreke,' responded Kythe miserably.

She and Annie stared at each other for a long, held moment, then both erupted into laughter. Kythe dipped her head, snorting and squeezing tears of mirth from her eyes; Annie held on to her snout, practically riding Kythe's long dragon head as they rocked together. Jonah smiled – the laughter was infectious – but he noticed that Gerent had turned away and was staring down through the nearest window, hands clenched tight behind his back.

'What about you, Esh?' asked Jonah much later, when night had fallen once more.

'I do not understand,' the Ypoth replied, staring down into the dark.

'Do you want to go home? What was it you said to me? – "You may find no further advantage in my presence." Do you *want* to stay in my presence, Esh? Is your work with me done?'

'Do you wish me to leave?'

'Don't avoid the question.'

Esh sighed. The sound was thin, like distant surf. 'I am here to be of service to you, Jonah Lightfoot.'

'But what do you *want*?'

'I want . . . I want only to be at your side. You are like no other; throughout eternity there has been no presence like yours on Amara. And . . . I love you.'

Dawn revealed a profound change in their surroundings. The air below the chequerboard windows was startlingly clear, clearer in fact than at any time since Jonah's arrival on Stone. What clouds there were straggled in thin, straight lines, looking less like ribbons than lines of chalk drawn into the sky.

And the sky – the sky was everywhere. It was as if Stone had vanished altogether.

They gathered around one of the windows and stared into the emptiness, trying to work out what had happened.

It was Kythe who saw it first. 'It's a mirror!' she exclaimed. 'The Dead Calm is a mirror!'

Once betrayed, the illusion was not perfect. It was no less disturbing for that however. The wall of Stone had been polished to perfection so that it reflected the sky flawlessly. All trace of sculpted block and engraved line was gone, there was only infinite smoothness. The only clue to Stone's continuing presence at all was the unnatural symmetry of the clouds, although these were so sparse it was hard to make them out. It was easier for the eye to believe Stone had been removed entirely, for there were no reference points on which it might rest. There was only the sky.

None of them could pull themselves away from the view. In the end Jonah lay down flat on his stomach, sprawled across one of the windows that was not smeared with the grisly residue of Archan's impact. By cupping his hands on either side of his head so as to shield his peripheral vision, he could believe himself a bird soaring above this alien sky. Free from concerns, free from the burdens of threat and hope, free just to fly.

Soon the clouds were gone altogether. There was only the infinite blue, paling as it fell away into the abyss. Then, suddenly, a flurry of movement attracted his attention – a cartwheel of white vapour tumbled downwards at astonishing speed, whirling in complex eddies as it tore itself apart. More followed until on each side there was a constant cloud-fall, twinned with its reflection in the endless mirror of the Dead Calm. It was like gliding through a kaleidoscope.

Jonah was struck by the immense speed at which the clouds were falling, much faster than any he had observed before. Nor were they straight any longer, instead they were contorted by vortices and rip-tides, angry knots of energy that disintegrated as soon as they were formed. Then he remembered Kythe's assertion that the wind was much stronger here, too strong for dragons to fly, and he understood what he was seeing: the turbulence caused by the interference of the monument with the normally unobstructed airflow.

Were I to venture outside, I would be sucked away in an instant.

The play of the clouds with their twins hypnotised him, and before he knew it the sun had moved round and the white clouds had turned to gold. Esh touched him gently on the shoulder.

'We have stopped,' she said quietly.

He had felt no lurch, nothing to signal the end of the journey.

'The Threshold?' he asked.

'It is down there somewhere.' She pointed into the golden mist, which now obscured the lower reaches of the sky altogether. 'If it exists.'

'Oh, it exists all right.'

He told them then about his experience with the basilisks – or rather their ghosts, as he had come to consider them. He did not know what had held him back from relating it until now; this simply seemed an appropriate time. They listened gravely, and sat in silence when he had finished.

'Then Stone is a made thing,' whispered Esh at last.

'We knew that all along,' said Annie. 'Didn't we? Didn't you know it, Esh? In your heart?'

The Ypoth nodded. 'To know a thing is not to accept it. Nor am I close to accepting it yet, for if Stone is made then I am made. I do not understand that. The thought makes me feel . . . small.'

'We're none of us big,' said Jonah. 'Look at me – I am but a faery.'

The clouds parted momentarily, affording them the briefest glimpse of a dark shape far below. It was little more than another chalk-mark sketched in the distance, but they knew at once they had arrived.

'To business,' Jonah said abruptly, climbing to his feet. 'We must find our way out of this place and go to work. Archan knows as much as we do now. If she manages to find her way here too then we have little time before she starts to make her mischief.'

'Can she?' asked Annie. 'Find her way here, I mean. That wind really does look too strong to fly in.'

'Kythe?'

Kythe flapped her wings uncertainly. 'Well, I suppose if she could have stayed underneath the monument, used it as a sort of shelter. But it would be difficult. And the pressure of the air will be low on the underside. It's very hard to grip thin air, even with all the charm she's soaked up.'

'Low pressure,' mused Jonah. 'Yes, I hadn't thought of that.'

'Dragons are good with air,' replied Kythe proudly.

Gerent interrupted them. 'I believe it is likely the red pedestal will provide us with the exit we need.'

The prince was standing next to the raised platform. At some point – none of them had noticed when – the etched lines had stopped glowing. All was dull again, except for the button, which was no longer depressed but had returned to its rest position, slightly raised from its surroundings. It was shining brightly.

'It will not be pushed again,' Gerent went on. 'I have tried.

I suspect it is time to put the pedestal away. Its work is done: we have arrived.'

'What do you suggest?' said Jonah.

'I raised the platform simply by climbing on top. I have no doubt the same action will cause it to descend into the floor. Then we may exit by the same means we used to gain access in the first place.'

'The ramp,' quavered Kythe. 'Oh, but the wind will be hopelessly strong on top! If we aren't crushed against the ground we'll be blown away before we can even stand upright!'

'We have no choice,' said Jonah softly. 'There must be a way. We would not be here if there were not. But climbing on the platform did not work before.'

'This is now. Are we decided?' demanded Gerent, looking directly at Jonah. Jonah returned his gaze, trying to measure the man. He was pleased the prince had asked his opinion, perhaps even his approval. Damnation! Could he not still like him?

He shrugged and Gerent climbed up on to the platform.

Immediately the button stopped glowing and the platform began to descend. Gerent crouched, his arms spread for balance even though the movement was slow and smooth. As the platform neared the floor he took a step forward, about to hop off again . . . but it continued to descend. Now it was level with the floor, now it was dropping *into* it. The others looked on astonished as the platform sank into the surrounding tiles to a depth of a foot. Then it broke clear.

A crack appeared around the entire perimeter of the platform and suddenly it was floating free, a massive child's building block dropping away unsupported from a square hole in the floor of the monument. Accompanying the separation was an anguished howling sound: the voice of the turbulence outside. It roared like surf, a constant idiot noise.

Air was sucked violently from the room. The wind was *in* the room, blasting from the four corners down into the trapdoor. Jonah rocked forward, overbalancing and nearly falling through the hole. Kythe's tail whipped nimbly across his path and he grabbed it to help steady himself.

'That's the second time you've caught me!' he managed to shout, though all the air seemed to have been drawn from his lungs. He was surrounded by brief rain as water condensed into the partial vacuum, and his ears throbbed. Then the pressures were equalised and the wind ceased; his ears still hurt however.

Still the platform descended at its leisurely rate. Gerent's head had already dropped below the level of the floor.

'We'd better jump!' exclaimed Annie, and without warning she slipped through the trapdoor and fell eight feet on to the platform. Gerent caught her around the waist, softening the blow. He continued to hold her even after she had landed, Jonah noted.

Esh followed at once, leaving Jonah dithering at the edge. With every second he delayed the platform dropped another six inches. Soon it would be too late; even now he might very well break his ankle.

'Jump,' whispered Kythe. His ears chose that moment to equalise the pressure inside his skull with that of the surrounding air and her voice popped audibly. The roaring of the wind dropped a tone and grew very loud. He hesitated a second longer, then turned rapidly and lowered himself over the edge. Then he closed his eyes and let go.

Esh caught him, quite literally. He felt the hard jolt of her bony arms against his back and opened his eyes to find himself carried like a baby, just as she had carried the unconscious Gerent. 'Thank you,' he gasped as she lowered him to the floor. Kythe appeared, descending lightly on her outstretched wings. They huddled together in the centre of the platform, none of them keen to approach the edges, not even those of the party with wings. Behind them, two hundred yards distant behind Stone's magical mirror, their reflections mimicked their actions perfectly.

Already the monument was out of reach. It receded swiftly, a tremendous rising ceiling of smooth, grey stone. The only marks on its surface, apart from a few vague blotches meandering their way across its width, were the windows against which Archan had hurled herself and the hatch through which they had emerged. Yet even they, large as they had seemed, were but barnacles on the belly of the whale. The monument was the biggest single construction Jonah had ever seen (disregarding Stone itself, of course), and its scale was made all the more impressive by the fact that it was now attached to its mirror-image.

The further they dropped the more the wind began to intrude.

It started buffeting them, sending exploratory stabs of air across the platform. Tendrils of clouds whipped past, backlit by orange-filtered light. The atmosphere thickened gradually as they drew away from the near-vacuum immediately beneath the monument.

Throughout all this there was no sign of Archan.

Nor was there any clue as to what was supporting the platform, nor by what means it was being propelled (or rather what force was preventing it from plummeting into the chasm). It was attached neither to Stone nor the monument by any visible means. It was, presumably, just a matter of charm.

The cloud was thinner now, and the roaring had all but ceased. Here, far below the monument, there was nothing to obstruct the airflow and so nothing to generate the noise. However they could hear a new sound: a deep whistle that grew louder the further they travelled. It preyed on Jonah's mind until he realised what it reminded him of: the hollow moan made by a glass bottle as one blew across its mouth.

Just then the clouds billowed apart and they were faced with their first proper view of the Threshold.

It was, as they had expected, a hole in the surface of Stone.

It was not, as Jonah had imagined, a smooth-sided, pinched oval: an eye.

Instead it was angry and irregular, the sort of hole that might have been gouged out by an angry giant overlord. It was rough and scoured, a crude slash in the seamless mirror of the Dead Calm. An aberration, dark and brooding. Something that clearly was not supposed to be there at all.

Yet there it was. And they were approaching it.

They were approaching Stone too. Their reflections were much closer, close enough to transmit their wide-eyed expressions. Kythe's wings were tented high, they and their magic silently deflecting the wind. Looking up Jonah saw them spread over the whole group like sails, the orange light of the setting sun glowing through a network of veins and slender bones.

The platform's rate of descent slowed noticeably as they drew near the mirror. Barely a yard separated them from their alter egos. Then, with the slightest of thumps, the platform met its twin. The descent continued.

All of them except Annie looked away from the mirror –

there was something unnerving about the perfection of both it and the reflections it contained. Jonah lay down again to peer over the edge of the platform; before doing so he glanced briefly at Annie. She seemed transfixed, and for a moment he thought her eyes were mirrors too. He gasped, his heart climbing into his throat. Then his view was obscured as she raised a hand to flick back her hair; when she dropped it again he saw that it had been a trick of the light. Her eyes were entirely human, almost aglow in the orange light.

They were very close to the top of the Threshold. Jonah remembered the vertigo he had experienced when he had first looked out across Stone, but he could not recall exactly how he had felt. It was an intellectual sort of remembrance, with none of the emotion.

Am I so much a part of this place already? he wondered, standing again as the platform reached the lip of the Threshold.

They dropped into the mouth of a tremendous cave. It was as if night had lifted from the depths; a dark curtain rose up and wiped away their reflections. As his eyes adjusted Jonah began to make out shapes in the gloom. He held his breath, waiting for his first glimpse of the memory rods.

The platform was floating free, dropping ever more slowly. The rim of the Threshold was studded with massive stones; each one was easily twice the size of Stonehenge's largest menhirs, which they resembled greatly. They were spaced more or less regularly around the cave's entire, ragged circumference; Jonah felt they should have reminded him of teeth, but they did not. Looking into the Threshold was not at all like looking into a mouth; it was more like looking *down*. Down the deepest well he had ever seen. He scanned the dark interior, looking for the familiar parallel lines.

The light was very bad now; the sun was an angry red ball about to strike the vertex of Stone. In vain he searched for the memory rods, crouched on the platform's edge and peering deep into the Threshold.

The platform halted between two towering, black slabs. The low whistling was all around them now. They were about to enter the neck of the bottle.

The instant he stepped off the platform and on to the gnarled floor of the Threshold Jonah saw them; he cried out in surprise.

Just as the cavern was a twisted, broken version of the lesser threshold which had delivered him here, so the memory rods it held were different too.

They sprouted from the curved and craggy walls in a reasonably orderly fashion, but no sooner did they enter the Threshold than the rods started to deform. They curved and spiralled, looping over their neighbours and thickening as they did so. They knotted themselves, wove themselves into great clumps, fattening all the while until near the centre of the cavern they were fused into a single, massed entity. From both sides the rods came, meeting at this confused nexus like the energetic roots of some unimaginable tree, a tree whose rings – if you could but cut through its trunk – would number not in the hundreds but the millions.

As he stepped forward between the giant menhirs Jonah saw beneath and beyond the knots: the rods extended far back into the blackness. It could take him a lifetime to explore this cathedral.

And I have only one lifetime, came the unsettling thought. *Archan has many.*

'Where do we have to go?' Kythe whispered in his ear.

'In there,' he answered. 'I suppose.'

'Is *she* here?'

'I think so.'

Esh grew more and more uneasy the further they proceeded into the Threshold.

'This is – not right,' she moaned. 'Not right at all, Jonah Lightfoot.'

'Only because it's not what you're used to,' replied Jonah, though if he was honest with himself he was terrified.

'Stone was meant to be whole. A cavity such as this should not be left exposed. It must be repaired.' She was jittering nervously. The bottom of her carapace, which she held behind the upper part of her legs like a bustle, was twitching – Jonah remembered the strange appendages the Ypoth kept concealed there and felt momentarily revolted.

'It is not your place to repair it!' he snapped. He pressed his hand against his forehead: it was hot in here, very hot. 'You don't see any other Ypoth around here, do you?'

Esh looked around apprehensively, saying nothing.

It was not long before the drunken memory rods blocked their way completely. The ground across which they had picked their way was grooved and pitted, the same black stuff Jonah was used to but wilder, like the surface of an ocean frozen in the throes of a storm. The light had almost gone; the mouth of the cave was a ragged line of black at their backs, an angry frame to the impenetrable night sky.

There was light here though. Hidden spaces deep within the tangled rods glowed palely. Not once did they see the actual source of the lights, which were gently coloured and transitory. No sooner did they draw near to one patch of phosphorescence than it winked out and their eyes were drawn by a new spark further away. Jonah could not help but think of mischievous faeries darting to and fro inside the maze, tempting them further and further in.

'We could lose ourselves in there very easily,' commented Gerent. This close it really did look like tangled tree roots, a veritable forest of them, looming high. Clambering up would be easy enough; getting lost would be even easier.

'I hope we won't have to go in there at all,' said Jonah. 'Esh, it shouldn't matter which rod I pick, should it?' She was not listening – one of the glimmers of light had captivated her. 'Esh!'

She jumped. 'Pardon me, Jonah Lightfoot. I was not paying attention.'

'Am I right in thinking I can touch any rod and find any memory?' he said impatiently. The random movement of the lights was irritating him. The rods towered, dwarfing them, a massive presence. 'They're all connected, aren't they?'

'That is right. At least, in all normal thresholds it is right. Whether or not it holds true here . . . I do not know.'

'There's only one way to find out.'

Jonah stepped on to the crest of one of the frozen waves of black rock. One of the rods was bent low here, its belly swollen like the saddle of a gigantic earthworm. Gingerly he extended both his hands and gripped its slick surface. For an instant he felt nothing, then . . .

. . . it was just as it had been before. A thousand cannons boomed.

White walls were drenched beneath searing mud. He heard an animal screaming far away, smelt the crispness of burning flesh . . .

A name stabbed into his thoughts: Herculaneum. *The Roman town fell away, became a puddle of ash in a vast emptiness. Liquid sped past, a thousand currents tearing through it, each one pulling him in a different direction. Again he heard the screaming – it was a horse. Without thinking he reined in the river, pulling it round like a liquid steed. Plunging forward he outstripped it, accelerating upstream until he met another river, more ash. Another volcano, another of the catastrophes pinning Stone to the worlds whose memories it tracked. This one snow-capped and immense. One whole side of it vanished and a million trees were laid flat. A steel carriage, its wheels wrapped in fat, black tyres, raced the ash-wall down a rocky slope, was consumed.*

The ash was everywhere, obscuring his vision, dulling all his senses. There was nowhere to go, nothing to do except . . .

. . . pull his hands clear. They dripped clear, sweet-smelling liquor. The others regarded him uncertainly. Gerent held Annie close; of them all she looked the most fearful.

'What did you see?' asked Esh. 'Did you find her?'

Jonah shook his head, for the moment unable to speak. He felt dizzy, as he had before, but he also felt strong. Touching the rods again was like diving into familiar water, shocking at first but then welcoming. 'No,' he gasped at last. 'No, I think . . . I think it's different here.'

'What is it you must do?' demanded Gerent. 'Tell us, Lightfoot, so that we might help you.'

'I can travel through the memories the rods hold,' said Jonah, the words blurting out in a sudden, sharp rush. His brief sojourn into the strange realm of the memory rods had brought startling coherency to his thoughts. He did not want to lose it. 'When I touch the rods I can go anywhere, to any world in any time. And when I get to where I want to be, I can change the memories that live there. I can change history. If I were to break one of the rods, I could make it stop altogether.'

'That's what Archan wants to do, isn't it?' cried Kythe. 'She wants to smash it all until there's nothing left!'

'Where is it you want to go, Jonah?' asked Annie quietly. She was in shadow, barely visible. Jonah wished he could see her eyes.

'I must find Archan in there. I must find the place in history where she is most vulnerable and . . . make her gone.'

'If you change the past,' said Gerent slowly, 'will you not also change the future? Was it not Archan who brought you here in the first place? By removing her from the past do you not also remove yourself from Stone, and hence from affecting her past at all. Do you not see it? The serpent eats its own tail.'

'Yes!' answered Jonah angrily. 'Yes, of course I see it! I don't understand it any better than you, Gerent. But I have to try. She cannot be killed. This is the only chance we have to get rid of her!'

He noticed Gerent's arm around Annie's waist. The prince was holding her tight enough so that her hips were tilted against his. A red veil washed across Jonah's vision and he lunged towards them, noting Annie's shocked look with something like satisfaction.

Gerent backed away, relinquishing his hold on Annie only at the last minute. Jonah raised his fist and swung, but Gerent ducked and he succeeded only in mashing his knuckles against one of the rods. Annie was calling out but he did not heed her words, whatever they may have been: he was tracking the prince, who was now ducking beneath his arm, trying to get away.

'You coward!' yelled Jonah, barely coherent. 'Your father was right if he thought you such! Fight, damn you!'

He was rewarded by a strong, clean blow to the point of his chin – Gerent had taken him at his word. Jonah staggered back, the red haze dotted now with stars. The back of his head struck the rod and for an instant he blacked out. When he came to he was still on his feet, swaying slightly. Gerent was crouched only a few paces away, fists raised, cheeks flaming; the burn on the side of his face was a livid pink.

'Jonah!' Annie was screaming. 'What the hell are you doing? There's no time for this!'

Jonah rushed him. Gerent side-stepped and helped him on his way. He cannoned into another of the rods, only just managing to extend his hands in time to absorb the blow. His fingers clenched around the ebony cylinder and again there was . . .

. . . hot, volcanic ash. Unbearable pain. Nothing more.

Flexing new-found muscles Jonah tried to rise above the ash as he had risen above the poor, doomed town of Herculaneum. But the air was folded, twisted round upon itself. The further he flew towards the blur of light that tempted him on the darker it got. Whichever direction he chose he could move only backwards.

He had no power here after all! There was nowhere for him to go!

Fire licked at him, dragon fire. He cried out and . . .

. . . broke contact. Gerent was standing close behind him, fists clenched at his sides. Jonah feinted a lunge; Gerent stepped back. Jonah laughed and wiped away the sweat pouring down his face. The red film had been replaced by a kind of white heat, a furnace driving out all thought from his head but clean, sharp fury.

'Curse you all!' he bellowed, clambering on to the rod. 'Especially you!' he added, pointing down at Gerent.

'Come back, Jonah!' Annie called. 'Come down from there!'

He continued to scramble higher. The anger was an intense light illuminating a path through the complicated inner world of the rods.

'Jonah Lightfoot – wait!' Esh's call seemed to come from very far away. 'I can hear something. I do not think you should go . . .'

Her voice dwindled to nothing and Jonah was alone inside.

The labour of climbing forced the anger back a little. Jonah became minutely aware of the tiny space occupied by his body; alone in a fragile shell of air, he made his way deeper. He was, of course, forced to touch the rods over and over again as he moved higher. Each time his bare hands made contact he received sharp jolts, varying in form from visions, most of them too brief to be understandable, to, most frequently, smells.

The further up he climbed the deeper he penetrated what he had come to think of as the forest, and each step was marked by a new scent: fresh poppies, the tang of vinegar, fried onions and woodsmoke, old sweat and fresh blood, oil, lemons, grass and honey. For a while he closed his eyes and moved blindly through the aromas, feeling his way by touch and smell alone.

The rods were grotesquely swollen here, huge and buckled, each as broad as a tree trunk. The gaps between them became smaller too, until it was impossible to proceed any further. A single, black curve blocked his way, the flank of the biggest rod he had seen so far. Its skin was pocked with warts and deep cracks oozing resin. Far to his left it bulged pregnantly. No jolts came when he touched these bigger rods; perhaps they were insulated, or simply thick-skinned. The memories were there though: all he had to do was concentrate to bring them swarming out as keenly as ever.

Suddenly he was exhausted. Turning his back he leaned against the giant rod and looked back through the labyrinth.

To his surprise there was a light blazing in the distance, throwing the crisscrossed rods into hard shadow. It was flickering hot and red – the unmistakable glow of fire. Jonah rushed back, ducking beneath the closest rods until he fetched up against one the size of a boiler pipe. Far from being enclosed he found himself on the brink of a sudden drop. Had the rods rearranged themselves without him realising it? His view of the Threshold was vast: he could see the entire width of the floor they had crossed to reach the rods from the entrance. A tongue of fire rose vertically and winked out. It came again, a short, fitful burst. The light it cast was enough for him to see that it came from the mouth of Kythe.

There was movement near the ceiling. Kythe delivered no more fire; instead Jonah saw his companions hurrying across the floor to the shelter of a deep cleft in the left-hand wall. Gerent stopped on the way and grasped a long spar of the black, resinous material, snapping it free and hefting it in his hands like a spear. By the time they reached the cleft the movement had resolved itself into an army of shapes dropping from the ceiling: at least fifty of the menhirs had detached themselves and were descending on long strands of glutinous resin. As they lowered themselves they hunched over and grew blockish legs, and he had no doubt that here were Esh's distant cousins: the Ypoth of the Threshold.

By the time they reached the floor the menhirs had metamorphosed into low-slung creatures with great beetle backs and long, thick limbs. They had no heads that he could see – indeed, their forms seemed unfinished, as though they had grown bored partway through the act of creation. The more he looked on them the less they seemed like animals at all: they looked like stones with legs, simple lumpish shapes perched on crude stumps with barely enough articulation to keep them balanced. Yet they were very many, and they were anything but clumsy; they *swarmed*.

They sped across the irregular terrain, these guardians of the Threshold, their legs striking sparks from the ground. The swarm moved with a dreadful intelligence, its movements smooth and co-ordinated. Jonah counted yards and doubted whether his companions would reach the sanctuary of the wall-cleft in time.

He jumped up on to the slippery black pipe, his quest forgotten.

A creamy white head rose smoothly before him. It looked like the point of an enormous needle, sharp and featureless. Then it split apart to reveal a gullet lined with chrome and alive with flame. The neck that bore it twisted languidly, rising higher and higher. A pair of wings, vast as clouds, appeared to either side, blotting out Jonah's view of the battlefield and sending draughts of warm air across his face. The sound of impacts, hard as metal, reached his ears, along with a single, human scream. Male or female? He could not tell.

Archan drew nearer, looking exactly as she had in his vision of the basilisks. She eclipsed the Threshold entirely, swallowed the night outside.

'So now the same air flows over both our wings,' she intoned. Fire enfolded her jaws, forming abstract patterns, from diamonds and waves to a shape like a human hand.

Jonah toyed with the idea of turning his back on her and continuing on his way before deciding it was madness. 'A human being might say that we are playing on a level field.'

'Are you human, Jonah? I wonder.'

'Why don't you burn me here and now? It is within your power.'

'We are, as you say, on "level ground". Therefore we have nothing to hide from each other. We are not so different, Jonah, though it pains me to admit it. Except I will still be young when your bones are long turned to dust. As to why I have not killed you already . . . I do not trust this place. Time has become soft here, as it became soft in our world near the moment of the Turning. We are very near to the Turning now, Jonah, nearer than you might think. It may be that I could burn you where you stand, but I cannot be sure you would not find time to cause mischief before the flames reached you.'

Jonah realised his hands were inches away from the nearest memory rod. 'Then you do fear me! Do you believe I can destroy you?'

'Do not forget that I arrived at the Threshold before you, Jonah. I have already travelled in time as you are about to do. My past is secure. You will find no weakness there. But . . .'

'But?'

'But I would like to see you try.'

She smiled, a thin dragon leer that split her streamlined head almost in two, then she coiled her neck back into an S-shape of repose and waited for Jonah's response.

'If you have used the rods yourself then you know the power they hold. Can you be so sure of your hold over that power? Can you be so sure I am not your match? In short, have you looked everywhere, Archan? You may be immortal, but that does not make you invulnerable. This may be your only chance to rid yourself of me, for when I leave here you have no idea where I will go.'

The white, faceless dragon before him closed its mouth abruptly. 'Do your worst, faery, and be quick about it. Time is thin. So is my patience.'

Jonah did turn away from her then, unwilling to let her see the defeat in his face (and wondering how she could see without eyes – charm, he supposed).

Yet I myself have no idea where to go. She has covered her tracks. She has herself gripped the memory rods with those charm-filled wings of hers and surveyed her whole life in its entirety. She beat me to the Threshold and used the extra time to fill the chinks in her armour. If it was ever anything but intact.

The pregnant memory rod loomed above him. He raised his left hand and touched it gently on to the surface . . .

. . . but not too hard. That was where he had been going wrong before – he had been trying too hard. The rods were connected, each capable of interchanging information with its neighbours, but each had its own unique scent, its own preferred stories. Its own memories. To travel in time, all he had to do was open himself to the memories of the particular rod he touched and let it carry him to its heart. Only from there could

he strike out into the wider flow of the great river of time and start exploring in earnest.

But did he have time for exploring, when Archan towered over his earthly body and his friends were in peril?

Time is soft, *he thought.* And very flexible. Here more than anywhere else.

This time it was not like entering another world at all. There was no thunder, no smoke and no ash. It was just like walking deeper into the forest of rods. If he looked over his shoulder, he imagined, he would see Archan still there. He did not try it: he had no desire to look on her any longer than he had to.

The rods parted of their own accord as he made his way forward. He was still in the Threshold, of that he was certain, but he was no longer on Stone. He had entered the store of memories and was therefore in some way within *Stone, yet as free of its confines as a bird is free of the ground. He sensed the fragility of this strange, new environment, could almost hear it crackle beneath his feet as he walked, and so he took great care.*

The Threshold contains memories of the turning of the world, *he reminded himself, trying to imagine what the world might have been like in that distant, mythical age. It seemed so remote, so meaningless, so unconnected to his own sense of the past – not just kings and queens and invasions but old history, prehistory, the history of man's rise from the crouched ape, his taming of fire and his working of stone and timber and metal. The hacking of a new life-force from the raw earth. What memories might he find here, in a time when dragons filled the skies and man . . . man was not yet made?*

The roots opened up suddenly, spilling him into a glade. It was laid sideways, of course, as everything of Stone was laid sideways, a dappled clearing in the horizontal forest. Something about the scale of the place made him feel tiny, like an insect clambering through an airspace in the soil.

Dust floated in the air before him, shining with inner light. It spiralled down as he watched, spinning ever faster until it became a solid shape. It grew limbs – long, delicate legs and slender arms – and diaphanous membranes. Walking soundlessly, its head tucked low, it approached him and bowed.

'My queen.' Its voice was like a caress. Still its body was only part-formed; in places he could see right through it to the roots on the opposite side of the clearing. A tiny bird no bigger than his fingernail,

its beak made from gold, darted through its chest, leaving tiny eddies to disrupt the dust from which the being was made.

Large eyes, a pointed face and pointed ears. Agonising beauty. A faery. A real *faery.*

'My queen,' the faery repeated, and Jonah realised it was addressing him. Raising his hand he suppressed a cry as he saw not his own familiar flesh but something soft and unmistakably feminine. He watched translucent fingers flex like wafts of air. 'All has been prepared. The twelve are ready. We await only your word.'

The faery turned slightly and a breeze blew through the glade, tearing its exquisite body into a thousand pieces. The pieces departed with a sigh.

Jonah was examining his new hands, turning them over in wonder and touching them against each other. Each touch sent sparkles of light into the air, and he knew he was making magic. He clapped and a billow of charm exploded across his face, transforming itself into a rainbow of colours, none of which he recognised.

His vision doubled and he was staring at another faery, except this time he understood that he was looking at himself, or rather the faery form he was currently inhabiting. He felt uncomfortable, remembering Archan's possession of Annie's body. The other faery smiled at him, allaying some of his concerns, though it was a sad smile, infinitely sad.

It was indeed female, the reflection in this magical mirror. Tall and willowy, with tiny breasts and smooth, hairless skin. Her wings, scintillating with stored charm, were immense by comparison to the rest of her body. Jonah looked beyond her to the roots defining the clearing and wondered just how big she was. Were faeries tiny as storybooks had children believe?

He looked closer, saw the shadow inside. Saw the beginnings of bones intruding inside her insubstantial flesh, understood that here was the natural faery, here was the man-to-be.

Here am I! *he thought with sudden, agonised clarity, as if he himself had pressed the crude, bony outline into this purest of creatures.*

Yet he knew it was not so. He knew that he was not really here, that he was simply observing what had once been in the world as a child might gaze into the pages of one of those storybooks.

The faery frowned, shockingly human, and pressed her hand – Jonah's hand! *– against her cheek, feeling the nascent skull beneath.*

I could be here, if I chose to be. I could enter this realm and change the faery's world. And she knows it!

Suddenly the urge to step fully into the memory of this moment was overwhelming. He could feel a pressure at his back, feel the tug of charm as it tried to spill him into the root-chamber. The faery queen spread her arms wide and held back her head, opening herself to him. Hair as clear as glass cascaded down her back, between her wings and pooled on the ground like water.

What I could not do here! *he marvelled, perceiving the faery's desolation, yearning to heal her wounds.* She grieves the fading of charm from the world. I could step in and sustain her!

He saw clearly how it could be done. Not that he could divert the Turning, that was beyond even his power, but he could grasp the memory rod thus *and twist it just* so *and a bubble would be made, a bubble of charm in which this lovely creature might be encased as though in amber, living still, retaining all her charm and as free in her spirit as she had ever been.*

He saw this, and was about to reach back into his earthly body, about to direct his own, meat-filled hands to mould the memory rod when he saw what else such a change might do.

To entrap this creature now would prevent her from completing the tasks she had yet to do. These tasks he could not see clearly but it seemed to him they too were wrapped up in the turning of the world. Everything nearby affected or was affected by the turning of the world – it loomed over these times and places like a thundercloud.

'The dragons are waiting at the summit,' whispered the faery queen. 'It is not my place to be saved.'

And so he let her go, weeping uncontrollable tears as she merged herself again with her reflection, then peeled her gossamer form away from his brutish humanity. He felt instantly soiled and stood there sobbing for what seemed an age, rubbing his palms repeatedly against his legs as though to wipe away the grime of nature.

But then she paused, looking back over her shoulder with the poise of a goddess.

'At least, not yet,' came her words. 'But . . . will you come back?'

Jonah nodded, not sure if he knew how.

She disappeared slowly, rising up through the glade like mist. Snowflakes ascended with her, huge and wonderful. Jonah's tears were freezing on his cheeks; he felt very cold.

On the other side of the glade was a tunnel pushed through the roots. Jonah crawled up into its spiral, trying not to breathe its foetid air until he emerged without warning on to a mountaintop. Though he was free of the tunnel he continued to climb, elevated now above the ground, only dimly aware that a group of faeries stood below him within a ring of towering stones. Two hunched forms lingered near them, but he could not make out what they were.

Above him the stars were coming out. When he looked down again the faeries, and the ring of stones, were gone. There was only fire belching towards him as the mountain split open.

This is it! *he thought wildly, careering into the heavens as the memory rod sucked him through the death throes of yet another volcano.* This is the moment of the turning of the world!

There were dragons all around him, briefly. Suddenly their wings folded and they dropped from the sky.

He rose higher, perceiving the world as the sphere it really was. Rings expanded from the brilliant ball of light, encircling the globe and painting it with light. He saw the world breathing in and out as if it were alive, and in that instant he believed that it was.

Thunder came then, the thunder of the cloud that was the Turning, the thunder of the winter it brought to charm, and then he was moving forwards through time. Something was calling him, something urgent. His quest? Archan! She was close beside him, he could sense her presence, calling him on, urging him forwards. He could not make out her words but he could hear her cries and he could not resist them. On he flew, on and on through the centuries as the world turned beneath him and the sound of thunder grew louder and louder in his ears. The fire brightened, flashing all around him, stabbing into him as it transformed itself into sheets of lightning. Rain lashed his body from every side and he was instantly soaked. He could hear the creak of metal, the occasional shatter of glass. Feel damp grass beneath his feet. He was no longer flying but fleeing, running and laughing, not just travelling through the memories but living them, breathing them. A fireball brushed his cheek and he heard a screaming, faint and so very, very far away. A horse, so human the sound.

His father's voice, calling him back.

Tree roots, dreadful, twisted things, yet right-sized at last. He jerked away from them, carried on running. The rain blurred his vision, softening the landscape so that for a breath or two he did not understand where he was. It seemed so alien, this flatness, the awful sideways slant of the horizontals. Then the scene locked into shape. He was back in the real world, his world, fleeing in the rain through the park on Sydenham Hill. Behind him the Crystal Palace towered. Faded outlines that were his father and brother scrambled through the murk in pursuit.

Before him: the dinosaur.

And he laughed, how he laughed.

17

Annie on the Inside – 4

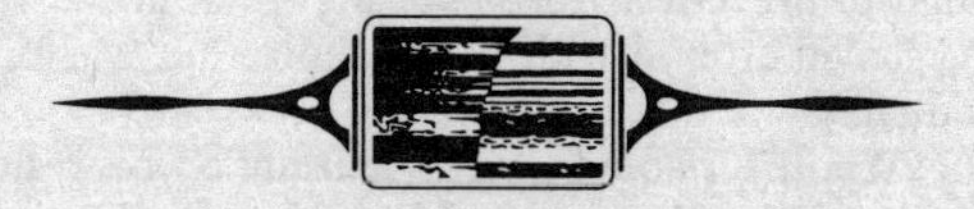

She was not aware of Archan until it was too late.

Bewildered by Jonah's unprovoked attack on Gerent, Annie had also been unaware of the descent of the Guardians. It was Esh who heard them first. Gerent wanted to stay amid the relative shelter of the rods but Esh urged them back down to the open floor, arguing that they could improvise weapons more easily.

'Why do we need weapons?' Kythe had asked plaintively.

Halfway across the floor Esh stopped and opened up her carapace. Insect limbs snickered out like busy machinery and suddenly there was a long spear of Stone-stuff lying on the ground.

'Pick it up,' she commanded, and Annie did so. Swiftly Esh carved off one for herself and one for Gerent. Kythe was already standing ahead of them, legs set wide apart, a jet of flame boiling from her mouth. It petered out after a short time and she looked round, an agonised expression on her face.

'I can't keep it up for very long,' she moaned.

'You're doing great!' said Annie with feeling.

The Guardians were descending from the ceiling on long strings. As soon as they landed on the floor the strings snapped and coiled around them like discarded lassos. They sprinted into motion at once, an army of black boulders moving on scarcely articulate stumps. Under different circumstances the sight of them might almost have been comical.

As it was it was utterly terrifying.

'Fly!' Annie shouted at both Kythe and Gerent. She shoved the winged Neolithic in the back, trying to propel him bodily into the air.

'And leave you alone?' he snapped back.

'Not on your life!' added Kythe.

They reached the crevice with seconds to spare. The foremost Guardian brought one heavy limb crashing down inches behind Gerent's heels before thumping into the overhang, which was low enough to prevent it from entering. It crouched as best it could and flailed around with its forelimbs, but was unable to reach its quarry.

'Are they Ypoth?' panted Gerent, leaning on his resin spear.

'No,' replied Esh. She sounded bewildered. 'No, they most certainly are not. Yet they are made from Stone as surely as the Ypoth are made from Stone, so . . . they may be regarded as cousins. Kin, of a sort. I have neither encountered nor heard of their kind before. They must be unique to the permanent Thresholds.'

'Whatever they are they're not happy,' put in Annie, jabbing at the Guardian with her own spear. It had been joined by three others, completely closing off the entrance, and more were massing behind. They were trapped.

The crevice was effectively a wide, low cave formed by a wave of Stone-stuff. Esh was bent almost double, and the two humans were forced to stoop. Kythe was desperately uncomfortable, constantly fidgeting as she tried to keep her delicate wing membranes and long neck and tail away from their besiegers. There was no other way out.

'Well,' Kythe cried, 'what are we supposed to do now?'

It did not take them long to establish that their weapons were largely ineffectual. Though the Guardians seemed to withdraw a little when struck, the spears did not even scratch their tough armour.

'These spears may be hard as diamonds,' grumbled Annie, throwing hers to the ground in frustration, 'but so are their hides!'

Kythe managed an occasional jet of flame, of which the monsters seemed at least a little afraid, but each effort cost her greatly, and there was little enough charm floating free in the Threshold for her to tap. The situation seemed hopeless.

Then the lead Guardian began to twist out of shape. Planting its stubby legs fast on to the ground, it flattened its body into a disc, whereupon it was able to force its way further into the cave. It was rewarded by a battery of heavy blows and was forced to retreat; its body expanded again as it withdrew, shedding tiny sparks of charm that chattered like infants.

'I have an idea,' said Esh, so quietly that her words were almost lost.

She opened her carapace while the others rallied round her, making sure she was not attacked. Those busy limbs worked with the undulating ground surface, trying to burrow into it. After several minutes she stopped, clearly distressed.

'It is difficult,' she gasped. A dull sheen covered the fragile limbs with which she had been digging. 'The Ypoth were built to repair Stone, not to wear it away.'

'What about them?' demanded Gerent, indicating the Guardians.

'I do not believe they can manipulate Stone at all. Such an ability would be a danger to a place such as this, which relies on remaining an open wound. These creatures are sentries, nothing more, mere automata with limited intelligence and certainly none of the subtler skills of the Ypoth . . .' She broke off, pale green eyes widening. 'Stand back,' she whispered.

Reluctantly they did so. Annie flung out her arm as Esh walked forwards, towards the entrance, but Gerent held her back. 'Wait and see,' he urged.

The Guardians held back too, waiting.

Esh approached the lead Guardian, the one that seemed most anxious to enter their stronghold. Her movements were slow and languorous, and Annie wondered if she was trying to hypnotise the beast.

Then she moved fast, very fast. Her shell lifted again and those infinitely articulate limbs were a blur of activity. Resin swelled from the floor, encasing the Guardian's legs and trapping it neatly in the entrance. It squealed, a high-pitched sound full of wrath, and fell sideways; its legs contorted horribly, bending in ways they were clearly not designed to bend. They did not break though – the stuff of Stone, from which these things were made just as their cousins the Ypoth were, was too strong for that.

Its neighbour took up the scream and lashed out at Esh, knocking her back against Kythe, who delivered a blast of fire straight into what passed for the beast's face. It backed away reluctantly. All the monsters were screaming now; the sound was almost unbearable.

Eventually Esh had the entire front row of the Guardians locked down to the floor. They continued to scream, rocking to and fro and heaving at their trapped limbs; gradually they stopped moving altogether, as if their inner workings had seized up. Esh squatted, looking tired; Annie rested a hand on her bony shoulder.

'That's got them under control, the nearest of them at least,' she said. 'But we still can't get out.'

Esh nodded. 'I am working on that, Annie West.'

Then the headache came, sudden and blinding.

Distantly she felt Gerent's hands clutching at her, felt the blast of superheated air as Archan's fire burned away the remaining Guardians and the whole front part of the overhang that had protected them. Then, briefly, she fell asleep.

When she came to, Archan was back inside her head.

Except it was not as it had been before. Before, Annie had been a prisoner, confined to a minute space deep in the recesses of her mind. Her tower.

This time she remained fully aware, fully able to interpret the data her senses brought her, able to see and hear and think just as well as she ever had. But she had no control over her body's actions. None at all.

She looked out through eyes that were moved by the unwelcome dragon presence, perceived the white lash of Archan's tail as it encircled her waist, drawing her away from Gerent's desperate attempts to pull her down. The tail deposited her gently on to Archan's smooth back. For the second time she rode a dragon steed, only now the dragon was in her mind as well as beneath her legs.

Archan allowed her a brief view of her companions waving after her amid the molten remains of cave and Guardians – Gerent distraught, Esh still bent double, quite exhausted, Kythe hovering in the air, wondering whether or not to follow.

'Go back!' she wanted to cry but her jaws were locked. There was a strange taste at the back of her throat; she wondered if it was the taste of fire.

The point of view changed and she was looking at the

approaching wall of memory rods. Archan penetrated the forest easily, alighting only once before reaching the deep, dark place where Jonah was waiting.

His body was erect and alert, but Annie knew at once that something was wrong – something was missing. Jonah's body might have been here but his spirit was somewhere else entirely.

'I could burn him,' came the dragon's voice, echoing both through her ears and across the tortured landscape of her mind. 'But I fear he would evade me. His absence is not as total as it may appear, and he might do me some mischief in the eternity it would take the fire to reach his bones.'

Annie did not understand, not fully, but she did recognise something for which she had not dared to hope: Archan was afraid.

'Why have you brought me here?' she demanded, her mouth not moving an inch.

'Oh, I think you have already guessed that, faery-whore.'

To her despair, she had.

18
Memory

He is sitting on Iguanodon's *tail.*

The rainstorm is brief but intense, turning the ground instantly to mud. The sun is already burning through the rim of the cloud when a solitary bolt of lightning rips into the ground. The thunder booms, inseparable from its electric twin.

The lightning strikes not Iguanodon *but an ancient elm some twenty yards distant. The tree explodes and Jonah yelps; it showers him with singed bark. In response to his cry, Albert peers out from behind the dinosaur and grins. Their father appears not to have heard. Jonah raises a finger to his lips; Albert shrugs and ducks back out of sight.*

The elm tips over, its roots groaning as they are pulled like teeth from the earth. One by one they give way and the elm is suddenly pointing not at the sky but at the Palace. The sunlight breaks through and bathes the scene with incandescence.

Everything stops.

Jonah slipped down from the dinosaur's tail, glancing warily at the tree which had been frozen in mid-fall. It leaned at an impossibly precarious angle, its upper boughs suspended just ten feet above the dinosaur's skull. Droplets of rain were hanging in the atmosphere like frozen fireflies.

Jonah gripped the memory rod tighter than ever, applying the bend to its inner structure with the instinctive touch of a sculptor. The memories it held paused in their endless flow, waiting to see what would change.

He circumnavigated the concrete beast. In the sky the storm-clouds looked like cotton glued on to a slate, their bellies still glowing with the after-light of the lightning flash.

Albert was there, of course, his finger still on his lips, grinning in Iguanodon's *massive shadow. And there was Henry, paused in mid-run. Both his feet were clear of the ground – he had been sprinting, a look of trepidation on his face. Jonah had not seen his father's face in those seconds before he had died. It had never occurred to him that Henry might have been afraid. He went up to his father and stroked his hair, weeping uncontrollably. The hair yielded; this was no statue.*

Quite free of the ground, his father looked as though he was flying.

And Albert, dear Albert, who had worked at life so much harder than his younger brother and who had never earned the full attentions of the father they shared. Where Jonah had daydreamed Albert had slaved, yet his diligence had only ever earned him more chores. Older, no less wise, he had never begrudged Jonah his special place.

There was sadness in his smile though. Funny how Jonah had never seen it until now.

Pulling the silent finger aside he kissed his brother once, on the lips.

He was dimly aware that Archan was returning. Strange – he had not noticed her leave. Annie climbed down from the dragon's creamy-white back and approached Jonah across the tumbled rods. With her dark hair awry and her face flushed she looked very beautiful.

Her lips parted. She was before him, startlingly close. Slipping her hand behind his head she drew him against her and kissed him, opening her mouth wide as her fingers clutched at his hair. Without breaking her hold she slithered over the memory rod and wrapped her other arm around his waist, pulling their hips together.

He kissed her hard. It felt so good, it felt so right, so long-awaited. One of his hands relinquished its grip on the memory rod – charm cascaded from his fingers as he let go – and slipped beneath the leather to find her breast. His hand seemed to move of its own accord, out of his control.

She was groaning, moving her body against his.

He opened his eyes, looked into hers.

Saw himself staring back.

Jonah pushed, as hard as he could, shouting, 'No!' as he propelled her back against the memory rod. Her lips peeled back to make a snarl, then the mirrors were gone from her eyes and she was Annie again, gazing back at him through a sea of tears.

'Jonah,' she sobbed, 'I'm sorry!'

Behind her, towering above her, Archan screamed her rage and poured fire straight towards Annie. It came slowly, so slowly Jonah could see every individual lick of flame. It would not reach her for hours. He still had one hand clamped to the memory rod.

They were not storm-clouds at all but the belly of a dragon.

'It was a good try, Archan!' he shouted into the motionless sky. 'But I fancy you have not distracted me at all. If anything you may have helped me. There's something I want to try before I leave this place behind me once and for all.'

The scene was straining now, anxious to regain its place in the ordered flow of time, afraid of being left behind while the river ran on.

Could I freeze this moment? *he wondered.* Could I make it so it remained like this forever? Would my father and brother be deathless then, like Archan?

The answer was yes, of course he could. He held this moment in his hand. It was his to do with as he pleased.

His brother with mischief on his lips. His father, flying.

Jonah approached the dinosaur again. Something was missing. There should have been a small boy sitting astride the tail: himself at the age of eight.

There was nobody there.

Because I am *here*. In order to see these memories I must enter the body of someone who was present at the time. Just as I entered the body of the faery queen. If I myself am part of the memory, then I will be drawn into my own body. At least that way I am never in danger of meeting myself.

What would he see if he looked in a mirror: the boy or the man?

He shook his head; he was wasting time, if such a concept had any meaning here.

But it did *have meaning, he could sense it. The scene was creaking audibly as the river sucked at it. He might return here afresh another time, have another bite at the apple as it were, but this encounter was drawing to a close.*

And back on Stone, Archan's fire was still crossing the space between her jaws and Annie's back.

Jonah ran to the dinosaur's tail, picked up what he knew was lying in the mud beside it and then swung himself astride.

'This moment,' he whispered. 'Oh God, forgive me.'

He bent his head and the storm clouds began to roll again. The dinosaur continued to fall forward, just as it had done in 1859.

The motion of the *Iguanodon*'s tail, lifting high as it had lifted high all those years ago, propelled him back into the world of Stone. He fell hard against the memory rod, taking care not to break contact with it, while behind him echoed the dismal thud of tons of concrete and steel embedding themselves into the ground, and his father and brother died again.

The tears would not be denied. Through their mist he looked at the thing he had picked out of the mud, which now lay in a sorry mess at his feet.

'I can bring things with me,' he sobbed.

Archan's fire had crossed nearly half the space already.

It was later, perhaps night-time, although how he knew this he was not sure. The root chamber was neither lighter nor darker than it had been. Something in the air.

He paced anxiously, wishing his control over the rods was greater and that he could gauge his arrival times more accurately.

I will grow more accomplished with practice, *he consoled himself, not convinced he* wanted *to practice.*

The faery queen was unsurprised to see him there. As she unfolded herself from a bough in the ceiling, assembling a rough, pastel body from parings of bark and a gloss of sap, he wondered just whose body he himself had entered. His question was answered when she reached out one of her slender hands – still translucent but green now and alive with flowing juices – and lifted him from where he stood low on the ground. She seemed extraordinarily tall, and he realised he was a bird.

'I came back,' he said redundantly.

'Your visits intrigue me.'

Jonah looked around with small, acute eyes. 'It feels different.'

'Winter has come. Charm has left the world and all is confusion. The dragons have done well – they have helped the world to turn true. But . . . colour has gone. The Old Earth Dwellers have scattered into the aether, into the empty spaces where the magic used to live. They are echoing halls now, haunted and cold.'

'Yet you have remained; you have waited for me. How is it you are able to perceive me at all? I thought – I think – it is unusual for people to travel through memories in this way. I thought the perception was one-way only, that I could only observe and not be seen.'

'I and my kin are near to the Deathless in many ways. We have long known of the existence of Amara, and a little of its purpose, though we have never travelled there. Our vision is keener than most.'

'Are you immortal too?'

'The word you use is emotive, and we are all emotion. But, to answer your question, we are not immortal in the way you would understand it, at least, not in both directions.'

'I don't understand – can you be immortal in just one direction?' Jonah was bemused, the faery amused.

'Why of course. The Deathless are immortal in both directions: that of the past and the future. Not only will they live forever, but they have already lived forever. Their perception of eternity is complete, though their memories are flawed. That is one reason they built Amara – to do their remembering for them.

'The Old Earth Dwellers – whom you might prefer to think of as faeries – were once created just as all other creatures of the worlds were created, in our case many aeons ago in a time when charm was the ruler of all and the troll lords still walked the land. Therefore we have no perception of eternity in our past.'

'What about in your future?'

Here the faery queen paused. With one, delicate finger she stroked the feathers of Jonah's head.

'You must understand we are not immortal in the same way the basilisks are. That is not to say we will die. Our fate is less . . . precise.'

'You talk in riddles.'

'I do not mean to. Faeries are aethereal beings. We reduce ourselves into physical bodies only once every hundred years, or when special circumstances demand. But I do not believe I shall be corporeal again. There is little enough charm left in the land; there will be none at all when the winter has passed.'

'So what will happen to you, if you will not exactly die? Will you sleep? Fade away?'

'None of those things, yet of them all perhaps sleeping *is closest to the truth. I do not know exactly what will happen, only that we will grow* less. *For some of us that means we will diminish, grow smaller by fractions. But we will never be completely gone. To halve a thing is not to destroy it. Others of my kind will simply go away to places where the flow of time is less demanding than it will be in the new, natural world. There are as many answers to your questions as there are stars in the sky, you see, and it would take me much of eternity to give you them all.' She peered closely at Jonah, her eyes like pearls. 'And it occurs to me that you have little enough time to spare.'*

'That's true enough.' He took a deep breath. 'Please, I need your help.'

A smile played about the faery queen's naturally upturned lips. 'Name your need. I promise nothing, but I am always ready to be amused.'

'She says she'll do it!'

Annie stared at him, paralysed.

I can't move my body, Jonah. What do you mean? Who will do what?

Her thoughts moved through the air like a trail of smoke. He caught them effortlessly.

'I'm cheating time, Annie! I can't stop. But I think there's a way to defeat her, I really do!'

So far he had been careering through the memories contained by the rods with little or no control. His second visit to the faery queen *had* been controlled, which was encouraging, but his first visit had been a quite random occurrence.

His journey back to the moment when his father and brother had died, he was convinced, had been engineered by Archan in an effort to distract him from the task at hand.

The task of making her gone.

If I had saved them then it would only have been so that she could take them apart again. Then they would never have lived at all!

He had turned his back on them, and he wondered if he could ever forgive himself.

But then he could always go back.

He had very little time now before Archan's flames burned

their way into Annie's frozen body. Coldly he wondered how much time would remain after that before they reached him.

If Annie died, he wondered how much will he would have to go on at all.

Very little time, and an entire lifetime to explore. One dragon's lifetime to be precise, in which there might only be a single moment of weakness. That the moment existed he had no doubt. Locating it would be like looking for a needle in the biggest haystack that had ever been made.

No time to lose then.

'I'm coming for you, Archan.'

Closing his eyes, he pushed down on the memory rod, seeking the past.

Darkness. He tried to breathe but his lungs were filled with sticky fluid. His eyes were open but saw nothing. He tried to move, and something yielded. He pushed at it, hearing it creak.

Exhaustion. He dozed, eyes glued shut.

Noise. Voices close by, dulled by the surrounding liquid. The urge to push came upon him again, impossible to deny. Straining his neck he pressed the top of his head against the hard surface holding him back.

Light. A hairline of light streaked across his vision like a shooting star. A second line bisected it: a perfect cross. Pushing harder, he managed to widen the cracks and open several more. A bubble stretched across the opening, popped. The voices sharpened and dropped into focus.

'Here she comes!'

'It's a he, I tell you!'

'Ssh!'

Jonah forced his head through the maze of cracks and squeezed his way out into the sunlight. It was blinding; his eyes began to water at once. It seemed to take forever for his neck to slide through the gap – such a long neck! Then his shoulders burst through and his world tipped over. He was rolling, struggling free of his prison, mewing into the cold, transparent air, thrashing his wings against the stony ground and kicking with all four legs into the gummy interior of the egg.

'I told you – she's beautiful!'

'No more than you, my dear.'

He rolled on his back, stared myopically into the faces looking back down at him as they swayed on the ends of their long, gleaming necks.

Dragon faces, smiling. Teeth like steel, eyes full of life and fire. Iridescent scales. Dragons like butterflies, gaudy and immense.

His parents.

'There's only one name we can choose.'

'There are many.' This voice, the deeper of the two, sounded wary.

'No.' The darker face, its snout longer, its eyes deeper, dipped towards him. 'No. It is a family name and it must be used. And it suits her perfectly. She will be Archan.'

'It was a name of ill omen for her grandmother. And you know what the plague is doing. Look at poor Neth's youngsters – only one left out of five . . .'

'Shut up, Reyland! Just look at her – she's perfect. Don't spoil it, please.'

'I'm sorry. She is beautiful. I just . . . I just want her to be all right. You know what I mean.'

'Yes, my dear, I do.'

They continued to talk but his attention wandered. It was Archan he was interested in, not her parents. Nevertheless, he might gain some clues from the peripheral characters in her life.

Her life! Her whole life! And he had to live it all!

So it began.

Keeping the merest thread of his consciousness attached to Stone, Jonah plunged himself wholly into Archan's infancy. He had hit his target unerringly; already he was an expert wayfarer of Amara's sea of memories. He adapted to life inside her dragon body easily enough, just as he had been unperturbed to be riding inside a faery form, or even that of a microscopic bird. Acutely aware of the unstoppable passage of time on Stone (it seemed he was unable to halt that altogether, only to slow it to a mere crawl) he sprinted through Archan's early years like a giant crossing counties in his seven-league boots.

She grew swiftly. Even given his accelerated perceptions it seemed to Jonah that as a species dragons had matured much more quickly than humans. He kept the flow of time fast – the sensation was disturbingly similar to the temporal acceleration he had experienced on the iceberg, with night and day flicking on and off like a lighthouse beacon and the seasons ebbing and flowing like tides. There was too much ground to cover for him to do anything else. He prayed that he would know when he needed to stop.

Occasionally he would dip into a particular scene, partly to orientate himself, partly out of plain curiosity. Also to test her defences.

The first time it was autumn. The large stand of trees to the south of the dragon settlement where Archan had grown up was ablaze with orange; the ground beneath it was thick with the leaf litter. Archan was playing there alone, only three years old. Another youngster waddled up, grinning and displaying a row of tiny white teeth. Its wings were almost transparent.

Before the newcomer could say anything Archan swatted it, knocking it on to its back and burying it beneath a cascade of leaves. She laughed and the other dragon burst into tears.

As its head emerged from the pile Jonah – through Archan's eyes – saw the dark shadows beneath its scales, saw how tight the skin was drawn across its face.

He moved on. A winter passed and he paused again. Archan was standing with her parents beside a shallow pit. The pit was filled with small bones. Other dragons – all of them adults – were ranged on the opposite side of the pit. Most of them were crying. Soon Archan turned away and found a stream in which to play. She set stones in the water, watching the way they dammed the flow.

No time, no time.

In adulthood Archan blossomed into a striking dragon. One day she flew far away from her home settlement, which was by now a bleak, unhappy place. Most of the infants had died from the plague and the adults they left behind were empty even of grief. Archan was one of the very few able to leave it all behind.

She lived alone in a cave near a place so small it had no name. She practised wielding charm and, in between teasing the male suitors who occasionally made their way up to her retreat, resculpted her body from the conventional charmed dragon shape into the form with which Jonah was now so familiar.

It seemed to drive the male dragons wild, the sight of this flawless, streamlined body, quite legless and boasting wings like clouds. She became a siren, an untouchable dragon idol almost permanently ensconced in her charm-filled cave . . .

No time!

No time to experience the miracle of charm that enabled Archan to share the thoughts of dragons on the other side of the world.

No time to delve into the murder she committed one moonless night, a night when the desire to taste the blood of a dragon was more persuasive than her conscience. Afterwards she felt guilt, but she did not understand its meaning.

No time to explore the complex hierarchy of the tiny dragon settlement to which she was loosely affiliated, their mores, their hopes and dreams. The way they had really lived, these mythical creatures who were so undeniably real.

No time for anything but instinct. And speed.

Flight. A castle clinging to a waterfall. (Jonah allowed himself a brief pause here – this was a basilisk structure, just like Stone! The architecture was unmistakable.)

But he was beginning to despair. He sensed he was nearing the end of Archan's time on Earth, at least in her original physical form. Already on this timeline the world had turned, and already Archan was flying north to meet the basilisks.

And at no time in her life had he detected any weakness he might exploit. There was nowhere in the stream of memory he might take hold and twist her out of existence.

Oh, he had tried. The day of her first flight, for instance. She had been so out of control he might have pulled the sky only a little out of shape and caused her to crash into a cliff. He had even reached out to grip a current of air.

But he was beginning to understand the subtle interrelationships of all the memories in the rods. They interconnected in unbelievably complicated ways. At first he feared any interaction at all: by removing just one blade of grass from a meadow might he not carve a great swathe through the whole of history? Soon he learned there were safeguards – the basilisks had seen to that. The memory rods were inherently flexible, so that future events rearranged themselves by the smallest possible amount in order to accommodate changes made in the past. He could *make changes without creating havoc. Jonah understood this at the deepest level, without the need for demonstration. He was now as much a part of Stone as the basilisks had ever been. Perhaps more so, for it had only ever been their last resort.*

But Archan had been here before him.

That was the real problem. She had already journeyed through her life as Jonah was journeying now. At every conceivable turning point, at every crack into which he might have driven a wedge she had sealed herself in. He could feel her presence here still; he could feel the barbed wire she had erected around her own memories of herself. She had barricaded herself into the past. Even here, inside her own mind, he was powerless to do anything to influence the life she had led.

And now that life – the part of it that counted – was nearly over.

He tried to push at the air to make Archan crash and die, but the air pushed back at him. She was surrounded by a shell of charm. Invulnerable.

He moved north with her.

It was a world of ice. Dazzling red light flared, marking the moment when the basilisks – all except one – died. The immortality they had shared crossed over into Archan's mortal dragon body.

For an instant, Jonah Lightfoot knew more than what it was to be a dragon. He knew what it was to be immortal.

The flood of memories swamped him, nearly destroying his mind. Again he recalled Krakatoa, the ocean-wide wall of ash bearing down, the tidal wave that had decimated the Javanese coast. Memories of past worlds, and all they had ever contained. All the knowledge of the Deathless dispensed in a single, convulsive insight.

Then his body was torn apart. So saturated was the air with charm at the moment of transfer that Archan was literally blown to pieces. He felt his awareness first separate from her then disintegrate, felt the first streamers of night fall upon his soul . . .

But he did not die, just as Archan did not die. As her living, thinking mind fell into the icy lake – where it would soon be frozen, to remain for a million years before patiently accumulated charm broke her free once more – so his tumbled down into yet another host: the one remaining basilisk. Ocher, the last of the Deathless.

This mind was different to Archan's. Ancient and weary. Filled with fresh excitement though: after a lifetime knowing only eternity it had suddenly become mortal. In the sky overhead dragons wheeled, singing. Beneath its claws the ice crunched.

And Jonah was in despair.

There was nowhere else to go. He had tracked Archan to the end and found nothing, no means by which he might defeat her. Each time he had reached out he had been repelled like a magnet. The defences she had set had been too good for him.

As the basilisk plodded on through the snow and ice Jonah took a chance. Rising higher into the creature's mind he took control and turned its head back to look at the lake into which Archan's disembodied spirit had fallen.

Nothing but a mirror-pool of water, already freezing over as the charm which had heated it into existence slowly ebbed away.

No hope, no time.

He held the basilisk there a moment longer, ignoring the quizzical mind probing beneath his own. The creature's vision was astonishing: he could almost see the individual crystals of the ice-shapes at the water's edge.

The shapes were strange, like sculptures. One looked like a fallen tree, another a little like a cat. One caught his eye – the basilisk's *eye.*

It was roughly diamond-shaped, slightly rounded with ragged threads jutting from one end. Though it was as clean and white as the snow in which it lay embedded, it did not exactly look like ice. He took the baslisk over to it. He made its claws pick the thing up.

'Archan,' he whispered, exhaling lethal basilisk breath. 'By God, Archan, I think I have you.'

This time the faery queen was waiting for him. It was much later in time than either of his first two visits. The root chamber had collapsed, leaving a low, sullen void in the earth. Her body was a fragile concoction of soil and worm-casts. Despite these lowly ingredients, she looked resplendent.

'I had almost given up,' she sighed as Jonah broke through into her hiding place. He reached down with his hand – a human hand! – and lifted her clear of the soil. The fingers he was guiding were short and podgy, their bitten-down nails caked with grime. The hand of a child.

Squinting through a pair of spectacles with thick, slightly smeary lenses, Jonah directed the child's hand to elevate the faery queen to his eye level. She stood erect in his palm, her wings spread wide like cobwebs, glistening in the low sunlight. An old oak creaked overhead, shedding acorns that dropped like tiny meteorites.

'I did not know where to find you,' he said. His voice was that of a young boy. Its sound filled him with nostalgia.

'Have you brought what you hoped to bring?'

'Yes, I have.'

'When we last spoke you did not know what it might be, this thing you need me to hold for you.'

'I know now. The funny thing is I think I knew all the time.'

'I am ready.'

Jonah hesitated. 'It is a dangerous thing I have asked of you. But . . I simply cannot be in two places at once.'

'But the thing you have brought – it can?'

'I hope so. If not, all is lost.'

'Then give it to me, Jonah Lightfoot.'

Holding the faery queen steady in the palm of the child's right hand, Jonah used the other hand to give her what he had brought from the Arctic lake.

The thing changed size as it passed from his touch to hers, shrinking to the size of a human fingernail. She clasped it against her tiny breast like a shield.

'It is hers. I can feel it.'

'Yes, it is. And now, I am afraid, you will have to wait again.'

'I will wait.'

'Pray that it is I who comes back for it, and not Archan.'

'The Old Earth Dwellers do not pray. But I will wish you good luck, Jonah Lightfoot.'

'Thank you.'

As Jonah departed the child's mind the faery queen turned sideways and vanished from between his fingers.

The last thing Jonah heard before returning to Stone was the child's voice crying, 'Mum, mum! Come quickly! I've found another one!'

The air was filled with Annie's cries. The fire was very close to her now. Archan's jaws were huge, her head was drawn right back as she belched out the flames. Jonah could feel his grip on the speed of time's flow growing weak. Already events were stuttering: the fire was jerking forward in tiny spurts, hungry to be let off the leash he had set on it.

'Hold tight, Annie!' he called, then he reached one arm behind him. Not taking his eyes off hers, he reached back a million years into a mythical past and again plunged basilisk claws into deep, Arctic snow.

For an instant he thought he had failed. In taking it once he had removed the thing from history altogether. It was gone!

Then his fingertips touched something hard beneath the snow and he had it!

Crying triumph, he held tight . . .

. . . and for the second time dragged a single dragon scale out of memory and into the world of Stone.

He raised it before his eyes, watching the ancient snow steaming as the heat of Archan's fire surrounded it. It glowed with inner light, more than just the scale of a dragon: this was the scale of a *charmed* dragon. An *immortal,* charmed dragon.

Keeping his other hand pressed hard against the memory rod he leaped in front of Annie and held the scale out towards the on-rushing fire. He thought of how the faery queen had held its duplicate, how it had looked so much like a shield. Well, that was exactly what he was hoping it was.

Suddenly, decisively, he pulled his hand away from the rod and time began to flow at its proper rate once more.

Archan's neck whiplashed back. The fire was exploding into his face, but not before it had struck the scale. The scale deflected it. Though it was barely the size of a dinner plate, the aura of charm it emanated was substantial enough to withstand the blast, and to divert the flames safely around the cowering humans. Still holding the scale aloft Jonah propelled Annie behind the rod before ducking down there himself.

'What's happening?' she cried. 'What's that thing you're holding?'

'I can't explain! There's no time! Can you distract her for me?'

Annie's eyes widened in horror but then she clamped her mouth shut. Jonah saw small muscles working at the sides of her jaw. 'Just watch me!'

Flinging herself back over the rod she sprinted directly towards Archan's exposed belly, ululating like a Cherokee. Archan was still spraying fire but wildly now; the flames went straight over Annie's head. It seemed to Jonah as he crept along the length of the rod that Archan had not seen her at all.

When he had gone twenty yards he began to climb towards her outstretched wing. He had stuffed the dragon scale inside his robe; he prayed it did not work loose.

Now Archan saw her. Twisting her neck she squirted fire downwards. Annie ducked sideways, dropping into the gap between two of the larger rods just in time. The flames splashed harmlessly. Archan bobbed her head from side to side, trying to see into the contorted mass of memory rods with whatever magical senses she was using.

Jonah had almost reached her wing – which was hovering motionless beyond a cluster of narrow rods – when she snapped her head round and pinned him with her eyeless gaze.

'Leaving so soon, faery? Did you enjoy my life?'

'Not as much as I enjoy my own.'

'There is little enough of *that* left!'

She plunged forward, obviously intending to grind him bodily against the rods. He pivoted, meaning to run, but his foot slipped and he fell headlong down a steep flight of rods; it was like falling down a never-ending staircase. Above him Archan's pointed snout crashed into the place where he had just been standing. When at last he reached the bottom his ankle caught in a narrow cleft and was wrenched sideways. There was a small, exquisite snap and a tearing pain, and he knew it was broken.

The fall had saved his life – for now. Archan was withdrawing again, shaking her head like a prizefighter who has just received an unexpected thump. Pulling his injured leg free, and biting his tongue against the agony the movement caused, he crawled forward and found himself not ten feet from her wing.

Meanwhile Annie had poked her head up and was shouting abuse at Archan. Each time Archan – distracted again – pumped fire towards her she ducked down again, scurrying around in hidden crevices so as to keep the giant dragon guessing. Jonah did not believe she could keep that up for very long; Archan was no fool, and would not tolerate such taunting indefinitely.

With an improvised war cry he pushed himself off from the last of the rods with his good leg and straddled the leading edge of her wing. If she noticed his presence there she did not show it; he could only hope she was engrossed in her pursuit of Annie.

He scanned the sleek arch of her body, seeking his target. There it was! There, in the middle of her back between her wings, was the dark space he had seen at the very end of his encounter with the basilisk ghosts. A hole where a single scale had fallen away. The chink in the dragon's armour.

He needed neither arrow nor spear to exploit this weakness. This was not a task for a conventional dragon-slayer. Pressing his hand against his chest he made sure the scale was still there, then began to traverse the wrinkled membrane, gripping the tough leading edge which, he was beginning to suspect, was quite devoid of nerves. Such a stroke of luck he could not afford to ignore – if she could not feel his touch he might get all the way to the cavity before she even realised he was there.

Then Annie stood up and screamed.

Fire was boiling up all around her. Archan had indeed grown tired of the game and had injected a stream of flames directly into the substructure where Annie had been hiding. So far untouched, Annie was fleeing a gathering conflagration that sent jets of fire shooting thirty feet above her head. It looked to Jonah as if she was dancing at the summit of an erupting volcano.

'Hey!' he yelled, cracking the edge of his hand against Archan's wing. 'Hey, dragon!'

Archan jumped, actually *jumped*. She had had no idea he was there at all! The sudden movement almost threw him free; somehow he held on. A chasm gaped below him, inviting him to fall. Both Archan's wings jerked upwards, a reflex action, and his fingers were torn loose. He was sliding down her wing membrane out of control, his broken ankle trapped painfully beneath his body. The wall of her arched back careered towards him and he struck it like an oncoming wave. It flipped him up and over. Desperately he flailed with his hands and found purchase on a line of scales flexed wide by the tight curve of her neck. He slipped his fingers into the narrow gap between two scales, trying to ignore the thought that if she were to turn her neck back the other way they would probably be sliced through.

All breath had gone from him. He could barely cling on. Dragging one hand clear he reached up and touched boiling metal. The sudden pain surpassed that in his ankle; he pulled his hand away with a shriek. He understood straight away where he was, and blessed the miracle of good fortune that had thrown him here. He slipped his burned hand into the folds of his cloak and withdrew the scale.

Archan's face hovered before him, rippling behind a haze of heat. An arm's reach away was the hole in her hide, the slot harbouring the searing chrome of her immortal interior. He held the scale over that slot now, feeling the heat baking his skin, seeing the perfect fit it would make.

'What are you doing?' Archan asked, her tone shatteringly ordinary.

'I'm about to make you gone, Archan,' Jonah croaked.

He thrust the scale into place like the last piece in a jigsaw puzzle.

Archan screamed, but he thought it was a scream more

of frustration than pain. Frustration because she still did not understand what he was doing to her. But she knew enough to be afraid. As she screamed she bucked, and this time Jonah was thrown entirely clear.

The fall was not nearly as spectacular as his fall from Torus's lair, but this time there was no Kythe to let him down gently. He hit with a crash that sent waves of agony throughout his whole body; no longer were ankle and hand the centres of the pain, now it came from everywhere. Immediately he tried to move, but he could not even breathe. Spread-eagled on his back, he could only look up, his throat a tight and useless tunnel, as Archan's dreadful face followed him down.

'You have been an irritation to me, faery,' intoned Archan as she leered at him through wreaths of smoke. 'And it brings me no small pleasure to know that the flow of eternity will suck you under as effortlessly as I have struck you down. I will grant you one small honour, however, as a token for the dance you have led me. I will say goodbye.'

'Not before I do, Archan.'

He gripped the rod on which he lay with both hands.

'It is time!' he cried, plunging into the blackness. 'I have come to relieve you of the burden I placed upon you.'

The blackness was thick and substantial. The faery queen coalesced immediately from crystalline strands, forming a body of coal threads woven into a sinuous, spiralling whole.

'Much time has passed for me here. I do not think you know how long I have waited.'

'I know. I'm sorry. But please, we have to hurry.'

'You wish to take the dragon scale now?'

He saw that she was still holding it against this new carbon body. It gleamed brilliant white, stark contrast to the darkness all around.

'Where are we?' He could not help his curiosity, despite the circumstances.

'Deep. Aeons have passed, Jonah Lightfoot. The time of the natural faery has come and gone. The world has turned again.'

'Again? Turned? Do you mean that the time of man has ended, and that you are still here?'

'Above us the trees are no more. This is all that remains. And the

natural faeries – your kin – they have become something other than what they were.'

'No men left,' Jonah murmured. 'What am I, here and now?'

The faery queen lowered her pearlescent eyes. 'Best you should not know.'

Jonah glanced down with a shudder, feeling the alien hardness of his exoskeleton, sensing alien fluids flooding his veins. His closed his eyes, unwilling to know the future.

'Give me the dragon scale, please,' he asked quietly.

'No.'

Panic slipped quietly into his system. Had he come so far and placed such trust to be betrayed? Before he could protest the faery queen went on, 'Rejoice, Jonah Lightfoot, and be glad, as I am glad. For I can perform this task far better than you ever could. And you have offered me a destiny that no other of my race has been promised. Even as I fade from the world so I shall be of use to it and others.'

'I don't know what you mean.'

'What did you intend to do with the dragon scale, Jonah Lightfoot?'

'You know very well what I intended to do with it! This scale was all that remained when Archan's original, earthly body was vaporised. I have stolen it and duplicated it, embedding the copy in her new body. If I can take this scale into the past by way of the memory rods Archan will be drawn back with me. And as long as I keep fleeing she will keep coming.'

'An endless chase into the eternal past.'

'All I have to do is keep one step ahead.'

'Your reasoning is sound. Except I choose to take the burden instead of you.'

'You . . . ?'

'You have done much of which you can be proud. You have brought Archan to this moment. You have fulfilled your quest, for as soon as she embarks on her pursuit she will be gone from both world and Amara in every sense which has meaning. Only if she catches up with her quarry will she be able to stop, and even if that should happen she will be abandoned deep in the abyss of eternity. Even she will find it hard to make mischief in that cold and lonely place.

'In short, you have done enough. Consider the advantages if I carry the dragon scale instead of you: I know charm, which you do not, and there is much charm in times past. Archan may use it to work trickery in her pursuit. I know dragons, and I know

the way they wield their magic. She will not find me such an easy prey.

'Consider too the fact that I am growing smaller. Do you remember how I talked about some of us diminishing? I am such a one. And as I grow smaller so my burden shall grow smaller too. Each day that passes I will be half what I was. Archan will have to work very hard even to see my trail, let alone follow it.'

A needle in a haystack, *thought Jonah, beginning to understand.*

'Finally, consider my desires. Do you not think I will find pleasure in such a task? Can you imagine what it is to be abandoned just short of immortality? The Deathless considered eternity a curse, and such it is, but the fate of the Old Earth Dwellers is no less tragic. This way at least I have a mission, and a threat. We all need such things from time to time. Even faeries.

'So,' she concluded. 'Will you let me go?'

'But . . . can *you go? Can you travel through memory as I can? I was told that I was almost unique – are you an adept like me?'*

'I am not. I need you to show me the way. If you will only open the door for me, Jonah Lightfoot, I will gladly take this burden from you and tread the path of the past in your name. Please, give me your permission.'

'Does my word mean that much?'

'Yes. Do you not know that yet?'

'Then go, faery, with my blessing.'

She hesitated. 'You are blessed with a gift, Jonah Lightfoot. The scale you have locked into Archan's flesh has in turn locked her into her past. Its twin, which I hold here, will indeed draw her after it as surely as night is drawn after day. But consider this before we part: once there was only one scale. Now, because of you, there are two. They may share the same heart, like reflections in a mirror, but they are two! *Not even charm can achieve the act of creation, Jonah Lightfoot. Not even charm.'*

He reached forward, closing his eyes as he did so: he had no desire to see what kind of hands belonged to this hard-shelled body. He could feel the charm busying itself around his fingers (claws?), *could hear it sizzling.*

The faery would need only the smallest of passageways. Opening it for her was easy, like cracking open an egg. The light of the past spilled out across the coal, vibrant and yellow, a living yolk.

'Goodbye.'

The faery queen stepped into the depths of the memory rod and disappeared into the distant past.

'Good luck.'

No sooner did he say it than he was . . .

. . . staring into the chrome of Archan's throat.

'Oh,' she said uncertainly. 'Oh. Oh, faery, *what have you done?'*

What happened to her then Jonah would never be able properly to recall.

At first it seemed as though she were turning inside-out, for the metal he had perceived inside her body flowed out and around her scales, turning them from creamy-white to polished steel. Then she seemed at once gigantic and yet at the same time very small. Throughout the transformation she screamed. Again, it was not a scream of pain, nor this time was it of frustration. It was a scream of the single, all-consuming emotion Jonah had come to associate most closely with this ancient creature.

It was a scream of uncontrollable anger.

'Oh! Oh you! Faery!'

Now she was exactly the size of the scale Jonah had pressed into her back, a dragon from a child's toybox. Her colour switched from chrome to white, white to chrome like the ticking of a clock.

There was a final, trailing scream, then her diminished body appeared to turn a corner and was gone.

Jonah's throat unlocked and he drew in a long, ragged breath that tasted like fire.

'Annie!'

Lurching to the side, ignoring the howls of pain from all around his body, he rolled down a bumpy slope of memory rods towards the flatter area where he had last seen her. Fires were still burning sporadically, though most of them had guttered now. There was no sign of her; the air was filled with smoke, thick and bitter.

Crawling on his knees, he waved his arms frantically, trying to clear a way through the smoke. 'Annie!'

'Jonah!'

For a moment he believed it was a ghost, then she broke

through the veil of smoke and fell weeping into his arms. He held her tight, unable to cry. Something hard cracked against his hip and he held her body away from his.

'I'm sorry,' she snuffled. 'It's just my painting box.'

He looked at it in amazement. One corner of it was charred black and the leather strap from which it dangled was almost chewed through.

'Well,' she went on petulantly. 'You didn't expect me to leave it behind now, did you?'

They cried together. Their tears turned gradually to laughter, and then subsided into a long silence.

'Is she gone?' asked Annie eventually.

'Yes,' replied Jonah. 'Gone a long way from here. As far as I could send her.'

'Is that far enough?'

'I think so.'

He thought about eternity, and the determination of the tiny faery queen, and he thought it probably was. He thought that everything was probably all right.

'What about you?' he asked quietly, touching her head. 'Is she gone from here, too?'

Annie furrowed her brow, then rewarded him with a radiant smile.

'Oh yes,' she sighed. 'Yes, I'm on my own again, Jonah.'

It was then that the memory rod burst open like a boiler pipe whose pressure gauge has gone far beyond the safety zone. Red steam gushed past them, hurling them against each other; they clung together as they had in the shadow of Krakatoa, shouting the same incoherencies, feeling the same blisters rise on their flesh.

In the wake of the steam came a cold suction. Annie managed to lock her legs into the space between two rods but Jonah was lifted bodily into the air. She grabbed his hand, trying to haul him back, but she could not maintain her grip. Jonah flew from her hands, spinning towards the yawning hole that had opened up in the side of the largest rod. The closer he got to it the bigger it seemed to get, so that he seemed to be simultaneously approaching it and flying away from it. At the same time his sense of balance flipped and he was moving not sideways but downwards. The hole had become a black well into which he was plummeting.

Wind flattened his hair and clothes. A shape appeared in the distant depths of the well: a crucifix spanning the chasm. He opened his arms in unconscious response, ready to meet salvation or damnation, whichever it may be. As he drew near he saw that the crucifix was Archan.

Her body was straight and rigid, as were her wings; snout, tail-tip and wing-tips were embedded in the smooth walls of the well, preventing her from falling. She was no longer white; her body had returned to its previous form – Torus's black and red stripes adorned a muscular frame bedecked with spines and barbs. Her hide was filthy, and scales were sliding away even as Jonah watched, dropping from the leading edges of her wings and tumbling into the darkness like falling leaves. She looked tattered and broken, but somehow she held on.

And there, in the centre of her back between her wings, shone the single white scale he had plucked from the snow. It was aglow, the only part of her that was *really* her. The bait on the fishing line he had cast.

Tattered she may have been, but she was taut as steel and anything but weak.

'You have been so clever, faery!' Her words were like venom – he could almost taste their poison. 'Or so you think. Did you believe I would not find her? Did you believe she could run forever? Because that is what we are talking about: *forever*!'

She gasped and spat a great wad of flesh out of her throat and into the chasm. It sparkled as it fell, as if it was encrusted with iron filings.

'She will prove more elusive than you think, Archan. She will not stop. And she has quite a head start already.'

Breaking one of her holds on the well lining, Archan lunged at Jonah and managed to snag his robe with her yellowed, rotting teeth. Several of the teeth shattered, showering him with ivory buckshot. A line of blisters beneath her right eye burst and runnels of black fluid cascaded down her cheek. Pinioned against the side of her face, he fought to free himself but could not. Glancing down he felt the pull of some deadly gravity, and wondered which was the worse fate: to fall or be consumed.

But she did not try to eat him. Instead she tossed him straight over her head and on to her back, then nudged him forcibly down her spine. 'Take it out!' she snapped. He was only yards from the scale now. The darker scales surrounding it had mostly dropped away, revealing a livid red skeleton. Looking inside Archan was like looking into a bizarre fossil exhibit: there was practically no flesh inside her at all, only strands of liquid metal and tiny threads of flame strung between her ribs. Yet that one white scale clung on . . . or rather it was Archan who adhered to it, entirely against her will.

'Never!' he shouted back. 'You've lost the race already, Archan!'

She smiled a dreadful smile and leered, 'On the contrary, faery. I have already won!'

Jonah felt his heart turn over. 'What do you mean?'

'Look inside, faery. Look *down*.'

He obeyed, not understanding at first. Archan's interior landscape was rapidly disassembling itself. Soon there would be only bones left, or perhaps just their shadows. Still, her essential, immortal spirit would remain. And the one scale, of course.

He saw something propped against the smooth flukes of her pelvis, something almost vanishingly small. Light grey, intricately made – more bones, bones so minute . . .

'Oh my God no!'

It was a skeleton so small it could only have belonged to a faery. The faery queen. Archan was right: she had triumphed already! 'How . . . ?' he blurted.

'Those who defy eternity do so at their peril! Remove the scale, faery. It no longer matters. It is over. You have lost.'

Suddenly he felt unutterably tired. His whole body slumped against the organic gridwork Archan's body had become. The chasm called to him; it would be so easy just to slip through her ribs and fall . . .

The scale glowed, pulsed, beckoned him.

He reached out his hand, then withdrew it, hesitating.

'Do not defy me, faery! If it is eternity you desire then it is eternity you will receive – but on my terms!' Archan's breath was hot on his back.

Something about the little skeleton intrigued him. Trying to ignore the yawning black abyss he lowered himself between two of her ribs. A single length of shimmering yarn trailed through the void of her chest cavity. Gingerly he grasped it; it was sheer, almost frictionless. Taking a deep breath he transferred his weight on to the yarn and began to slide down it, slowly at first then with increasing speed. He tightened his grip and managed to slow himself a little, but not enough. He looked up, expecting to see the skin burning from his hands, but he saw nothing, felt nothing. Already he was approaching the wide shelf of Archan's pelvic girdle; in a second or two he would overshoot and spill out into the chasm.

He let go and fell fifteen feet on to solid bone.

High above, ghostly through the rib-lattice, Archan was trying to force her head into her own ribcage. The sight of it made Jonah feel sick. He turned his back on her and scrambled up the shallow slope to where the tiny skeleton lay.

It was no bigger than a doll and bleached almost white. The bones were so small and fine; the fingers were no thicker than pencil-leads. He could have held the entire skeleton in the palm of his hand. Tears came – she had been so beautiful, one of the last of her kind. Nothing remained of her gossamer wings, nothing at all.

He looked closer. There were more bones here than he had realised, long strings of them slung around the faery's waist.

And a second skull lying at its side, this one no bigger than a pin-head.

'No bigger than a doll,' he gasped. And he knew that this was no faery. 'Frey!'

He turned to see Archan's angry face, reduced to nothing more than a dragon skull bearing a few flaps of skin and a couple of cracked scales, thundering towards him like a steam engine.

He sprinted along the length of the bone platform and jumped into the chasm.

They were both falling now, turning over and over. The memory rod was no longer a well but an open throat swallowing them down. As they fell it widened towards infinity. Archan was right beside him, screaming incoherently. She stopped screaming just long enough to stretch out her neck – which was now just a line of tangled vertebrae – and trap him once more between her jaws.

He managed to turn his head. There, infinitely far above yet almost close enough to touch, was the blinding light of the world he was leaving behind: the light of Stone. An angel was moving in the light, holding out its hands for him.

'Jonah!' The angel's voice was hard and strong. *Gabriel*? 'Jonah, take my hand!'

He was so tired. The press of Archan's jaws was like a cocoon. He was a mummified Egyptian pharaoh, travelling not down but up, ascending to greet the sun, preparing himself to live forever . . .

'Lightfoot! Take my hand, damn you!'

Odd, that an angel should speak in such a fashion. He squinted into the light, angry that he should be disturbed.

The angel's flight was hasty and barely controlled. It lurched from side to side; perhaps it had only just won its wings. Its wings – they were like Archan's wings, black and red.

'What sort of angel are you?' he murmured.

The creature crashed clumsily against his shoulder, jerking him out of his reverie. The light was eclipsed completely and he found himself staring into the face of Gerent. The Neolithic prince was shouting.

'Come on! You can free yourself easily! Just take my hand!'

Jonah balled his own hand into a fist. Gerent stared back at him, his face as hard as stone. Jonah turned and punched the row of teeth that held him prisoner. They exploded like plaster ornaments and he lurched forward into Gerent's embrace.

'Are you coming now?' asked the prince quietly. Jonah could think of nothing to say, so he simply nodded.

The unseen gravity of the memory rod tugged at his legs but Gerent's hold was true. Archan's remaining teeth drew a great line of scratches down his calves as he was carried up into the light. Her eyes bulged. All that remained of her now was a raw, red skeleton surrounded by a cloud of fragmentary scales. In the centre of her spinal column was embedded the one, true scale, the magnetic core that held her locked inside this new prison cell. And try though she did to twist herself round to reach it, she could not even come close.

So Archan fell into the many pasts of the world, and though Jonah knew her fall would soon become a pursuit, he was satisfied that he had done his best. Her final deception had so nearly worked, but the faery queen was down there somewhere, fleeing still. He imagined her striding over the surface of an atom, the white scale's twin still clutched to her breast and her hunted face forever cast over her shoulder.

He did not believe she would ever be found.

Archan's bones lingered in the gloom like a strange ideogram, never quite vanishing.

'Will she ever be gone?' Gerent's voice came in his ear.

'She is gone,' replied Jonah as the prince lifted him out of the gaping hole in the side of the memory rod and back into the thick, warm air of Stone. 'Gerent . . .'

'Say nothing.'

'No, please let me speak, before we rejoin the others. Before we rejoin Annie.'

They alighted. Behind them, without either of them noticing, the memory rod had already sealed itself. Of the wound through which they had emerged, and the bottomless well that lay beyond it, there was not a trace.

'Please forgive me, Gerent. I do not know what possessed me to attack you.' He was panting, barely able to catch his breath, but the words spilled out all the same.

'We have all been possessed, one way or another. I forgive you, Jonah.' Gerent paused. 'Do you love Annie?'

Jonah gulped. 'Of course. Don't you?'

'Yes,' Gerent nodded, 'I do. But Malya . . . I knew her my whole life. She has left a void in me and I must be sure I am not simply filling that void with the first thing I find.' His chest swelled, and for a moment he seemed taller than he really was. 'A king must consider such things. Do you not agree?'

Jonah touched the nearer of his wings. 'Of course. Even a faery king. Gerent, will you shake my hand?'

Gerent took the hand he offered uncertainly, and gave Jonah a puzzled smile when the Englishman pumped it up and down. 'I presume this to be a ritual of your era,' he said cautiously.

'The hand of friendship.'

'Our friendship has never been in doubt, Jonah.'

Jonah bowed his head, feeling small.

19
Esh

Behind Jonah and Gerent the memory rod was seriously buckled.

'Gee!' exclaimed Annie, surveying it with wide eyes. 'Did you do that?'

'Come on. Let's find the others. I hope they're all right.'

Climbing down from the mountainous tangle of rods was hard work. Annie and Gerent took care not to handle the smaller rods, though it seemed safe enough to walk on them; the larger ones, with their thicker skins, offered no peril even when touched with their bare hands. After going only a short distance they had to stop and improvise a strapping for Jonah's ankle using fabric torn from his cloak. Even with the dressing he was limping badly and had to take frequent rests. His hand was not badly burned, and with determination he was able to ignore the throbbing. Annie urged Gerent to fly ahead but he complained of aches in his wings.

'They are truly a part of me now,' he added ruefully, running his hand along one of the membranes.

Eventually they reached the relative flatness of the entrance plain, where a nervous Kythe greeted them.

'You're safe! By the skies, we saw all the fire but we weren't sure whether to come or not. It all happened so quickly.'

'Did it?' asked Jonah, feeling a little dazed. He had no real idea how long he had been up there at all. It felt like a lifetime – which in many respects it had been.

'Yes, of course it did! It was all over in the blink of an eye!'

'Jonah's hurt,' explained Annie, and at once Kythe helped support him.

'Where's Esh?' began Jonah. Waving him silent, Kythe answered his question by pointing towards the entrance.

Esh stood poised before a long line of Guardians. This new regiment, Kythe explained, had detached itself from the floor only minutes after their predecessors had been despatched. 'No sooner were they dead than this lot started to rise up. Esh has kept them at bay somehow, but she's getting awfully tired I think.'

Looking closely Jonah could see the Ypoth's entire body was shaking. This struck him as truly dreadful: she had always been so poised, so controlled. 'We must help her!' he said.

'How can we?' wailed Kythe. 'We don't have any idea what she's doing out there.'

'Well, I'm going to find out!' answered Jonah, and he limped towards Esh. He had gone only a few paces when his leg gave way. Gerent's arms caught him before he fell. Then Annie and Kythe were there too, and so with hands and wings joined this motley band crossed the short distance to their companion.

Esh was standing perfectly erect with her carapace wide open, exposing the organic machinery inside. She looked to Jonah like some glorious beetle with its wing-cases unfolded, about to take flight. But she was suffering in some way he did not understand, for the look on her alien face was one of abject misery.

'Esh?' he whispered, touching her gently on the arm. 'Esh, we are here to help you. We will stand by you.' She did not respond. Her body still shook; her pale green eyes were wide and blank. 'Esh! We're here!'

This time she swivelled her head to look down at him from her prodigious height. 'There is nothing you can do here, Jonah Lightfoot.' Her voice was a barely audible croak. 'Flee to the platform while you have time. I have nearly summoned the energy I need.'

'Need? Need for what?'

'Do you remember how I said I would no longer be of use to you?' She allowed herself a brief smile. 'Well, I believe I may have been wrong. I am privileged to be able to save you, Jonah Lightfoot. It is the very least I can do for you, since you have saved all Amara.'

'What are you talking about, Esh?' Jonah was scared now – there was something in her tone he did not like at all. He grabbed her arm and tried to pull her away but she was as solid as stone.

'Come on,' Annie said in his ear. 'We should do as Esh says. She knows what she's doing.'

Jonah ignored her, looked instead at Gerent. The Neolithic prince nodded once. Jonah bent his head, an immense sadness weighing down his whole spirit. At length he raised it again, feeling like Atlas trying to lift the world. Leaning on Gerent and Annie, he reached up and kissed Esh on the shoulder – she was too tall for him to reach her cheek.

'We won't leave you behind,' he choked.

'Go,' she whispered.

Even as they stumbled over the waves of the floor the line of Guardians was beginning to stir. They changed course, making not for the platform but moving to the side, opening a clear space between the Guardians and Esh.

Then Esh moved.

She looked to Jonah like a ballet dancer preparing some elaborate set of steps. First she bent almost double, spreading her arms wide and touching the floor with her head. Then she folded up, a Chinese puzzle of limb and shell becoming one with the shadow on which she stood.

As the Guardians surged forwards the floor extended black tendrils up and around Esh's pleated body. Her carapace flowed like tar, blended into the floor, became a part of it. She sank back, allowing herself to rejoin the stuff from which she had first been made.

And still the Guardians bore down on her.

The melting process slowed and then stopped. There was something absurd in the sight of Esh's top half protruding from the congealed mass in the floor, but none of the onlookers was laughing. The nearest Guardian was barely five yards away from her.

Esh laid her torso back as if she were reclining into an armchair. Placing her arms to either side she grasped great wads of the floor, stretching it up like toffee. Then all the floor started to move, even under the feet of the humans and their dragon companion. The first three Guardians lurched sideways, hurled off-balance by a sudden explosion beneath their awkward legs. A whip, looking exactly like a thick strand of liquorice, lashed out of the ground, looped itself around all three of them and contracted. They squashed together, their bodies squeezed to pulp by the serpentine lasso. More whips followed, attacking the Guardians immediately behind them.

So it was that Esh brought the whole floor of the Threshold to life, except for a roughly oval zone around Jonah and the others which remained unaffected but for a gentle ocean swell. The Guardians bellowed discordantly as they were systematically decimated by Esh's onslaught. Behind the whips came machete blades; behind those came enormous scoops that reared over the lumbering creatures' backs and enveloped them, drawing them down until they were gone, absorbed into the ground.

And with every tremor that passed beneath their feet, Esh sank a degree or two further down herself.

Soon only one Guardian remained. This one she despatched with a single loop of black stuff that encircled it and cut it neatly apart. The two halves fell lifeless. Esh's head fell back.

The floor ceased its rippling straight away. The only sound remaining was the eerie hooting of the wind as it plunged past the entrance. Wordlessly they made their way over to what was left of Esh.

Most of her body was lost in the ruins of the floor. The top of her torso protruded from a mushroom-growth of resin. Her upper arms were still recognisable, but they degenerated quickly into a sticky mass that even now was melting into the rest of the semi-liquid debris. The ground was still soft, but already a tough skin had formed itself over the surface; soon it would be quite hard again.

Her face was unharmed, but from the back of her skull an ugly growth had burst and latched on to the floor. Green eyes peered out, pale and unfocused.

'Esh?' ventured Jonah hesitantly. 'Esh. Can you pull yourself free?'

She coughed up a glutinous purple fluid. It congealed before it had run fully down her chin, leaving her face lopsided.

'I think . . .' she choked, 'that is beyond even me.'

'We must be able to help you!'

'You have done all you needed to do and more, Jonah Lightfoot. Go now, before the next wave of Guardians cuts you off.'

'She's right, Jonah,' murmured Annie in his ear. 'We can't waste the chance she's given us.'

'But . . .' Jonah was distraught. He grabbed what was left of Esh's arm and tugged at it. It did not yield an inch. To his horror he felt his fingers sink into it, just a little, and he let go with a cry. 'Oh, Esh! Why did it have to be like this?'

The Ypoth's face had softened, or so it seemed to Jonah. Her features were simpler somehow. 'Do not weep,' she sighed as her body shifted another few degrees. 'It is the way of the Ypoth, to return to where they were made. It is as it should be.'

'But you were made far from here,' moaned Jonah. 'Far away, upStone. If you had to go back it should have been there.'

'But Amara is everywhere. You know that. That is the wonder of the memories it holds, for the past is inseparable from the future. I am as near to my home as I have ever been – as are you to yours.'

She coughed again, and this time she changed visibly. The floor heaved up, rolling her over on to her side and exposing her misshapen carapace. Her features blurred and flattened; her arms thickened. 'I . . . I will be home soon. I have spent too long from my kin. They call to me. I . . . I do not recall your name.'

'Jonah Lightfoot.' His voice, a whisper.

Smaller now, Esh began to curl up. 'Yes, yes. You have done a great thing. It . . . it escapes me now but . . . I will remember. I know I will remember everything, given time.'

Now she looked very much as she had when Jonah had first seen her. Her limbs had entirely sunk away but her neck still held her head proud of the surface and her shell still made a smooth, black curve on her back. Her original tortoid form had reasserted itself, claimed her back for its own. 'Nothing is forever.' Hardly a voice now, just a susurration on the air. 'Not even forever. But I will remember. I will do that at least. I . . . I hear them calling now . . . so close. Unmade.'

'Esh,' Jonah whispered.

'Esh . . . do not remember . . . name . . .' She relaxed into the floor's waiting embrace, her eyes glazing over black. One last word escaped her mobile lips: 'Remember.'

If I looked away and then looked back, thought Jonah, *I would not know she was there at all.*

Except that was not strictly true. Though the outline of her body was scarcely distinguishable now, one marking remained as clear as it had ever been: the red sigil on the side of her shell. The mark of the Red Dragon.

'We go!' declared Gerent before Jonah could face his grief. 'We go now!'

Already scraping sounds were coming from their left as yet another squad of Guardians began to form itself from the menhirs lining the mouth of the Threshold. They hurried back to the platform and stepped on one at a time. Immediately it began to move, not upwards as they had expected but sideways.

DownStone.

Jonah did not care. He felt drained of all feeling, even of the pain he knew was racking his body. He simply sat there with his head in his hands, a head that felt filled with wool and dust and hot, motionless air. It was too much effort even to think.

He was vaguely aware of Annie barking a sudden command and a breeze blowing against the side of his face, as if one of his companions – it could have been either Kythe or Gerent – had spread their wings and taken flight. After a space of time, the length of which he was powerless to judge, a second gust signalled the return of whoever it was that had gone.

He did not even look up.

Later on he slept, and he remained asleep even when the sun rose and bathed the miraculous, charm-held platform with clean, morning light.

20

Waterfall

Most of the morning had gone by before they began to emerge from the Dead Calm. Jonah woke shortly before midday. The others were lying on their backs, staring up at the far-off rectangle of the monument as it tracked its way across the Dead Calm's flawless mirror high above them. Evidently the platform was still very much attached to its parent, if only by an invisible thread of charm.

Soon the mirror started to show defects. Large expanses of it became warped, so that the reflections it threw back were wildly exaggerated. Then cracks started to appear in it, and the cracks became filled with growths and trailing vines. As if displeased with the irregularity of the surface, the platform drew away slightly, leaving a disconcerting gap between it and Stone.

By the time the sun was at its horizontal noon position they had passed into a region that looked more or less familiar: gigantic blocks repeating at regular intervals into distant haze; ledges and crevices; a thousand indeterminate structures adhering to the ten-degree slope.

It was almost like coming home.

The platform stopped adjacent to a wide, cobbled ledge. The cobbles were very like their London counterparts, only in true Stone style they were greatly enlarged, each one as big as a cartwheel. Luckily they were almost flat, curving down only near their perimeters into a maze of grimy mortar which was filled with all manner of noisome undergrowth, so it was not hard to walk across them.

Before they set off Annie removed the strapping on Jonah's ankle. It had swollen up, but not as much as he had expected.

She carefully felt around the joint (causing him more than a few stabs of pain, which he endured doggedly), pronounced it well-positioned and reapplied the strapping, taking the opportunity to wind it with more care than she had been able to manage previously. To his surprise he found he could even put a little of his weight on it when he stood.

'I think the charm of Stone may promote the healing process too,' he suggested.

They all felt starved. Although Stone had sustained them well enough with the magical properties of its atmosphere, still their stomachs rebelled. More importantly they needed water, which the air seemed less adept at supplying, despite its high humidity. It was the hope of sustenance that carried them along the cobbled highway for the rest of the afternoon, although they were at first reluctant to leave platform and monument behind.

'I suppose they will remain here should we choose to return,' Jonah speculated as they set off.

'Let me try something,' said Gerent, and he jumped impulsively back on to the platform. It did not move so much as an inch; he stepped off again, tried once more then rejoined the others. 'Stepping on and off was the trigger. It appears the trigger no longer works.'

'It was always picky about working at all,' commented Annie. 'I reckon it's shut down for good.'

'It makes sense,' agreed Jonah. 'It too serves the Threshold, I suppose.'

Both Kythe and Gerent exercised their wings as they made slow and steady progress along the ledge. The dragon-child swooped joyously around their heads, lunging into streamers of cloud and rolling on to her back in a dizzying display of aerobatics.

'Oh, it's wonderful to be in the open sky again!' she rejoiced. The others could not help but smile at her simple pleasure.

In contrast Gerent's flight was more a series of experimental hops. He had used the wings several times already, but his approach now was decidedly circumspect. He was, Jonah decided, rather like someone riding a penny-farthing bicycle for the first time – more conscious of the dangers of falling than the pleasures of perambulating. His dragon wings had acquired a striking gloss, as if the human blood he was pumping through them had imbued them with new vitality.

Towards the end of the afternoon, with the sun in their eyes, they came upon a waterfall cascading from a precipice fifty yards above their heads. It struck the cobbles with a deafening roar, and they all rushed to stand beneath it, to wash themselves and to drink its pure, sweet water.

Nearby grew straggling brambles on which hung the largest berries Jonah had ever seen, ten times the size of strawberries, which they greatly resembled. Their flavour was unexpected: bland, but undeniably wholesome. They all wolfed the berries down, not caring if they ate too much, just eager to appease their hunger. Large blue damselflies busied themselves around their heads, darting in and out of the brambles and squabbling with each other in their high-pitched voices. When he looked closely at one, Jonah saw it had the head and mane of a tiny, blue lion.

'How's your ankle, Jonah?' asked Annie. Her lips were slightly swollen and stained bright red from the berry juice. The low sunlight set her hair ablaze.

'It feels good, thank you. Better all the time, in fact.'

'It's very sad about Esh.'

'Yes.' They were silent for a moment. 'You know, I cannot help but wonder if we might see her again one day.'

Annie shrugged. 'Maybe. Anything's possible in this topsy-turvy place.'

'I still feel bad about Gerent.'

'Don't. He doesn't. If you ask me, I think you needed to go a little mad to do what you did.' She stopped and considered this for a moment. 'What I mean is, I think memory is all about emotion, when you come right down to it. I think that to get into the memories like you did takes an intense emotional effort. I think that something was in there with you, making damn sure you were fired up enough to do what you had to do.'

'I must say I had not actually thought of it like that,' Jonah laughed.

'It didn't have to be anger. Could have been anything – love, for instance.'

Jonah pondered this, then said, 'You haven't spoken much

to Gerent.' He added hurriedly, 'It's all right. I mean to say, I'm not trying to pry . . . I just . . .'

'Oh, Jonah! You just don't get it, do you?' She sighed, exasperated. 'Look, I lived a hard life back in our world. You'll probably never know just how hard it was. I had a husband who touched me more with his fists than he ever did with his heart. I saw too many people I loved die in the droughts and famines, and the stupid brawls that blew out of nowhere when the stages came by. I'm not complaining about it, Jonah – it's a part of me I'll never let go, just as I'll never let *you* go. Or Gerent, or Kythe. Or Esh.

'Gerent has lost far more than I ever have. I never loved a man as Malya loved him. We cannot imagine how he feels. All we can do is offer him our own support, and our own love. That's all I've been doing, Jonah, helping a man who needs my help.'

'You mean . . . you don't . . . ?'

'God damn you, Jonah Lightfoot! Don't you ever give up? Or are you just plain dumb!' Her tone was scornful but her eyes – her eyes were full of affection. 'I don't love Gerent. I might do one day but then,' she eyed Jonah mischievously, 'I might just as easily love you!'

Jonah opened and closed his mouth, feeling a little like a goldfish, while Annie turned on her heel and strolled away, glancing back just once over her shoulder and pinning him with her smile.

He smiled back; he couldn't think of anything else to do.

There was little point in debating which way they should go. The way back upStone was effectively blocked by the shining desert of the Dead Calm, and with the platform apparently inoperable, the monument was unreachable.

Besides, they had been journeying downStone for so long it had almost become a habit.

The cobbles took them on through another morning, but by early afternoon the scene began to change. A dark line had appeared out of the haze, a projecting wall completely cutting off their view of the distance. It ran upwards and downwards as far as they could see, an exclamation mark emphatically blocking their way.

As they approached they saw a mesh of gantries and catwalks affixed to its broad vertical sweep. Most of these were made of metal, though they looked more as if they had been grown than constructed. Jonah could see no sign of bolts or welds. The piebald wall – gunmetal and terracotta – to which they were attached was also seamless.

'We are near to the age of charm,' announced Jonah suddenly, as they gathered before one of the gantries. 'We have travelled back beyond the turning of the world. Anything we encounter here that has come through from our world will have come from a time when the world was ruled not by nature but by charm.'

He paused, expecting a thrill, but the realisation quickly sank out of sight. Had he not experienced magic already? What more could there be that he had not yet seen?

They walked along the gantry with a marked lack of enthusiasm. The illusion of freedom in their journey had quickly worn off, leaving them tired and disconsolate. Jonah decided that his own mood matched that of the rest of the party exactly: he wanted nothing more than to find a warm, sheltered place where he might rest for a very long time indeed.

Kythe was not comfortable on the metal path and soon took to the air. The clouds were quite thick here, but they moved swiftly and broke apart easily so their view was not hindered. The air was, as ever, very humid.

'Stay close to us,' warned Jonah wearily. 'We have no idea what might be on the other side of this wall.'

The gantry took them far out, until they were hundreds of yards distant from the surface of Stone. When they were within striking distance of the outer edge of the wall it occurred to Jonah that it reminded him of a dam.

A single, wide catwalk extended around the outer edge, turning them round the corner and opening up their view downStone once more.

Jonah gasped and leaned heavily against Annie, who barely caught his weight. Kythe was hovering at their side, laughing merrily as she too drank in the sight. Even Gerent, who had been trudging mostly in silence, cried out in astonishment.

Expanding before them, tilted up at the same vertiginous

angle as all the rest of Stone, was a gigantic expanse of water. An entire ocean, tipped on to its side.

Jonah tilted his head, trying to turn the distant line of the ocean into a horizon. But he could not do it – so accustomed was he to Stone that he felt more comfortable accepting its impossible slant. Tipping his head back again he looked out over the water and grinned.

The clouds were racing downwards, hauling their blurred reflections through the deeps. White foam crested far out to sea, while nearer the shore dark combs crashed against great breakwaters. It was the epitome of Amara: the familiar turned on its side. And made beautiful. A sudden spray of water caught his attention. Scanning the middle distance he just saw an ebony back breach the waves before rolling under again, followed by the briefest glimpse of a fin's sharp edge. He looked hard at the place where he had seen the beast, but he saw nothing more.

Jonah noticed Annie's hands fingering her painting box, saw how her eyes were drinking in the view.

Then she grabbed him.

'Oh! Oh, Jonah! I forgot! How could I have forgotten?'

She was practically dancing a jig at his side, slapping her head with the flat of her hand and fumbling inside her leather garments.

'What.' He could not help but smile. He suspected he might be doing a lot of that from now on. 'Annie, what is it?'

'What I made Gerent go back for!' she exclaimed. 'Dear Gerent. I didn't think he'd be able to find it and as soon as he went I cursed myself for an idiot. But he didn't grumble, not once. And he found it straight away.'

'Found what? What are you talking about?'

She was babbling; whatever it was had got stuck. 'Damn thing! I saw you put it down and meant to get it for you when you forgot to pick it up again, but then *I* forgot about it what with Archan and Esh and everything. Ah! Here it is!'

And she held it out to him, the thing he had brought out of the world and on to Stone, the thing he had retrieved from the mud of Sydenham Hill in the shadow of the rebuilt Crystal Palace. It was a book, covered with mud but otherwise intact.

Pristine, in fact. Brand new.

He traced his fingers over the title on its spine:

On The Origin of Species

and its author:

Darwin.

It was a first edition, and Jonah's father, Henry Lightfoot, had bought it for him on the day of publication – 24 November 1859. He had been eight years old. He had often fancied that in years to come, it might become a very valuable item indeed.

How right he had been.

Something splashed his face. At first he thought it was his own tears, then he saw Annie wiping her own cheek and assumed it was sea spray. The wind was getting up.

Then they were all standing, lined up to face the sea with their heads turned up into the constant wind of Stone. Water was falling all around them in huge droplets that exploded like kisses against their skin. The droplets were filled with gold and silver, ablaze with their own, internal light as if a minute sun burned within each and every one.

Jonah opened his mouth and felt the droplets spreading across his tongue, inflaming his senses. He held the book his father had given him close to his chest and looked up into the cloud-filled sky. It was not sea spray at all.

On Stone, it was raining pure magic.

Author's Note:

A great deal has been written about Krakatoa. An invaluable reference for me has been Rupert Furneaux' excellent *Krakatoa,* which draws heavily on ships' logs and eye-witness accounts to reconstruct the extraordinary sequence of events that occurred off the coast of Java between May and August 1883. Thanks to Mike Colledge for unearthing that book for me. So enormous was the scale of the disaster that the truth about it seems indefinable: reliable sources directly contradict other equally reliable sources, and the people best-placed to observe events simply perished. I think my version's pretty accurate – you can be sure that any mistakes are down to me, not the quality of the source material. Likewise the description of the destruction of Herculaneum by Vesuvius in AD 79, and another volcano mentioned only in passing . . .

My thanks as always to Helen for those crucial early readings, and constant support and badgering. To Matt Bracewell for an invaluable later reading and Ridge too, for constantly dropping the manuscript. Thanks also to Joy Chamberlain, Jane Johnson and John Jarrold, and to Lucas for inspiring the title.

Graham Edwards

Dragoncharm
Graham Edwards

The ultimate dragon saga

THE WORLD IS TURNING

The bones of trolls are turning suddenly to stone as nature draws apart from the Realm, the mysterious source of charm. It is a young world, but soon it will be old, and no magic is strong enough to resist the onset of a new era.

Instead, a young natural dragon named Fortune, with no fire in his breath nor magic in his power, holds the key to the survival of charm.

The malevolent Charmed dragon Wraith knows this, and he awakens the basilisk in a desperate bid to gain power over Fortune . . .

Myths handed down since the dawn of time tell of dragons, the most strange and magnificent creatures of our mythical prehistory. In this glorious epic fantasy, Graham Edwards captures the terror and the beauty of the days when dragons roamed the sky.

ISBN 0 00 648021 7